A

Heist

A Beautiful Heist

Kim Foster

KENSINGTON
Kensington Publishing Corp.
http://www.kensingtonbooks.com

KENSINGTON BOOKS are published by

Kensington Publishing Corp.
119 West 40th Street
New York, NY 10018

Copyright © 2013 by Kim Foster

All rights reserved. No part of this book may be reproduced in any form or by any means without the prior written consent of the Publisher, excepting brief quotes used in reviews.

All Kensington titles, imprints, and distributed lines are available at special quantity discounts for bulk purchases for sales promotion, premiums, fund-raising, educational, or institutional use.

Special book excerpts or customized printings can also be created to fit specific needs. For details, write or phone the office of the Kensington Special Sales Manager: Kensington Publishing Corp., 119 West 40th Street, New York, NY 10018. Attn. Special Sales Department. Phone: 1-800-221-2647.

Kensington and the K logo Reg. U.S. Pat. & TM Off.

eISBN-13: 978-1-60183-064-7
eISBN-10: 1-60183-064-5

First Electronic Edition: June 2013

ISBN-13: 978-1-60183-209-2
ISBN-10: 1-60183-209-5

Printed in the United States of America

For my boys: Ken, Griffin, and Holden.

Chapter 1

Everyone breaks the rules eventually. It's just that some of us make a career out of it.

Lingering by the bar, I sipped my Veuve Clicquot and, with the utmost subtlety, tugged at the short neoprene wet suit concealed beneath my cocktail dress.

The warm September evening air swirled with lush jazz; the chime of crystal mingled with the laughter of socialites and millionaires. It was a graceful affair. But I, for one, was far from relaxed. My eyes roved the party restlessly and my nerves sizzled with anticipation. And fear.

My safety that evening hinged on my skills of deception. On my ability to conjure the illusion that I belonged at this party. Whether I got my assignment done, however, depended on an altogether different sort of talent: the particular skill-set I happened to be born with.

As always, I needed to keep my fear in check and stay focused on my goals. *Do the job, Cat. Make it out of here alive. Don't get arrested.*

I tucked a short lock of my platinum blond wig behind my ear. A saltwater breeze teased the hem of my black Dolce & Gabbana gown. The party occupied the lido deck of a 280-foot luxury yacht moored in Seattle Harbor. Which should explain the wet suit. Rule number one for every professional thief: always have as many getaway options as possible.

Now—before you judge too harshly, consider this: everybody in this world is guilty of something. Everybody has dirty truths they keep tucked in linen closets and shoe boxes, secreted away in diaries and letters and the dark alcoves of their minds. Maybe yours isn't anything all that grievous. Maybe you just cheat a little on your taxes. Maybe you sneak into a different movie once you're inside the theater. Or, perhaps your dark secret is something worse. The point is, sooner or later, everyone behaves badly. Some of us are just better at it than others.

I curled my way through multitudes of rich and beautiful people who were busy rubbing shoulders and sundry other body parts. My muscles were coiled tight as a librarian's bun, my face was impassive. I watched for signs that someone suspected what I was up to. The people at this particular party—and their hired security staff—would not react well knowing someone like me was in their midst. Weapons would be drawn. Blood would be shed. This was a state of affairs I preferred to avoid. Just thinking about it made the hairs at the nape of my neck curl with sweat. My mouth felt dry; I took another sip of champagne.

Maybe this was a mistake. I glanced at the exit points. Should I really be attempting this tonight? It was risky pulling a job on the night of a gala.

But no—I was prepared. Besides, I couldn't pass up this opportunity—it meant too much to me. I *had* to do this. I couldn't back down now. This could be the job that would finally banish the shadow.

I selected a vantage point on the upper deck and wrapped my palms around the cold chrome handrail. Stars dazzled in a tuxedo sky high above, reminiscent of the shimmering gowns and sparkling flutes of champagne below.

I kept my face expressionless and methodically scanned the glittering party below me. Glamorous young things lounged on curved banks of white tufted leather sofas, orchids spilled out of crystal vases, hundreds of fairy lights twinkled along the sleek lines of the yacht.

I was scouting for telltale signs: the distracted expression of someone listening to an ear-receiver, unusual body language, a waiter or a musician who looked strangely uncomfortable. Markers of a person who could interfere with my ability to do my job tonight, be it security staff, FBI, or—worse—one of those damned concerned citizens.

Then my stomach tightened: was that red-haired man by the oyster bar watching me? I narrowed my eyes and slid to my left, concealing myself behind a post. There was something odd, something furtive about the small actions of his hands. He was standing beside a woman, his date or girlfriend, but he seemed to be avoiding her gaze. Very strange. The set of his jaw betrayed a degree of anxiety. I bit down on the inside of my cheek. Then, I saw him reach into his jacket pocket and a small Tiffany box appeared in his hand.

Ah. I rolled my eyes and focused my attention elsewhere. He was going to propose tonight. Fine. Not interesting.

I continued raking the crowd of partygoers. But as I did so, I must confess to a small twinge of envy. As they sipped their mojitos and nibbled their canapés, everyone looked so, well, relaxed. I glanced back at the couple by the oyster bar.

For a moment I considered stuffing this assignment and simply enjoying myself, perhaps trying my chances at meeting my own Prince Charming equivalent, of which there appeared to be plenty.

No, Cat. I scolded myself and pushed those thoughts firmly from my mind. That was not for me. I had to get this job done. Besides, the truth was, people like me were not destined for storybook endings. Dreams of the moon belonged to much worthier people; I'd abandoned those hopes a long time ago.

No. This girl didn't deserve the fairy tale. It wasn't usually the *villain* who got the happily-ever-after.

A white-gloved waiter approached and, after mentally clearing him as a nonthreat, I accepted a divine smoked salmon crostini from his silver tray. I smiled at him, confident in my disguise: the wig, of course, plus chocolate-brown-colored contact lenses and painstakingly applied theater makeup conveying much sharper cheekbones than I myself, sadly, possessed. I took a mouthwatering bite of the crostini and allowed a small shiver of delight. Another fringe benefit to the job.

On the surface, becoming a crook is an ill-advised choice. I get that. Very few people would see the appeal and, fair enough, it's not a way of life that would suit everyone. But let me assure you: it's a thrill like no other. And isn't that what we all want, ultimately? A life purpose that we're good at, and that we love?

Of course I'm making it sound like I had a choice in the matter. As if being anything other than a criminal was an option for me. It wasn't. The universe made it clear, long ago, that being a thief was my role in this life. Bucking that fate was not only futile, it brought dire consequences. I know. I had tried it.

At the party, I popped in one last bite of crostini and was on the move again. I buried myself in the crowd and wove my way to a less populated area of the party on the aft deck. I needed to choose my moment precisely. It was a matter of sharpening my awareness of other people's attention. I needed to have a clear perimeter in my peripheral vision, to know there were no eyes directly on me.

But although the crowd here was thinner, there were still a lot of people. I experienced fresh anxiety about doing this job tonight. It was never my first choice to do the actual heist on the night of a gala. Too many potential complications. Most crooks will tell you: parties are better suited for reconnaissance.

Unfortunately, I didn't have an option. Davis Hamilton Jr, the steel magnate, sailed the *Elysia* into Seattle this morning and he was staying one night only. The next morning he would sail down the coast for California and I wasn't about to miss the opportunity. I had done that before; it would never happen again.

Then, I noted that in the nearby knot of people a man was entertaining the group with an anecdote. I readied myself—this would be my chance. As he wrapped up the story and delivered the punch line, the group was laughing and distracted. That was my moment. I made a sharp right turn, melted into the shadows, and dove down the steps leading belowdecks.

The corridors were dark, narrow, and quiet. The ceiling hung low. The layout of the yacht and its suites was firmly etched in my mind, memorized from the blueprint. Fourth door on the left, just after the corridor took a sharp right turn. I was skulking along when a large, lumpy man suddenly emerged from a doorway and lurched out, smashing into me. *Damn.*

I'd have to bluff it. "Oops!" I giggled, stumbling against the wall. "Where's the little girls' room?" I said with an intentional slur. The man possessed an unfortunate physique: slopy shoulders and barrel torso. His small eyes were too close together, his teeth tiny and spaced apart, like those of a third-grader.

Unfortunately, the man moved closer. And started leering. "Hey, sweetheart, what's your hurry?" A hot cloud of liquor-spiked breath floated my way. And now I had a problem.

Memo to self: Take a moment, next time, to size up your audience before knee-jerking into drunk, giddy female bit.

"What's your name?" he said, taking another step closer. I cringed. Even an expensive suit couldn't minimize the impact of hair like a Brillo pad. Why, oh why, was it always this type? Why couldn't this be that Hugh Jackman-lookalike I noted by the Jacuzzi upstairs? I was sure I wouldn't have been quite so irritated.

This was exactly the sort of thing I was afraid of. I should have aborted the job, right then.

But I didn't.

I put a hand firmly on his shoulder, to stop any further advances. "Just slow down, there—"

He glanced down at my hand on his lapel. "Uh oh—wedding ring?" he said, cross-eyed gaze focused on the cheap plastic, fake diamond ring on my finger.

I flinched and pulled my hand away, tucking my ring within my fist. *No, genius, it's not a wedding ring. Not on my right hand.* But to me, it was no less meaningful than if it were. That ring had been on my finger since I was fourteen. My heart constricted at the thought of who should be wearing it. An old wound opened, and gnawed like a raw tooth nerve. My sister's ring, her lucky charm. What a cruel joke that turned out to be.

At the mention of the ring, however, my resolve became firm again. I had to do this job.

"It's not a wedding ring," I said absently to my lumpy suitor. My eyes flicked over his meaty shoulder, looking for an exit, alert for witnesses. The longer I stayed there, the uglier it might get. I glanced over his form—should I attempt to take him down? I could knock him out, drag him into the supply cupboard I knew was four feet behind my left shoulder. Though I wasn't confident he'd fit—

"So how come a girl like you isn't married?"

My focus snapped back and I glared at him. Who was this guy— *my mother*? I'd have liked to tell him the real reason: a professional jewel thief tends to make poor marrying material. But getting into that can of worms was probably a bad idea.

It was time for me to get out of there. I needed a change of tactics. I clamped a hand to my mouth, opened my eyes wide, and did my very best to turn green. "Ooh. Rough waters out here."

He hesitated and moved infinitesimally away from me. His left eyelid twitched, just a little. "Are you—um, going to be . . ."

To close the sale, I made a gagging sound. "Toilet—around here—somewhere?"

"Oh, er—go that way." He beat it out of there, stumbling surprisingly quickly down the hall.

Within moments I arrived at my target: the master stateroom. I slipped on my gloves and tried the smooth nickel door handle. Locked. In the time it takes the average woman to rummage through an overstuffed handbag and locate her keys, I opened my Kate Spade clutch and withdrew my lock pick, cleverly disguised as a mascara wand, and had the door open. I slipped inside and closed the door.

It was dark and quiet, apart from the faintest throb of music from upstairs. A little light was coming from the bathroom, illuminating a king-size bed buried under a mountain of pillows. Raw silk curtains were artfully arranged along the far wall. Sparkling mirrors adorned the walls. The room smelled of aftershave, ammonia mirror cleaner, and money. And dirty money, at that. Davis Hamilton Jr. was widely known to have a lot of friends in the mafia. Real nasty pieces of work. I crept across the room toward the bathroom light, my feet sinking into the plush carpet, and peered through the crack in the doorway. Clear. Speed was my top priority; I was committed. Being caught in there would be tricky to explain. And in terms of escape, it was the worst spot to be. I had only one option available—through the en suite window, back out to the starboard side of the lower deck. I knew this yacht like the back of my hand, thanks to the blueprint. The blueprint supplied by the Agency.

Oh yes, we're very organized, here in our little corner of the underworld. Although people don't realize it, most major thefts these days are executed by thieves working on commission, hired by an agency. The system has been perfected over the years.

Let's say, as a hypothetical, you're a gentleman of substantial means. Your wife's got her heart set on a very rare, absolutely divine chocolate diamond pendant. You promise you'll buy it for her. But the owner, irritatingly, refuses to sell. You're in a bit of a pickle. That's when you call the Agency.

Intake opens a file for you, and a thief is matched to the job. After that it's pretty simple. The thief grabs the diamond, you pay the Agency, and the Agency pays the thief a fee. It's very businesslike. Very clean.

Once upon a time, thieves and burglars worked freelance. That is, no connection to an agency. But that's messy work. Like trying to do your own bikini wax.

For one thing, you have to worry about selling the stuff you steal. Finding and dealing with a fence is a time-consuming and dicey business. There are a lot of unscrupulous double-crossers out there.

My particular agency is known as AB&T Inc. Officially, that stands for Anderson, Bradford & Taylor Inc. Unofficially—and somewhat more truthfully—it's the Agency of Burglary & Theft Inc. AB&T is the premier agency for thieves in Seattle. And it's definitely the oldest—it's been operating for generations. How many generations? No one knows.

I flipped out my penlight and started scanning the walls. The safe was in here somewhere, according to my intel. I spied a large oil painting. Degas, I believed. I tilted it and yes, sure enough: I found myself staring at a large steel square in the wall, a fat combination lock staring back at me. *Please.* How clichéd can you get? But no matter. It was time for a little safecracking.

Just as there's more than one way to make a margarita, there's more than one way to crack a safe. You could drill into the face of the lock and use a punch rod to push the door lever out of the way. There's also the truly caveman method of slicing through the side of the safe using a plasma cutter. Or even worse, using a jam shot—a small explosive—to blow the door off the safe. But these approaches are terribly crude and leave the safe looking like cat food.

Me, I prefer to finesse a safe. My first choice is to manipulate the lock itself and gain entry without damaging the safe. Leave as few clues as possible.

Some professionals use a stethoscope to amplify the sounds of the contact points clicking into place. But I've always found that I can manipulate a lock better by feel than by sound. Even through gloves, my fingertips are highly sensitive. This was something, incidentally, that helped me realize being a thief was written into my genetic code.

In the hushed stateroom I removed the Degas from the wall. I needed free hands so I clamped my penlight between my teeth. It clicked against my incisors; there was a faint metallic taste. The light illuminated the safe door in a glowing gunmetal gray halo.

I gingerly took hold of the combination lock and began rotating the dial, searching for the contact area, the notch in the drive cam. As I worked, I could tell this lock was not going to particularly stretch my talents; it was a very basic safe. Typical. Splurge on the best champagne; scrimp on a crappy safe.

I kept going, methodically feeling for telltale clicks and formulating an image in my mind of the wheel pack, the pattern of the lock. I was in the groove. I was the Lock Whisperer.

At last, all the notches aligned. The lock sprang open. I was in. I shone my penlight inside the cave-blackness of the safe and like Aladdin, I was rewarded with the gleam and shine of jewels and gold. I rifled through, my hand caressing chains and brooches and pushing aside thick rolls of bills in various currencies. I unearthed an enameled jewelry box, opened it, and—*ah, there we are, my lovely*. I pulled out the diamond ring and admired it. The diamond was a golden yellow, big as an ice cube, like hard sparkling honey. Fire flickered inside the cushion-cut stone. This baby, eighteen carats, was the largest fancy yellow diamond ring in existence. And it had a pedigree. At one time it was part of the Iranian crown jewels, but it was smuggled across Iran's borders with the revolution in 1979, sold and traded on the black market several times since then.

A feeling of triumph blossomed inside me. I knew this was a jewel that Brooke had coveted. Brooke—my one-time mentor turned vile betrayer. Not that any of that mattered anymore, because she would never get this stone. She was safely behind bars.

I took one last admiring look at the riches within the safe, but I left everything else inside. I closed the safe door, extinguishing the sparkles. The ring was the only item on my shopping list for today.

I had this little thing I called my "Thief's Credo":

1. Never steal from anyone who would go hungry.
2. Never steal anything that's not insured.
3. Never steal frivolously.

For example, say I was shopping and I spotted a divine pair of Gucci sunglasses with a prohibitive price tag. Although I could have stolen them, I wouldn't have. If I'd really wanted them, I would have bought them. This fell under the jurisdiction of guiding principle number three.

Generally speaking, I tried to keep stealing limited to my job, not my daily life.

I closed the safe with a soft clunk and gazed at the ring. My breath slowed and I bit my lower lip. Would it happen . . . now? If this jewel was, in fact, to be a talisman for me—the thing that released me from my guilt about Penny—would *now* be the moment I felt the change? I was balancing on a knife's edge, waiting for some sort of shift, some kind of sign.

But—I didn't feel anything different. I stared hard at the diamond; it represented a job accomplished, sure, but I felt nothing more than that. I frowned, confused and disappointed.

And then, I heard footsteps in the corridor. I froze. The footsteps grew louder.

The room went into sharp focus. My muscles contracted and my skin prickled with a sudden adrenaline blast. I needed an escape. Now. I jammed the ring on my baby finger, over my glove. The door opened and I sprinted toward the bathroom. I leaped over the bed and heard someone enter the room behind me. The lights flicked on. I lunged for the bathroom door . . . I was almost there—

I heard a sharp intake of breath, and then the question every burglar despises:

"*Hey!* What the hell are you doing in here?"

Chapter 2

I dove into the bathroom, slammed the door and locked it. I spun; where was that damn window? The bathroom was enormous, all marble and glass mosaic tiles and polished nickel and gleaming halogen lights. Ah, there. The tiny square window was high above the toilet, beckoning me to freedom.

I ripped off my dress, revealing the wet suit beneath. I crumpled the dress and zipped it inside my suit.

In the next second I was clambering on the toilet tank up to the window.

The bathroom door suddenly vibrated with pounding and hollering. My mouth was dry and there were thundering hoofbeats in my chest. My mind flickered with slide-show images of police, courts, prisons.

I shoved the glass open and lunged through the space. Halfway out, my hips got stuck. *No.* It was supposed to be big enough—were the blueprint dimensions wrong? I wriggled and squished myself—*damn, damn, damn* those extra caramel macchiatos last week—and three precious seconds passed, an epic.

I grabbed onto a bar outside on deck and gave one mighty pull. My body popped out like a cork and I landed on my knees. I was outside on the cold smooth deck, an unoccupied part of the yacht. I rose, scanning for the quickest way off.

"Hey! You there!" a voice behind me shouted. *Okay, just go, Cat.*

A gunshot cracked the air.

And it was a good thing the liquor had been flowing freely on the boat. The gunman's aim was way off; the bullet zinged a distant pole. Still, I was not feeling inclined to wait around to see if they could find a designated driver to operate the firearm.

I sprinted toward the railing. Unfortunately my stiletto heel stuck in a drain grate. I crashed onto the deck. A shot zoomed just above me, roughly where my thighs would have been. The gunman was getting better.

I yanked at my heel but it wouldn't budge. I whipped off the strap and slipped my foot loose. The edge of the boat was two feet away. I could have crawled it in a fraction of a second, but—

Shit—I didn't want to leave my shoe. They were Louboutins for chrissake, the most perfect black patent sling-back pumps, and those babies cost me $725. Besides, I was no Cinderella. I did not need anyone searching me out with a handy little clue like an abandoned shoe.

I turned, hesitating. The man carrying the gun, with two others behind him, was standing on the lido deck high above. The yacht reverberated with shouting, rapid footsteps, the sounds of panic and anger. We locked eyes. He took a step down the stairs that led to the lower deck, and slipped, ever so slightly. As he regained his footing his gaze flicked downward for a moment.

That was all I needed. I lunged back to my shoe, wrenched it free, and in one fluid movement dove into the water. The cold took my breath away.

Underwater, I reached back and ripped the other shoe off and clutched them both in my hand. I swam hard. I torpedoed on, underwater the whole way, thankful for the competitive swimming lessons my parents made me take as a kid.

I surfaced briefly, halfway to the dock, silently gulping air and hoping my head would be unseen on the shifting dark mirror of the harbor. Angry shouts of alarm skidded across the water. I quickly submerged again, muffling the upper world. At last I reached the dock, swam under it, and got myself lost among moored boats. Although my lungs were shrieking, begging me to breathe something—*anything*— I kept going, avoiding searching flashlight beams.

At last I came up for air and silently glanced around. I was surrounded by faintly rippled, moonlit water, and the hulls of boats resting like great whales nudged against the wharf. I heard water slapping lazily against the dark-wet wood of the docks, and distant shouts, somewhere over my left shoulder. Nobody was in sight. I breaststroked my way through the slumbering boats. Then I spotted the ship I was searching for, the *Rumpelstiltskin.* I slithered out of the water, up the spindly metal ladder, and onto the uninhabited *Rumpelstiltskin.*

This was yet another handy aspect of working for an agency. They could do the legwork and learn which boats have out-of-town owners (i.e., the type who tend not to kick up a fuss should someone, say, stash a getaway kit on their boat). Belowdecks I stripped off my wet suit, dried quickly, and climbed into the pair of jeans and sweatshirt I had hidden earlier that evening. I stuffed my Louboutins into a backpack. I checked the remaining contents of the backpack: a cell phone, a wig, a thick bundle of emergency cash in a pink billfold, and a passport, for getaway purposes.

I smiled; it was all there. An electric thrill ran through me. I felt fabulous—tingling and fully alive. *I did it.* This was my thing. Totally my thing. The one thing I could do in this world.

I removed the yellow diamond ring from my pinky finger and peeled off my wet gloves. As I did it I caught a glimpse of my own ring—my sister's ring—on my right hand. I stared at the cheap, fake pink stone, the yellow-toned band, and I twisted the ring to reveal a glimpse of my finger, paler and skinnier underneath. That flesh hadn't seen sunlight in a long time. The ring felt like a part of me, like my blood vessels and nerves and skin had grown through and into it. Yet I would cut it out of me, give it away instantly if I could have my sister back.

But that could never happen. And it was all my fault. My stomach twisted. *My fault.*

I tucked the stolen ring into a padded envelope. I stuffed it into the backpack and then frowned. I'd been so sure, so hopeful that tonight's job would be the one. And yet . . . the shadowy emptiness was still there.

I shook my head as a jumpy sense of urgency crept up on me. I had to get going. I couldn't sit here all evening. My escape was not complete just yet.

To cover my wet hair I slipped on a wig: dishwater blond and utterly forgettable. I climbed from the boat and onto the dock. The marina was scattered with people: a dreamy twentysomething couple promenading hand in hand, sipping from Starbucks cups, a family of five wearily trailing balloons and strollers, wearing glowing necklaces and faces painted like tigers and superheroes. It was Labor Day weekend and people had wandered to the marina, overflow from the massive annual music and arts festival at Seattle Center. I forced myself to stroll slowly, casually. I could make out the drumbeats and cheers and instrument sounds of a concert several blocks away.

Then I noticed marina security staff scanning the water with flashlights, speaking urgently into walkie-talkies. A small crowd clustered around, murmuring with curiosity. I ambled over.

"Hi, what's going on here?" I asked. Innocent and mildly curious was the tone I struck.

"Theft on a boat out in the harbor," said the man, keeping his gaze tethered on the water's surface. Flashing lights swung into my peripheral vision, a siren sharply cut off. "See anyone climbing out of the water? Wearing a wet suit?"

"Nope. Sorry," I said, shrugging.

Fireworks from the festival crackled the sky as I strolled away.

I coiled my way home, a circuitous route—as usual—to ensure I wasn't being followed. I stuck to busy streets of downtown Seattle, losing myself within crowds. Buses rumbled by. The night was illuminated by streetlights, headlights, and massive store logos: Old Navy, Banana Republic, Williams-Sonoma. Brown leaves were just beginning to gather in the gutters.

I stopped at the Greyhound bus station to change my clothes in the public restroom. The station was a plain brown brick building, skirted with wet newspapers and coffee cups. The sidewalk outside was lumpy with the bedrooms of the homeless. I entered the deserted restroom, which smelled overpoweringly of urine and marijuana and harsh industrial cleaner. I locked myself in, removed my wig and, without the benefit of a mirror, quickly dried my hair using the hand dryer. After changing into skinny black pants, it was time to slip my Louboutins back on my feet. Of course they were still wet and cold, and felt about as comfortable as small talk with a new boyfriend's mother, but when has *that* ever mattered when it comes to shoes?

I re-emerged on the downtown streets. Crisp city air swirled around me and I had a bubbly, champagne-inside-my-chest feeling.

I passed a homeless man just outside the bus stop; he was slumped on the grimy sidewalk. His unfocused gaze registered utter defeat. He had eyes that were already dead, waiting for the rest of him to follow. A dried leaf fragment adorned his tangled beard. Dirt was lodged not just under his fingernails, but all around the edges in a grimy frame, worked into the lines over his knuckles. He carried the yeasty-sweet-sour smell of someone who hadn't washed in weeks—maybe longer. I paused, opened my bag, pulled out the pink billfold. I bent forward and placed the stack of cash directly in his open hand. He startled but I was already gone, striding down the street without looking back.

Further on, I stopped at an intersection waiting for the light to change. I gazed across the street to the opposite side of the crosswalk and my eyes landed on a man. Actually it wasn't fair to call this a man—this was a man-god, Adonis in mortal form, cheekbones you could open soup cans with, shoulders of a blacksmith. And wearing an Armani suit that would make Giorgio himself break out in opera.

With a quiver in my gut I noticed he was checking me out. I was feeling pretty good about myself as the light changed and I stepped onto the street. Even though my hair was looking ragged, I'm sure, I was still able to attract a little attention. Not bad, Cat Montgomery.

Feeling bold, I flashed the man-god a broad smile as we passed each other. He smiled back. I experienced a strong urge to giggle. I resisted, of course, and played it cool. When I reached the other side I turned and looked at my reflection in a shop window. In a horrid moment I realized why the man-god was looking at me and smiling.

Wide black smudges of mascara—hopelessly smeared from my swim in the harbor—circled my eyes. I looked like I was auditioning for *The Rocky Horror Picture Show*. Perfect.

Twenty minutes later I climbed the broad steps to St. James Cathedral. I entered the enormous doorway and, to my great relief (and moderate surprise), failed to burst into flames upon crossing the threshold.

It was dark inside, hushed and reverent. Candlelight flickered beneath a soaring ceiling; a scattering of people occupied the pews, kneeling, praying, or sitting in quiet contemplation. I slid into an empty pew at the very back and glanced at the old man to my far left with his head bowed. And at the young woman near the front, staring forward. Good people, obviously, praying and looking for guidance.

For a moment, I wondered what that would be like. To be someone who could whisper a confession and receive forgiveness. It sounded so easy. But for me, it had never been that simple.

At any rate, I wasn't there for that. I was there for a scheduled rendezvous with my handler from the Agency. And Templeton was late. Which was unusual for him, but there was no reason to worry just yet.

I shifted on the glossy wooden pew. As I tried, fruitlessly, to find a comfortable position, there was just one thing I wanted to know: was there a specific *reason* they made church pews so damn hard and uncomfortable? I mean, stained glass here, gilded whatnot there—surely there wasn't a lack of money in the budget. Comfortable seating—would it have killed them?

My insides felt prickly, my hands fidgeted in my lap, then at my sides. Where was Templeton? Dependability was a crucial quality, particularly in the thieving world. Could something have gone wrong? No. Templeton was the best.

I did another scan of the people in the church—all the good people. My gaze unfocused. *Good people.*

I wasn't always bad. And I didn't set out specifically to become a thief. Some kids are born with natural musical talent, or they're the fastest runners in their class. I, on the other hand, was born with the skills of a thief.

It took me a while to recognize it. Growing up, I was always just okay at everything. Always vanilla. Garden variety. I did fine in school but not great. I was so-so at sports, ballet, music, but never really excelled at anything.

Until I realized I had my own special knack.

First, I was stealthy and quick. Growing up, I could enter and exit rooms before my parents had any idea I'd been there.

And I had nimble fingers. Sure, I wasn't the only one of my friends who shoplifted. Most kids try it out from time to time. The one big difference: I was the only one who never got caught.

I rose abruptly from the church pew. I couldn't stay sitting any longer. I wandered quietly, softly to the stained-glass windows in an alcove. The candle smoke, normally a pleasant smell, was starting to irritate my eyes, and the air in there felt increasingly stuffy—how did people handle it?

I told myself to calm down. It was just nerves making me feel this way. Still, I wondered: at what point should I abandon our rendezvous? I patted my backpack and felt the faint crinkle of the padded envelope inside. I pressed my lips together. Should I dump the envelope somewhere? Just get the ring—the evidence—out of my possession? No. Not a good idea. *Hang in there, Cat. He'll be here.*

I needed a distraction so I gazed up at the stained-glass windows. I focused on the colors: emerald and indigo and amber. Rich, beautiful tones, painstakingly cut and fashioned into luminous works of art. My eyes panned to a portrait of the three wise men, carrying gifts. It made me wonder. How had *I* received the gifts I'd been born with?

As a kid my parents enrolled me in gymnastics classes. Perhaps a mistake on their part, but how were they to know? Here I learned some rather nifty skills. Things that would come in handy later on, for situations requiring me to scale downspouts or balance on chandeliers. Standard stuff.

As I got older I set challenges for myself. Like locks. One afternoon, home alone, I studied our back door lock by unscrewing it and taking it apart. After a couple of hours I had it figured out. I practiced picking the lock, over and over. After that, every chance I got, I tried other locks. And I became good at it.

Then I turned my attention to pickpocketing. It's an art, really, lifting things from people without them detecting it. I grew up here in Seattle, and the best place to practice was Pike Place Market: a part-underground jumble of fish markets and curiosity shops down by the pier. The market is always teeming with people, especially tourists (read: distracted and oblivious), so there were oodles of opportunities for an enterprising young crook like me.

Flexing my newfound skills—and getting away with it—made me feel special. I would never be ordinary or garden variety again. I was different than other people. And that gave me a place in the world.

I turned away from the stained-glass window in St. James, and pulled out my iPhone, anxious for a message from Templeton. Nothing. I circled the cathedral in an effort to soothe my nerves. I glanced at the time. Seven minutes late. I decided to wait three minutes more, and then I was out.

My circuit brought me to the ceremonial bronze doors. I gazed at the carvings, the likenesses of Mary, the saints, a handful of apostles. I looked at the faces. They appeared solemn, remorseful, and strangely . . . guilty.

Which is something I knew all about. As I'd honed my burglary skills when I was young, I felt increasingly guilty. This was not something good girls did. And I had always been a good girl. So one day I decided: that was it. No more. Things were getting out of control, and it scared me. I promised myself that I would never steal again. And, had things turned out differently, I'm sure I would have kept that promise.

I walked away from the bronze doors and slid into a pew by the side. I glanced at my watch. One more minute.

Then, there was a creak of wood as someone slid into the pew behind me.

"Good evening, my dear," said a low British voice. "Anything to confess?"

Relief wrapped around me like a warm bath. "Jesus, Templeton. What took you so long?"

"Had to ditch a tail. Sorry, darling."

"Sure you weren't followed?"

"Lost them thoroughly. Nothing to worry about."

Templeton was my handler. We usually arranged to rendezvous like this—strangers in a public place. It was the best way of maintaining the hush-hush of the Agency.

"You sure, darling? No sins to confess?" asked Templeton, a playful lilt in his voice.

I smiled. "I can't think of a thing."

"Anything to deliver, perhaps?"

"That, yes."

"Excellent," he said.

Templeton was fifty-nine and a lifelong bachelor, just the way he liked it. He was tall and distinguished looking, with the hands of a concert pianist and the carriage of an earl. Templeton took his tea with two lumps of sugar—lumps, not spoonfuls, mind you—and preferred his eggs soft boiled. Letting an egg boil for one second more than four minutes was a crime of the highest order as far as Templeton was concerned. And he would know about crime.

He used to work at Weatherspoon's, the illustrious auction house in London, until he got sick of the endless lying, backstabbing, cheating, and politics. To escape all that—*ahem*—he came to work for AB&T.

That was thirty years ago. I'd known Templeton for five years and, together, we'd been through a lot.

I allowed the envelope containing the yellow diamond to drop to the floor. I slid it backward with my foot. Templeton leaned down to retrieve the envelope. The paper rustled faintly as he tucked it away. My numbered Swiss bank account would shortly reflect my commission for this job. A healthy figure—which was good. My account had been looking pretty ugly recently. Let's just say I had received some exceedingly bad investment advice.

"Another job completed to marvelous perfection," he said. "Wouldn't you agree, my dear?"

I hesitated momentarily. "Sure." I nodded, smiling, staring straight ahead. But my mood wasn't quite as big and shiny as it should have been. My smile flattened a little and I fiddled with the ring on my finger.

"What? What is that tone about?" he asked.

"Nothing—what tone? Everything's fine. The job was fine. And now it's done."

He sighed. "Oh no. Not that again."

"What?"

"You thought this would be *it,* didn't you?"

I said nothing.

"You thought this would be the job that finally brings you closure over your sister."

I shrugged weakly. "You know, it was a ring. Like Penny's. But . . . I don't really feel any different."

Templeton clucked his tongue. "Of course you don't. And that's because you can't change the past, Catherine, my dear. You can learn from it, certainly. But you can also become consumed by it. Besides, what happened to Penny was not your fault."

Shortly after I promised myself I wasn't going to steal anymore, my sister came to me, begging me to help her. Penny was twelve and I was fourteen. She, unfortunately, had not been blessed with a natural physical ability. She tried figure skating, but sprained her ankle. She rode her bike, but fell off and sustained a concussion. She took ballet lessons, but ended up with a fractured nose. Penny had, however, been born a natural math whiz, which didn't exactly make her the social star of the school. But it gave her an identity.

Penny had one other talent: she was great at keeping secrets. In fact, she was the only person I'd ever told about my little moonlight hobby. She never judged me. In fact, Penny had this idea that being a thief was simply my calling. "It's your destiny, Cat," she'd say. "Look how easy it is for you, how good you are at it."

This usually made me feel better, and just a little less guilty.

Anyway, Penny had a lucky ring. A cheap trinket from a vending machine, but to her it was lucky. And she was very superstitious.

One day, one of the girls who bullied Penny on a regular basis stole her lucky ring. Penny came to me, begging me to steal it back for her. "Cat, I need it," she said, her big brown eyes growing red and glossy with tears. She was sitting on the edge of my bed, her fingers clutching at my pink bedspread. "She just . . . *took* it from me, stole it out of my PE bag when I was getting changed, and put it in her locker. There was nothing I could do to stop her. Cat, I need it back. I have a really important math competition tomorrow. I can't do it without my ring. I need you to steal it back for me."

I looked at her sitting on my bed, so small and helpless, and I said gently, "Penny, you don't need that ring for the competition. You'll be amazing no matter what. You know that. It's silly to think that something like that would make a difference."

Her small face grew even more pointed and worried. "No, Cat, I really need it."

Little demons tugged at my heart. Could I do it? *Should* I? But I'd only just promised myself—I couldn't go back on it already. "Penny, I can't," I said, looking down. "It's not right. I swore to myself I wouldn't do it anymore."

I ventured a look upward, into her face. Her normally flushed cheeks were pale, her mouth trembling. I stroked her hair. "Listen, why don't you just get it in the morning? Go talk to the vice principal. They'll open her locker, and then you'll have it."

She twisted her anguished fists into my pillow. "That'll be too late! The contest is early in the morning, before school starts, and it's at a different school. Please, Cat. I really need you. This is what you do. It's who you are. You can't just deny who you truly are."

The thing is I knew I could do it. Breaking into the school would be no problem, and getting into a locker would be as easy as checkers.

I closed my eyes. "Penny, I just can't."

Penny was crushed. She wandered away, out of my room, without saying anything more.

What I learned later was that, out of desperation, Penny grasped at a reckless plan. She packed a backpack with the things she thought she would need, snuck out of the house, got on her bicycle and rode toward school.

It was a rainy, blustery night. I can imagine Penny, head bent against the cruel, slanting storm, pedaling hard, her small fists knuckled around the handlebars.

On North Silver Creek Road a blue Ford Explorer came around a dark bend too fast, and the driver saw Penny too late. I don't actually know that it was a blue Ford Explorer, that's just what I've always imagined, when I've gone over and over that image in my mind. The reason I don't know the make of the car is because the driver didn't stop.

It wasn't meant for my ears, but I overheard the doctor in the hospital saying that Penny hadn't died right away; she had likely been conscious for a while as she lay there, alone, cold, in the darkness, slowly bleeding internally.

In Penny's backpack they found a ski mask, a pair of gloves, and a lock pick. Of course they didn't know it was a lock pick. They said it was a sort of small screwdriver, maybe to tighten some part of her bicycle. But I knew.

"Listen, petal," Templeton said, "this twisting yourself up in knots and flagellating yourself—no good can come of it. You're never going to be happy or a complete person like that."

A weight crushed down on my chest. *My fault.* Entirely my fault. Penny should not have been there. If I'd just done the job—done what has always come so easily and naturally to me, she'd be fine. Or, perhaps, I'd have been the one lying crumpled on the road. Except that my reflexes were much better than Penny's. I could have avoided that Ford Explorer.

Or maybe not. But, truth be told, if someone was destined for that accident—I wish it had been me, not her. I snubbed the powers of the universe, thinking I knew better. *Hubris,* they called it in ancient Greek literature. And I had paid dearly for it.

"I'm quite serious, Cat. This endless quest for atonement—or whatever it is you're looking for—can lead to serious self-destruction.

You need to let it go, and move forward with your life. Besides, do you really think you would quit if you ever did manage to find atonement?"

"Yes. Of course," I said without hesitation.

Templeton snorted. "Rubbish. It's too much a part of you."

I clenched my teeth. It drove me crazy when he said things like that. "You don't understand, Templeton. She shouldn't have been there. If I'd just done the job for her, she'd still be here today. I had the power to get her ring back. And I didn't do it."

"Yes," Templeton said, his voice softening. "It was awful. I know. But, Cat, you need to forgive yourself. Or you'll never be happy."

I sat for a moment, staring up at the vaulted ceiling. *Maybe I didn't really deserve to be happy.*

"Listen, love, I know what might help. I've got a little tidbit I've been dying to tell you." He sounded mildly breathless. "I really shouldn't . . . . but, naturally, I'm going to."

I turned slightly and glimpsed his flushed, open expression and gleeful smile.

"AB&T is considering you for the Elite level of their jewel department," he said.

My eyes widened.

"That means, my dear, that you'd be getting a premium commission for all your jobs. And some perks. A car, an expense account. A *penthouse.*"

I whispered, "Are you serious?" I licked my lips, in spite of myself, and my breathing quickened.

"Dead serious," he said. "And I haven't even told you the best bit yet."

"What?" A gym membership? Contribution to my pension? I shouldn't have been feeling so excited. But I couldn't help it.

He paused for dramatic effect. "International assignments."

"Get *out!*" I expressed my shock, here, at an apparently unsuitable volume, judging from the heads that snapped in my direction. A woman in the front of the nave—who possessed the pinched face of a constipated goat—speared me with a very nasty glare.

I smiled weakly, apologetically.

International assignments. It was the dream of every thief. Why bother mucking about with small potatoes in the Pacific Northwest when you could be jetting off to New York, Hong Kong, Marrakech to pull off much more glamorous heists?

"Don't get too excited, Cat. You haven't got it yet," Templeton said in a low voice. "They're going to be watching you carefully over the next couple of jobs you do for us, and then confirming their decision."

It was odd that he told me not to get excited. Sensible, sure, but that had never been a particularly strong feature of Templeton's personality. Was he worried about whether I could pull this off? Naturally, as my handler, if I received a promotion, he would, too. He had a lot riding on my performance.

"So what do I have to do?"

"Just keep doing your job," he said. His voice carried the hint of a warning. "No mistakes. And stay out of trouble. I'll keep you posted."

I decided to ignore Templeton's peculiar mixed messages and focus on the positives. This was incredible. In my mind I saw the Hall of Honors at headquarters: the wall of plaques, each etched with an Elite thief's name. Okay, well the thief's name in the code we used at AB&T, of course, but the effect was the same. And no photographs. We tried to avoid that sort of thing.

The most recent inductee to Elite status was a thief named Ethan Jones, from the art department. I remember feeling terribly jealous. Mine would be the first female name up there.

I felt a warm billow of pride at that. And then I frowned. Why was I getting so feverish over this? I thought I wanted out. I thought once I had made amends for Penny I was going to go straight. Wasn't that the deal I'd made with myself?

"One other thing," Templeton said. There was a sudden wisp of smoke in the air as a side door opened and a row of candles was snuffed. "There's been a new FBI agent assigned to the jewel theft desk in the Seattle office."

"Oh?" My jaw clenched. New agents are trouble. Always trying to assert themselves, striving to impress the boss—just the sort of thing that made my job more difficult. But I shrugged. I didn't want Templeton to worry about my confidence. An Elite thief wouldn't worry.

"She's young and zealous. Name of Nicole Johnson," Templeton said.

The name didn't sound familiar, nothing I'd heard Jack mention. She must have been very green. "Do I need to be worried? What have we got on her?"

"Nothing much yet. But the intel team is working on it." His tone was vaguely dismissive.

An uncomfortable prickle scaled my spine. If I was going to be doing bigger jobs, riskier jobs, I needed to know my adversary. I needed to know about the new FBI agent who could be hunting me down. It was a matter of survival.

"I can help with that intel," I said. I could probably find her photograph in the time it takes to order a pizza. "I could get to know her—"

"Cat," he said firmly, with a side order of irritation. "Stay away. They can handle it. You do what you're good at. Besides, it really didn't work out so well the last time you tangled with the FBI, did it?"

This was a punch in the stomach. *Jack.*

"That's in the past. And clearly a mistake. I've learned from my mistakes."

"Yes, well, I don't think we can take the chance of you getting personally involved again, can we? You need to stay far away from anyone involved with the FBI." He paused, for emphasis, I assumed. "The last thing we need is you getting back together with Jack."

I knew Templeton hadn't quite forgiven me for this yet. I was reminded every time it came up. And I got it, I really did. What had happened with Jack threatened everything. I could understand why Templeton didn't want me getting close to anyone in the FBI. The thing was, he had nothing to worry about.

"That is never going to happen, Templeton, because Jack and I will never be back together." Somehow, it didn't seem to matter how many times I'd said that exact phrase to myself. Whether lying in bed at night, alone, staring at streetlight shadows on the ceiling, or leaning against shower tiles as warm water streamed down the nape of my neck and hot tears sluiced down my face—saying the words out loud just never got any easier. My heart, just then, felt rather old and sore and tired.

"Just stay out of it, Cat."

I said nothing.

"I'm serious," Templeton said. His voice carried the weight of warning. "If you get personally involved with the FBI again, you could put us all in jeopardy. I'm afraid the Agency would be forced to remove you from their roster. Permanently."

I nodded. "I understand, Templeton." And I wasn't specifically planning to go against his wishes. But a part of me was thinking I could easily do a little digging. It's not like I would have to act on the information I gleaned, right?

"I'll be in touch with your next assignment. Remember, stay out of trouble."

With that, Templeton's pew creaked and he slid off into the shadows, the diamond ring I stole tucked safely in his jacket pocket.

I waited a few minutes, then I, too, slipped away into the darkness.

Chapter 3

A thick mist curled around the discarded armchairs and rusted shopping carts that littered the dark city alley of Delridge neighborhood, not far from downtown Seattle. Jack Barlow walked among the shadows, fists clenching and unclenching within the pockets of his brown leather coat. Against instinct, he maintained an unhurried gait and schooled the muscles of his face. To an outsider he might have looked comfortable, unconcerned. Which is exactly the way an FBI agent ought to appear at any given moment.

In reality Jack was anything but relaxed. His stomach muscles tightened. An FBI agent should not be on the way to the meeting he was. An FBI agent should not be meeting with criminals and underworld types. It would be different if it were to bust or trap them. But to *collaborate* with them? He had worked his whole life to capture people like this, and now he was going to rendezvous with them, because he needed their help, and they needed his.

These thoughts made Jack's insides crawl. These, and the fact that he was not carrying a gun. Firearms and other weapons were prohibited where he was going, to the very hornet's nest of Seattle underground. And they had told him he'd be checked at the door. Which Jack could live with, in any other part of the city. But not in this neighborhood.

As he passed under a cracked, leaning lamppost, Jack heard something that did not belong. A faint stifled sound, abruptly cut off. He turned sharply and peered into the shadows. At the far end of the alley there was movement and sharp scuffling sounds—unmistakably, a struggle. There were three lumpy shadows, two of them much larger than the third. Two men were attacking someone. A woman. Jack ground his teeth. He felt a hot surge of rage. Without hesitation Jack acted. He moved like a predator toward the struggle, assessing the situation as he went. His vision sharpened and his pulse hammered. He sized up his opponents. They hadn't seen him yet. He guessed they were hopped-up on something, meth perhaps. Jack had a few inches of height over the taller one. He could take them down. Then he saw the flash of a knife blade.

"Back off. Now," Jack growled. He moved toward them, always moving, something his training and experience had taught him. The men turned their heads. The taller had small steel bars piercing his eyebrows. The other wore a grimy baseball hat; filthy hair stuck out beneath the hat in scraps. Both men carried knives. They held the woman on the ground with her hands behind her, driving their knees into her back. Her clothes were torn and she stared at Jack with terrified eyes. She looked about forty, with plain shaggy brown hair and a long nose. Her shoulders and knees jutted out at bony, gawky angles.

"Help me—" she choked out.

Jack's rage turned to steel, his vision expanded to include all surrounding details, and his mind rapidly advanced, playing out the next few minutes with cold, hard efficiency. He continued moving forward.

"Who the fuck are you?" said the pierced one.

"Buddy, just turn and walk away," the grubby one said. "This is not your problem."

The thought of turning and leaving was not even a glimmer of an option for Jack at this point. "Actually, it is my problem," Jack said.

Jack continued to advance, forcing one of them to come at him. The pierced one, eyes rabid, rushed him with a knife. Jack bobbed and caught him in the jaw with a powerful kick, sending him to the ground. The woman curled up like a potato bug, protecting herself from the surrounding maelstrom.

The grubby one jumped Jack's half-turned back, attempting to stab his knife into Jack's ribs. But Jack was ready. He reached back and grabbed the man's wrist, twisted hard and drove his elbow into the man's throat. The man dropped like an anvil. But the other was up again, uttering a primal growl as he flew at Jack. His knife ripped the air in a violent arc. Jack dodged it and smashed him in the cheekbone, then chopped him at the base of the neck. The man's eyes fluttered and he too crumbled, unconscious.

Jack instinctively reached to his left hip. *No handcuffs.* He scanned around and ripped a dangling chain off the grubby one's belt. With it he tangled the inanimate men together, arms behind their backs.

Jack strode to the woman. "You okay?" His gaze raked her for major bleeding or other injuries. She trembled all over but nodded and mumbled something vaguely reassuring, barely comprehensible. Her face was swollen and bruised but Jack found no sign of major trauma.

Jack placed an anonymous 911 call using the woman's cell. He then hid in the shadows just long enough to see the woman safely put inside an ambulance, and the thugs in a cop car. He didn't need the hassle of being involved, officially. Especially considering where he was headed.

Weaving through alleys, he felt a warmth inside, satisfying and genuine. Doing that sort of thing, being that guy, it felt right. It *was* right. Then Jack frowned, mulling over his true purpose tonight, his meeting with the underworld.

Screw the meeting, he thought. He stopped and swiveled. And then hesitated again. Jack scrubbed his hair and took a deep breath.

No. He had to go.

If this were a perfect world, Jack would keep his life simple. He would stay on his side of the law and the crooks would stay on theirs. But life was never that straightforward.

Jack liked things to be black and white. And these days, his life consisted of way too much gray. He squeezed his jaw tight. Damn his father for doing this to him. Damn his father for—even beyond the grave—being able to reach up and screw with his life.

Jack pivoted and continued on his way, toward the meeting that would make him no better than all the other criminals in this world.

The two supersized humans at the back door of the club checked Jack for weapons, as he knew they would. Jack's every fiber sizzled with caution as he stepped from the cold, dark night into a warm, glowing, fragrant restaurant. His eyes never stopped flicking around the room, noting white tablecloths, a string quartet, chilling champagne. Jack blinked, briefly distracted. This was not what he was expecting to find in such a seedy part of town. But then, even underworld types liked to have a nice foie gras now and then. And lord knows they can afford it. The round tables were filled with men. Old men, battle scarred and dead eyed, and young men, jumpy and twitchy and lavishly dressed.

The hostess approached Jack. She was a woman well past her prime, wearing a high ponytail and too much makeup. *That cake layer might be thick,* Jack thought, *but it's not going to protect you from gunshots, sweetheart.* She ushered him through to a private room at the back of the lounge. It was dark, velvet-wallpapered, with brass lamps and mahogany bookshelves. Two men were seated in leather armchairs surrounded by tendrils of cigar smoke. One was older, at least in his sixties. He carried the appearance of a gentleman: sterling hair, well-groomed hands. Jack knew him as Mr. Oliver Cole. Jack could recognize many of the local criminals. Most had done time, or at least been brought up on charges, even if they'd managed to slither through the cracks.

The younger man, however, Jack did not recognize. He was lean and puckish, with the teeth of at least two grown adults jammed into his mouth.

"Welcome, Jack," Cole said with a smile. He introduced the younger man by the name Wesley Smith.

Jack simply nodded. He was not about to pretend to be nice. He was here and, as far as he was concerned, that was enough.

Jack's eyes roved over the bottle of single-malt whiskey on the table, the Rolex on Smith's wrist. All bought with dirty money. Jack's mouth twisted as if he were tasting something sour.

He could have easily ignored the summons, the message he'd received on his phone that had led to his coming here. *Your help is requested,* it had said. The directions to this meeting had followed.

His heart had stopped, briefly, when he'd read that message. After all this time he was finally being called upon to take up his father's quest. Jack had made a promise to his father, long ago. He would keep his word. He would help the criminals in their quest. And—God help him—he would probably help them steal.

He wondered, what had changed now? What was happening, now, that had caused these people to contact him?

Jack took a seat. They offered him a drink and after a moment's hesitation Jack accepted a glass of single malt. He took a sip: burning molasses smoke, an exquisite pleasure.

"I must tell you," said Oliver Cole, swirling his drink, "it's been a long time since we've had an FBI agent in here. And any visits we've had in the past . . . well, let's just say that we tended not to offer them drinks." He looked at Wesley and the two laughed.

Jack cringed. He felt an immediate impulse to get up and leave. He should not be here. This was a mistake. And yet . . . and yet. He had good reason to stay. He forced himself to remain where he was. It was time to find out.

"Let's get to business, shall we?" Jack said in a low, humorless voice.

"Of course, Jack, of course." Cole smiled, but his tone wasn't condescending or dismissive anymore. He needed Jack's help—that much was obvious. He didn't want him to leave.

"In your message you asked for help," Jack said. "Why now? What's happening?"

Wesley opened a file and produced a glossy color photograph. He passed it to Jack. It was a picture of a magnificent jeweled egg.

"What's this?" Jack asked. "A Fabergé Egg?"

"Not just a Fabergé Egg," Wesley said. "The interesting part is what's contained inside."

Jack gripped the photograph tightly. "Are you saying—"

Wesley nodded. "This is where the Gifts are now."

Jack looked at the Egg. Black enamel, gold filigree, jewel-encrusted surface: it was stunning. A thin seam ran around the center of the Egg, clamped tightly shut, containing an amazing secret. If they were right about it.

"So where is this Egg?"

"Well, that's why we've contacted you, Jack," Cole said. "The location has been traced here, somewhere in Seattle."

Jack processed this, his breathing shallow. It was hard to believe. After all those generations, all the men and women who'd spent their lifetimes searching. Could it finally be surfacing? A small warmth flickered to life deep inside his chest—could he possibly be part of the team that finally revealed it?

Mostly Jack didn't believe it. They'd been fooled before. When it came to hunting down biblical artifacts, there were always false leads and wild goose chases.

"So why was I called in?"

Wesley looked at the elder man, who gave a single nod. "We're going to need you to do some work for us, Jack," Wesley said.

Jack knew that by *work*, here, they meant things that Jack would not be able to share with his department. Or anyone, for that matter.

The older man scrutinized him with a penetrating stare. "Are you sure you're up for this? Can we count on you?"

It took Jack a long time to answer. There was no easy choice here. If he entered into this, at the end of it his career could be in ruins. And would he be able to live with himself? After spending his whole life working against crime, now he was contemplating crossing to the other side? The danger level would be far higher than in a regular, aboveboard investigation. But there was his damn promise to his father, before he'd died.

Growing up, Jack had despised everything his father had been about. Except one thing. His father had been part of a larger quest: the hunt for the long-lost Gifts of the Magi. Yes, the biblical artifacts of lore, the legendary gold, frankincense, and myrrh. It was a quest that had been passed down through countless generations, always in secret, always within underworld circles. Jack knew that, for his father, it had been more than a pet project. It had been his reason for living. And the last time Jack had seen his father alive, John Robie had made his son promise that one day he would, when called upon, continue the quest.

Jack couldn't simply scrub that from his memory, much as he might like to.

Of course there was something else, too. A feeling of doing the right thing, of helping with something that was bigger than him. Jack knew if there was any chance of finding, and reclaiming, what was held inside that Egg—if that's where the Gifts were now concealed—it would have to be done outside the bounds of the law. He could have sat there forever, trying to figure out another way. But there wasn't one.

When Jack finally spoke, his voice was firm. "Yes. I'm in."

Before they could get any further, however, the hostess knocked at the door. She informed Cole of a telephone call. "I have to take this. Wesley, fill Jack in on the rest," he said, and closed the door behind him with a soft *click*.

Jack took another sip of his whiskey and watched Wesley Smith over the rim of his glass. He didn't trust new people. This man was no exception.

Wesley reclined in his chair and spoke. "Before we get into it, Barlow, I want to know why you're doing this." He rubbed his chin and cast Jack a direct look. "I'll be honest. Mr. Cole says you can be trusted, but I need a little more convincing. So tell me, what's in it for you?"

Jack studied the other man's thin face. He saw in Wesley's countenance the same dislike and distrust that he, himself, felt. If they were to work together, they were both going to have to deal with that.

"Did Mr. Cole tell you who my father was?" Jack asked.

"Nope."

Jack shrugged and looked up toward the coffered ceiling. "His name was John Barlow. But his alias, and the name he was known by in your circles, was John Robie."

Wesley's eyes went wide. "Well, fuck me," he said. "That's *you*? But—everyone says that Robie's son didn't want to have anything to do with him."

"That's true. I didn't."

"So why do you care now?"

Jack sipped his whiskey again and attempted to formulate the words. It was a good question, one he'd asked himself many times. "Because he was my father, I suppose." Jack left it at that, but it wasn't that simple. Jack's father had been a career criminal. And in spite of being the sort of man Jack came to despise, Jack knew there was one part of him that was honorable at its core. And it was something he'd died trying to do. That was the part Jack felt compelled to honor.

Jack had more than atoned for his father's sins by becoming an FBI agent. But he had a different guilt to deal with now. He'd rejected his father. And in doing so, he'd broken his heart. Jack had been his only son, and they hadn't spoken since the day Jack left home.

Jack's stepmother had pleaded with him a few times to reconsider. He refused. And once she passed away, there was no further contact between father and son. They were estranged. There was a part of Jack that always assumed they would reconcile someday. It certainly didn't occur to him that his father would die. Then one day Jack received a letter. After that, everything was his.

"Can we get on with things, here?" Jack said irritably.

"Sure thing, Jack." Wesley smiled that toothy smile, like fingernails on a chalkboard for Jack. "So. There are two involved parties, other than us."

Two parties? Jack thought. He felt fresh doubt. Nothing about this was going to be simple. "Involved in what way?"

"The family that calls themselves Gorlovich is one party. They have the Fabergé Egg. But we don't know where they're keeping it."

"And the other party?"

Wesley regarded him carefully. "Have you heard of the group known as the Caliga Rapio?"

Jack's jaw tightened and he felt a prickle go up his spine. "I know about them."

"Well, they're the other party."

Jack nodded grimly. This job had just become a lot more difficult. And dangerous. But how could he walk away now, after everything he'd heard? An image flashed in Jack's mind of what would happen should the Caliga get their hands on the Gifts. His stomach turned sour.

"Are they here also?" Jack asked. "In Seattle?"

Wesley nodded. "They're close. They know it's here. They know the Gorlovich family has it. And, we're afraid, they just might know its exact location. Which is what we've got to figure out."

At this point Wesley handed Jack a file with further information. Jack began thumbing through pages of intel, photographs of the Gorlovich family members, details of their endless series of homes and office buildings and warehouses. This search was not going to be easy.

"So I'm wondering," Wesley began as Jack scanned pages. "Sounds like you couldn't stand being in the same room as your father. You gonna have a problem working with a thief now?"

Jack turned a page. "Not all criminals are unpleasant to spend time with," he said. His mind flashed to a memory of sitting with Cat at a sunny sidewalk café. He was smiling, watching her pour endless packets of sugar into her cappuccino. Then the image changed and they were curled on a sofa watching a movie in his fire-warmed living room. He rubbed her feet while she cradled a giant bowl of butter-fragrant popcorn.

Wesley cracked his knuckles, frowning at Jack. And then a look of understanding dawned. "Oh, that's *right*." He smiled. "You were dating a crook. According to rumor anyway. Cat Montgomery?"

Jack's head snapped up before he could curb his reflex.

"Yep, that's the one," Wesley said with a self-satisfied smile. "And—yeah, I remember now—you're the one who let her off the hook in that Camelot job." Wesley's smile spread to a full, toothy grin. He let out a short bark of laughter. "The girl sure knew what she was doing, sleeping with you."

Jack lunged across the coffee table, grabbed Wesley's throat and pushed him back into the leather armchair. Wesley's eyes popped.

"It wasn't like that," Jack said in a dangerously low voice. "And if I ever hear you saying anything like that again—"

"Okay, okay!" Wesley choked "Just a joke, dude."

Jack forced himself to release Wesley. A few moments of silence passed. Jack looked away, frowning fiercely, willing himself to let it go. The nerve that Wesley had touched throbbed like a toothache.

The guy was wrong—completely wrong about Cat, about their relationship. But why did Jack care anyway? It was over. It didn't matter anymore. Being with Cat had been a mistake. A huge mistake. But it was all in the past now.

After everything that happened with Cat, Jack had applied for a department transfer out of property crimes. He just couldn't stand the conflict of interest, even though the only person who knew was him. He now worked in the Counterintelligence Task Force, Seattle division.

Being the low guy on the totem pole in that department, Jack was mostly shuffling paper around a desk these days. His supervisor was a hard-ass, and wasn't letting him out in the field until he'd paid his dues. Which, when Jack thought about it, was probably going to work in his favor now. He could do what was essentially an office job with the FBI during the day, and work with Cole's crew at night.

Wesley was rubbing his throat and straightening his jacket. Jack shook it off. He looked directly at the other man. "All right," Jack said. "Unless I'm mistaken, we've got work to do. What's our next move?"

Wesley stopped rubbing his throat and smiled. "Glad you asked." He reached into a drawer and handed Jack a thick, engraved invitation, embossed with a small Venetian mask.

Jack read it and looked up. "What's this? A masquerade ball? What's this got to do with anything?"

"You'll see."

Jack stared back down at the invitation and rubbed the heavy card stock with his thumb. So it began. Question was, would he be able to live with himself, when it was all over?

Chapter 4

I unpacked a bagful of pencils, charcoal, and erasers, and looked furtively around. I arranged my instruments on an easel in an art studio that was ablaze with the last rays of evening sun and wondered what I was going to do with it all. The studio smelled of chalk dust and oil paint and herbal tea.

If Templeton knew I was here he'd kill me. A pang of guilt and anxiety centered between my shoulder blades. He could never find out I came here.

I couldn't leave it alone, though. It hadn't taken me long to ferret out some personal information about the new FBI agent. And what I'd learned about Nicole Johnson was that she attended a figure drawing class every Thursday evening. I had attempted to go through proper channels with this information—called the right department at AB&T and everything—but they said they didn't have the manpower to deal with it right now. Not a priority. So what was I supposed to do, just squander this opportunity?

The art instructor strolled over to me. He was short, almost hobbit-like, with a shaggy sweep of brown hair and round, wire glasses. He smelled strongly of cigarette smoke. "So you've studied figure drawing before?" he said, eyeing my pencils and other gear.

"Oh yes. Absolutely," I said confidently. He nodded and wandered away to speak with the other artistes in the room.

The truth was, not only had I never studied figure drawing, I didn't have the first idea what figure drawing actually *was*. But I'd faked more difficult things, I was sure.

In the class, I'd recognized Nicole Johnson right away from the photograph I'd found online. Heart-shaped face, sharp eyes, blond bob. It had taken a bit of musical chairs, but I'd managed to finagle a spot right next to her. I copied the way she attached paper to her easel and scanned my brain for a suitable opening line.

Before I had a chance to speak, an overweight man wearing a ratty brown robe strode to the center of the room and up onto the podium. It clicked then. Of course: figure drawing. We draw *people*. Okay, no problemo. And then, Mr. Plump dropped his robe. Now he was Mr. Nude.

I didn't know where to look. *Are you kidding me?* He struck a catlike pose, without a hint of irony. There was just *way* too much flesh and bits and pieces and hair, and it was altogether an entirely alarming sight. The room was hushed. People were quietly contemplating his form, taking out their charcoal sticks and starting to sketch.

For me, contemplating and sketching the sight before me was the absolute last thing I wanted to do. My deepest wish right then was to squeeze my eyes tight and scrub away the image I feared was permanently seared onto my brain. Memo to self: *Wikipedia*, Cat. A little background research on what, exactly, is involved in figure drawing might have been useful preparation.

Somehow, I forced myself to raise my eyes again and hold my piece of charcoal as steadily as I could. Oh God. How do people do this? More importantly: *why?* I started moving my charcoal over the page, concentrating on his left foot.

"Okay, people," the instructor called out with an artistic wave of his hand. "Remember: move your hand quickly. Fly over the page. Don't just draw. I want you to capture the essence of the model's gesture. Not just the physical body, but the *mood*."

I had my own approach: attempt to forget what I was looking at and instead pretend I was drawing a bowl of fruit. Okay, so it was a large, fleshy, hairy bowl of fruit, but still . . .

After a few minutes, Mr. Nude changed poses and settled into a reclining position on a chaise lounge. Everyone flipped to a blank page. I took the opportunity to turn to Nicole and glance at her first sketch.

"Hey, that's really good," I said.

Nicole flicked a brief glance in my direction. "Thank you." Her voice was tight; she kept her torso turned away from me.

"That highlighted bit—how did you get that effect?" I asked, pointing to a body part I'd rather not name.

"Chalk."

Hmm. This was going to be tricky. Somehow, I needed to get her to relax and open up. While I brainstormed on this, I kept drawing. The instructor advised us to stay loose and draw quickly, which I tried, until—"*Whoops!*" I cringed. "Oh, that's not good," I muttered to myself. "Pretty much every guy's nightmare . . ." No man likes to see *that* particular piece of his anatomy portrayed at one-third its real size.

Nicole glanced at my drawing and a smile twitched on her lips. We made eye contact and both grinned, suppressing laughter.

But then, under her gaze I had a moment of panic. What if she'd seen a file on me? What if she recognized my face? It was a little late for these thoughts, of course. I was all in now.

I pointed to her sketch with my piece of charcoal. "Yours is good," I said. "You're an artist?"

"No, no," she said, shaking her head dismissively. "I just do this for fun. My day job is much less artistic."

"Oh? What do you do?" I kept my voice light and chatty.

She hesitated briefly. The guard had not been fully dismantled. "I work in criminal investigation, actually."

"Cop?"

"FBI."

"No kidding," I said. I did my best to sound impressed and interested, while fighting down the natural impulse to flee in terror at the sound of someone introducing themselves as an FBI agent.

I did note that Nicole's spine straightened as she said the word. She was still a little suspicious—normal for an agent, I imagined—and although she tried to be discreet, it was obvious she was proud of this.

"Yeah, I do this sort of thing as an escape," she said, resuming her sketching. "Although I have to admit, some weeks are more pleasurable than others." She leaned toward me and lowered her voice. "You should have seen the guy who was the model last week. . . ." She flashed me a wicked smile.

"Good?" I said, raising an eyebrow.

"Think Ryan Reynolds."

"Wow," I said, smiling back. "Nice."

Hmm. So she had good taste in men. Interesting. We continued working on our sketches.

"So how about you?" she asked me. "What do you do?"

I suffered a sudden paroxysm of coughing, and then strove to keep my heart rate steady and my voice even as I said, "Oh, I'm a grad student at the University of Washington. French lit."

Actually, this was true.

Naturally, I maintained a mild-mannered alter ego. Every self-respecting felon has a cover. Mine was a graduate student in nineteenth-century French literature, to be specific. Hugo, Flaubert, Dumas . . . all those great, romantic writers. For me it was more than a fake cover, however. I really did enjoy it.

I yanked the conversation back around to her. "So, being with the FBI must be pretty exciting," I said. "Have you been doing that for long?"

"A few years."

I nodded. I needed to pace my questions a little. "You hunt serial killers and stuff?"

"No, I'm in property crimes. I head the jewel theft team."

"Wow, how cool is that?" My voice was unnaturally high. "A whole team for jewel theft."

"Yeah. Although our department needs a bit of a whip-cracking. We're completely disorganized, and totally bogged down with work."

Perfect. Disorganized was good. I smiled and then quickly schooled it. "Lots of jewel theft in Seattle?"

"You'd be surprised."

"Mmm," I said, nodding, and concentrating hard on my drawing, hoping I wasn't displaying an inappropriate response to that. "I'm sure I would."

As I applied the finishing touches to a particular piece of male anatomy (and doing not a bad job, if I do say so myself), I stopped to consider my sketch, and started giggling.

"God, it's a good thing I don't have a boyfriend anymore," I said offhandedly. "I'm not sure how thrilled he'd be that I've been staring at another man's naked body for the past hour."

She laughed. "My boyfriend thinks it's hilarious."

I looked at her; she was glowing. "Sounds like a good guy." Must be nice to have one of those, I thought. Although I suppose I did, once upon a time. My mood darkened a shade, smeared over with charcoal.

"Yeah," she said. "He is a good guy. He's FBI also."

"Really?" I said, turning to her. "You work together? Isn't that difficult?"

"Sometimes. But it's fun, too."

"Huh," I said, considering this. "I wouldn't know about that. I've never actually dated anyone who does the same thing that I do."

She looked at me with a frown. "But you're a student. You've never dated another *student*? Ever?"

Shit. I was supposed to be disarming her and getting her to open up—not the other way around. "Umm, no. I mean in my exact discipline. Other students, sure, but nobody in French studies."

"Ah," she said.

When the class ended, we packed up our supplies. Despite the fact that I was probably scarred for life from the experience of figure drawing, it was very fruitful talking with Nicole. Getting the inside track on your adversary was always time well spent.

We walked outside together. The sun had set now, and the sky shimmered with gauzy twilight. The air was fresh and cool.

"Hmm . . . where is he?" Nicole glanced around, frowning slightly.

"Who?"

"My boyfriend. He's supposed to be picking me up. . . ." And then she smiled over my shoulder. "Oh, there he is. Hi, honey."

I turned and found myself looking into the face of Jack Barlow. My ex. The man who, two months ago, completely crushed my heart. Shocked, I dropped my portfolio. Out tumbled one of my drawings: a perfectly artless—but nonetheless recognizable—portrait of a big, fat, naked guy in full-frontal pose. It fluttered down like a feather and landed at Jack's feet.

Jack bent down and picked it up with one long, carved arm. I froze as he studied it with a smirk. He looked into my face with those melting brown eyes that had so often turned my knees to syrup, and handed me the drawing. "Is this yours, miss?"

And just like that, I was dying.

I walked across the darkened parking lot in a trance; my cheeks still retained the remnants of a hot burn. At least I could comfort myself with the knowledge that Jack was not going to rat me out to Nicole. He'd kept up the charade that he didn't know me.

Good guy, I thought. And that, right there, was our problem. Right from day one.

It might seem improbable that a thief and an FBI agent could become romantically involved in the first place. But ours had been a pretty typical love story, really. You know how it goes: Boy meets Girl (by investigating the crime ring to which she secretly belongs). Boy and Girl fall in love (while Girl tries madly to keep her true vocation hidden from Boy). Boy loses Girl (partly due to his utter shock at catching her red-handed, but mostly due to his decision to arrest her for a major felony). Then, of course, we get: Boy covers for Girl, lies to his supervisors, arranges for her release because he's realized that he really does love her after all and will somehow have to come to terms with her criminal tendencies but for now is simply going to whisk her away to Paris.

In other words: Boy wins Girl back and the two live happily ever after. Well, that's what was supposed to happen. The happily-ever-after bit. Unfortunately, in the true version of the story, the romance ended rather prematurely, when Boy finally realized he just couldn't tolerate Girl's criminal lifestyle.

After our breakup I did consider giving up my career, leaving my life of crime. But I just couldn't do it. Every time I contemplated it I felt repelled by the idea, like a reverse-polarity magnet was pushing me away. I'm sure it was because of Penny, because of promising myself that I wouldn't quit until I'd made amends. Although, in my darkest moments, I've wondered if there was something else.

I didn't stay long in that cozy triangle outside the art class, making small talk with Nicole and Jack. I extracted myself as quickly as possible. And now all I wanted to do was get to my car, get home, and nurse my wounds with a bubble bath and a vodka.

Midway through the parking lot I got a prickly feeling of being watched. I glanced around. Nothing moving. Nobody to be seen. Only a scattering of motionless cars and minivans, and a pair of battered garbage bins, barely illuminated by the single, dim yellow streetlight. Ruffling maple trees bordered the parking lot, their vibrant autumn colors transformed to black silhouette against the darkening sky.

Okay, Cat. Just your imagination. I kept walking.

And then all the hairs on the back of my neck lifted upward. There it was again.

I ducked down between two cars, crouching low. I scanned for moving shadows and listened hard for footfall. Still, nothing. I began creeping toward my car.

This parking lot was empty, I told myself. Deserted. Okay, fine, my sensors must have been thrown off from the trauma of seeing Jack again.

I reached my car. There was a note taped to the driver's door:

Go to the diner across the street. You will see a man with a white rose in his lapel. Sit down at his table.

I snatched the note and looked quickly around. I *knew* it. But still, I couldn't see a soul anywhere nearby.

In spite of myself I was impressed. Whoever this was, he was good. I glanced back at the note. It was a small square of heavy bond. The message was scrawled in thick, fountain-pen black ink. I didn't recognize the handwriting. It wasn't Templeton. It wasn't any of my friends or anyone else I knew.

Well, this guy certainly favored the cloak-and-dagger routine. Which was fine by me, of course. Cloak and dagger? Totally my thing.

I squinted across the street and spotted Roxy's Diner written in neon, flickering slightly above a low building with glowing plate glass windows. Looked like my bubble bath would have to wait.

Chapter 5

The door chimed as I entered the diner. Which was unfortunate, because I'd wanted to slip in. I was wary as I stepped into the warmth, with tense shoulders and senses going full throttle, but I was also bursting with curiosity. My eyes swept over the red vinyl-covered stools lining the Formica counter, the red vinyl booths with chrome trim, the chalkboard listing the specials. The diner smelled of coffee and onion rings and chicken noodle soup.

Within seconds I'd assessed the degree of danger in there. I scouted the exits (one by the restroom, and another through the kitchen) and the other customers (a family with two teenagers, three grizzled road workers at the counter, a retired couple at a booth in the corner, and a smattering of single diners sitting alone huddled over their platters of French fries and country-fried steak).

But where was Mr. White Rose? Maybe he wasn't there? Maybe this was just someone's joke?

No, wait—there he was.

Hmm. What made me think this would be a man? This was a kid. No older than twenty, I would have said. Sporting curly brown hair, John Lennon-esque glasses, and falling asleep in his seat.

But I wasn't ready to approach him yet. I ran my gaze over the other customers there. Yes, the man seated by the window was clearly a lookout, judging from the tension in his body, his hyper-alert gaze that didn't belong in a diner at supper time. And there was another, lingering by the restroom. His weight was just a little too far forward, a little too ready to make a move if necessary.

Despite this, I didn't see an imminent threat. Their eyes were wary, but not malevolent. There was no finger twitching, preparing to grab a weapon. These guys were just watching. They were leery, but then so was I.

I strolled across the diner and slid into the booth to sit across the table from Mr. White Rose, keeping track of the watchers in my peripheral vision. I observed Mr. White Rose for a moment. His head lolled forward, a small line of drool was escaping his mouth, and his face was smooth, slack, and peaceful.

I cleared my throat. He awakened with a start.

"What? Oh! Miss Montgomery." He sat up, flustered and wild eyed. "Was I asleep?" He raised a hand to rub his face and spilled his coffee across the table.

I nodded, mopping up the mess with a wad of napkins from the tin dispenser on the table. "Looks like you just dozed off a little," I said. I struck a casual tone here, but my brain was churning. He'd used my *name*.

"No problem, no problem," he said, straightening his glasses and wiping the crusted drool from the corner of his mouth. Could this possibly be the person who so skillfully drew me here? No, surely the true mind here was behind the scenes. I flicked a surreptitious glance at the lookouts; nothing about them said "leader," however. Was someone else involved? At that moment a waitress in a peach-colored apron arrived. She placed a fresh cup of coffee on the table, refilled the spilled one, and said she'd return for our order.

I lifted the warm mug and sipped, watching him over the rim. I didn't usually drink coffee black, but fiddling with packets of sweetener and little pots of cream would have created the wrong impression at a clandestine rendezvous, I felt. Bitter, strong flavor punched my tongue, but I swallowed it down.

"So, Miss Montgomery," he said, lowering his voice and leaning toward me, "I'm here to ask for your help."

"Oh?" I said lightly. "You need a French lit tutor?"

He smiled but shook his head. He lowered his voice further. "We know who you are and what you do."

My gut squeezed. "I'm sorry. I don't follow," I said, keeping my features smooth. Who *was* this guy?

"Please, Miss Montgomery. We know you are skilled at . . . *procuring* certain items."

I glanced swiftly around. No other patrons were within earshot. "I don't know what you're talking about."

He shrugged. "Okay. Does the Camelot Diamond sound familiar? The Bianca necklace?"

I tightened my jaw. Those were recent jobs of mine. "Maybe you'd like to tell me who you are," I said sharply. "And who you mean by 'we.' Other than the lookouts you've got posted by the restroom and that table over there." I flicked my eyes in the direction of the two men I'd spotted.

His eyes widened. He blinked. "I must say, Miss Montgomery, they told me you were good, but I'm impressed."

I maintained a cold stare. "You were about to explain who you are, exactly."

"Yes, of course. My apologies. My name is Sandor." He rubbed his chin and pressed his lips together. "My family is—well, have you heard of the Romanovs?"

At that, my mind conjured images of imperial Russian splendor, snow-covered Saint Petersburg, and the lavish Winter Palace.

"Are you telling me your ancestors were the *czars*?"

Sandor nodded. He slid his coffee cup on the table, rolling it between his hands.

"But—they were all killed," I said. "In the revolution. A mass execution."

"Well, that's what you were supposed to believe. But you know as well as I do that the public story is often completely different than the private one."

A good point.

"Okay, fine." I took another sip of coffee and shifted in the slippery vinyl booth. "Let's just say, hypothetically, that this is all true, and you really are who you say. How do you know who *I* am?" Little fluttery shocks of anxiety were going off inside me, like the uncomfortable zips you get with static electricity. I had a lot of questions besides this one—like who else besides Sandor knew these things about me.

"A family like ours has a lot of resources and connections," Sandor said. "How do you think we've survived all this time?"

"Fair enough." I folded my arms over my chest, leaned back and narrowed my eyes at him. "So, what do you want, exactly?"

He bolted down the remainder of his coffee. But he winced slightly as he did it. It was endearing, really, to watch this kid try to play the big man. I was starting to get the picture. I imagined the patriarchs of his family pushed him forward for this task. I wondered why him, though. Did they think he would be the least intimidating? Were they trying to disarm me? What?

"Have you heard of the Fabergé Eggs, Miss Montgomery?"

"Of course." Any self-respecting jewel thief knew all about the Fabergé Eggs. They were masterpieces, designed by the virtuoso jeweler Fabergé for the Russian imperial family to give to each other as Easter gifts. Today, a Fabergé Egg is worth several million dollars. The Rothschild Egg was sold by Christie's auction house a few years ago for nearly nine million pounds sterling.

"In that case, you probably know," Sandor continued, "that many of the Eggs went missing during the revolution."

I nodded. There were fifty known Imperial Eggs originally. When the palaces were looted during the revolution, several Eggs disappeared. Some were found, but eight were still missing.

"It's been my family's quest ever since to right that wrong, to track down the lost Eggs and recover them for the family. One of them, in particular, is called the Aurora Egg. Its existence has been seldom documented. Even so, we've traced its path over the years, and we've finally located it here."

"In Seattle?" A thrill traced up my back. The only things better than priceless jewels are long-lost priceless jewels that have just turned up in your own backyard. And a Fabergé Egg, at that. It's like the holy grail for a jewel thief.

"Believe it or not, yes. And this is where you come in. We want to hire you to steal it back for us."

I said nothing for a moment. I sipped my coffee to partially hide the expression on my face. This sort of job would be a thief's dream.

Sandor looked at me uncertainly. "Maybe this wouldn't mean

anything to you, but it would be a chance for you to right a very old wrong."

I froze, midsip. My heart soared at the very idea. Could this be the job I'd been waiting for? Reflexively, I touched my old ring and twisted it back and forth.

But there was a problem: I couldn't take work outside the Agency. It was a major no-no. It was the sort of thing that could terminate my contract with the Agency—and end my career. He was going to have to go through AB&T. But that might mean the assignment would go to someone else. I squeezed my hand into a fist beneath the table, weighing the sides. I really didn't have a choice. I couldn't jeopardize my future.

I exhaled. With a great deal of effort I said, "It's an intriguing proposition, Sandor. But what you need to do is contact my Agency—"

"No," he said abruptly, his nostrils flaring. "No agencies. Listen, Miss Montgomery, our family is extremely uptight about the possibility of betrayal. We've been deceived in the past; history is familiar with the disasters that befell our family. The fewer people involved, the better. There's no way we're going to be betrayed again."

"Oh," I said. "I see. That's nonnegotiable?"

"Totally." The set of his jaw was firm.

This was a problem. Taking extracurricular work was strictly verboten. Besides, it was risky. There would be no backup, no support team should something go wrong, that sort of thing. And the timing was terrible. I was just at the point of climbing the ladder at AB&T. If I were caught doing a freelance assignment, I'd be out. Likely blackballed, to boot—it would be near impossible to find another agency willing to take me on. I gazed around the diner and quelled the urge to fiddle with the sugar packets.

"So," he said, sitting back and taking a calming breath. "Will you help us?"

I was torn in pieces. The idea of it had me salivating, but the realities of my situation were not good.

"Well, I don't know. I mean, I don't usually work this way. My assignments always come to me through my Agency." I toyed with my coffee spoon. I contemplated the other thieves who might clamor for this job—other, more seasoned thieves. "Why me, anyway?"

"My family believes that you've got the exact skills needed to make this happen. We know all about your recent jobs. The Camelot Diamond heist, for example."

I smiled, reflecting. Yes, I was quite proud of that one. The Camelot was a famous diamond on traveling exhibit from the Louvre. It had been on display last year at the Seattle Museum of Natural History and I . . . *wait a minute.* "You know I was caught during that job, though?" I said. Not before handing off the jewel, I remembered with some pride.

"We know," he said, nodding once and smiling. "We also know that in spite of that, you managed to escape not only arrest but also public exposure. You seem to be a thief of unusual resources."

Yes, well. It helps if the FBI officer who catches you is someone you're becoming romantically involved with. I didn't think I could count on that for future jobs, but I declined to raise that issue with Sandor.

I watched his face carefully. It occurred to me: might he already know about Jack? He seemed to possess a lot of information. A prickly discomfort returned. I disliked it when strangers knew things about me.

"One other thing," Sandor said, leaning forward once again. "I should probably mention that you will be compensated handsomely, should you decide to take this job. We're a family of great means. If you were to help us, we would appreciate it to the highest degree."

Now I liked the sound of *that.*

"In fact . . ." He dug through his canvas bag and pulled out a Cerruti leather checkbook. "This is a show of good faith. No strings attached."

He scribbled onto the check, ripped it from the book, and slid it over to me. My eyebrows elevated. Five thousand US dollars.

"Just so you know, this is simply a gift. Yours to keep. However, if you accept our request, we'll be paying you many times this."

I knew I should walk away. I knew I should turn it down. But when I thought about what this job could mean to me . . . I wasn't so sure. I thought about what happened the last time I turned down a job, when I refused my sister, all those years ago. If I took this job now, might it not help heal that old wound? And what about the sheer challenge of it? I wondered . . . was I even good enough to pull off a job like this?

I chewed my lip. "I need some time to think about it," I managed to say.

He rubbed his face, then nodded. "Fine, I understand. We'll give you twenty-four hours to consider it. But after that, we'll need a commitment."

He slid an envelope adorned with an embossed Venetian mask toward me and I opened it. It was an invitation—engraved on heavy, cream-colored card stock—to a masquerade ball.

"Your appearance at this event tomorrow night will signal that you have accepted this assignment."

Chapter 6

Mel's face darkened. "You're crazy to even consider it," she said with characteristic bluntness. She turned away from me with exasperation and went to my refrigerator to rummage for something to eat.

I turned to Sophie. Her blue eyes were wide with concern. Sophie's face had always been a plate-glass window without drapes or blinds—you could see her every emotion through it. "Sorry, Cat, I'm with Mel on this one."

I had just told my two best friends about my strange rendezvous with Sandor earlier that evening. They came over as soon as I called. I needed some help getting my head straight over it.

I knew they were right, of course. I should just forget about Sandor's offer. So why couldn't I get it out of my mind? I fidgeted with the sofa cushion. "The thing is, I really think this job could be the one," I said at last.

"Oh, not *that* again, Cat," Mel said from the kitchen. She held up two containers: cocktail olives and a jar of mayonnaise. "By the way, these items represent the entire contents of your fridge. How do you *live*?" she said with a disparaging tone.

Mel was not a thief; she was a pediatrician. Which, as it happened, was the perfect career for her—except for the fact that she didn't like children. To Mel, children were grubby, snotty, squirmy little creatures. Naturally kids adored her. My personal theory was that Mel actually loved kids, deep down. And they could sense that. They were like dogs, I figured. They could sniff out a person's true emotions.

"It sounds dangerous," Sophie said worriedly, sipping her wine. Her armful of bangles jingled as she lifted her glass. "You don't know anything about these people. And I have to tell you, Cat, I'm not getting a good reading from your chakra energy right now."

"Sophie, please. Spare us the hocus-pocus," said Mel. She slid onto a bar stool, pushing aside the take-out containers and unopened mail that adorned the countertop. She slid off her dark-framed glasses and buried them in the mound of blond, curly hair on top of her head. "The whole thing sounds like bad business, top to bottom." She lifted her wineglass and took a sip. She gave me a level stare over the rim of her glass. "Cat, don't you think it's time to stop all this? Isn't it time to look for a new job? A new career?"

"You know I can't do that," I said quietly.

Mel and Sophie have been my closest friends since before we could walk. We all grew up in the same neighborhood and still lived near one another. My girls both knew the truth about what I did and had for a long time.

After my sister died, I tore myself apart with guilt and grief. Mel and Sophie knew something more was going on than what I was telling my parents. They took me aside and I told them everything, all about what Penny had been trying to do and my secret little hobby. Had I been a little older than fourteen when all this came out, I never would have told them. I would never take such a ridiculous risk now.

But they'd been by my side ever since, though I knew they wished I would choose a safer—and somewhat less illicit—line of work.

The two of them would never have dreamed of breaking the law themselves. But they didn't hold it against me. Or, at least, they hadn't up till now.

"Let me ask you this," Mel demanded. "How will you know when it's time to let that go? How will you know if you've done enough, so you can stop feeling guilty about Penny?"

"I'll just know."

"And do you really think you would leave it all after that?" asked Sophie.

I frowned into my wineglass. That—I didn't know.

"Know what I think?" said Mel. "I don't think you're capable of leaving it, of not being a thief. I think it's too much a part of you. And I think there's something that keeps drawing you into it. Something more than what happened to your sister."

"What do you mean?"

"I don't know. But there's got to be something. Really, Cat, any normal person would have gotten out long ago."

"Oh, thanks. So I'm abnormal now?"

"What makes you use the word *now*?"

"Ha. Funny."

I looked at my two girlfriends. They only wanted the best for me. "Okay, fine," I said. "Maybe you're right. I'll try to forget about this job."

Traffic sounds floated up and over my balcony, into my living room. The city was coming to life for the evening.

"Why don't we get out of here?" Mel said abruptly. "If we hurry, we can get to Bar None for a drink before happy hour ends."

"Good idea. I need a distraction. Just let me get changed."

I darted into the bedroom. While I was digging around in my closet I called out to my friends in the kitchen. "Hey, Mel! I need my black sandals, the ones with the rhinestones and the killer heel— can you grab them for me?" I flopped onto the bed, struggling into my dark, super-skinny jeans.

"Uh, sure," Mel said. "Where are they?"

"The oven." I stuffed lip gloss and some cash into my handbag.

Momentarily, her head popped around the bedroom door frame. "I'm sorry—I don't think I heard you. . . . Did you say the *oven*?"

"Yes."

She didn't move, staring at me with concern.

"Forget it," I said, sighing with exasperation. I walked briskly past her to the kitchen. I opened the oven door with a creak. Inside was a neat line of several pairs of shoes. I grabbed the sandals and closed the door, turning around to see Mel staring at me. A smirk grew on her face.

"What?" I said defensively. "I ran out of closet space. Besides, it's not like I *use* the oven for anything."

"Good point."

Then, there was a knock at my door.

"I'll get it," said Mel, striding toward the door. I frowned, wondering who it could be—I wasn't expecting anyone.

Mel swung open the door. In the hallway stood Bradley, my neighbor from across the hall. Bradley, my fortysomething, balding (but in denial), personal-injury-lawyer neighbor. I cringed when I saw him. What now? I wasn't in the mood for interruptions; I was keen to get going. Mel folded her arms and leveled Bradley with a caustic stare. "What do you want?" she asked.

Bradley ignored Mel. "Good evening, Cat!" he said, using his cheerful and important tone. This was the one that was like a cheese grater on my mental state. His smile was oily car salesman. I could see his eyes flicking about my apartment, noting the dishes piled in my sink, the damning heap of laundry parked by my front door. He held out an envelope with a flourish. "This registered letter was being delivered to you yesterday, and you weren't here, but it seemed to be an urgent matter, so I agreed to take it and deliver it personally. . . ."

I strode over and snatched the letter. "Thanks, Bradley. That's really helpful," I said in monotone. I glanced at the envelope: registered, government-looking.

Mel closed the door and I tossed Bradley's letter on top of the stack of mail.

"Aren't you going to open that?" asked Mel.

"It looks important," Sophie said with concern. She picked up the letter and studied it.

"Nah. I'll look at it later," I said. "Let's get going."

I stood in front of the hall mirror and touched up my mascara. There. Ready. When I turned back, Mel was opening the envelope with a knife.

"Mel, what the *hell*?" I stared at her with outrage.

"What? I can't help it. I can't stand it."

She started reading the letter before I had a chance to stop her. As I walked toward her, ready to snatch the letter away, a small prickle of warning crept up my neck. Her eyes opened wide.

"Um, Cat, I think you should look at this."

"Why?" Her face was ripe with worry. Mel never worried, so I took the letter from her. The seal at the top read: *Internal Revenue Service.* The IRS? What did they want with me? Mel tucked in behind me, reading over my shoulder, as I scanned the words.

Dear Miss Montgomery:

We have recently conducted an audit at Anderson, Bradford & Taylor Inc. You are registered there as an employee and have been receiving wages for the past five years. Our records, however, indicate that you have not filed income tax returns for the past ten years. We have calculated your income taxes for the last five years, using the data provided by AB&T, and we have assessed your amount payable below. This includes delinquent taxes plus interest plus fines.

You are herewith advised of 30 days to pay the following, or we will be forced to levy your assets. We would like to take this opportunity to remind you, Miss Montgomery, of the grave nature of tax evasion and fraud. Certain crimes are punishable by incarceration.

My eyes zipped down to the dollar amount at the bottom of the page. I gasped and clenched the counter for support.

"What?" Sophie had been frozen to her bar stool, watching this whole thing. "What is it?"

"Looks like I'm in some trouble with the IRS." My voice sounded faraway, in someone else's apartment. I was still staring at the letter, crumpling slightly in my sweaty hand.

"Trouble? With your last tax return?" Sophie asked.

I looked up at them. "Um, no. It's—well . . . I've never actually filed a tax return."

"What do you mean? Never filed?" Mel said, staring at me incredulously.

"Well, I'm a *criminal*," I said with exasperation. "I really didn't think criminals did that sort of thing."

Mel snatched the letter from me. "Okay, but your organization clearly files tax returns. Didn't you know that? Do you remember signing something when you were first hired?"

I pressed back in my mind, trying to remember. "You know, that sounds familiar. . . ."

A fuzzy memory pushed forward. It was years ago, on my first day with AB&T, Templeton saying something to me about AB&T setting up a legitimate shell company, carrying all of their employees on their books. Something about protecting themselves, and that we needed to do the same thing. But I hadn't really paid attention. I was too excited—my first day at a new job.

"Didn't they send you W-2s?" Mel demanded.

"I hid them. I thought the whole operation was secret," I said miserably.

"Oh my God, Cat, how can you be so naive?" Mel shook her head.

"Okay, now you sound like my mother." I crossed my arms.

"I'm sorry about that, but this is a big problem. You have to pay that bill. ASAP." Mel looked at me with genuine fear in her eyes.

An icy hand touched my spinal cord. She was right. The last thing I wanted was the IRS conducting a full-blown audit on me. If they came sniffing around they could find out what I do. Even if they didn't imprison me for tax evasion, they would get me for my real crimes. My head began to swim. I couldn't let that happen.

"Do you have enough to pay the bill?" Sophie asked, eyes wide.

"No," I said, rubbing my forehead. "I gave a lot away—UNICEF was in major need last year, and the Red Cross had a very persuasive fund-raiser . . . and the rest I lost in that bad investment scheme, remember? My Swiss account is bare bones right now."

Mel closed her eyes. "Okay," she said, with a deep breath. "Is there some other way you could come up with that sort of money? In thirty days?"

I stood there, chewing a fingernail.

Mel closed her eyes and shook her head. "Oh no. No you don't."

Chapter 7

After a long, restless night filled with dreams about Fabergé Eggs and prison bars and—inexplicably—figure drawing classes, I still wasn't sure what to do. In bed, I cracked my eyes open and glanced at my alarm clock. Highly inconveniently, it read 10:12 a.m. I sat bolt upright.

Crap, crap, crap. My mother was going to kill me. I should have been up an hour ago. I was supposed to be going to a baby shower with her this morning. I flew out of bed and started tearing clothes out of my closet.

It's not that I was keen to attend. On my list of things I'd like to be doing that day, a baby shower in the suburbs fell somewhere between swimsuit shopping (I've long suspected they use fun-house mirrors in those changing rooms) and having my car serviced (curse those mechanics and all the damn extra repairs they "strongly recommend" knowing perfectly well I have no idea what they're talking about).

The trouble was, my mother lived for these social graces. She also possessed an athletic talent for administering guilt trips. I'm convinced mothers learn this skill in Lamaze classes. You know: *This is how to breathe in the second stage of labor, this is how to change a diaper, this is how to deliver an effective guilt trip. . . .*

So it was fine. I would just make a brief appearance, make my mother happy, then get out of there.

I got dressed for the shower in a whirlwind. I bolted through the rain, threw everything in my black Mini Cooper—including my pitiful potluck contribution of a bag of frozen edamame chipped away from the back of my freezer, and my makeup bag—and leaped behind the wheel. I had luck on the freeway and made pretty good time. I even managed a half-decent job at applying my makeup as I went. The concrete and glass of the city quickly changed into leafy streets and houses of the suburbs. I careened off the 520 to Kirkland, and drove on autopilot. My mind roamed away. Thoughts of Sandor, and his offer, bubbled like soup in my brain.

Mostly, I wanted to take the job. For practical reasons: I needed the money. Badly. And for less practical reasons, too. The thrill, the challenge, and—no matter what my friends said—the irresistible possibility that this job could be *the one*.

But I knew it could be a big career error. It could ruin my future. Of course, being behind bars for tax evasion tended to ruin one's future, also.

Yesterday, I'd called Templeton and demanded, "Did you know that AB&T files corporate tax returns? And that I'm listed as an employee?"

"Of course, Cat. The company is not about to get caught for tax evasion, now are they? That's very unfashionable."

"Shit, Templeton. I haven't filed tax returns."

"For how long?" His voice was quiet and apprehensive.

"Like, forever."

There was a long pause. "Oh. That's not good."

I chewed my lip and asked, "Are there any big jobs coming up? Anything that could make me a lot of money in the next thirty days?"

"I'm sorry, kiddo. I don't know of anything that major right now. But I'll see what I can dig up."

I arrived at my parents' house and walked straight to the kitchen, which carried lingering smells of breakfast sausage and dish soap. No sign of my mother. I frowned, wondering what that meant, when I heard, *"Pssst."*

I turned. It was my dad, poking his head around the back door. "Cat," he whispered, "is your mother nearby?" My dad's sixtieth birthday had been that year. He was bald on top, with gray hair fringing around the sides and back. His eyes were smiling at me—they were always smiling, with permanent crinkles at the sides. His nose was slightly pointed, like an elf's. To me, he looked anything but old.

"I haven't seen her yet," I said.

"Perfect." He stepped into the kitchen.

"What are you doing, skulking around?"

"I've got *this*." He showed me the corner of a large package tucked under his arm. I knew right away it was a folded sail. Probably a new spinnaker for his sailboat. This was strictly contraband. It enraged my mother when he "wasted money" on his Leif Eriksson fantasies.

My dad and I loved to sail. When I was growing up he'd take me to the yacht club every chance he got. These days we met there once a week. My mother, on the other hand, despised sailing—she suffered terrible seasickness. "Mom will kill you," I said.

"I know," he said. "That's why I need you to help me get it upstairs. Be my lookout?"

I grinned and helped him sneak it up, keeping guard while he went up first. We climbed into the attic, ducking through soft streaks of filtered light, breathing musty, mothball-scented air.

I unfolded the spinnaker a little to admire it. The sailcloth was first rate. "It's beautiful, Dad. Good choice." We hauled open a trunk, and my dad placed the sail inside. "Good. Your mother never needs to know." We closed the lid and latched it with a soft *click*. He winked at me. "My little partner in crime."

I was stunned for a second, until I realized he was only talking about the sail. I laughed—a brittle laugh.

I could never tell my father the truth about what I do. My dad might sneak a sail or two into the house, but he would never do anything truly wrong or illegal. He wouldn't dream of it. His income tax forms were honest to the penny. Even in a snowstorm, he waited for the crosswalk light to turn.

"Hey, do you remember the time we had to sneak in that enormous new boom and hide it in the garage?" He grinned.

I laughed again. "Yeah, that wasn't easy."

I glanced around the attic. My eyes were drawn to my dad's

model boats, beautifully constructed, intricate works of art. He'd always had craftsman's hands. Something I'd inherited, I figured. I stared at my hands. Craftsman's hands that I applied to an altogether different purpose.

"What is it?" asked my dad, yanking me from my trance. "Everything okay, Kit Kat?"

"Yes, I'm fine," I said quickly, snapping on a smile. "It's nothing." I could never tell him the truth. Could I?

I gazed around the attic again, the dusty space inhabited by remnants and relics of our family's history. A large trunk rested under a dormer window, labeled *Penny*.

An emptiness opened before me. I glanced at my dad, but he was looking elsewhere, moving boxes in a corner. I'd never been able to bring myself to tell him that it was all my fault that Penny died. Although my dad and I had always been like partners, like two peas in a pod, Penny had been his baby. He had never recovered from losing her. His hopes for both his daughters had been high; he was always our biggest fan. And now, all those hopes were pinned on his one remaining daughter.

No. Telling him the truth about me would crush him.

We descended from the attic and returned to the kitchen. My mother was there, waiting.

"Oh, there you are, darling. Chop, chop, we're going to be late." My mother had frosted gray-blond hair, cut precisely in a sharp bob. She swathed herself with pashminas and shawls at all times. She was short, yet carried herself with the posture of a marching band leader, so you didn't notice her true height as much.

"Have fun, you two," said my dad, slipping away to the living room.

My mom turned to me. "All right, plans have changed. We're not going to the baby shower."

"We're not?"

"We're going to Barnes and Noble." She narrowed her eyes at my choice of footwear and then ran her gaze over my outfit. "You're going to need a sweater—it's chilly out there." She shuffled me out the door, grabbing a pashmina for me on her way.

"Um, why are we going to a bookstore, exactly?" I asked.

"Research," she said plainly. She all but pushed me into the passenger seat of her Volvo, then went around to the driver's side. She reversed the car out of the driveway, checking her lipstick in the mirror as she did so, and said, "Oh, I almost forgot, Catherine. You have an appointment with Templeton next week to discuss your commission."

For years I had successfully concealed my true job from my mother. This was no easy task. My mother had a black belt in prying and a PhD in meddling. But several months ago, I couldn't take all the nagging ("you need a career, darling") and all the pestering ("do something meaningful and make something of yourself for goodness's sake, or no man will ever be interested in you"). I told her exactly what I did for a living, and exactly how good I was at it. At first she was—as I expected—shocked. Traumatized, even. But over a period of months, that twisted mind started manipulating things around. Pretty soon, not only was she okay with the whole thing, you could actually say she was on board.

"Mom, I've told you before, I don't want you contacting Templeton," I said through my teeth.

"Now don't go getting all miserable," she said, fussing with the car stereo as she sailed through an intersection. "I'm only trying to help you."

"I don't need your help. This is *my* career. Mine."

"Yes, and I'm not certain you're handling it all that well, from what I can see." I rolled my eyes. She saw nothing of my career. But this was not a new conversation. "Are they paying you enough? It's dangerous work you're doing, do they realize that? They're probably not even paying for your disability insurance, are they? You *do* have disability insurance, don't you?"

"Mom, please," I said witheringly. "Do you think I'm an idiot? Of course I do."

Memo to self: Look into disability insurance policies first thing next week.

"Anyway, I took the liberty of scheduling this meeting with Templeton," she continued, accelerating through a left turn and cranking the wheel.

I gripped onto the handle above my window. "Okay, first: how did you get a hold of Templeton? Second: why are you meddling about in this?"

"We've discussed this. I'm your business manager, darling."

"My *what*? We have most definitely not discussed this."

"Really, Catherine," she said, glancing sideways at me. "You need someone to keep things organized. Let's face it, dear, orderliness is not exactly your strong suit. That's why I've appointed myself to guide your career."

This had taken things to a whole new level. But I shouldn't have been surprised. My mother had always been overly involved in her kids' lives—and of course it became much worse after Penny died. She explained to me once that her own mother was essentially absent. My grandmother was depressed, miserable, and hardly ever there for her kids. My mother swore she would be different.

"One other thing," she continued before I could formulate a cohesive argument to the business manager issue. "You're going speed dating. Next Tuesday."

I closed my eyes and took a calming breath. "Excuse me?"

"Now don't give me a hard time on this, Catherine. You know as well as I do that a stable, committed relationship would help with your cover." She pressed hard on the brakes to come to a sudden stop at a red light. My seat belt locked. "A married woman is far less suspicious." Sitting at the light, she turned her scrutinizing gaze on my hair and reached up to fuss with the pieces closest to my face. I removed her hand.

"Possibly," I said. "But—just so you know—I don't need to do anything so desperate as *speed dating* to get a boyfriend, Mom."

Her eyes sprang wide with surprise and delight. "Are you telling me you *have* a boyfriend?" She gasped. "Wait—has Jack taken you back, darling? I can't believe you didn't tell me!"

"No," I said firmly. "Jack has not 'taken me back,' as you so charmingly put it. And no, I'm not dating anyone."

She scowled, disappointment at our breakup renewed. I could see the blame in her eyes. After our relationship ended, my mother questioned me incessantly about it, trying to deduce what I'd done wrong, how I'd ruined things. It wasn't novel behavior—with every boyfriend I'd ever had, she'd done the same thing.

Jack, however, was going to be a particularly tough act to follow, in her eyes. And in mine, too, I supposed.

My mother pulled the car into the Barnes and Noble parking lot. With a great deal of relief I unbuckled myself and climbed out. "So why are we here, anyway?" I asked.

She smiled gleefully. "They're having a book signing. It's very important for your career."

"Okaaayyy," I said doubtfully, and awaited the explanation that was sure to follow.

"A reformed thief has written a juicy exposé," she said. "A tell-all. It'll be good research."

"Mom, that's not research," I said flatly. "You know what else isn't research? *Ocean's Eleven.*"

My mother seemed to think I needed to be watching heist movies like *The Pink Panther* and *The Italian Job* to stay brushed up on my industry. Reminding her these were works of fiction never seemed to make any impact.

She flung her shawl about her shoulders and strode toward the bookstore. I must admit my curiosity was piqued. I wondered who the thief-turned-author was. Still, I wasn't about to give my mother any satisfaction. I emitted an exasperated sigh. "Fine. Let's get this over with." I grabbed my pashmina and followed her.

The moment we entered Barnes and Noble I was enveloped with that wonderful bookstore smell that's part roasting coffee, part book paper. People were just beginning to gather for the reading and find seats.

We were still early, as it turned out, which gave me a chance to browse the bookstore briefly. I found myself drawn to the Art section . . . Decorative Arts . . . Antiques and Collectibles . . . *aha*. A book on Fabergé Eggs.

I picked it up, flipped through some pages. I was dazzled by full-color photographs of the exquisite jeweled eggs. All familiar images—like old friends. My mind spiraled away, tracing around the decision I had to make by that night, revolving around the same issues, no closer to a resolution.

My mother found me. "It's almost time, Catherine. Let's get coffee."

I ordered two lattes from Starbucks and handed one to my mom. As she steered a direct course for the front row, I sipped my drink and glanced at the poster propped on an easel.

Hot coffee spurted out of my nose.

Oh. My. God.

The author of this juicy exposé was none other than Brooke Sinclair, my old friend. And by *old friend* I actually meant loathsome, vile, abhorrent archenemy. How could this be? Brooke was supposed to be in prison. I'll admit I didn't—thankfully—know a lot about prison, but I was pretty sure she was not supposed to be walking around freely, never mind publishing memoirs and gallivanting on book tours. But this wasn't the first time Brooke had turned up in my life, unexpected and unwelcome.

I took a closer look at the poster. Prison certainly hadn't changed her appearance: same raven hair and deceptively angelic face. The title of the book? *The Good Girl's Guide to Jewel Theft.*

Oh, please.

The funny thing was, Brooke and I hadn't always been enemies. In fact, we started out as friends. We were both undergraduate students at NYU. One day, many years ago, I was leaving the old stone library on campus and saw an opportunity too good to ignore. After bumping, just lightly, into a gentleman who was passing me, I apologized. For bumping into him, that is, not for lifting his wallet—which had been dead easy.

Anyway, the moment I lifted the wallet I noticed a young woman seated at a table looking directly at me. She raised an eyebrow and smiled knowingly.

My stomach squeezed. She'd seen me. It was something that had never happened to me before—getting caught. I didn't know what to do, so I turned and hurried down the broad marble steps to the foyer and out the door.

Nothing happened until the next day. I was reading *Madame Bovary* on the campus lawn when the same woman sat down beside me.

"We've got something in common," she said, and smiled.

And that was how I met Brooke Sinclair, professional jewel thief. I was thrilled when she took me under her wing. Over the next couple of years she transformed me from a common, amateur burglar into a true professional. She taught me the finer points of the craft: circumventing high-tech security, analyzing blueprints, maneuvering ledges in high heels, etcetera. The thing is, I don't think she expected I would become any good.

But I did. In fact, I became really good. And I loved it. I loved the thrill, the excitement, the challenge . . . everything. Even better, I began to get the attention of the chief officers at Larceny New York, the prestigious agency that Brooke worked for.

They began asking Brooke about me. It was just at this time that Brooke had started discouraging me from pursuing jewel theft as a career. But by that time I was hooked.

Really, I should have seen it coming.

In Barnes and Noble, Brooke breezed by me on her way to the podium, in a swirl of Christian Dior perfume. Her long dark hair was smooth and glossy and her slender figure was perfectly defined in a tailored white Donna Karan suit. Before she got any farther I grabbed her elbow and pulled her aside. Her eyes popped wide and she stiffened, then relaxed when she saw it was me.

"Oh hello, Cat," she said smoothly, looking bored now.

"Brooke, what the hell is going on?" I spat in a low voice. "How did you get out of prison? What's this book garbage?" I waved my hand in the direction of the poster. "*Good Girl?* Please. Are you kidding me with that?"

She shrugged. I rolled my eyes. "Never mind that," I said. "What are you doing here?"

"Um, I'm signing my books." She reached for a book and cracked open the front cover. "How shall I address yours?"

"Brooke, cut the crap. You know what I mean."

The manager of the bookstore approached, a man with a too-long neck and ears like portobello mushrooms. "Miss Sinclair, are you ready to begin?" he asked in a whispering voice, gazing at her like she was a rare butterfly. "The crowd is getting a little restless."

I looked out to see the eager faces of blue-haired ladies, young moms wrestling toddlers, preteens with braces, all turned to Brooke like she was some kind of movie star. I scraped my teeth together. I guess it had been naïveté on my part thinking I'd seen the last of Brooke Sinclair. Because there she was, back to haunt me. Like the roots of your natural hair color growing back in.

In New York, as I had been learning the trade and gaining an excellent reputation as Brooke's protégé, LNY hired me on probation. They gave me an assignment—my first solo job, and it was a crucial test, to see if I had the chops to work for them. The target was a famous diamond necklace, from a guest room at the Plaza, no less. It was better than being asked to the prom by the high-school heartthrob.

As I was reviewing blueprints in my dorm, preparing for the theft later that evening, I received a text message from the agency.

Good job. We'll see you at 5 p.m. for the transfer.

What? Then I saw the headline on the news: FRENCH DIAMOND NECKLACE STOLEN. My mouth hung open. Someone else had scooped it before I had.

I rushed directly to LNY's head office. As I attempted to explain, they received a call from the team that had been dispatched to search my room. They'd found the necklace tucked under my mattress.

Needless to say, I was immediately fired. Truth is I was lucky that was all that happened. I suppose they took mercy upon me, being young and inexperienced.

I was angry and confused. Who would have done this? Brooke flashed into my mind—but why would she betray me? We were friends. Brooke was my mentor. And she already *had* everything. What would she have to gain?

Still, I had to know for sure. I gathered my nerve and went to find her.

"Tell me this wasn't you," I said, standing in Brooke's dorm room. One look at her smug face gave me my answer.

I struggled to stay calm. I felt like the carpet had been ripped out from under me. "Why?"

"Because someone needed to show you, Cat, how these things are meant to work." She began filing her nails. "I saw what was happening to you. You were getting overconfident. You needed to be brought back to reality a little."

"A *little*? I was fired from the agency!"

Brooke rolled her eyes. "Don't be so dramatic. You'll find other work." Then she paused. Knitting her perfectly shaped eyebrows together, she said, "You know, I'm not so sure LNY was the best fit for you anyway. I mean *I'm* the professional jewel thief here. I just taught you what I know. But the truth is, it's really not your thing, Cat. You do *okay*, I suppose. But you'll never truly excel. You're not anything special. In fact, I've been quite concerned you would make a mistake and get caught. You should probably consider a different line of work. I hear there's a lot of money to be made pickpocketing on the subway."

My response to this was to buckle and retreat home to Seattle, where I transferred to the University of Washington. That was a very dark time for me. But I eventually recovered and started working again. That was how I came to be at AB&T.

"Two minutes, please," Brooke said to the bookstore manager, in a silken voice. He grinned, flushing to his ears. I expected him to return with a latte and an offer to rub her feet.

"Unbelievable," I whispered angrily. "Come here."

I dragged her into the ladies' room. We needed to talk and we needed some privacy. Unfortunately, there was another woman in the restroom standing by the sinks. We paused and waited for her to leave. The woman was notably overweight, bent toward the mirror, carefully applying lipstick.

Seconds ticked by. Brooke cleared her throat and made eye contact with the woman's reflection. "Please. Do you really think that lipstick makes any difference?" She looked the woman up and down, just once.

The woman blinked, hand frozen in midair. And then her face crumpled as she stuffed the lipstick in her purse and stumbled out.

I glared at Brooke, who wore a smug smile and brushed a piece of lint from the shoulder of her jacket. "There. Problem solved," she said. She twisted the lock on the restroom door, ensuring us privacy. "Now. You were saying?"

This was vintage Brooke, ruthless and cruel, doing whatever it took, no matter who got hurt. "You haven't changed," I said.

She shrugged.

"Why aren't you in prison?" I demanded.

"Did you honestly think I would be kept there? Really, it didn't take long . . . a few phone calls to the right people, you know, and voilà."

"If it was so easy for you to get out, why did you stay there at all?" I asked, narrowing my eyes suspiciously. She'd been behind bars for at least six months.

"Well, I had to call in a couple of favors that I was hoping to save for later," she said, a look of mild regret on her flawless face.

I dug my nails into my palms. This was so typical. Brooke's career was ruined. She was locked away. And what did she do? She came back stronger. And better. And famous. *Arrggh.*

"So how much truth is in this thing, anyway?" I asked, poking the hardcover book in her hands.

"Oh, some," she said. "But I haven't named names."

"Right. Well, I guess I should thank you in that case."

"You know, Cat, I wouldn't be so quick to do that." With that, Brooke's bored expression rearranged into something nastier. Her eyes became hard black chips. "I haven't forgotten how I ended up in prison in the first place."

I swallowed. "Oh, right."

Okay, so that was true. Brooke had been incarcerated because of me. But in my defense, she had it coming. Last year, Brooke tracked me down in Seattle after she began hearing rumors about my successes, and she set out to ruin my career. She systematically undermined everything I did.

But I fought back—something I hadn't done the first time we'd clashed. In the process, Brooke ended up losing. Of course, I didn't exactly win fair and square. I did have some help from the FBI, in the form of Jack Barlow. I frowned, wondering. Would I have been able to best her, if I hadn't had that advantage? I pushed the prickly thought away.

"Fact is, Cat, I'm *never* going to forget it," Brooke said. She folded her arms over her chest and leaned back against the row of sinks.

My attention returned to Brooke. "Oh," I said quietly. "Meaning?"

"Meaning, I'm going to make you pay."

I fidgeted with the edge of my cardigan and forced a light laugh. "Please, Brooke—could you come up with something a little less clichéd?"

She ignored me. "It's called—in a word—revenge, Cat. Pure and simple. You ruined my ability to do what I was put in this world for. In this life I had one true thing, and that was my career as a thief." Her chin was high. Her voice cracked—ever so slightly—and for just a moment I felt like I was seeing behind the polished, lacquered surface and into the true Brooke. "I'm going to do the same to you. Not right away. I'll watch you squirm a little first."

Her face was ice-queen cold. There was no trace of humor. A dark discomfort crept up my neck. Brooke flipped open the lock to the restroom.

"One more thing, Cat," said Brooke, her hand on the door. "You'll always be second rate, and you know it. You can never be as good as me." She strode from the restroom back to her adoring crowd.

The applause sounded muffled to me, underwater. My face was hot with anger, but doubt crowded into my brain. Was she right? I splashed cold water on my face.

Well then. Only one way to find out.

Chapter 8

A driveway curved in front of the looming mansion in Madison Park, a leafy Seattle neighborhood. Sequined masks glittered in the darkness as partygoers arrived. A warm breeze ruffled the burnished leaves of grand oak and chestnut trees. Lights glittered in the endless stretch of windows across the front of the house. Lanterns glowed along the serpentine path and up the steps to the front door. There was a crisp smell in the air of early autumn: apples and pine and wood smoke.

I drew the peacock-feather mask down over my eyes and climbed from the cab, clutching my invitation to the masquerade ball.

Finding a mask that was formal-ball suitable had been surprisingly easy: Yellow pages under *Costume Shop*. Finding an outfit to coordinate with said mask? Not so much. But I did okay. I swished my black silk Marchesa gown (a loaner from Mel) and glided up the steps in sparkling evening sandals.

My heart thrummed with excitement. I loved a party. Loved it even more when it involved an intriguing new assignment. There were a lot of reasons I decided to come here tonight. The deeper reasons—the ones involving my feelings about my sister, and proving myself, and proving Brooke wrong—were distracting and thorny so I attempted to ignore them. I focused instead on the practical stuff: namely, the money. Nothing like a threatening letter from the IRS to push a girl into a little moonlighting.

Even still, I couldn't completely quell the feeling I was making a big mistake. The assignment was going to be dangerous, and I could risk my entire career. Were those risks worth the potential gain?

I'd had a friend run a background check on Sandor (a friend who happened to be a retired intelligence officer from AB&T). I wanted to be sure Sandor was telling the truth. And, indeed, his testimony about being a Romanov descendant held up. An official AB&T assignment would have come with a much more detailed dossier, of course. But that couldn't be helped.

I approached the glossy black doors to the enormous manor. I'd never been here before so I was on my guard.

And so, apparently, was the large German Shepherd stationed next to the two security staff at the entrance.

"Nice teeth," I said, attempting friendliness. The blocklike, uniformed guards stopped me with a glare, as they did everyone. I produced the invitation Sandor had given me. They scrutinized it, scrutinized me, scrutinized it a little more, and finally let me in. I passed through a foyer, then French doors swung wide and I entered a grand ballroom.

Ice sculptures of swans and dolphins sparkled beneath enormous chandeliers; the vaulted ceiling was hung with crimson twists of velvet and satin garland. Dancers glided over the black-and-white checkerboard marble floor, clad in sequined and feathered masks, tuxedos, and satin gowns. A big brass orchestra filled the room with bright swing music.

I surveyed the room full of strangers. Well, I was assuming they were strangers, but of course I couldn't be certain because of the masks. That guy over there? Could have been my dentist. Who knew?

By the same token, of course, I wasn't particularly recognizable. Which was a state of affairs that was definitely within my comfort zone. What was not comfortable was the dress. Mel was a half size smaller than me and the gown was cut to fit.

Never mind. Shallow breaths.

The other source of discomfort was not knowing what was coming next. Did I need to find Sandor? Should I wait for him to find me? What?

A waiter appeared with a tray of fig and prosciutto canapés. I helped myself to one of the proffered canapés and sank my teeth into it. It was salty, sweet, and crunchy all at once—delicious.

I sauntered over to the bar and casually scanned the room. And then I saw someone I recognized. In spite of the gilded Venetian mask, he was unmistakable. And he was the last person I expected to see here. I can't say how I knew it was him, exactly. Something about the set of his shoulders or the angle of his jaw and the self-assured, sharklike way he moved as he made his way through the crowd.

What the hell was *Jack* doing there?

I did not want him to see me. I looked frantically for a gap in the crowd, but people were shoehorned in by the bar. Had he spotted me yet? I hazarded another glance. Yep. Definitely seen me. On his way over, in fact.

And all I could think was: *Damn,* why did he have to look so good in a tuxedo?

"Hi, Cat," he said in a low voice. There was no hint of doubt in his tone. Evidently, I was just as identifiable to him. I wondered how? What were my tells that he knew so well?

I noticed that his eyes were shifting. He looked around constantly, and his muscles were tense, like compressed springs. Interesting. He was working. I wondered what was going on there. What case was he working on? Was there something worth stealing? Some other criminal activity about to go down?

"Hello, Jack," I said, and I was pleased at how cool and aloof my voice came out considering the burning sensation in my chest and the brisk rate my heart was clipping.

"I'm surprised to see you here." His voice sounded tight: by *surprised* he clearly meant *unhappy.*

"Why?" His comment set off an alarm. Why wouldn't I be here? What was going on? My questions quickly turned to indignation. Did he think I wasn't good enough to be invited to an exclusive party like this?

Jack sipped his amber-colored drink—a Manhattan, I suspected—and looked around again. He then leaned in and lowered his voice even further. "Cat, this isn't a good place to be."

I barely registered his words as the scent of his cologne curled its way into my nose and I could feel the warmth from his body as he leaned close. The room went into soft focus. But then I noticed something: a small black earpiece in Jack's left ear. My attention snapped. Who was he communicating with?

"What do you mean, not a good place?" I asked, my eyes narrowing. The orchestra grew a little louder, swinging into full dance rhythm rich with trumpets and clarinets and drums.

"I can't get into it here. Just listen to me: *go home.*"

I felt an angry heat rising up my neck, and my fingers clenched around the stem of my glass. "Excuse me?" I snapped. Issuing vague, veiled warnings was one thing; ordering me away as though I was a helpless child was something altogether different.

"It's dangerous here," he said.

My teeth went on edge. "And just where do *you* get off telling me what to do?"

He straightened. "I'm only looking out for you."

"Listen, you broke up with *me,* remember? You don't have the right anymore. Besides, I can take care of myself." The crowd was thickening; someone bumped into me from behind, jostling me.

"I know that, Cat, but—"

"But nothing. You just do your job, and I'll do mine," I said.

He was about to take a swig of his Manhattan when his hand froze with his glass midway to his mouth. "Your job—you mean you're working right now?"

Crap.

"No. I mean—maybe. Whatever. It's none of your business." Memo to self: Keep a clear head in future when tearing strips off ex-boyfriends, to avoid incriminating slipups.

"Cat, you know I'm just worried about you."

"Once again, *not* your problem."

With this, I turned abruptly and strode off. I marched by a knot of masked, laughing women, and past the carving station rich with scents of roasted meat, to the far side of the room.

Did he think I was incapable? That I was a complete rookie? He knew what I did for a living, for Christ's sake. The last thing I needed was an egotistical ex-boyfriend playing the hero, behaving like I was some sort of distressed damsel in need of saving. I screwed my hands into fists as I imagined his thought process: the kid's not necessarily worth keeping around as a girlfriend, but still let's rescue poor helpless little Cat. . . .

And just as I realized that I was muttering aloud—"arrogant, self-righteous . . ."—I sensed someone close behind me. Hairs lifted at the nape of my neck.

"Hello, Miss Montgomery." I recognized Sandor's voice. I turned.

Sandor wore a red and black harlequin mask. His white tuxedo hung awkwardly on his shoulders, and he looked decidedly uncomfortable in such a formal garment. The effect was endearing, actually, like that of a kid going to a junior high prom.

"So you've decided to accept our offer?" he said.

"Yes." My insides flip-flopped like a fish in the bottom of a rowboat. I hoped I was making the right decision.

He nodded and clasped his hands together. "Excellent. Come with me. We've got a lot to discuss."

Jack stood beside Wesley on the mezzanine, surveying the masquerade ball after his argument with Cat. Wesley adjusted his lime green jester's mask and placed his hands on the iron banister. "Cat Montgomery is here," Jack said in a grim voice, scrutinizing the crowd, sipping his Manhattan.

"What?" said Wesley, abruptly turning to Jack. "What is she doing here?" His voice was low, ripe with suspicion.

"I don't know. But I don't like it."

Jack kept his gaze tethered on Cat, who stood by the piano swirling a glass of champagne. He had been shocked to see her here. Even so, he'd recognized her instantly. His impulse on first spotting her had been to sweep her away. Far away, to safety.

That, Jack thought, would not have gone over well. He'd seen the fire in her blue eyes, just moments ago, as she had advised him she could take care of herself. The corner of his mouth twitched, not quite a smile, in spite of himself. Life had never been dull with Cat. Different than life with Nicole, now. Not that things were boring with Nicole. Just different. Comfortable. Nicole was like Thanksgiving at a cozy country cottage; Cat was a weekend in Vegas.

He watched her sip her champagne. The intriguing thing about Cat, of course, was that she was so much more than she appeared. Like now, for instance, looking exquisite in her cocktail dress but so much more fascinating than any other beautiful woman in the room. Beautiful women were easy to find. But a woman with secrets, with hidden talents and skills and an unexpected familiarity with the dark side . . . Jack inhaled deeply, then clenched his fists. *No, Jack. Not what you need.*

"What's she doing here?" Wesley muttered, repeating himself. "Maybe she's after the same thing we are. She could ruin everything," he whispered harshly.

Jack could see that Cat was talking to someone now. He strained to make out the portion of face not covered by the harlequin mask. Who was it? Jack couldn't tell.

Despite everything he knew about Cat, an uncomfortable itch traveled up his spine at the thought of leaving her down there, knowing the dangers in the room. Treacherous underworld types were here. The Caliga specifically, and they were not a friendly bunch.

They were very good at disguising this, of course, consummate wolves in sheep's clothing. The leader, in particular, was reported to be extremely unpleasant, but with the face of an innocent. They'd had great difficulty obtaining a clear photograph.

Still, what was Cat doing here? Could she possibly be wrapped up with the Caliga?

No. It was impossible. She was a thief, not a gangster or a murderer. He'd always felt confident that Cat was a good person at her core. Could he have been wrong about that? No, she must be here for another reason. He looked down at the party. There was a lot of glitter here that would attract a jewel thief. Had she simply stumbled onto the wrong party?

The trouble was, he had work to do. He had an important contact here at this ball and the rendezvous was crucial. The contact, a Caliga insider, had information on the whereabouts of the Fabergé.

"Listen," Jack said to Wesley. "I want you to follow Cat, see what she's up to. I'll make the rendezvous with our informant. I'll let you know when I've made contact." Jack lightly touched his earpiece.

Wesley nodded. "No problem. I'm on it."

"You can handle this, right?" Jack turned to Wesley, eyeing him carefully. Wesley was sharp, Jack knew that. And he had experience in covert operations. But Jack had never worked with him, and Jack tended to not trust anything until he'd seen it with his own eyes. "She's good—very good at making herself disappear," Jack warned.

"I can handle it," Wesley said in a clipped tone. He glanced around the ballroom. Then he frowned. "But—where is she now?"

Jack turned back to look at the dance floor. "She's over by the piano—"

But Cat wasn't there. Jack's brow lowered. She had been right there just a second ago. The two men scanned the crowd. She had to be there somewhere.

Damn, Jack thought. They had to find her, needed to have her whereabouts pinned before undertaking the delicate rendezvous operation they had planned. He did not need wild cards like Cat Montgomery at large here. Jack rubbed his forehead; he felt a headache coming on. This was going to complicate things.

Where was she? And what was she up to?

Most importantly, was she in danger?

With quick steps, Sandor led me from the ballroom. I followed him through a labyrinth of corridors richly carpeted with handwoven Persian rugs. We entered a small drawing room with dark green walls and a stone fireplace, and he closed the door behind us. Tapestries and a large full-length ornate mirror decorated the walls. He turned to me. He pushed his mask up off his face, and I did the same. I saw his face clearly for the first time tonight—the smooth skin, a small shaving nick on his chin.

"Now, before we continue, Miss Montgomery, you have to understand that this is an irreversible decision."

"Right," I said, nodding, waiting for him to elaborate. My insides tightened. He said nothing. "So . . . could you clarify what you mean by that?"

"I mean there is no going back. Once we've shown you what we're about to show you, you can't back out. There's too much sensitive information here. Do you understand?"

Okay, that sounded ominous. Maybe this was a bad idea. Sandor stood close enough that I could smell the peppermint on his breath. I glanced at the doors we entered through. What did he mean, no backing out? What if, once I learned the details of the job, I didn't think it could be done? Aborting a mission, even in the thick of it, had always been my fallback position. What would happen—what would they *do*—if I were to back out? I shuddered slightly and realized that I didn't know much at all about these people. I had no idea how far they would go.

Trouble was, I knew exactly how far the IRS would go. And I knew I couldn't risk sacrificing my freedom. I couldn't go to prison. And that was the bottom line.

Besides, how could I have lived with myself if I gave up this opportunity?

"Yes, I understand. Absolutely." I strove to keep my voice level, without tremor, and I mostly succeeded.

He walked toward the full-length mirror, touched an area on the carved frame, and the glass of the mirror swung slowly inward. A secret doorway. I smiled. The guy really did love his cloak and dagger.

We stepped through the mirror and descended a dark staircase; my shoes made faint scuffle sounds on the stone steps. The air was cold and damp, mushroomy. The staircase twisted to the left and ended at a large oak door. Sandor opened four separate locks with a large ring of skeleton keys. He pushed the door open.

I chewed my lip and kept my breathing steady. I couldn't see past him, see what was behind the door. An irrational question flashed into my brain—*if I go through, will I ever come back out?*—and I pushed it down scornfully. I followed Sandor and stepped through into the room beyond.

Chapter 9

My breath quickened; we entered a room carved out of rough-hewn stone. The ceiling was low but arched, like a medieval wine cellar. There were half a dozen people gathered around an old oak table, men, mostly, some with gray hair and the pregnant bellies of a long rich life, others young and sharp eyed. All were formally dressed. Wall sconces flickered and the honeyed scent of candle smoke infused the room. An old-fashioned slide projector rested in the middle of the table, and a screen that was slightly off kilter with a small tear hung on a wall.

Everyone stood as we walked into the room. Two people took the opportunity to shake my hand, smiling: the lone woman, middle-aged with a steel gray bob, and a tall man with an asymmetric nose and warm eyes. I smiled uncertainly back. These were all strangers to me, yet they were behaving like we were old business colleagues. I couldn't help wondering what they knew about me. My skin crept. I didn't like people knowing things about me when I knew so little about them.

But all that was going to change soon. It was time to find out exactly what was going on.

"Okay, people, as you know, this is Catherine Montgomery," Sandor said, addressing the room. I looked around and it hit me that all these people were gathered there because of me. And in spite of myself, my chest swelled with a radiant pride. I was special—they all thought I could do this. They brought me here because they thought I was the best. I clenched my hands behind my back. Would I be able to prove them right?

I realized, belatedly, that Sandor had removed his mask and that I, unfortunately, still had mine pushed up on my head like a ridiculous peacock headdress. I whipped it off.

I took a seat.

"Would you like some water?" the man to my left asked with a faint Russian accent. Ice cubes clinked as he poured from a pitcher and handed me a glass.

Before I could ask any questions the servants snuffed the wall sconces and everything went dark. My pulse ramped up a notch. A pale square flicked onto the projection screen and the ancient slide projector whirred into operation.

Flick.

A picture of a Fabergé Egg appeared on screen. "This is your objective," Sandor said. "The Aurora Egg."

My eyes widened. It was absolutely gorgeous. Every inch of the black-enameled Egg was adorned with gold filigree, seed pearls, and onyx.

"Hugo is going to give us some details on the Aurora's heritage," Sandor said.

A man with an unreasonably large chin and a thin mouth rose. He stood beside the screen. "The Aurora Egg was stolen from our family during the Russian Revolution of 1917." Hugo's voice ran low and rich. "In the lists of Fabergé Eggs, no Eggs are noted for the years 1904 and 1905. It was assumed that no Eggs were produced during those years. But that was an inaccurate assumption. The czar kept these secretly produced Eggs apart from the others. The knowledge of their existence has been passed down through our family."

"Why were they a secret?" I asked abruptly.

There was a tense silence and a cough in the room. I got the distinct feeling my questions were neither expected nor particularly desired. Still, after a moment, Hugo addressed me.

"It was a time of war between Russia and Japan. It was also a time of unrest that eventually led to the revolution. Like many other luxuries, the jewelers' craft went underground. Unfortunately, this made these particular Eggs easier to steal and smuggle away. The revolution wiped out most of the trail, but we have finally traced the Aurora here to America. It is in the possession of a powerful family of criminals."

Flick.

The screen changed to show a black-and-white photo of a man, flanked by two other men who could have been his brothers. They were dark haired, with the thick, heavy features highly prized by the casting directors of films like *The Godfather.*

"The Gorlovich family," Sandor said. "They run a chain of casinos, and one of them is here in Seattle. The Starlight Casino. We know there's a vault beneath this casino. The family holds many of their personal valuables in that vault. Our information leads us to believe the Aurora is in that vault."

"What kind of information?" I asked.

"Our operatives have gathered intelligence from one of the security staff there. Mikhail?"

Heads swiveled to Mikhail. He had a peculiarly flat head at the back, like someone had smashed him with a heavy frying pan. The lack of contour on the back of his head was compensated by the extreme architecture of his face—deep-set eyes, prominent nose, large cleft in his chin. He stood and took over the presentation. "We have learned of a rumor about an old Russian treasure being kept in the vault," Mikhail said with a reedy voice.

"We're going in based on a rumor?" I asked. This was not what I considered good recon. Someone cleared his throat at the end of the table. I heard water pouring into a glass.

"No. There's also this," Mikhail said. He produced a file. "These are official papers from the casino, taken from the casino's security room. It lists the vaults under the casino, but the one that interests us is the Bagreef Vault. The list of contents are described only as 'classified.'"

"So?" I asked. Classified could mean anything. "What does Bagreef mean? What language is that? Hindu?"

"No," Sandor said. "It's an anagram. *Fabergé.*"

A chill ran through me. "So it is." With that, I knew we were on. The screen flicked again to another shot of the Aurora Egg. I stared at it. The intricacy and craftsmanship were stunning. Gold detail scalloped the ebony surface, and the enamel was quilted with jewel-work. "So . . . what's inside the Egg?" I asked.

Sandor and Hugo exchange a flicker of a glance. "Inside?" Sandor asked.

"Yes, the 'surprise.' Fabergé Eggs were all created with an interior chamber containing a little surprise, weren't they? Like a charm." I smiled at the steel gray woman next to me.

"Mmm. Right," Sandor said. "Just a carving, we think. A figurine or something. Not important." He waved a dismissive hand.

I frowned. Was it really possible they didn't know what was inside? Why didn't they seem interested?

Whispers eddied around the table and the picture on the screen changed, flicking to a shot of the casino.

"Here—you should examine the security file." Sandor slid the manila folder across the table. "Everything you need to know should be there."

I flipped through the pages in the file. I scanned some superficial listings of systems—CCTV, entry alarms, that sort of thing. But as far as everything I needed to know? Not even close.

"Now, is there anything else you can think of?" he asked.

I took a deep breath. "Actually, yes. I need detailed schematics. Cameras, locks, other security features. I need to know how their computer and wireless systems work." Murmurs fluttered around the table. "I need to know about the casino staff, their hours," I continued. "And I'll need blueprints of the casino. Windows, doors, exits, and a schematic of the underground passages, and the vault, specifically."

"Okay," Sandor said, licking his lower lip. "You really need all of that?" Hugo, Mikhail, and all the others stared at me with varying degrees of suspicion and unease.

They clearly didn't get it.

"We could try, perhaps—" Sandor snapped his fingers and the tall man with the asymmetric nose at the end of the table started frantically scribbling notes.

"You know what?" I said quickly. "Why don't I do the recon myself? That way, I can get what I need."

Sandor shrugged and nodded.

"But maybe you could tell me more about this casino guy?" I asked. "The family—Gorlovich, is it?"

"The Gorlovich family is dangerous," Hugo said in his rumbling voice. "They are underground, and very secretive. They are aware of our presence. However, they do not feel we are a threat."

I wondered if this was what Jack was referring to upstairs. Were members of the Gorlovich family at the ball? My stomach kicked inward—this was going to make things more complicated. Although, if Jack was on the case they wouldn't be a threat for long. A flush of pride unexpectedly glowed inside me, thinking of Jack's ability to do his job. I reached for the condensation-beaded water glass that rested in front of me.

"Okay, so we should discuss the deadline," Sandor said, rubbing his hand through his hair.

"Deadline?" My hand froze midway to my glass.

"We've been hearing rumors about plans to move the Fabergé to a new location. Somewhere in Prague, we believe."

"Okay, so what's the deadline?" I asked. "When are they moving the Egg?" I lifted the cool water glass to my mouth for a sip.

"Three weeks," Sandor said.

My hand jerked suddenly and ice cubes clinked and water splashed down around my mouth and onto the front of my gown. I hastily replaced the glass on the table and mopped at my mouth with my pashmina.

"Is—is that going to be a problem?" Sandor asked. He frowned slightly.

Yikes. Three mere weeks to do recon, get prepped, and do the job was shaving it very close. Typically, that sort of heist would take at least three *months.* But let's face it, I didn't have that sort of time if I was to keep the IRS happy. I looked at the faces around the table, all hopeful and needy and apprehensive.

I swallowed. "That should be fine. No problem whatsoever."

* * *

The next day, I wasted no time. I plunged straight into the job.

Now, when casing a target there are various strategies for obtaining key pieces of information. There's the old-school method: dress like a bag lady, root through garbage, and pull out bills, bank statements, etcetera.

One word: yuck. Modern-day equivalent? Pay a visit to your friendly neighborhood computer hacker.

This was precisely the reason I was driving out to the suburbs on this honey gold and crisp September morning. I turned down a leafy, glowing street and parked outside a gingerbread-cute bungalow.

I rang the bell and the door opened. A grandmotherly figure—all round arms and ample bust and cinnamon-bun hair—greeted me, blanketed in the tangy, buttery smell of freshly baked rhubarb pie. She welcomed me with a warm, wrinkly smile. "Well, Cat!" she said, planting a hand on her hip. "What a lovely surprise. You're just in time for some pie."

"Hi, Gladys."

She ferried me inside. The house was warm and tidy, trimmed with lace curtains and avocado-green appliances, circa 1972. She took my suede coat and I sat at the kitchen table, scraping an aluminum chair across the brown linoleum floor. She sliced an enormous wedge of pie and placed a steaming mug of tea before me.

"So," I asked, "is your grandson at home?"

Gladys wiped crumbs from the counter with a cloth. "No, dear," she said pleasantly. "He's out skateboarding or some such thing. He'll probably be gone until later this afternoon."

I paused and took a sip of hot, sweet tea. *"Good,"* I said. I raised an eyebrow and looked at her over the edge of my teacup. "Got a little favor to ask, Gladys," I said.

"Oh?" Her eyes twinkled mischievously. "In that case, step into my office."

She led me through the living room, past the chintz-covered sofa with lace doilies on the arms, and then to a small nook. She stepped around an easel that supported an unfinished watercolor of a seascape, pushed her knitting basket aside, and closed thick brown curtains, plunging the room into darkness.

She twisted a skeleton key in a wardrobe lock and flung open broad doors to expose a pair of top-of-the-line CPUs, four LCD screens, and a wireless router.

Gladys was my hacker. And she was the best.

She sat and began booting up her machines. The computers hummed, the LCD screens flickered to life. I began explaining what I needed: details of Starlight Casino's security. Schematics, blueprints, as much information as possible.

I took a seat and peered over her shoulder. "Maybe we should start with the security company the Starlight Casino has under contract? I don't know which one it is, though."

"No problem," she said. Her knobby fingers flew over the keyboard. "For starters, let's get into the casino's e-mail." She scrolled down the screen. "Okay . . . here we go . . . ah, yes! There." Her face brightened like a child's on Christmas morning. "This is the accountant's details."

Then, quick as a finger snap, she was into the bookkeeping system. She went from screen to screen like she was changing television channels, then cracked into the casino's bank. A grandfather clock ticked in the corner of the room; I could hear the faint buzz of talk radio from the kitchen. As she trolled through the list of bills, I got a familiar bubbly feeling inside my chest. We were getting close.

And then, Gladys frowned. She clicked a few more buttons. She sat back and folded her arms across her chest with a grumble. "Well, Cat, you're not going to be happy with this."

"I'm not?"

"It's York."

Just like that, the bubbles faded.

York Security never stored any of their information in computers. No hacking. It would be impossible—Gladys could do nothing more for me at the moment.

As I walked back down her front steps I slid my hand along the cold metal handrail and ground my teeth. I didn't have time for snags. *Damn.* I hoped this didn't mean I was going to have to break out my bag lady costume after all.

When I returned home, lost in thought about what I was going to do next, I walked through the door to my apartment and heard the phone ringing. I raced and caught it just in time.

"Cat?" said a woman's voice.

"Yes," I said, slightly out of breath.

"Hi, Cat. This is Nicole. Do you remember me, from the figure drawing class?"

I was stunned for a moment, then found my voice. "Oh, um, yes, of course."

"You asked me to let you know if any good art classes were coming up, and I just heard about a lithograph workshop that sounds great. So this is me, letting you know. . . ."

There was no way I asked her to do any such thing.

Oh, wait—maybe I did. In my haste to get out of that awkward little scene with Jack I might have said something along those lines. What the hell was I thinking? Of all the people in the world to befriend, the least appropriate was the FBI agent sleeping with my ex-boyfriend. No matter how pleasant she may or may not have been.

"Oh. Well, that sounds nice." I frowned and pinched the area between my eyebrows. I had to end this conversation.

"It's this Sunday. Are you interested?"

"I'm not sure. I'm going to have to check. . . ." I rustled some random papers on the counter, pretending to fumble through a calendar.

"Ooh, no, wait," I said, giving my voice a disappointed tenor. "I've got"—brief pause for frantic scanning through mind for suitable excuse—"an appointment that day with my ob-gyn."

A brief silence followed. "On a Sunday?"

"Yes," I said quickly. I started fanning my face with one of those pieces of paper, suddenly feeling hot. "He's, um, very accommodating."

"Oh. Okay, well, maybe some other time." I could tell from her tone that she wasn't buying the ob-gyn story. She thought I was brushing her off.

Inexplicably, I started feeling badly about my pathetic lie. So I began overcompensating. "Yes. Absolutely," I said emphatically. "Let's do it."

She paused and then said, "I hope—was it okay that I called you?"

"Yes!" I said, with an excess of cheer. "Absolutely! Honestly, I just can't make it that day. He's a very popular gynecologist. Impossible to get an appointment with him. He's very good. A genius at Pap smears . . ." *Okay stop, Cat, for God's sake.*

"Okay, well, I'll call you again sometime then. If I hear of anything interesting."

"Yes, please do."

Pathetic. Seriously pathetic. After I hung up, I rolled my eyes and flopped down in an armchair. Memo to self: Must develop a decent strategy for dealing with unwanted acts of kindness from people with the ability to ruin my life. Or, just let voice mail take the call.

Then, as I was sitting there, a nasty little doubt slithered into my consciousness, curled up, and made itself at home. Was that all that was? An act of kindness? Or—perhaps there was something more behind it. Why would Nicole make the effort to call me? Was there another reason? My throat constricted. Did she know something about me? Did she suspect me? Did Jack tell her who I was? *Shit.* Now, what was I going to do about *that*?

Chapter 10

Jack shifted and did his best to ignore the burning, cramping muscles in his shoulders and back. Stakeouts were rarely what you could call comfortable and this one was no exception. He and Wesley were crouched in a small copse of dogwood bushes with their binoculars trained on a suburban house several yards away. Wesley's Ducati motorcycle was concealed behind a nearby stone wall.

Thunder rumbled softly in the distance and heavy clouds brewed overhead. Rain was common on the West Coast, of course, but thunderstorms were peculiar. It left Jack feeling ill at ease. He hoped they didn't have much longer to wait; he was not interested in being struck by lightning.

The house they were staking out was ordinary, one you would barely notice driving by: plain white siding, double-car garage, a tidy flower bed in the front yard. But Jack knew who lived here, and they were anything but ordinary. The Gorlovich family—or so they called themselves now—had chosen a house that was the opposite of the high-profile restaurants, hotels, and casinos they owned.

Jack stretched his neck, inclining to either side, then refocused his binoculars. From their vantage point they could see both the front and rear entrances of the Gorlovich house.

"You sure this is going to work?" he asked Wesley, his voice on edge. Although he wanted the stakeout to end, he wasn't particularly eager to do what they were about to. Breaking and entering was uncomfortable territory that chafed with his nature. On the other hand, he knew that the information they needed, about the location of the Fabergé, was in there somewhere.

"Trust me," Wesley said. "They'll be leaving the house any time now for a business meeting in town. After that the house will be virtually empty except for the housekeeper. It's our best bet."

Jack scowled. "Remind me why this has to be covert? Couldn't we just approach Gorlovich directly? Surely he's unaware of the full truth about what he's got in his possession. If we explained it, let him in on the full story, maybe we could strike a deal with him."

Wesley shook his head. "Tried that twelve years ago. It didn't fly. That was the last time the Egg disappeared and it's taken us this long to locate it again. We're not taking that risk again."

Jack clenched his jaw. *Fine*. They would wait.

At that moment a yellow taxi pulled up to the front drive. Jack stiffened, sharpening the focus on his binoculars. Two men climbed from the rear seats of the cab. Jack's eyebrows shot up at the sight of them.

"Well, what do we have here?" Wesley said, staring through his binoculars.

Jack's thoughts exactly. These two did not appear to be men so much as small brown sparrows—their monks' habits grazed the ground as they stepped from the car and walked up to the front door. Jack squinted to make out their faces.

He flicked a glance at Wesley. "Any idea what this is all about?"

"Your guess is as good as mine."

Jack continued frowning through his binoculars. He didn't recognize them. One was tall, with shoulders that sloped away from his neck like playground slides. The other, much shorter man, had dark, Latin coloring. Whoever they were, they didn't look comfortable. It was a cool day, yet they were both sweating profusely. The tall one peered behind him, twice, as they shuffled toward the front door.

"Think they're actually monks?" Wesley whispered. "Or is it a disguise?"

Jack squinted. "No idea."

The monks arrived at the front door and stood beside the geranium planters. Jack watched keenly, leaning forward. The arrival of these two men was important, he could feel it. But what did it mean? The taller monk reached out and rang the doorbell. Jack's breathing was loud in his ears. Several seconds passed. Then, the door opened and the monks disappeared inside.

"Looks like they were expected," Wesley observed.

Jack nodded, thinking furiously.

"Well," Wesley said, rubbing his face, "if they really are monks, I suppose it wouldn't be a huge surprise if the church was involved."

Jack scowled. "But why now?" After all this time, after denying the existence of the Gifts again and again, why would the church only now be concerning themselves with it?

"Okay," Wesley said, "if they're in disguise, who are they? You think maybe they're Caliga?"

"How should I know that?" Jack snapped. "I thought you guys were all over this—I thought your team had done all the intel."

"Hey, you're the *cop,*" Wesley said venomously, his eyes flashing. "Aren't you supposed to be familiar with the members of organized crime rings?"

Jack pushed his jaw forward but said nothing. Squabbles were not going to help them now.

"I'll see if I can find anything out," Wesley said. He pulled out his iPhone and began sending messages, while Jack kept an eye on the house. An hour passed, which felt like several to Jack. Background checks and cross-references on two monks came up blank.

And then, the monks emerged. As they did, another taxi drove up to the door, ready to receive them.

"Do we follow them?" Wesley whispered urgently.

"I don't know—"

This was an important lead. They needed to know who these two were; if they let them go now they might never find out. Following them would be the best way to do that. The monks were folding up the hems of their habits, climbing into the cab. Jack clenched his fists, trying to decide.

Then he heard Wesley say, "Oh shit."

Jack whipped his head around to stare at the house, where Wesley was looking. Gorlovich and entourage were exiting out the back door. Jack closed his eyes and looked down. Their hand was being forced.

Jack snapped his head up. "You follow the monks," he said to Wesley. "I'll do the house."

"No way. You can't break in alone."

"Yeah, I can. And you'll be able to follow that taxi on your Ducati. It's the only way this can work."

Wesley stared at him for a second, eyes narrowed. "You sure you can handle this?" he asked.

Jack nodded. He glanced back at the taxi—one monk was in, the other just climbing in the other side. Wesley hadn't moved, was still looking at Jack doubtfully. "Do I need to remind you who my father was again?" Jack asked.

"I thought you disowned him."

"Not before he taught me some things," Jack said grimly. This statement, this confession, felt like something he'd ripped from the roots, cleaved from his bones.

Wesley hesitated one more heartbeat, then said, "Okay. You're going to need this." He slapped a small kit of tools in Jack's hand, then disappeared from the bushes, sliding backward to his motorbike. Jack watched as the taxi's passenger door closed, the brake lights went off, and the car pulled away. A few seconds later, Wesley's motorbike slid like a shadow, quietly purring, following the route of the cab. Jack returned his gaze to the house. His mark. He tucked the kit of tools inside his jacket, his mouth tight. It was time to do it.

Jack's feelings about theft were complicated, to say the least. Growing up, he had thought he'd known what his father did for a living. He'd always been told that his father had his own security company. That was the reason why he was out of town on "business" so often. When Jack was about seven years old, his father started taking him places: grand houses, museums, jewelry shops. His father needed help with the business, he'd said.

Those were the times, Jack realized later, that John Robie was using Jack as part of his cover while he did recon. A man was less suspicious when he was with his young son.

Then there were the times Jack's father asked him to sneak into the back rooms, the security offices—Jack was small, he could do it—and check out the systems, take photos and report back to him. Jack had been thrilled to help his father. He felt special, useful. His father's pride and esteem was like an energy source for Jack, illuminating him like a lightbulb. He wanted to grow up to be exactly like his dad.

Jack's first awareness of the concept of stealing wouldn't happen until he was a few years older, when their house was the target of a break-in. Jack's most precious possession—his mother's locket—was one of the stolen items.

Jack's memories of his mother had been slowly dissolving like soap bubbles in a kitchen sink. He'd been five when she'd died. The locket was the only real part of her he had left. When it was taken from him, he discovered rage for the first time. Stealing became an unspeakable crime to him.

But it wasn't until Jack was twelve that he learned of his father's true vocation. It happened because Jack got in a fight at school, after Billy Millar said that Jack's father was a thief. The boy had brayed in front of everyone that John Robie had been arrested, just that weekend. As far as Jack knew, his father had been called away on a last-minute business trip, and that was the reason for his absence the past two nights. At least that's what his stepmother had told him.

Jack fought Billy Millar, then, defending his father. Unfortunately Billy was further along the pubertal scale and Jack's thin shoulders and fine fists, however impassioned, were no match for Billy's androgen-spiked musculature.

When his dad came home later that day, Jack, through swollen eyelids and bloody lips, had confronted him. Jack's father had sat down on his favorite orange armchair and rubbed his temples. Yes, it was true. He'd just been released on bail that afternoon.

"What are you saying—you're actually a *criminal,* Dad?" Jack had demanded, his face contorted with disbelief and betrayal.

At this, Jack's dad had laughed. "Hate to tell you this, son, but so are you."

Jack had wanted to tear his own skin off when he put it all together, when he realized how he'd been used. Jack would later discover the full extent of his father's renown. In the thieving world, Jack's father truly was a legend. It's said that the old Hitchcock film *To Catch a Thief,* the one with Cary Grant and Grace Kelly, was based on John Robie's life. John Robie got off that time on a technicality and the family shortly left town, moving overseas. The distance, the fresh start, wouldn't be enough for Jack to surmount his shame and anger. He spent the next several years wrestling with that burden of guilt and trying to atone for it. Which he did, mostly, in the end, by becoming an FBI agent.

There were a few things, of course, that Jack's father had taught him at a young age, during the time when Jack was too young to know what he was doing. One of those things was how to pick a lock.

It was something Jack had never managed to scrub from his brain.

Jack slipped along the side lawn of the Gorlovich house. He reached the side door, tucking himself into the shadows of the porch nice and tight. He glanced at the lock, sizing it up. He unfolded Wesley's kit and swiftly selected the tools he'd need. He began working at the lock, gritting his teeth the whole time.

Chapter 11

Under my umbrella, I climbed the rain-slick steps of an old stone building at the heart of University of Washington's campus. The sky was black and thick and the heavy air was laden with the scent of moss and wet leaves. Students in woolly scarves were hurrying by, heads bent down inside their hoods. Once inside I shook the chilly drops from my umbrella and squelched down the dark stone hall to Professor Atworthy's office. I was here to pick up my *Les Misérables* paper.

After hanging up the phone with Nicole yesterday, and agonizing over what to do, I'd called Templeton. His response to my concern was brief and dismissive. As far as he knew there was no warrant out for me in Nicole's department and no intel suggesting she was on to me. However, he said he would put someone on it to confirm. He also told me to not worry but to stay out of it.

Which had made me feel better. Sort of.

I pushed open the heavy oak door to my professor's office and pulled my brain around to the task at hand. Atworthy, as my academic advisor, had told me he was concerned about me. This probably had something to do with the fact that I'd turned in every assignment late and my attendance at tutorials had been patchy to say the least. So he'd been all over me, more than usual, and had stated that every major paper or assignment must be accompanied by a discussion.

I admit my academic performance had been lacking lately. Overall, I was a pretty average student. Nothing special. I wasn't an embarrassment, but I didn't particularly shine—*not like I do in my other life,* I thought reflexively.

"Hi, Barbara," I said to Atworthy's secretary as I entered the office.

"Oh hi, Cat," Barbara said, looking up from her desk. She was in her midfifties, with a round, blond bob, red plastic-framed glasses, and extremely thin lips. She smelled like hairspray and had an amazing memory for names. "He's not here at the moment," Barbara said, "but I'm expecting him back soon. You don't mind waiting, do you? Just go on in."

"Any idea how long he'll be?" I asked.

"Shouldn't be long, maybe ten minutes."

I opened the inner door with a creak and entered his private office. Every bit of wall space, and a great deal of floor space, was crammed with books. A tiny little window allowed a thin shaft of light into the dusty space. I took a deep breath, enjoying the smell of the old leather that bound the books. The tension in my shoulders released. There was something very comforting about this academic shrine.

Jack had once asked me why I persisted in pursuing an academic life when I didn't need to. It wasn't easy to juggle the two, so why did I do it?

The truth? It was my backup plan. One day I would leave my life as a thief. And when that day came, I planned to retire to a leafy college town, teach French literature and live a quiet, poetry-filled existence.

But that couldn't happen just yet. Not until I'd made amends for my past.

As I took a seat in my professor's office, I contemplated that far-off future. I imagined my nice, safe life. My sensible life. It was a good plan. But . . . I found myself feeling empty, somehow, at the idea of a life without thievery.

After waiting seven minutes, and playing several rounds of Sudoku on my iPhone, I grew excruciatingly impatient. I couldn't stand the suspense. At the very least, I wanted to know my grade on this paper.

I sat, arms crossed, for another minute, jostling my foot, then abruptly slid out of my chair. No more waiting. I maneuvered around to the other side of the desk and slithered into Atworthy's chair. My paper had to be around here somewhere, close at hand. I was sure I could find it quickly.

I foraged and rustled, peeking under stacks of files and books. I tried to think back to previous meetings. Did he keep them in the file cabinet? His out-box? No, that wasn't right. My skin began to prickle—this was taking longer than it should. Messing about in my professor's desk would be hard to explain.

And then I remembered. He always reached in *this* drawer to get marked papers that needed to be discussed. . . . I opened the left-hand desk drawer.

So here was the good news. My paper, indeed, was in here. And on the top page was a B plus scrawled in red ink. Okay, a pretty good grade, about what I usually got. Nothing spectacular. Now here was the bad. When I withdrew my paper, there was a Smith & Wesson Model 945 lying underneath. A .45 caliber semiautomatic pistol.

My eyes bolted wide. *Well, hello there.* Not exactly what one expects to see in the desk of an academic, is it? At that moment, I heard Atworthy's voice in the outer office, greeting Barbara. I froze. My heart slammed into my throat.

"Good lunch, Professor?" Barbara asked. "Here's your mail. Oh, and Cat Montgomery is in your office."

The next instant, I was in motion. Papers flew, books straightened, drawers drove home, and I leaped over his desk in a single bound, more or less—

"Barbara," Atworthy's vaguely distracted voice grew louder as the door to his office opened, "can you dig out my Flaubert files? I need to look them over for tomorrow's lecture."

And in he walked. Which was my cue to look up, innocently, from deep focus on my iPhone, seated in my own chair, everything left exactly as it should be. "Oh hi," I said with extreme nonchalance, belying my lurching heart rate.

"Sorry, Catherine. Have you been waiting long?"

"Few minutes," I said, yawning with boredom. "Not too bad."

He sat down at his desk. Professor Atworthy was younger than most of my other profs. I'd say early forties somewhere, although his age was a little tricky to pinpoint. His face, while mostly young, had an aged quality to it. Like he'd seen a lot, been through a lot. There were deep lines around the outside of his eyes, like those of a sailor, someone who'd spent a lot of time squinting ahead, intently staring toward the horizon. He had a sharp nose and a sweep of muddy brown hair. "Right then. Your paper on *Les Misérables.*"

I held my breath as he opened the left-hand drawer and pulled out my paper. He showed no sign that anything was amiss.

Over the next several minutes he nose-dived into an in-depth analysis of my paper. As I sat there, nodding dutifully, I suspected that the conversation would have been useful for the furthering of my academic career. But I couldn't stop my brain from curling back around to the firearm that rested in his drawer.

And then my iPhone bleeped: a text message. I glanced down to scan it quickly. As I read the message I chewed my lip. I peered up at Professor Atworthy. He paused.

"Yes, Catherine?"

"I'm so sorry, Professor, but I really have to go. Something important has come up."

I glimpsed my phone once more before erasing the message, and tried to ignore the anxious fist that had gripped my stomach.

The message read: **Me. Now. Hippos.**

When I arrived at Woodland Park Zoo, I walked to the hippopotamus pond and immediately spied Templeton standing by the railing, wearing the tourist's uniform of khakis, sneakers, golf shirt, and Windbreaker, peering through a digital camcorder at the slumbering hippos.

I stood next to him, staring at the enormous wet lumps floating in the water. As I waited for him to say something, I cracked my knuckles nervously. Why the urgency of the meeting? Did he know about the masquerade ball? Know about Sandor and my new, unauthorized assignment?

"Cat, love, you are going to a conference," he said to me, keeping his eyes fixed ahead on the baby hippo. I shot him a sideways glance. He didn't look angry or upset. In fact, he looked like he was trying to contain his excitement. Not what I was expecting.

I blinked, mind spinning. "Um, what?"

"Yes, they've put in a special request, the board members that is, to have you attend the Twelfth Annual Conference of the Museum Security Alliance. All paid, of course."

I did rapid calculations, trying to figure out if this was a good or bad thing.

"Do you know what this means?" Templeton demanded, working hard to not crack a full-face grin.

"Not exactly. Am I supposed to?"

"It means they're taking you seriously, my dear. They don't send mediocre thieves to this conference. Your shot at the Elite level is looking increasingly like a real possibility."

Now it was my turn to try to contain a smile. *Elite level.* Could it really happen? In spite of myself, my stomach did a back handspring. *International assignments,* it sang, as it stuck the landing . . . *expense accounts. . . .*

"The conference is in New York," he said. I glanced at Templeton, who was beaming now. At once it struck me that he really wanted me to succeed. He was completely on my side. A cramp of guilt centered on my chest. I was lying to him. Betraying him, going behind his back with the Fabergé job.

"So, in more good news," Templeton continued, "I've got an assignment for you. It'll be an easy job. A good one—you're going to like it. And it should help a little with that IRS bill."

I maintained a neutral expression. The last thing I had time for was another assignment—I had heaps of work to do on the Aurora job and time was perishing. But I couldn't exactly explain that. And there was no way I was going to turn down an AB&T assignment.

"The Washington Dinner Train," he began, "is an old, restored luxury train that takes people on a circle route from Seattle around Lake Washington. They serve a six-course dinner as the coast and the mountains slide by. Mostly it's for well-heeled tourists."

There was a stir in the smattering of people watching the hippo pond. We both looked up. Hippo A was passing Hippo B while floating from the west side of the pond to the east.

Templeton flicked on his camcorder—precisely the same action that several other onlookers took. He started recording what I was sure would be a riveting piece of filmmaking.

"So the target is on the train?" I asked. I shuffled my feet and pulled my jacket around me.

"Davis Harrison the third. Absurdly rich—and absurdly obnoxious. Inherited his grandfather's pulp and paper company. We know he's going to be giving a trinket to his latest trophy wife, and he'll be doing it on the train."

"And by trinket you mean?"

"Emerald and diamond necklace, recently acquired from a Sotheby's auction in Amsterdam for 97,000 pounds sterling."

In spite of myself, I felt a tingling in my fingertips. Templeton was right—this would be a good one.

He continued with further instructions. "While they're having dinner, the necklace will be kept in the train's safe. He'll be giving it to her during dessert. You're to procure it before dinner is through, get off the train, and get back here."

I smiled once more—genuinely this time. "Okay. Consider it done."

"Good girl," he said. "I knew I could count on you."

My smile grew somewhat wooden. But I said nothing. I stared at the hippos another moment, and then said, "What about Nicole Johnson, Templeton? Have you learned anything more?"

At my question, his expression clouded. "What?" I demanded. "What does that face mean? You look worried."

"Nothing, Catherine. There is nothing to worry about. Your actions should not change at all. Continue to be cautious. Continue to do your job well. And leave everything else to us."

I clenched the handrail and did my best to quell the heat that was rising up my neck. "Templeton, that's crap. You can't keep me out of the loop like that."

"You're not out of the loop. There's nothing to report." He paused and pressed his lips together. And then added, reluctantly, "It does appear that Nicole Johnson is investigating something significant, but we do not yet know what it is. We're looking into it. That's all. You don't need to think about it further, and like I said, your actions should not change."

With that admonition, he zipped up his Windbreaker and swiftly clipped away. I squeezed my eyes tight. If his words were meant to be reassuring, they were not.

Chapter 12

The dealer placed the king of spades in front of me. I winced. *Bust.* I watched as his stubby fingers swept away the last of my chips, which clicked as they disappeared down the hole. I sighed and pushed myself up from the padded edge of the card table. Never had been all that lucky at blackjack.

But it was fine because gambling was not my primary purpose there. I was at Starlight Casino doing a walk-through. My objective today was to get a sense of the security, a feel for the place. It wouldn't replace a thorough review of the schematics, once I managed to get that—somehow—but it was still a critical recon step.

And I had a second purpose. I knew that some of the security systems here depended on biometric technology—courtesy of the security file, albeit thin, that Sandor's people gave me. The devices used the casino owner's DNA. Which meant I needed a DNA sample from Gorlovich himself. Easiest way to get it? Obtain one of Gorlovich's hairs. Piece of cake.

I began touring the casino floor. I was immediately assaulted by a sensory overload of flashing lights, bleeping machines, smoke-laden air fortified with pumped-in oxygen and air-conditioning. I lingered by the roulette table and played "spot the security cameras." Hundreds of them dotted the ceiling—typical for a casino—and of course they were encased in dark domes so it was impossible to tell which direction they were facing.

Paradoxically, instead of feeling daunted by this, the hairs on my arms thrilled upward at the challenge. It was not going to be an easy job. And it was going to be great.

I loitered by the high-stakes poker room and picked out the security staff, both uniformed and plainclothes. I noted the elevator locations. I mentally mapped out the entrances, emergency exits, and staircases.

As I strolled through the casino floor and into the main lobby, I ran my hand along the backs of smoothly grained leather armchairs and gazed at the sweep of a gold-veined marble staircase. Everywhere I looked, an embarrassment of riches bubbled out and overflowed like a cloying chocolate fountain.

And these were the people who had needed to steal a Fabergé Egg from the Romanovs? Typical. And oh-so-consistent with the dirty little truth I'd observed ever since enlisting in this profession. Something I liked to call the Secret Sport of Kings.

The truth is, über-rich people are constantly stealing each other's goodies. Why? They're bored, for one. Also, they have the means to make things happen. Legal or otherwise. Plus they're always trying to one-up the other guy.

Whether it's a Picasso, the Orlov Diamond, or a 1787 bottle of Château Lafite Bordeaux, these rich old guys practically trade this stuff back and forth like baseball cards.

It's certainly not a modern phenomenon. Throughout history, the elite in society have always delighted in nicking each other's toys. It's like a game to them. Consider the Hope Diamond. How many times was it stolen, conveniently ending up in various aristocratic hands? Many, I assure you.

Only a fraction of these cases make headlines. Most of the time, the general public never hears about this stuff. But keep in mind that in this Secret Sport of Kings it's usually not the *kings* who do the stealing. As a rule, they hire someone to do the dirty work. Someone like me.

Basically, it's a high-stakes chess game. And I was just one of the players.

I passed through a gilded archway and returned to the casino floor. At that moment I spotted three men walking toward the gambling tables. A tall man in the center, who I recognized as Gorlovich himself, was flanked by two men with grotesquely distorted neck-to-head-width ratios. These I took to be his "assistants."

I frowned slightly, scrutinizing the man. It was funny—Gorlovich looked much more like a thug in Sandor's photographs. In person, his posture and carriage had an aristocratic air. The air around him crackled with intensity.

The refrigerator-sized men flanking him also had a certain presence—but theirs seethed with seedy underworld. As Gorlovich entered a private, high-stakes poker room the bodyguards broke formation. They approached a middle-aged man seated at a blackjack table. The man was thin, with a shiny bald patch on the crown of his head and glasses that were too large for his narrow face. I was standing too far away and couldn't quite hear over the cacophony. When the first thug clapped a heavy hand on the man's shoulder he startled and spun. His face crumpled into fear and recognition.

They grabbed the guy and wrenched his arms so violently behind his back that I winced. They hustled him off the casino floor, breaking their stride not at all as the man's flank glanced off slot machines that stood in their path.

I chewed my fingernail and reminded myself, forcefully, that this did not involve me. I dragged my attention back to Gorlovich, who was settling in to his poker table. I needed an opportunity to get close to him and somehow obtain a hair. But this setup wasn't a good one. Too many people around and paying attention. Still, I scanned my brain for a suitable pretext that would allow me to approach his table.

After five minutes the two thugs returned but there was no sign of the man they had carted away. With the expressions of men who had scratched a very irritating itch, they took up position around Gorlovich. The blond-haired one glanced down at his fist and noticed a large amount of blood smeared on his knuckles. He grabbed a towel from the bar and started rubbing at it, unconcerned.

I shuddered. Crossing these guys was clearly not a good idea. I swallowed. Good to know.

I retreated to a nearby bar counter, continuing to keep watch. And then, my opportunity arrived. Gorlovich left the table and headed for the elevators with a redhead draped on his arm. They must have been going to one of the rooms in the hotel. A plan formulated in my mind.

His two executive assistants were also escorting him to the elevator and I followed the entire group. I glanced at my watch and gave a faint sigh, for it was late and I, too, was going to my hotel room. Clearly.

My heart was skipping along, double-dutch. The thugs briefly looked at me as I waited in front of the thick brass elevator doors. Really, they looked through me more than anything, plainly deeming me a total nonthreat.

When the door opened Gorlovich waved his security staff away and entered the elevator with his lady-friend. They stood inside, canoodling. I slipped into the elevator and pushed a floor button at random. I moved to stand behind them. They couldn't care in the least. A beige instrumental version of the Beatles "Hey Jude*"* floated out from the speaker in the ceiling. The floor buttons politely flashed on and off in sequence.

Gorlovich leaned over to his redhead, nuzzled her earlobe and whispered something. This was my moment. My heart experienced a brief seizure as I reached up and plucked a hair from the shoulder of his jacket. I moved fast and grabbed it in a sliver of a second. Neither of them had any idea.

I exited the elevator the moment the doors slid open, relief and triumph setting off fireworks in my chest. Time to get out of there.

I hopped the next elevator down, heading for the lobby. I took the opportunity to check my iPhone for messages. I was still staring at the screen when the elevator car reached the ground floor and the doors glided open. I stepped out and bumped right into someone.

"I'm sorry—" I lifted my head and looked directly into the face of Nicole Johnson.

"Cat?" Her face was stern, different than the way she looked the other evening. I recognized the look. It was the patented FBI agent-on-the-job face.

My mouth went dry. Was she here because of me? My mind wheeled in terror. "Hi, Nicole. So, having much luck?" I asked, quashing the squeak in my voice and striving for a friendly tone. Nicole's eyes roved over my shoulder, watching the room.

"What?" she asked distractedly. She focused on me again. "Sorry?"

"Luck—you know. In the casino?"

"Oh. Yes. I mean no—I don't gamble."

My pulse slowed fractionally. She was clearly working, clearly investigating something, but I wasn't sure it was me. She didn't seem particularly concerned about me. *Could she be faking it?* World's best poker face if she was.

Still, I didn't like it. I started mentally rifling through my various getaway lines, when she said, "Listen, Cat, I was wondering. . . ." She was looking at me more attentively now, like she had driven work things out of mind for the moment. This gave me vague hope, but I was still holding my breath at what she was going to say next. "You wouldn't be interested in going to a golf tournament next weekend, would you? It's this thing I'm organizing as a benefit and I have a lot of spare tickets. It's just for fun, and for a good cause."

I stared at her dumbly for a moment, much the same way as I stared at my bathroom scale immediately after the holidays. Vaguely horrified, vaguely disbelieving.

An invitation to a golf tournament? *Not* what I was expecting.

It was a beautiful evening for a sail: clear skies and a fine wind. Which was perfect, because I really needed this. My every nerve needed soothing. Between balancing my regular life (graduate student) with my moonlighting job (jewel thief) with my even more illicit moonlighting job (jewel thief going rogue from her agency), I was feeling pulled in all directions, like a cat's cradle string. But for tonight, I had a brief respite from all that. I was meeting my dad at the yacht club for our ritual Thursday evening sail.

I hadn't exactly accepted Nicole's invitation last night at the casino. I'd made a vague comment about having to check my schedule and then got myself out of there quickly. Why would she have invited me to a golf tournament? I simply didn't get it. Was she investigating me or trying to befriend me? Or did she know about my history with Jack and was she trying to rub my face in it?

I got to the yacht club and found my dad preparing the boat to set sail. I walked down the dock, reveling in the sound of waves lapping on the dock, boats gently knocking on the wood, and the smells of the seaside: fish and seaweed and salt. The masts of the sailboats pierced into the rosy evening sky like a hundred church spires. As I approached I saw that he was checking the lines. I could already feel my stress melting away like butter on toast.

"Hey, Dad," I said, approaching him, resting a foot on the side of the boat.

"Hi, Cat," he said, without looking up. Immediately, I knew something was not right. My stomach twisted.

I watched him pull the ropes. His normally fluid movements were jerky. His hands were stiff.

"Dad, what's wrong?"

He finished tying a knot, then turned to look up at me. Hurt and disappointment darkened his face. A gaping hole opened in front of me. I stopped moving and held my breath, staring at him, waiting to hear what was so terribly wrong.

"Cat, I *know*," he said quietly.

All the air left my lungs, collapsing my chest. I knew my dad and I knew what would make him look and sound like that. He'd found out about my secret.

Chapter 13

"You know . . . what, exactly?" I asked, my voice pale as I grasped at the tiny possibility that I was wrong. I studied his face: he looked tired, older, his gray eyes cold oceans of disappointment.

"Please, Cat. Don't insult me. I know about your so-called career."

My wisp of hope disappeared. I didn't know what to say. He bent to his work again, shaking his head.

"Dad—let me explain—"

But he cut me off. "I really didn't think we'd raised you to be like that. I feel like I hardly know you. I just can't understand it."

A wave of nausea hit me. All these years I'd worked so hard to keep this secret from my dad. I'd never wanted to hurt him. He had never truly recovered from Penny's death and the last thing I wanted was to be an agent of pain for him. It was bad enough that it was my fault Penny was taken from him.

I wished I could rewind, wished I could walk back down the dock again and see my dad smiling at me. Everything would be normal, and we'd go out sailing.

I had a crushing, twisting feeling that nothing would ever be the same between us.

But there had to be a way I could fix it. My mother had always been my number one critic, but my dad had always been my number one fan. He had always been on my side. Maybe I could make him understand. "How did you find out?" I asked softly. I gripped onto a rough, taut rope from the sailboat. The fibers stuck into my palm like tiny thorns.

"One of your friends, she called for you. I answered. She said she'd been trying to get you at home, and wondered if you were visiting for the weekend. She then asked me if you were off on assignment for Templeton. I asked her what she meant and she said something about your handler and the thief agency. I had no idea what she was talking about, but when I started questioning her she backed down and got off the phone quickly. But I'd already heard enough. After that I forced your mother to confirm the truth."

One of my friends? I didn't understand. The only people who knew were Mel and Sophie and I couldn't imagine either of them doing such a thing.

"Who was it?" I asked.

"Brooke somebody," he said.

I closed my eyes and fought the red rage that filled my vision. *How dare she.* I had an urge to find Brooke. Right. Now.

But first, I had to fix things with my dad. I had to make him understand. "Dad, I can explain. You don't understand—"

"Cat, there's nothing you can say." He looked so sad. And that look was killing me. I had to make it better. Somehow.

"Don't you want to know how this all came about?" I asked desperately. "How it works? Anything?"

"Not really. No."

"It's not as bad as you think," I said, grasping. "In fact—"

"Listen, Cat," he said, climbing onto the boat. "I think I'm just going to go out on my own tonight." There was complete finality in his voice.

I swallowed against the dry rock in my throat. "Oh. Okay."

He looked back at me with anguish on his face. "I have to say, Cat, I feel like I've lost two daughters now."

It wouldn't be difficult to find her. She was practically a celebrity these days. No, finding her wouldn't be the hard part. Keeping myself from throttling her would be.

Sure enough, after a little detective work, I burst through the door to a shoe boutique in Belltown. Brooke was there, seated on a tufted leather Barcelona Chair, trying on Jimmy Choos with the help of a twig-sized salesgirl. The shop was thick with the smell of shoe leather and expensive perfume; rhinestone sandals glittered under halogen lights and the air pulsed with British pop.

"Brooke, what the hell is your problem?" I demanded with rage. I was holding on to my self-control by a hair—a very dry and overbleached hair, at that, brittle and apt to break.

"Cat, I already explained that to you," Brooke said, completely unruffled. She stood and swiveled her foot toward the floor mirror to get a better view of the Choos. The salesgirl was not so serene. She glanced with alarm between the two of us. She was frozen in a half-crouching pose before Brooke's feet, evidently debating whether to stay or go. Brooke said to her, "Darling, do you have something with a slightly higher heel? Just like this one . . ."

An expression of relief lapped over the salesgirl's face and she scampered off to the back room. My eyes traced her retreat, then flicked back to Brooke. "Telling my father? That is really low. And . . . incredibly fourth grade."

She shrugged. "Innocent mistake, Cat. Really. I thought he knew. So sorry." Her tone carried no sincerity whatsoever. "It's a problem, though, isn't it? When people know your secrets? You never know who might find out next."

There was a distinct possibility I might kill her. I squeezed my fists and tried to remain calm. I stared out the window to regain my composure, focusing on the people walking by, the late evening shoppers and strollers—a young mother with uncombed hair pushing a baby carriage, three men in the classic suiting of corporate lawyerhood emerging from an après-work martini bar.

And then I got to play my card. "Listen, Brooke. Do I need to remind you that I know your secrets, too? You do not want me as an enemy."

Brooke recrossed her legs. "Are you kidding, Cat? I don't have any secrets anymore. Haven't you read my book?"

Memo to self: Find time to read that damn book.

I stood there without knowing what to say. Just glaring. And flaring my nostrils, I'm pretty sure.

The shoe salesgirl returned balancing a tower of shoe boxes. Brooke and I were squared off, firing imaginary poison darts at each other. The salesgirl froze. And then swiveled, retreating to the back room again.

Beneath the anger and infuriation, I felt a cold hand clamped on my spinal cord. Brooke could end my career as a thief. For a moment I visualized the life I would be left with—after all, Brooke's career as a thief was over, wasn't it? How would I cope with it? Would it be so bad, really? A small voice inside me said: *yes, it would*. But wait—wasn't that what I wanted eventually, anyway?

I walked home from the shoe store, although there was a brisk, cold wind. I was hoping the air would cool off some of my anger toward Brooke. I realized, shortly, that this was a bad plan. My anger at Brooke had allowed me to—temporarily—forget the ache in my heart over seeing my dad so disappointed. But as I walked, the pain crept back in.

I stopped and looked at the window display of a perfume shop. My hands went down to rest on the aluminum windowsill but I barely felt the coldness of it. I was staring at the display of cut-glass bottles but not particularly seeing them. Somebody bumped into me as the crowd bustled by. I was scarcely aware of it.

There had to be something I could do to repair things. The idea of my father not forgiving me, not understanding—how could I live with that? I pressed my nails into the cold windowsill. I'd fix it. I had to make him understand.

"Wake up, sleepyhead," said a voice, pulling me from sleep.

I cracked my eyes open to see Templeton standing in my bedroom.

"Templeton, what the hell?" I groaned, rolling over and squeezing my eyes shut against the bright, very early morning sun.

"Tsk. I knew you'd forget."

"Forget what?"

"The security conference. Our flight is today, darling. Time to get up. Here. I brought coffee."

I sat up and blinked at him as he held a steaming Starbucks cup. The aroma of coffee infiltrated my nose and started touring through the house of my brain, switching on the lights and firing up the appliances. "Templeton. There is no way you told me it was today."

"No?" He paused, thinking. "Hmm, perhaps you're right. My bad." I rolled my eyes. "Anyway, off you go." He pulled me from the warmth of my bed and pushed me toward the shower.

"Did you say *our* flight?" I asked. "Are you coming, too?"

"As it happens, I've got business in New York myself."

"Business?" I asked wryly. "Or . . . shopping?"

"Cat, please, I'm a busy man—"

"Saks Fifth Avenue holiday sneak peek sale?" I said.

He shrugged. "Guilty."

The timing here sucked. I did have one or two other items on my list of things to do—planning a casino heist sprang to mind—but I couldn't skip the conference. It was too important for my future career with AB&T. And how could I explain my refusal to Templeton? Besides, it was just two nights out of town, right? Then I'd be back.

But in the shower, blanketed with steam and hot water, I started thinking. This was my opportunity to get Templeton to spill the beans about Nicole Johnson. He was clearly in a good mood and totally relaxed. He wasn't shutting me out any longer.

On the plane we settled into the luxurious leather seats of business class—courtesy of the Agency. Soothing chamber music piped in. Our flight attendant furnished us with cocktails and warm cashews. I clicked my seat belt and flipped through a magazine as the engines rumbled and we began to roll down the runway. As the plane lifted into the crystalline sky I turned to Templeton. "So what's this conference about, exactly?" *Step one,* I thought: warm him up, get him relaxed and discussing a topic he's happy about.

"Well, it's all about the latest developments in museum security. The newest technology, and the most cutting-edge thinking on how to stop, well, people like you," Templeton said, grinning. "*You* are attending, my dear, because you happen to be the head of security for a small modern art museum just outside Seattle. You know, a minor, independent institution that nobody has heard of. Mostly because it doesn't exist." His eyes glimmered.

Templeton's smile was bright and his speech was quick. "I think you're going to find it quite enlightening. Always a prudent idea to know everything your enemy knows. And, I must say, the Agency is thrilled that you're going. You and I are making a rather good move here."

His excitement was contagious. But a barb of guilt tugged on a corner of my mind. My success clearly meant a lot to Templeton and here I was keeping secrets from him. Doing things that could potentially unravel all his work. I watched him carefully as he rummaged in his briefcase, head down, and I found myself wondering— would he be so loyal to me?

"Here, this is the program," said Templeton.

I scanned the list of workshop titles.

Beyond Fingerprints and Iris Scanners: What's New in
  Biometric Security?
Security Guards: Challenges and Best Practices
Internal Theft Boot Camp: Detection and Prevention

He was right. This was going to be fun. And highly educational. I glanced sidelong at Templeton, who was grinning like a schoolboy at the brochure. I chewed my lip and ignored the guilt. I returned my attention to the page.

Advanced Intruder Detection: Photo-Electric Beams
  and More

I raised an eyebrow—now that sounded interesting. "So who else is going to be attending this conference, Templeton?"

"Mostly industry types. Museum representatives, security consultants, and the scientists and engineers working on the leading edge of security technology."

"So, the exact people looking to stop people like me."

"Precisely."

I nodded and chewed my lip.

"It's not something we throw novices into, petal. Your skills of blending in and staying inconspicuous will need to be at their sharpest. Obviously, you're going to be entering the lion's den."

I experienced a twinge of uncertainty. Was I up to this? It wasn't going to be easy. On the other hand, it was undoubtedly going to be fun.

At that moment the flight attendant draped a linen tablecloth over my tray and placed a platter of antipasto and a frosted glass of pinot grigio before me.

Okay, *now*, I told myself. Get into it now. I decided to go for the direct approach.

"Listen, Templeton," I said, nibbling on an olive. "I need to talk to you about Nicole Johnson."

Templeton sighed. "Cat, I have been perfectly clear. Stay away from her. Do not get involved."

I frowned and shifted in my seat. "Well, that's just the trouble. I'm trying my hardest to avoid her but she seems to want to be friends. And it's freaking me out."

"Why?" he said sharply. "When did you last see her? Did you speak?"

"She invited me to a golf tournament." I winced, preemptively.

"She what?" he hissed. "Catherine, this is not acceptable. When did this happen? Where did you see her?"

"Um . . . it was a few days ago. And—" At this point I began scanning my brain. Could I tell him about the casino? Should I lie? What if he knew something about the Aurora Egg? He might be suspicious at the mention of the Starlight Casino. Fine—I'd have to lie. Okay, casino . . . money . . . "It was at the bank," I pronounced.

"The bank?"

"Yes." I reached for my wine and took a swig. This was not going the way I envisioned. "Anyway, that's not important. What's important is that she invited me to a golf tournament. Why would she do that?"

"I have no idea. But you are absolutely not to attend." Templeton plucked at his platter of prosciutto and cheeses.

"I know. I have no intention of it."

He looked directly at me. "Was Jack with her?"

"No."

"You haven't seen Jack lately, have you?"

Ugh. Another lie coming up. "No." I had no choice; I couldn't tell him about the masquerade ball.

"Good," he said. "We cannot have you becoming involved again."

"Okay, but, Templeton, you still haven't answered my question. What do you know about Nicole?"

He rubbed his temples and gazed out the window. "The team, from what I gather, is having more trouble than usual accessing her file. As it stands, her past is a bit of a mystery."

With a sip of his wine, he refused to say any more on the topic. Great, Cat. Smoothly handled.

After we deplaned, a car maneuvered us through the wilderness of downtown Manhattan directly to the hotel and convention center. After a solid night's sleep (P.S.: 600-thread-count Frette sheets are a miracle), I met Templeton in the lobby and we made our way to conference room B. I was dressed plainly in business-casual trousers and white blouse. Nothing memorable or flashy about my clothes or my hair. My job today was merely to blend in.

A black and white poster board was set up outside the main conference room. It read:

WELCOME TO THE 12TH ANNUAL CONFERENCE
OF THE MUSEUM SECURITY ALLIANCE.

"Okay, this is us," Templeton said, leading the way.

Were security professionals the only people who needed to know about the latest advances in security technology? Of course not. We had that need.

And, really, let's face it. These people existed because people like *us* existed. If there were no burglars, no bad guys, there would be no need for all this expertise in security. These people, to put it plainly, would be out of a job if it weren't for us. Truth is, crooks kept this whole industry going.

At that moment I received a message on my iPhone. It was from Gladys.

Might have a good lead on York Security. Sit tight; will get back in touch as soon as possible. Stay close to your phone.

"What's that about?" Templeton asked, suddenly at my elbow. "You look concerned."

My head snapped up and I instantly deleted the message with my thumb. "Hmm? Oh, just a stock tip. It's fine. No big deal."

Templeton's mouth twisted with disapproval. "Catherine, no. You are not to go chasing those tips again. Haven't you learned from your last mistake?" I gave a helpless shrug.

We strolled into the conference room; I scribbled onto a *Hello, my name is . . .* sticker with a Sharpie. I looked around. Hundreds of people were seated at round, linen-covered tables. A small crowd bunched around a buffet table at the side, helping themselves to coffee, tearing open little packets of sugar. I wondered how many other attendees were thieves and burglars, too, just like me.

"All right," Templeton said. "This is where I leave you to your own devices." He surveyed the group of attendees. "Oh, wait," he said, grinning enormously. "I'll just introduce you to someone first," he said. "Come with me."

I followed him as he deftly wove through the tables. He stopped at a table far to the left that was occupied by only one person. "Cat Montgomery, this is Ethan Jones." He lowered his voice and said, "Ethan is also with AB&T. Our man in the art department."

The man stood up and my stomach jolted backward. Green eyes, fabulous jaw . . . a little short, perhaps, but otherwise gorgeous. If you liked the Brad Pitt look. *Hello,* Ethan Jones.

I frowned slightly. Now, how did I know that name?

Chapter 14

"Hello, Cat Montgomery," Ethan Jones said with a voice that sounded like a long sultry afternoon in bed. He wore a suit that must have been custom-sewn by a tailor with a man-crush on him, and was sporting a smile that could bring women, small countries, and heads of industry to their knees. "It's a pleasure to meet you."

"Yes . . . um, hi," I said.

Memo to self: At next available block of leisure time, generate list of charming and intelligent opening lines. Anything would be an improvement upon "um, hi," for Christ's sake, Cat.

But I wasn't here to flirt. I was here to learn, to improve my skills. And then fly home to get on with more important things. Also, I needed to stay on top of my iPhone in hopes that Gladys would send me some good news about the York Security file on the casino.

"Is this chair available?" Templeton asked.

Ethan nodded. "Join me?"

"She'd love to," Templeton said, and pushed me down into the chair. I glanced at Templeton and he gave me a none-too-subtle wink.

"Right," Templeton said cheerfully, clapping his hands together. "Well, I'm going to leave you two kids to enjoy your champagne breakfast. Pip pip!"

Which left me feeling like I was in junior high. An awkward silence ensued. I stole a glance at Ethan, who looked perfectly at ease as he poured me a glass of ice water. As I struggled for something clever to say next, a waiter came by with breakfast and mimosas, saving me from my exertions. Cutting into eggs Benedict suddenly became the most absorbing task I'd ever encountered.

"Templeton's quite a character, isn't he?" Ethan said, just at the exact moment I inserted a large forkful of food into my mouth. All I could do was smile and nod. I glanced around, assessing the proximity of the other people in the room. The fact was, we were alone at our table and the room was vibrating with loud chatter. Nobody was paying us any attention. We were secure in our conversation.

"He's an excellent handler," Ethan continued. "You're lucky to have him."

I swallowed my food in a hard lump. It stuck in my chest. "Yes, definitely, I am," I said. There was a pause. I sipped my mimosa. I hazarded a sidelong glance at him—*Ethan Jones.* . . . I swear, the name was familiar from somewhere.

"So, Montgomery," Ethan said with a devilish smile. He leaned toward me and I could smell his aftershave, a citrus-musk scent. He pitched his voice low. "I've got to tell you—lately I've been hearing a lot of fantastic things about someone in the jewel department at AB&T. Very talented, apparently. Great intuition. However, if I'd known she was going to be this cute, I think I would have found a way to meet her sooner."

My face got hot.

Okay, pull it together here, Cat. I had to make some sort of conversation. "So, you're in the art department, huh?" I said. "In Seattle?"

"You got it." He sprinkled salt on his eggs and began eating.

"Done any work I'd know about?"

"Did you hear about the Cézanne at the Seattle Art Museum?"

I put down my fork. "That was you?"

He nodded.

"I'm impressed," I said. "That was a tough job." I wondered if that was how I knew his name. Agency gossip perhaps?

Ethan raised an eyebrow. "Tougher than the Camelot Diamond?"

I blushed again. "Ah. You know about that one."

At that moment, someone stood at the podium and started introducing the opening speaker. The room bloomed with applause. Conversation ceased as we listened to the speaker's heartwarming and inspirational speech about overcoming adversity—adversity in this situation being a highly skilled team of burglars. I paid rapt attention, making mental notes on where the team had gone wrong. After the applause ended people gathered their papers and folders and iPads and moved off to the first workshop.

"So where are you headed?" Ethan asked me.

I glanced at the agenda. "I was thinking about The Art and Science of Security Electronics."

"Hmm. Sounds interesting. Mind if I join you?"

My insides kicked about like an epileptic who forgot to take her meds and I worked hard to suppress a smile. "Not at all."

In spite of being distracted by a pressing need to check for messages from Gladys, and the presence of the very fine man sitting to my left, I found the seminar to be brilliant. I gleaned some extremely useful pointers on the latest intruder-detecting sensors—weighing advantages of the various types and troubleshooting the potential glitches. Very interesting. Particularly the glitches part.

At lunch I distracted myself by diving into the mouthwatering gorgonzola risotto. The strategy proved effective. As Mozart floated up from the string quartet in the corner of the ballroom I felt the tension in my shoulders turning warm and soupy. I turned to Ethan. "This conference is fabulous," I said, breaking into a crusty French roll. "Why haven't I gone to one of these before?"

"Guess you've been invited up with the big boys now, Montgomery. You must be doing something right."

I smiled, but something he said had me thinking. *Big boys, big boys . . .* aha. That was it. I remembered where I'd seen Ethan Jones's name: inscribed on a plaque at Agency headquarters. He was Elite.

After lunch, we went separate ways. Ethan was going to a workshop specifically about art theft (the tragedy of) and I'd signed up for a master class on jewel theft (the modern scourge of). Before we parted he turned to me and said, "Going to the Varma Kalai seminar after this? It's in the Advanced Skills for Security Guards: Subduing Intruders stream."

I nodded. Varma Kalai is an ancient Indian martial art that targets vital pressure points throughout the human body. Ethan asked me to save him a seat and schoolgirl-vintage butterflies flickered through my insides.

The Varma Kalai workshop was entirely hands on, which was fabulous. I learned a nifty little trick involving a strike just below the occipital ridge with the marvelous effect of instant confusion and disorientation in your opponent. I was looking forward to trying it at the next possible opportunity.

The final seminar for the day was titled Safes and Vaults: What's New? I scanned the room. No Ethan. *Good.* I was glad. Who needed the distraction?

But just as I was taking a seat, in walked Ethan. My pulse quickened and I felt a warm flush all over. I was officially in trouble.

After the seminar we walked down to the chandelier-lit dining room and took our seats for dinner. I was irritated because I still had no message from Gladys. Why was she leaving me hanging? Holding my iPhone beneath the tablecloth, I tapped out a quick message to her: **Any word?** Two more people squeezed into our table, forcing everyone to jostle a little closer together. I became acutely aware of Ethan's leg touching mine.

I focused fiercely on my peppercorn rib eye.

"The workshop on Infra-Red Security was excellent, didn't you think?" asked a middle-aged man with a bulbous, flushed red nose and gentle eyes sitting on the other side of me.

"Yes. Superb. Very informative," I said, nodding. There was applause then, as the keynote speaker was introduced.

In the hotel lounge, after all the speeches and acknowledgments were finished, Ethan and I were tucked away having a drink in a quiet corner. He took a sip of wine. "Mmm. Is there anything better than a great red wine?"

I nodded, lifting my wineglass from the table.

His lips curled into a mischievous smile. "Well, I suppose I can think of one other thing, possibly," he said quietly. And left it at that. My hand wobbled as I raised my glass to my mouth.

"So, Montgomery," said Ethan, taking a sip of his pinot noir and pulling my attention back to him. "How did a nice girl like you get into this business?"

I shrugged. "I just always had the knack, from a young age. You know, stealthy."

"Parents never knew you were there, could sneak up on them from anywhere?" he asked, with a knowing smile.

"Exactly!"

I told him the whole story, my version of the making of a crook. When I was finished Ethan was watching me with a thoughtful expression. "God, it must be easy for you to keep your cover. Nobody would suspect a young, gorgeous woman of being a thief."

Fortunately I didn't have to produce a response to this because at that moment a waiter passed by, too close to us. We said nothing as he cleared away a nearby table and then moved off.

"So, Montgomery . . . you married?" Ethan asked innocently.

"That's pretty impressive," I said, swallowing my wine and laughing. "Just right out with it. Not the type to ask me what my husband is doing while I'm at the conference? Something like that?"

"Nope. Too cheesy."

"Agreed," I said.

"So?" he asked, waiting with eyebrow raised.

"No. Not married," I said.

His smile broadened.

The wine was making my legs feel a little tingly. And other parts, too. Unfortunately.

"You know what's nice?" I said, sloshing my wineglass a little. "It's nice to hang out with someone who's not judging me. I don't have to worry that I'm acting too criminal, talking too much about various felonies and other off-limits topics, you know?"

He sipped his wine. "Sounds like you've been involved with somebody on the other side, Montgomery."

I nodded.

"I've tried that," he said, uncharacteristically solemn for a moment. "Waste of time."

I had a hard time coming up with an argument to this. In fact, he was making a lot of sense. Gladys and the York Security dilemma were a distant memory.

"Well, Montgomery, you can be yourself with me. I'm not going to judge you. We're the same, babe."

We sat in silence a few moments, drinking our wine.

Then, a group of people from the security conference sat down at the table next to ours. One man nodded to us, recognizing us as fellow conference attendees. They continued chatting loudly about the day's workshops, about the success of the conference.

Which left us completely unable to continue our conversation. I became acutely reminded of where we were and who surrounded us. I shifted in my seat.

I caught Ethan looking over at the table of security professionals, also. And I could see that his relaxed posture had changed to something much more guarded. Our nice little cocoon of criminal camaraderie was gone.

"Listen, Montgomery," said Ethan, leaning in close. I could smell his cologne—and a faint undertone of sweat and soap—that did very dangerous things to my insides. "Maybe we should relocate somewhere a little more . . . comfortable. I've got a bottle of wine in my room. Care to join me?"

I took a long sip of my drink and swallowed. It seemed like a reasonable suggestion. But the last shred of rational thought in me said this would be a very bad idea. I knew exactly where it would lead. This guy was the kind who left a trail of shattered hearts. Which was the last thing I needed. Again.

I knew myself. As much as I liked the idea of a one-night stand, I'd never been terribly good at it. I always got wrapped up and I always fell hard.

"I'm not sure that would be a good idea." This is what the logical side of me—the winner of a major internal battle—managed to say.

He raised an eyebrow. "Ah, but that's where we disagree."

I laughed lightly. "I'm sorry, Ethan. I—I had a bad breakup recently."

He smiled wickedly. "You know, I specialize in rebound. I can make you forget this guy."

Oh, God. Must . . . resist . . . temptation. . . .

Think heartbreak, I told myself. Think crushing pain of rejection.

Think insomnia, sitting at your kitchen table alone in the darkness with a pint of *dulce de leche* Häagen-Dazs and a spoon.

"Sorry, Ethan, I don't think so."

"I can't change your mind?" he asked.

I shook my head. We finished our drinks and, like a perfect gentleman, he walked me to my room. He made no further moves.

Alone in bed, I stared at the ceiling. Ethan's words echoed in my head. *"We're the same, babe."* And, truth be told, how could I deny that?

Chapter 15

Jack walked to his car, footsteps marking a lonely beat in the dim, deserted parking garage. His stomach rumbled and he readjusted his grip on the take-out bag from Maria's Greek Taverna. The smells of roast lamb and tzatziki were getting to him.

His pace was quick. He wanted to get home fast, eat, and do some serious thinking on this case. Things were not going well with the Aurora hunt. After breaking in to the Gorlovich mansion, Jack had not gleaned a lot of information.

Apart from one small, but vital, fragment. He'd found a ledger entry that confirmed the receipt of an overseas delivery a few weeks ago. And the details of that delivery had curled a smile on Jack's lips. A rank amateur must have been the one to make the entry, originally, because Jack could make out the words beneath harshly scribbled out pen marks: *weight: 23 lbs 6 oz; make: Fabergé.* For that matter, the supervisor who had scratched out the words must have been a rank amateur himself. Very sloppy, not destroying that record.

But the trail was cold after that. He could find no further mention of this shipment in any ledger, file, or notebook. Where did they take it from there? There was no way to know. Could they possibly be keeping it in the house? No, Jack thought. They'd never leave it under such light security.

But he didn't get the chance to confirm this suspicion: before he could begin a search he was interrupted by the housekeeper. She'd screamed; he'd had to improvise an escape out the second-floor window. As he bolted from the scene Jack spat with anger at himself. *Speaking of rank amateurs.* How could he make such a mistake? Why hadn't he heard her coming? Distracted by his find, he supposed. Not much of an excuse.

Maybe he hadn't learned quite so much from his father as he'd thought. Surprisingly, this idea bristled him.

He'd stopped caring about those skills long ago. He did not want to be like his father. And yet—here he was, feeling shamefaced by his failure.

Jack wove his way through the rows of stationary cars in the parking garage, the garlicky aromas from his take-out dinner prodding him onward. The garage was completely empty of signs of life. Parked cars stared at him with empty, unlit eyes as he squeezed through a narrow space between two vehicles.

Jack heard a faint scrape on the concrete floor—a shifting foot—just beyond the car he was passing. That slight sound gave him a microsecond of warning to prime for the attack. But it wasn't enough.

A man with a balaclava mask and bare hands slammed into him. The impact of the tackle, coming at him from his left, knocked Jack to the ground just in front of the hood of a car. The blow winded him and he struggled for breath as he fought to lift himself off the ground.

The attacker loomed over Jack and punched him in the face. Searing pain ricocheted through Jack's skull and brain. He had to do something, had to get out of this. He blocked out the pain of the blows and focused all his energy into powering a great swing of his leg, kicking his assailant's feet out from under him. The man went down and landed hard and Jack was on top of him in a second. Jack rained blows on the man's chin, jaw, kidneys. He picked the man up and pressed his face against a concrete pole.

"Who are you?" he hissed into the man's ear. "Did somebody send you?"

The guy blinked, didn't flinch, didn't cower, and was barely breaking a sweat. "Guess," he said, voice flat as pavement.

Jack didn't have to. That degree of coldness, that degree of detachment—the man was Caliga. Jack realized too late that his grip on the man's arm was awkwardly placed. The Caliga twisted and smashed his elbow into Jack's throat and Jack's grip loosened as he gasped for breath. The man turned and ran.

Jack heaved for air and gave chase. The other man was two car-lengths away and sprinting through the grid-work of vehicles. Jack hurled himself over a hood foot first, sliding over it and crashing to the ground beyond. He came out of it running. His eyes clamped on his target and his pulse hammered in his ears. His own ragged breathing was the only sound that existed. But Jack was gaining.

He tore between two tightly spaced cars and then his hip slammed into a side-view mirror. The impact knocked him back; searing pain fired through to the ganglia in his spine and black rain exploded in his field of vision.

With a grunt Jack rebounded forward in pursuit once more. At that moment a silver Volvo squealed up to the Caliga and the door swung open. The man dove in. The car peeled away.

Jack glared after it with nostrils flaring, fury and frustration boiling inside him. No license plate. He spat blood-streaked saliva to the ground and roughly wiped his mouth with a rapidly swelling fist.

He leaned against the hood of a black BMW and felt his heart rate decelerate. He became aware of aches and pains germinating in various joints and muscle groups. And then Jack smiled, just a little. That attack, seemingly pointless, was clearly meant to issue a warning.

It was a good sign. It meant he was getting close.

Chapter 16

Notice and Demand for Payment

Dear Miss Montgomery:
*This is a second notice. Please be reminded that you have
20 days to fully repay your debt. If you fail to do so, we will
be filing a Notice of Federal Tax Lien. This is a notification
of the claim we have on your personal assets and property.
The Levy will take place following this, when we will seize
your personal assets to satisfy payment.*

I crumpled the paper in my fist. This was the letter waiting for
me when I returned home after the conference.

Enough messing around. I had to get the Fabergé. On the flight,
on the way home from the conference, I had finally received Gladys's
message. York Security was a no-go. She'd tried her best, beyond her
best, and the information was simply not available online.

At home I opened my cupboard to search for something to eat.
A virtually empty jar of peanut butter and a can of chickpeas stared
back at me.

There was only one thing to do now about York Security. I'd have
to physically break into their headquarters and retrieve the information the old-fashioned way. I chewed my thumbnail. I'd hoped to
avoid that.

I was going to need a plan and I couldn't do it on an empty
stomach. I pulled on my boots, grabbed my wallet and stalked to
the 7-Eleven on Maple Street, a few blocks down.

As I turned a corner I saw a black Audi parked across the street, next to a mailbox, and I recognized it right away. Jack's car. My shoulders dropped. *Not now.* But it wasn't Jack seated behind the wheel. It was Nicole. I immediately stepped back behind the edge of a garage.

Nicole, again? I pressed my lips together. Something wasn't right. Why did she keep turning up?

Of course Jack did, in fact, live in this neighborhood. And they were a couple. My heart shrank away from this admission. The sky started to lightly spit rain. My glance flicked around—was Jack here somewhere? Nicole was in the driver's seat. Which meant that Jack was not with her. He always drove.

I could feel the sweat gathering at the base of my neck—what if she *was* staking me out? If she was, she was doing a poor job of it. Also, why would she be here, not at my apartment? No, I was just being paranoid.

However, *paranoid* had saved me many a time.

I exhaled with irritation. The smart thing to do would have been to go home. But my stomach groaned and rumbled like an old train engine. I was still starving. Then I got an idea. I backtracked half a block and zipped into a dollar store and bought a cheap umbrella. I used it to cover my face as I walked back into the 7-Eleven and pushed through the door. A cheerful chime tolled overhead and I was greeted by the familiar convenience store smells of stale coffee, Slurpee syrup, and one overcooked hot dog rotating on the grill.

I found myself drawn to the candy aisle to seek out comfort, in the form of chocolate. As I scanned the rows of red-and-silver-papered bars my mind trawled back to my York Security conundrum. Breaking into their headquarters was going to be about as easy as eliminating bread and sugar from one's diet. But what choice did I have? I couldn't go into the casino without that information.

As my eyes focused again on the chocolate in front of me I noticed a small piece of paper taped to the Snickers and I felt the hairs lift on my arms. It read:

Miss M: Walk to the canned food aisle. Baked beans.

I flipped my gaze to either side. Nobody around. I snapped off the note and tucked it in my pocket. I sauntered innocently to the designated area and stood in front of the rows of Bush's tins. The aisle was deserted. I frowned and pick up a can of beans. *Wait.* There was a space behind it. I peered through the space and saw Sandor loitering in the adjacent aisle holding a jumbo pack of toilet paper and trying to appear surreptitious. He turned to look toward me.

"Hello, Miss Montgomery," he whispered.

"Hello," I whispered back. His methods may have been a little too spy-movie to be taken seriously but I had to admit, he was good. He must have seen me as I approached the 7-Eleven and then anticipated my beeline for the chocolate. But I wondered: how long had he been watching me? And why didn't I know about it? I played with my earlobe as I studied him; that skill level was not what I expected from this apparently innocent, bumbling guy. A vague discomfort prickled under my skin.

"I'm here to check on your progress," he said. "With the assignment. Everything coming along okay?" He sounded worried, doubtful.

I gnawed the inside of my cheek. Should I tell him about my difficulties getting the security information? Before I could say anything, he added, "I should tell you, Miss Montgomery, the board has decided to line up another . . . professional to do the job, if you're not up to the task—"

"I'm fine!" I said quickly. "Everything is going beautifully, in fact. All falling into place." A panicky feeling pushed into my throat. I needed this assignment. I couldn't let it go to someone else.

He smiled and looked relieved. At least I thought he did, based on the fraction of his face I could see through the bean cans. "Good," he said. "That's good. Of course I have every confidence in you, it's just some of the others—"

"No problem. I understand. But believe me, it's well in hand."

After that, Sandor went to the counter and purchased the package of toilet paper he'd been holding. I returned to the chocolate aisle and reached for a Baby Ruth bar. I paused, reflecting on my dilemma, then grabbed four more bars.

I was standing by the front shop window as I watched Sandor exit the store with a jingle of door chime. He walked briskly away, head down against the wind. Then, Nicole's car abruptly pulled away from the curb. As she drove, her gaze was clamped on Sandor.

My eyes went wide with surprise as I realized the truth of the situation: Nicole was staking out *Sandor*.

Chapter 17

This was not good. Why was Nicole tailing Sandor? Did she know who he was? Did she know what he was involved in? Worse—did she already know about the crime he had commissioned but which hadn't yet come to fruition?

I tightened my hold on my umbrella—thank God I'd been wary enough to buy it. If she was staking out Sandor, I did not want to be connected. I thought back and replayed the last five minutes. Given the orientation of the store, the windows, I was sure she couldn't have seen me talking to Sandor.

I slipped out my phone and sent Sandor an encrypted text message: You've got a tail. Black Audi.

I paid for my Baby Ruths and, after conducting thorough cross-checks for any sign of Nicole or other FBI agents, I exited the store. I began power-walking the five blocks to my apartment. I could feel the tension spreading in my shoulders and a headache developing. The faster I planned this job and got it done, the better. The FBI was on the scent and obviously getting closer.

I knew I had to break into York to get their security file on the Starlight Casino. But quite frankly, their security was going to be every bit as tight as the casino's. I wouldn't be able to wing it. If I had a little more time I could access the information from York in another way. Going undercover, for example. Scoring a job as a secretary or something, working there for a few weeks and then lifting the information from the system. Of course for that matter, I could have gone undercover at the casino.

But I didn't have time for any of that. The deadline was looming. What was I going to do? After walking two blocks with my dilemma circling my brain like a terrier chasing its tail, I felt no further ahead. And then my scalp began to tingle. I was being followed.

At the next crosswalk, I stopped and casually reached into my purse. I pulled out lip gloss and a mirror. As I applied the gloss I looked behind me through the mirror's reflection—an old trick and yet another advantage to being female in this business.

Within the crowd waiting at the light, two men were staring intently in my direction. Yep. Definitely being shadowed. I steeled my jaw—time to vanish.

I walked half a block further and made a sharp turn into a Starbucks. I continued to stride directly behind the counter, pulling a green Starbucks apron out of my handbag. I glanced at one of the baristas behind the counter. "I'm so sorry," I said, flustered. "Gosh, I can't believe I'm late for my very first day. . . . Do you think the manager saw me come in late?" I immediately went to the coffee grinder and started pouring in beans.

This was my patented shake-off plan. It's perfect for several reasons. One, because there is, at bare minimum, a Starbucks on every block. Two, because coffee shop staff are virtually invisible. Anyone following me would hardly spare a glance at the workers. And three, there always seems to be a new trainee; nobody is ever surprised when I turn up.

The key is acting like you belong. Sell it and nobody will question you. And then you're hiding in plain view.

As I stood there operating the grinder and listening to the shift manager rattle off my duties and responsibilities, I trained one eye on the door. Soon enough, the men who'd been shadowing me walked in. Once I got a good look at them I turned my face away and rolled my eyes with scorn.

They were dressed as monks. It's a highly amateur move to dress in memorable disguise when tailing people; it only serves to highlight your presence. Worse, these two were doing a poor job of hiding the fact they were looking for someone.

I snuck another furtive glimpse. I frowned, drawing a complete blank on their faces. One was long boned and tall, with narrow-set eyes. The other was shorter and olive skinned, with a gentle, almost handsome face. They scanned the coffee shop for a few minutes, casting nary a glance at the staff. When they didn't see me among the patrons, they left, adjusting their cloaks and scratching their heads with confusion.

I slipped into the tiny, cracked-tile staff restroom, stuffed my handy apron in my bag, and crawled out the window. In the alley I doubled back and took an alternate route home, vigilant for monks. I mentally catalogued the list of people who would have reason to follow me: Someone connected with Brooke? Possible. Someone with Nicole and the FBI? Definitely possible. Somebody else altogether? Always an option.

So now I would have to watch my back even more than usual. The throbbing headache that I'd been cultivating earlier ratcheted up a notch.

I got home and checked my messages. Ethan's voice floated, smooth as bourbon, over the line.

"Hi, gorgeous," he said. Typically a very cheesy line, but in the capable hands of Ethan Jones, it worked. "Listen, Montgomery," he continued, "I've been thinking about you. When can I see you again? Call me."

As Ethan recited his phone number, a beacon suddenly flared in my brain. Ethan did the Seattle Art Museum job. And York Security was the company in the soup for the security breach. Maybe he had some ideas on prying information out of York.

I picked up the phone and dialed Ethan's number.

"Montgomery," he said. I could practically hear him grinning. "I had a feeling I'd hear from you."

"Listen, I need a little help with something," I said. I caught a glimpse of my face in the hall mirror and noted that my coloring was high.

We made a plan to meet at Glow martini bar, in Belltown neighborhood, in one hour.

As I was putting the finishing touches on my makeup my door

buzzer sounded. With extreme reluctance I let my mother in. "It looks like you're going out, dear," she said, following me from the front door into my bedroom.

"Very astute, Mom."

Her eyes opened wide. "Do you have . . . a *date*?" she asked breathlessly.

Reluctance, validated. "No."

"But you're meeting a man?"

"Yes. But it doesn't matter." I dug through my closet searching for my Kate Spade handbag. "Anyway, Mom, what exactly are you here for?"

"I wanted to bring you these books that I checked out from the library." I looked down at the stack that she unloaded from her fabric tote bag, and scanned the titles:

The Complete Book of Locks and Locksmithing
The World's Greatest Heists
Disguises for Dummies

My mother was grinning at me, puffed up and proud. "I thought you could use these," she said.

I closed my eyes and exhaled. "Please don't tell me you checked these out with your own library card?"

"Yes, of course I did." She gave me her condescending look.

"Mom, are you insane? That is exactly the sort of thing that could get you—and not long after, *me*—red flagged."

She looked thoughtful and tapped a manicured finger to her lips. "Mmm. Good point. I suppose I need an alias, don't I?" Her expression turned quite gleeful.

I sighed deeply and pinched the bridge of my nose. "No, Mom. You don't need an alias. Just don't do stuff like this."

She pouted. "Spoilsport."

Later that evening I strolled into Glow. Blue under-bar lights gave a moody vibe to the room. The air swirled with the blended scents of perfume and cologne and exotic liqueurs of every variety. Prepubescent hostesses teetered about in black minidresses and stilettos. I scanned the room for Ethan. My heart rate picked up in spite of myself. This was *not* a date. I started regretting my outfit: slim black pants, embellished top, and fabulous Jimmy Choo pink sandals. Way too datelike.

Still, I was allowed a little fun, right? Nothing wrong with an innocent drink with a man. Nobody needed to get hurt. I finished surveying the room. No Ethan. I frowned slightly. I walked over to the bar, slid onto a sleek plastic bar stool, and ordered a mojito. As I sipped my drink, sweet and cold and minty, I couldn't help remembering that Jack absolutely never left me waiting. Never. And he would always have my drink ordered and ready.

Just as I was pondering this, Ethan walked in the front door. My insides went to jelly. He looked fantastic. Just as good as I remembered. He was wearing a crisp white shirt, jeans, and a cocky strut as he made his way over to me. God, the guy was hot. The thing was—he knew it.

He leaned over and kissed me on the cheek. The scent of his cologne flirted with my senses. "Sorry I left you waiting, Montgomery."

Ethan ordered a Heineken and we moved to a table in the corner. We needed something a little more out of earshot.

"So listen," I said, placing my frosty glass on a paper coaster. "I have a question to ask you. But you have to keep it confidential."

"Naturally." His face sported a crooked smile, as always. It was like life was one big amusement for him.

"What do you know about York Security?" I asked.

He raised an eyebrow. "Why do you want to know?"

"I need details on the security system they put together for a client."

"Hmm. Which client?"

"Can't tell you." I sipped my mojito innocently.

"Aw, come on."

"Nope. Can you still help me?"

He sat back, thoughtfully. "I imagine you've already found that you can't get anywhere online, even with a hacker?"

I nodded.

"Breaking into their offices is almost impossible," he said. "However, I *did* get in there once."

I felt a flutter of hope. "So it can be done?"

He took a swig of beer and nodded. "Yep."

"Can you tell me how?"

"Nope."

I paused. "Excuse me?"

He grinned. "I could show you, though. We could do it together."

"No," I said, shaking my head. "No way. I work alone." At that moment I started having second thoughts about this plan. Ethan was AB&T Elite. And here I was consulting him on a moonlighting job. Could I trust him to keep this a secret?

He shrugged. "Guess you'll have to figure it out yourself then," he said, glancing at his watch. "Listen, babe, there's somewhere I've got to be—"

"Wait, wait," I said, seizing his forearm as he stood. *Damn,* I was desperate. And he knew it. "Okay, fine. We'll do it together."

He smiled wickedly. "See how good that sounds?"

I rolled my eyes. "Okay, but listen. This is just between you and me, right? I mean—nobody else needs to know what we're up to. You get me?"

"Of course, Montgomery." All joking was aside now, as he said this. There was uncharacteristic seriousness in his gaze.

I took a deep breath. "So when can we do it?"

"Tomorrow night work for you?"

"Absolutely."

I was totally fascinated to see how Ethan planned to pull this off. Breaking into airtight security headquarters was no easy task. However, as we both knew, every security system had seams.

"They've got one weak point," he said.

"Which is what?"

"You'll see."

After Ethan left I gathered my things and walked to the front entrance. I was just passing by the bar when I heard my name called.

"Cat?" said a surprised voice.

I turned. Nicole was at the bar, perched on a sleek acrylic stool and holding a martini glass, looking at me. I swallowed. This was getting ridiculous. And way beyond suspicious.

"Oh, hi," I said awkwardly. I reluctantly moved to where she was seated. A blender suddenly whirred behind the bar, crushing ice. "What are you doing here?" I tried to make the question come out as pure curiosity, instead of the guilt-ridden accusation it was.

But Nicole didn't seem bothered. "Just here with some friends," she said. At that point one of her friends, seated at the next bar stool, turned to face me. This friend was none other than Brooke Sinclair.

I almost choked on my own tongue. It took me a second to process this jarring image. Nicole smiled at me, apparently oblivious to my shock. "Brooke, this is my new friend Cat." She looked at me. "Brooke is a work colleague."

"Oh, um, hi," I managed. I shook Brooke's hand. "Nice to meet you." It was surprising that I could actually hear any words being spoken, what with all the alarm bells and sirens going off in my head.

Brooke smiled at me. "Well, I'm not *exactly* a colleague."

"Oh?" I asked, feeling a groundswell of nausea.

"I used to be one of the bad guys," she whispered confidentially, with a show of remorse. "But I reformed. And now I work as a consultant of sorts for the FBI."

My mouth went dry as her words sank in: Brooke was now an FBI informant. Or possibly just posing as an informant. The distinction was a bit academic because either way, I was screwed. The walls of the bar appeared to be closing in. It was definitely time for me to exit stage left. I mumbled some excuse about having to feed my cat, uttered a hasty good-bye and then turned abruptly away. I was almost at the door when I felt someone at my right elbow.

"It's time for me to get home also," Brooke said with a serpent's smile, "as it turns out."

I nodded stiffly and buttoned my jacket. As we walked out the front door the cold city air entered my lungs, spiked with car exhaust and the spicy curry aromas from a nearby Thai restaurant. I hazarded a sidelong glance at Brooke. "So I assume you're going to tell Nicole all about me now," I said in a low voice.

"Mmm, not just yet," Brooke said.

"Why not?"

"I like watching you squirm, of course. A little game of cat and mouse. So to speak."

And what could I do? I had nothing over her. No leverage. Her secret had been laid out in the public domain. As I struggled to come up with an appropriate threat or otherwise satisfying response, she filled the silence with, "So anyway, Cat, have you read my book yet?"

I blinked, and stared at her for several seconds. "Actually, I have." Truth is I devoured it late one night, sitting up in bed surrounded by a heap of pillows and the remains of two boxes of Chips Ahoy. To my supreme irritation, I couldn't stop reading.

"Really. What did you think?"

"The most self-indulgent thing I've ever read."

Instead of looking hurt by this, Brooke smiled a Cheshire grin as though I just paid her an enormous compliment. I crossed my arms and scowled at her. "I suppose Bertha, in the book, well . . . is Bertha supposed to be me?"

Bertha was Brooke's protégé in her book. Based on many of the details, specifics about heists and such, it was clear that Brooke intended this character to represent me. Bertha also happened to be extremely unattractive, overweight, and as smart as a paper clip.

"Oh, you noted the resemblance, did you?" Brooke asked, blinking innocently. I bit hard on the inside of my cheek.

The fact was, Brooke didn't unveil much truth in her book. For one thing, she made it sound as though she was an independent thief. No agency. No naming or finger-pointing. Clearly, she wasn't about to burn any bridges. Which I admit, grudgingly, was smart.

I narrowed my eyes, studying her. "If you're so hell-bent on destroying me, Brooke, why *didn't* you name me in your book?" I asked. "As far as I can see, that would have been the perfect way to screw me."

"Ha," she barked. "Right. And give you a portion of the spotlight? I don't think so. You're nothing, Cat. A speck of lint on my skirt. A scuff mark on last season's Manolos," she said, with her most unpleasant expression.

I folded my arms over my chest. "If I'm so insignificant to you then why are you going out of your way to hurt me?" Brooke said nothing. She stared at me. Her hard gaze faltered, infinitesimally, but she recovered and glared at me with renewed loathing. And I felt a small glow of triumph. A tiny spark kindled in an otherwise bleak landscape of frustration.

"So," Brooke said through her teeth, "what were you and Ethan Jones talking about tonight, in the bar? You looked pretty cozy. Planning a new heist, by any chance? What are you working on, Cat?"

I shuddered. There was no way I could tell her—or allow her to find out—what job I was planning. There were too many ways she could screw me. I thought of Brooke sitting with Nicole at the bar. I made tight fists inside my pockets. It was never a good thing to have a sworn enemy hanging around, bent on vengeance. But give that person a cozy little friendship-slash-working relationship with the exact person who possesses the authority to end your life as you know it? Not good.

I would need to be a lot more careful, knowing Brooke could be watching my every move. It was even more urgent, now, for me to get this Fabergé job done. And then, somehow prevent Brooke from ratting me out. Either that, or hop a plane to Bora-Bora.

For the hundredth time, I contemplated backing out of the Fabergé job. I could contact Sandor, tell him it couldn't be done. I had a vaguely uncomfortable feeling about how they would react—what they would *do* with me—if I were to abort. There was that warning they'd issued. I knew all the details about their plan—did I know too much now? But was that threat more significant than the one coming from the general direction of Brooke? Or Nicole? Or my Agency, for that matter? So why was I making life so hard for myself?

I gritted my teeth and turned for home. I fidgeted with my ring. I knew why. And I knew why I wasn't going to call Sandor, and why I wasn't going to quit.

Chapter 18

The following evening Ethan rolled his BMW to the curb in
Pioneer Square and we parked in front of a bar called the Ginger
Room. It was a place I'd been to once before, and I knew it to be
a cheesy tavern-type spot, all red velvet and brass fixtures, bad
lounge singer by the piano. My nerves were fizzy with the familiar, intoxicating cocktail of anxiety and eager anticipation that I
always felt before a heist. We were going to bust into York Security tonight.

"Wait here," Ethan said. He hopped out, offering no further explanation. I had no idea what we were doing there but he'd assured
me it was a crucial part of the plan. I shifted in the smooth leather
seat and fiddled with a lock of hair. After a few minutes I saw him:
he appeared in one of the front windows, standing before a bejeweled cougarlike woman who was sitting alone sipping a martini. At
the sight of Ethan, the woman positively ignited. She stood and
kissed him affectionately and hungrily looked him up and down.

He talked. She listened. He had a drink. She lit a cigarette. She
touched his arm with her lacquered, talonlike fingers in a very familiar way. And just when I started getting cranky at watching what
appeared to be a date, he kissed her hand and walked out.

"Okay, mission accomplished," he said, climbing back into the
car. He brought the cold air into the vehicle with him and I shivered
slightly. The ignition warning bonged until he closed the door
behind him.

"Okay, so who was that?" I tried to keep my voice as minimally shrewish as possible.

"Mrs. York," he said, peering in the rearview mirror and wiping the lipstick from his neck. "Wife of the CEO."

"You've *got* to be kidding me."

He grinned. "That brief intercourse—*ahem*—just provided us with the codes that disarm the security at York headquarters."

"Let me get this straight. You're sleeping with the wife of the CEO?"

"Well, not anymore, no. Now we're just friends." He twisted the ignition key, turning the engine over and revving it gently. "But I make it a practice to stay close to key people." He looked at me and raised an eyebrow. "Jealous?"

"What?" I laughed. "Of course not," I said, with slightly more heartiness than strictly necessary. "So she just *gave* you the entry codes?"

"That's what friends do," he said with a broad smile.

"Does she know you're a thief?"

"Yep."

I narrowed my eyes. "And . . . she doesn't care?"

"It's her little way of getting back at her husband, pissing him off. A power struggle thing between spouses, I gather."

"Sleeping with another man isn't already enough to piss him off?"

He shrugged, shifted the BMW into first gear and glided away from the curb.

"How can you be sure she's not going to rat you out? Or that this isn't a trap?" I asked.

"I just know." He looked at me and saw that I wasn't convinced. "Trust me, Montgomery."

The trouble was: what choice did I have?

"Okay, so are you sure you can do this?" Ethan asked in a low voice as we rounded the corner, on foot, in front of York Security's office building. We were in the heart of downtown. It was well past midnight. The strips of sky that sliced between glass skyscrapers were chalky black and cloudless. "Last chance."

"I'm ready," I said. My stride was brisk and my fingertips tingled with eager anticipation. Even so, all the risks and possible pitfalls were swirling about my brain—but I didn't choose to share this with Ethan. I didn't want him to think I wasn't up to it. He was Elite. And I was . . . well, I still had some things to prove.

"Good girl." He stole a sidelong glance in my direction. "By the way, have I ever told you how sexy it is when a woman wears glasses?"

I touched my tortoiseshell frames self-consciously. They were part of my disguise. Fleshed out by a gabardine wool pencil skirt and crocodile pumps. A law firm happened to occupy an office in the same building as York Security so Ethan and I were posing as corporate lawyers. He looked unreasonably good in his ten-thousand-dollar Armani suit.

We strode into the lobby toting coffee and yammering away importantly on cell phones. My pumps clicked on the high-gloss marble floor. The after-hours security guard, an overweight man with a cleft chin and skin the color of milk, stopped us and asked us to sign in.

Ethan hung up his phone and greeted the guard. I kept talking feverishly as we approached the desk. I reached for the pen, cradling my cell phone and placing my coffee on the corner of the clipboard that rested on the desk. All it took was a minuscule tilt of the clipboard. My cup teetered and spilled all over the place.

"Shit!" said the security guard, jumping up. He started madly mopping at coffee.

"Damn," I said, wiping at the spill on my skirt. I started muttering about having a bad night, everything going wrong . . . big project . . . didn't know how I was going to get it done, that sort of thing.

I spared a brief glance at Ethan. He was taking the few seconds of distraction to flip back in the records to find the names of people who worked in the law firm.

"I'll fill yours in," Ethan said to me. "Don't worry."

I mustered up one or two tears and the quivering chin that is part of every woman's arsenal. The security guard looked at me sympathetically and finished soaking up the remainder of the coffee.

"Here," Ethan said, "just sign."

"Thanks," I said. I leaned over and signed quickly, a nonspecific scribble.

We entered the elevator. After the doors slid shut I pulled out my camera jammer—a sleek little thing that looked like a mini-remote control. I pushed a few buttons.

"Nice gadget," he said. "Does it scramble or block?"

"I've set it to freeze mode. Much less obvious than a black screen, as long as there are no people in the shot." He nodded appreciatively.

The doors opened on the twenty-seventh floor. My device detected three CCTVs in the hallway outside, which were automatically disabled. The corridor was dark and hushed, lined with a plush carpet. It smelled like carpet cleaner. Small streaks of ghostly light from the city filtered in through a long bank of windows. We slid on night-vision goggles and ultrafine black leather gloves that Ethan produced from his briefcase. We slipped down the dark hallway and arrived at the door to York Security's head office. To get into the offices required multiple layers of security.

Ethan glanced at the piece of paper provided by Mrs. York. He punched the first code into the pad outside the main door. My palms went sweaty as I watched. What if she'd given him false codes? What if she was bitter about the end of their affair?

The door latch blinked green and clicked. Ethan turned the handle and entered. I exhaled. We were through the first layer. This was as far as Mrs. York intended Ethan to go, but we had other ideas.

Ethan pulled a security card from his jacket—something he'd pickpocketed from Mrs. York at the bar. He swiped it.

I checked my CCTV device at each step, automatically disabling each camera before we got to it. We were functioning like a well-oiled machine. At each doorway there was not a lot of space, which forced us into close proximity. As a result, I found that I was growing increasingly warm.

We reached the door that required fingerprint ID. I passed him the latex mold of the fingerprint we'd lifted from Mrs. York (specifically from the cocktail glass Ethan had pocketed from her at the bar). Creating the latex mold had been my job, in the car as we drove here. It had been easy work—like playing with a kid's science kit.

Ethan gingerly placed the mold in position. It worked; the door unlocked.

As we tucked through the alcove of the doorway and paused to disable the CCTV, his rock-hard thigh was suddenly touching mine. Oh dear. *Focus,* Cat.

Memo to self: Endeavor to *not* bring hot, distracting males on sensitive recon missions in future. No matter what information or resources they bring to the table.

At last, we were in the inner room, essentially a cold, concrete vault with two workstations and endless banks of old-fashioned steel filing cabinets. This was where they kept all the specifics of their clients' security systems. The only information Gladys had been able to glean was that Starlight Casino's security detail would be in filing cabinet 907.

Cabinet 907 turned out to be a three-foot-square safe, bolted to the wall beside the bank of filing cabinets. But it was fine. Safe-cracking was my specialty.

Ethan watched as I worked my magic with the safe. The lock was a challenge: a new-model Sargent and Greenleaf with nine tumblers and very tight notches. I licked my lower lip and concentrated hard. After seven and a half minutes, it emitted that beautiful *click* and opened. The inside of my chest felt warm and hot-chocolaty. I sat back and glanced at Ethan. He nodded and smiled with approval— gorgeous white teeth flashing—which set my stomach cartwheeling. It was nice to be admired, for once, for the one thing I was truly good at.

The only other person in this world who had admired me for that was my sister. I felt a renewed sense of purpose. This job, this quest for the Fabergé, was the only authentic gift I could give her now, because that's what I was. I was a thief.

I rummaged through the safe and quickly found the file for the casino. I flipped it open, took out my microcamera (cunningly con-cealed within a Chanel lipstick tube) and snapped photos of the schematics, blueprints, and specs. Finally, *finally* I had what I needed.

"This is some pretty heavy-duty security," Ethan said, looking over my shoulder. "The Bagreef . . . that's the vault that interests you? Looks like it's got much heavier security than any of the other vaults."

I was frowning because I'd just noticed this exact thing. All that security—just for one Fabergé Egg?

"They've got a lot of biometric measures," he commented. "Blood match, even. It won't be easy to disable that stuff."

"No, it won't. But I've got a head start in that department." I wondered how far along my lab was with processing Gorlovich's hair sample.

I sat back on my heels and felt my knees pressing into the cold concrete floor. I scanned all the security details. I was breathing fast. "This is gonna be great," I said quietly.

Ethan was looking at me. "Are you doing this for fun, Montgomery?"

"Not exactly. I mean, it *is* going to be fun. But, no. That's not the sole motivator."

"What then? Come on, spill it. I won't tell. This is more to you than just an assignment—I can see that."

I wondered how it was so obvious. I turned a page in the file and came across the details of a particular alarm deep within the Bagreef Vault itself. It was essentially a booby trap. If tampered with, the vault would lock down, trapping the trespasser and emitting a gas into the enclosed space. The gas, according to the file, was something called Kolokol-1.

Ethan whistled, reading over my shoulder. "That's pretty unfriendly."

"What's Kolokol-1?"

"It's the gas that was used in that Russian hostage situation a few years ago. Causes pretty quick unconsciousness."

"That's all?"

"Well, a bunch of people died—but the official word is they got the dosing wrong."

My eyes widened. Okay. So it would seem the Gorlovich family favored the shoot-first-ask-questions-later approach. Of course, this I already knew.

As I captured photos of the remaining pages, a creeping doubt sent tendrils into my brain. This would be a mighty tricky task; was

I up to it? Was I truly good enough? I snapped one last image with my microcamera. "This is everything I need," I said, tucking my equipment back inside my pack. It wasn't morning yet, but it wasn't far off. The sky outside was infinitesimally lighter.

We returned everything the way we found it. We reversed our steps out of the inner vault, recalibrating the alarms and resetting the cameras as we went. So far, everything had gone smooth as glass.

But now came the riskiest part: we had to return the way we came, and exit past the security guard. If any suspicion had been raised while we were upstairs, now we'd have a problem.

I compelled my legs to walk slowly as we exited the elevator. I controlled my breathing. As we turned the corner I caught a glimpse of myself in the lobby mirror. I was surprised that my outer appearance didn't betray my inner jumpiness. Ethan, of course, looked as cool as a peppermint Frappuccino.

We approached the front door. If all went well, the guard would be behind his desk, we'd sign the form and then get out.

The desk came into view. My shoes were impossibly loud in my ears—echoing through the marble-clad lobby. The guard was not seated at his desk. Instead, he was standing in the middle of the grand expanse of floor, feet planted, arms folded, staring us down.

Every molecule of air was forced out of my lungs. It was all over, I was sure of it.

Ethan and I were staring down the security guard in the lobby at York Security. Time came to a screeching halt. The guard's face was expressionless—I couldn't tell what he knew—but he had definitely been waiting for us. I could feel the tension in Ethan as he stood next to me. What should we do? Run for it? Dart back into the elevator and look for an escape from another floor? Keep up the charade as long as possible?

And then, it all changed. The guard's face softened into a smile. "Ah, there you are." He walked back to the desk and reached over. "Look what I managed to get for you, miss—to replace the one you spilled." He produced a large steaming coffee cup. "I wasn't sure how you take it."

The sheer effort of not making eye contact with Ethan made me break out in a sweat. I thanked the guard graciously and accepted the coffee. We signed out quickly—but not too quickly. We were so close I could taste it. Then came the long stroll across the foyer, and out the front door to the cool night air.

My heart leaped with triumph. We had done it.

We went our separate ways, as previously agreed. As Ethan closed the door of my cab he leaned in the open window. "You've got to admit it, Montgomery," he said. "We make a great team."

Chapter 19

Jack glowered at his watch with impatience. *How long does a woman need for a shower?* He listened with hope, then frowned. Water was still running.

Outside, water was also streaming down the windows. It was a vintage Seattle autumn morning, gray and drizzly. The sun hadn't quite risen yet. Jack gazed at his million-dollar view of the harbor. The streetlights still glowed with hazy halos, pushing valiantly against the gloom. The view from the penthouse was always spectacular, just a little less so on a day like today.

It was odd; this was a fact that almost made him feel better. A little less guilty. He knew he should get rid of the penthouse. His conscience dictated it. Of course there was no real external pressure. Nobody knew where his father's money had come from—nobody in his circle of friends and colleagues, anyway. Still, he was a hypocrite. And he knew it.

Jack glanced at the clock again. He jiggled his knee and snapped the page of the newspaper he wasn't really reading. Nicole didn't usually take such long showers, he thought, with irritation. On this particular morning, he needed to get her out of his apartment. Wesley was scheduled to contact him with information first thing. He did not want Nicole around while he was dealing with this.

He could have lied, of course, but Jack was loathe to do this. He didn't want to start on that path, spinning a web of tales. He was already guilty enough by omission. Everything would be fine if she would just go to work—the sooner the better.

At last, Nicole entered the breakfast room. Jack's shoulders relaxed a little. *Good.* It wouldn't be long now.

"Morning, sweetheart," she said, smiling and squeezing his arm. Jack didn't look up from his newspaper. She sat at the table, wearing a bathrobe. Her hair smelled freshly washed. Her hand was warm from the shower.

Jack slid a mug of coffee over to her. He had considered pouring it into a stainless steel commuter cup and hustling her out the door but changed his mind. It was just coffee, it wouldn't take long. She never had breakfast upon first awakening, anyway.

Jack's housekeeper bustled into the breakfast room. Evelyn was in her sixties, her gray hair in a short, tidy bob. She was five feet tall, with thick forearms from years of rolling pastry and peeling potatoes and scouring bathtub tile. "What can I get you two for breakfast? French toast, perhaps?"

"No thank you, Evelyn," he said. "Just coffee this morning, I think. We should get going." Jack smiled warmly at his housekeeper. Evelyn had been working for Jack for a long time. She was like family. In fact, in many ways she was the only family he had left.

"Actually," Nicole said brightly, "breakfast sounds wonderful."

Jack turned to her sharply, but quickly regained composure. Nicole flashed him a conspiratorial smile. "I called work—told them I'd be in late. I thought we could spend a little extra time together this morning. You said you weren't going in until later, right?"

"Yes, but—" He tightened a fist under the table. "Okay, Evelyn . . . looks like French toast it is."

It will be fine. Evelyn was a quick cook. They could eat right away and then Nicole would go, surely.

The sounds of butter sizzling on the griddle and the smells of bacon frying soon drifted in from the kitchen.

"Jack, I was wondering," Nicole said casually, sitting back and sipping her coffee. "Have you heard anything around town about a Fabergé Egg?"

Jack's throat seized. *How the hell did she know about the Fabergé?* "I'm sorry, a what?" With a great deal of effort Jack kept his voice smooth and unconcerned.

"There's scuttlebutt on the street, something about a long-lost Fabergé Egg. A potential target, possibly involving a jewel theft ring. I'm keeping tabs on a couple of people we suspect are wrapped up in this. Just checking if you'd heard anything." She shrugged. "Let me know if you do."

"Sure." Jack turned the page of his paper. "Sounds like an interesting case. Keep me posted."

They sat in silence for another minute. Then, as Jack downed the last of his coffee he heard footfalls in the corridor just outside the breakfast room. But it was someone with an entirely different gait than Evelyn. Jack's hand went instantly to his side—no firearm—and he was halfway out of his chair when Wesley Smith strolled into his breakfast room. "Morning, Jack," Wesley said with an impish smile.

"What the hell—how did you get in?" Jack demanded. His gaze flicked to Nicole, whose eyes were wide with alarm. Her hand was also on her hip, where her gun would be if she were wearing something other than a bathrobe. "It's okay, I know him," Jack said.

Wesley shrugged. "Have you looked outside? It's brutal out there. Thought we could meet here instead of out there—much cozier." He looked around and rubbed his hands together, warming them. "Nice place, Jack."

Jack's hand clamped around his coffee cup handle, but his face remained stony. Wesley flipped a kitchen chair backward and sat astride it. "Hey, sorry for the surprise," he said comfortably. "I rang the bell. Nobody answered. And the door was . . . unlocked."

Jack ground his molars together. *Unlocked, my ass.*

"So you're a friend of Jack's?" Nicole asked, sipping her coffee, relaxed again.

This was exactly the sort of thing Jack had been hoping to avoid. How was he going to explain Wesley? Couldn't be a work colleague. Nicole knew everyone Jack worked with, a problem with working in the same office.

"I'm Jack's accountant," Wesley said, smooth as butter. "We've got some income tax issues to review."

Not bad, Jack thought. But dammit, now he was going to have to remember that. He didn't like keeping secrets.

Unbidden, Cat flashed into Jack's brain. This must have been how she felt when they were together, Jack thought. His stomach tightened in empathy. It must have been difficult, always keeping secrets. It's not that Jack hadn't known about her line of work, but he'd always made it clear that he didn't want to know the details of her jobs. He'd never considered how Cat must have felt keeping things from him.

"Listen, we should go—" Jack began, moving toward the door.

Just then, Evelyn walked in with a tray laden with French toast, warmed syrup, bacon, and orange juice.

"Oh, why don't you stay for breakfast, Wesley?" Nicole asked, smiling kindly. "Do you like French toast?"

"As a matter of fact I love French toast," Wesley said, turning his chair around without hesitation and grinning at Jack over the coffee pot. Jack sat down again.

While they ate, Nicole and Wesley chatted about the traffic and the weather and the dismal performance of the Seahawks. Jack chewed his breakfast in silence. This was partly out of anger and irritation but mostly because he was afraid of saying something wrong, tripping himself up.

Then Wesley asked directions to the bathroom. As Jack watched him disappear down the hallway his skin crawled. The last thing he wanted was Wesley Smith wandering around unaccompanied throughout his apartment. But what could he possibly say to stop him? He glanced at Nicole, who was finishing her last few bites of French toast, seemingly oblivious to his discomfort.

Just then, Nicole's phone made bleating sounds. She looked up sharply and reached for it. "Jack—do you mind if I take this? It's a video Skype call I've been expecting from an informant." Her coloring was high; Jack could tell she was excited about the call.

"Of course," Jack said, smiling. "Go ahead." Maybe this meant she'd want to leave and get back to work right away, he thought, slurping his coffee happily.

She touched the screen of her iPhone and pulled up the video feed. Jack couldn't help glancing at the image. Brooke Sinclair's face came into focus.

Jack's coffee suddenly tasted bitter. He knew all about Brooke. And he certainly knew about the long-standing rivalry between Brooke and Cat.

Brooke Sinclair was a piece of work. The fact that she was now an informant was laughable to Jack. Typically, he was a fan of criminals going over to the right side of the law and helping out the FBI. In Brooke's case, he had the distinct impression she was doing it for all the wrong reasons.

As Brooke began to speak on the video call, Jack stood up to retrieve more sugar from the cupboard. Of course he could hear her every word.

"Hello, Nicole. I thought you might be interested in a potential burglary I heard about. It's planned for tonight on the Washington Dinner Train."

Nicole frowned. "Who's doing it?"

"You know that thief who did the Moonstruck job? Word on the street, same thief."

Nicole sat up straighter and started talking very excitedly, pressing Brooke for more information.

An uncomfortable churning centered in Jack's stomach. The Moonstruck had been Cat's job. But only he knew that.

The call lasted only a few seconds more. Brooke had very few additional details. After Nicole hung up, Jack said, "Well, that sounds like a good lead. Who's this thief she was talking about?" He tried hard to keep his tone casual.

"Someone we've been trying to track down for quite some time." Nicole's hands were moving with animation over her breakfast plate. "A jewel thief who's very active in the city."

Jack's discomfort mushroomed larger as he sat down at the table again and forced himself to eat. "Oh? Got a name? A photo?"

Nicole's eyebrows stitched together. "No, unfortunately. But we will—soon."

Jack nodded. He replaced his fork carefully on his plate.

The Dinner Train theft had to be Cat's job. He was certain Brooke knew it, too. She just wasn't providing that key piece of information, for some reason.

But—and here was the sticking point—what was he going to do about this? The logical side of him insisted he stay far, far out of it. But the side that wasn't so concerned with self-preservation, the emotional side . . . well, it had other ideas. Jack stood again and strolled to the window. He kept his face turned from Nicole. Rain streamed down the plate glass. Jack stared through it and rubbed his face angrily. He did not enjoy this, this squeezing sensation, with the distinct flavor of a rock and a hard place.

Cat could be in real trouble here. And that fact fired up all his protective urges. But he was already risking so much, stepping over the line for this Fabergé Egg. How much further could he go, before he completely lost sight of who he really was?

Chapter 20

The elevator doors slid open and I walked through to the observation deck of the Space Needle. I looked around; I was supposed to be meeting my mother there. It was the day after the York Security job with Ethan, a blustery, windy day under a steel gray sky, and I could feel the Space Needle rocking slightly under my feet. The restaurant was in the throes of brunch. I could smell omelettes and frying potatoes and grilled seafood.

My mother had said she needed to talk to me about something important. She'd be here at a private charity function and had asked me to meet her. I reluctantly agreed, though I had a lot of planning to do for the Fabergé job. On top of that, the Dinner Train job was tonight. But she said it would only take a minute. And she sounded . . . odd, on the phone.

I spotted my mother next to a coin-operated telescope, waving to me. My line of vision slid to her left and I froze. I shot her an accusing look. Standing beside her was my father. He hadn't seen me yet. He was gazing out the window and he looked tired. I bit my lip. I hadn't spoken to my dad since the evening at the yacht club—he'd refused to take my calls.

He turned then, and when he spotted me his eyes widened. He speared my mother with much the same look that I just did. Clearly, we'd been set up. When I walked over to them my mother blurted out quickly, "Listen, you two, I'm sorry I had to trick you like this. But it was the only way. You have to talk."

She slid away and melted into the background. Which was a first for my mother I was pretty sure. I smiled at my dad, trying to stay hopeful. I hoped I could find the right words. I had to make him understand. After strained small talk, he looked down.

"Listen, Cat," he said. "I'm really struggling, trying to understand all this."

"I know," I said softly. I noticed how much gray there was in his hair—when did that happen? It's a strange thing to see your parents aging. For a long time they just look the same, nothing is changing. And then one day you look at them, standing with you at the bank or the grocery store, and you notice the lines in their faces, an age spot on their left cheek, a more pronounced curve of the spine and the shoulder.

He looked me in the eye. "I just can't believe this is the only choice available to you. What about your studies? I thought you loved French literature." His tone was not accusing; he sounded more bewildered than anything.

"I do. But I've got a lot more school ahead of me. Finishing my masters, then doing my PhD. Lots of students have part-time jobs, you know—"

"So this is about money?" he said abruptly, grasping at this. "This thing you do is because you're short on cash?"

I shrugged. "Well, partly, I suppose."

"Cat, honey, you've got to know that I can lend you money if you're having trouble."

My heart twinged at the term *honey. Honey.* He hadn't written me off completely. "It's not money I want, Dad," I said. "I don't do it just for the money. I'm actually good at this," I added quietly.

And I do it for Penny, I wanted to say. *She wanted me to do it.* I wished I could explain this to him. But telling him would mean admitting that it was my fault she died. And I couldn't do that.

He turned his face to the window. The skyline of Seattle was etched in dull gray. "Okay, then let me help you in another way." He paused. There was a spark in his eyes, suddenly. "I could line up a job interview for you at my firm."

I blinked. This was not what I was expecting. Before he retired my dad had been a certified public accountant at a large accounting firm. As much as I loved my father, I had always hated the idea of following in those particular footsteps. I twisted the end of my sleeve. "Oh, Dad, I don't know. . . ."

"Just hear me out." He held up a hand. He was speaking quickly now. "You could try it out, entry-level of course. But then, if you liked it, you could take the courses, the exam, get your CPA license." There was a glimmer of hope in his face as he made this pitch.

I said nothing for a moment, chewing the inside of my cheek. I was trying to keep the revulsion from showing on my face. "Dad, I really don't think I'm the accountant type—"

"How do you know if you don't give it a chance?" He shrugged and smiled. "Please, Cat. I want to help you find a . . . legitimate lifestyle. Okay?"

A legitimate lifestyle. As an accountant. I was swept up in visions of sensible shoes and bad perms. And a life that added up to utter insignificance. I shuddered. "Dad, I really don't—"

"Just do it for me, please? Just try?"

I just couldn't turn him down. How could I crush his hope without even trying? I sighed. "Okay. I'll give it a try. I'll go to the interview."

I can't fully explain why I agreed to this. But seeing his relieved, hopeful look confirmed that I'd done the right thing. For the time being. He leaned over and wrapped me in a hug—big and strong and warm. He smelled of soap and Old Spice, as he always had. We didn't hug often anymore. I noticed his shoulders felt slightly bonier than I remembered them.

I descended the elevator, leaving him happily imagining a nice, safe future for his daughter, I was sure. Which left me with a large fist of guilt in my stomach.

But it was a first step. I'd have to figure the rest out later.

Several hours later I was skulking about on a train platform, slipping in and out of shadows and clouds of steam, dressed entirely in black. The air echoed with announcements of train departures and sharp whistles from conductors. Metal clanged as trains rolled into the station. Every inch of my skin tingled. I felt exhilarated. Alive.

I was sneaking onto the train because I didn't want to be a registered guest—I didn't plan to stick around once I stole the necklace. The last thing I wanted to be was the girl who ordered the crème brûlée for dessert but never returned from the restroom to eat it. I didn't need anyone worrying about where the missing guest had gone and raising an alarm prematurely.

I was pleased with myself and the new skill I'd tried out—the Varma Kalai trigger point from the security conference worked like a charm to take out an overzealous security guard and render him unconscious. He was sleeping soundly in a storage cupboard.

But even as I worked, creeping along the platform, I couldn't help a small tug of guilt. If my father could see me now—well, it would devastate him. But I had to put that out of my mind. Lapses of concentration could be very dangerous for a thief. Besides—why should I have felt badly? This was what I did best. It was who I was.

I was tucked in close to the body of the train, to attract a minimum of attention. I could feel the heat from the engine. With ninja stealth, I dissolved into the shadows of the train and the steam. I slipped between cars and slithered onboard through the emergency door.

I stole into the restroom and changed into the cocktail outfit I had tucked in my pack: sheer black blouse, bias-cut silk skirt, pashmina, black patent sling back shoes. As I was changing in the tiny restroom, I felt the train jostle and pull away from the station with a faint squeal of wheels. I glanced out the window. The shadows and flickering lights of the city slid by. I made my way to the club car and ordered a dirty martini. Next phase: some light mingling, being careful to not have any memorable conversations. Mostly I was assessing the staff, appraising their degrees of alertness. I was also determining how often they entered the baggage car—because that was my target.

Being an old-fashioned steam engine, it had been built with a train's safe in the mail car for packages and valuables. When the train was revamped, the mail car became a baggage area and cloakroom. They kept the safe. After a little updating of the locking mechanism, they were all set to provide a tidy little service to their customers. Or so they'd thought.

In the club car, sipping my martini, I was waiting for just the right chance. It would be when the staff was fully into their routine, lulled into complacency, when we were well away from the departure platform. Timing was everything here. This was a finesse job. As there was no high-tech security, per se, it was all about the art of burglary. Which meant that failure would be a major career error. I knew the AB&T board was expecting a stellar performance from me. I knew that Templeton was counting on me. But, more than that, I felt a bone-deep aching to prove to myself that I could do this. At last everything gelled. It was time. I strolled through the club car, backward through the train, and slid the door open into the baggage car. The door clicked gently behind me, shutting out the noise of the dinner party, and I was in darkness. The train rocked gently beneath my feet and the only sound was the rhythmic clacking of the track. My eyes adjusted to the darkness and I pushed my way back between plush coats, through the heady scent of leather jackets and luggage, toward the rear wall. The safe came into view, a small black-enameled iron box. I slithered on my second-skin gloves and reached out to put a hand on the safe.

At this point someone—in a highly deliberate manner—coughed. I froze. My throat constricted as a figure emerged from the shadows. I made out an all-too familiar face.

Jack Barlow.

Chapter 21

"Jack, are you kidding me?" I managed to croak, once my heart resumed beating. I stood my ground but my eyes swung wildly, looking for an escape route. *Damn.* How did he know I would be here? He was waiting for me. This was not good. Into my panic pushed a small, dark ache of betrayal. I knew he was FBI, but somehow I'd thought after everything we'd been through he would never actually bust me. He would turn a blind eye, perhaps, when the time came.

The train was clacking quickly over the track, the horn sounding its muffled warning as we passed through a level crossing. The hanging coats swung slightly with the jostling of the train.

Jack stood before me, holding his hands out in the gesture one might use to calm a wild horse. "Don't worry, Cat. I'm not here to arrest you." His voice was low and level.

I narrowed my eyes. Was he telling the truth? Jack was never a great liar. He was watching me with patience, and something else. Concern, maybe? "Okay," I said slowly. "Then what are you doing?"

"I'm here to warn you. The FBI received a tip about a job happening on this train. Agents will be waiting for you at the Seattle station when we pull in."

I raised my eyebrows. Not what I was expecting. A warm spark filled that dark hole of betrayal. "That's fine," I said, shrugging. "Because I was never planning to be at the Seattle station anyway."

Now it was his turn to be surprised. "You weren't?"

"Nope."

He blinked and did that half-smile half-frown that people do when they're intrigued by something. He then shook his head and closed his eyes. "Wait—don't tell me any more. The less I know the better."

"Agreed."

Jack took a step toward me. "Cat, even so, it's a big mess. They'll have people all over it. Why don't you give this one a miss?"

I pressed my lips together and considered this. Maybe he was right. Maybe it was too risky. But to give up so early would not look good from the Agency's point of view. I pictured the look of disappointment on Templeton's face.

"Absolutely not." I turned my back to him and resumed working on the safe.

"What are you doing?" he demanded behind my back.

"What does it look like?"

"Cat, you can't . . ." He trailed off. I rotated the wheel of the lock with the lightest of touches. I blocked out the outside world. The clicks of the contact points transmitted through to my fingers and an image began to formulate in my mind. It was a fuzzy, sketchy drawing at first, which began to sharpen as I turned the wheel.

"How are you doing that, exactly?" Jack's voice penetrated my concentration. I glanced at him over my shoulder. He was chewing on his lip and watching me intently, eyes wide, arms folded, trying to fight the crooked smile that was besieging his face.

I raised an eyebrow. "Would you like me to teach you?"

His face swiftly rearranged into a scowl. "No." I turned back to the safe to hide my smirk, and kept working. "Listen, Cat, this is not a good idea—"

My shoulders dropped and I exhaled loudly. "Jack, I'm trying to concentrate here. So . . . either bust me or shut up." I took a sidelong look at him. His fists were clenched and his jaw was working. "Jack, if you want me to stop, you're going to have to force me. Are you willing to do that?"

He made an incomprehensible sound of exasperation, which I took to mean no. I returned to the task at hand while Jack watched. After several more minutes working my magic, I cracked the safe. The door sprang open with a soft *thunk*. I shivered with gratification—it was the most delicious sound in the world.

I pawed through the various items inside the safe and found the treasure I wanted: the diamond necklace. I grabbed it, slipped it into my handbag, and closed the safe door.

Jack made a peculiar sound. "You're just leaving everything else? Just taking that one thing?"

"Yep. That's all I've been hired to do."

He frowned slightly, a pensive look on his face. "Is that how you always work?"

"Always."

"How come we never talked about that?"

I sighed. "You never wanted to know, Jack."

At that moment, I turned around and saw a uniform hat framed within the small square of glass in the baggage car door. The security guard was looking downward at the latch he was about to pull to enter the baggage car. My eyes flew wide. The guard wore a bored expression; he hadn't seen us yet.

But I knew it was too late to hide.

Instantly, I ripped open my blouse. In the next beat I tore open the shirt of a very bewildered Jack. And then I heard the door unlatch.

"Quick, kiss me. . . ." I hissed urgently. Jack's eyebrows sprang sky high. "Guard coming."

Comprehension dawned on Jack's face. In the next second he dug his hands into my hair and pulled me close. With hands and lips and tongues entangled, we did an excellent job of impersonating a pair of illicit lovers.

"Hey!" a male voice hollered. The sound pulled me, sadly, into the present reality. And then there was some grumbling and throat-clearing from the guard and he continued with, "Oh . . . umm . . . you—you aren't allowed in here."

I turned toward the guard, looking up bashfully from beneath tousled hair that I knew hid most of my face. "Oops," I giggled. "Guess we've been caught, honey."

Jack cleared his throat and muttered a "So sorry, officer."

The guard glanced at my exposed bra and averted his eyes,

flushing furiously, and hustled us out of the room with more gruffs and grumbles. I rebuttoned my blouse as we exited.

To my irritation, I found that I was having difficulty walking in a straight line. I could still feel the heat of Jack's hands on my neck, my face. We returned to the cocktail car. As my head gradually cleared, I could see that we had a big problem now. Jack and I moved to a quiet corner of the car, by the window, and I turned to him with urgency.

"Listen, are you a registered passenger?" I demanded in a low voice. "Does anyone know you're here?"

He shook his head. "I snuck on, just like you. I'm off duty."

I tugged hard on my earlobe. "Well, that decides that."

"What?"

"You've got to come with me now."

"Excuse me?" He took a step back and looked at me like I needed urgent admission to the nearest psych ward.

"We're getting off this train. Now."

He laughed. "No way."

I stared at him and I was not smiling. "Think about it, Jack. When the train arrives in Seattle, the necklace will be gone. The police will be questioning everyone. It won't be long before they make the connection. They'll find that you weren't registered. And when that guard gets a good second look at you, he'll be able to say that you were the one in the baggage car at the time. But I'll be missing. You'll be the guilty party."

"Cat, forget it. I'm an FBI officer."

"Who was present at the scene of a crime. In a highly compromising position with the probable thief. That will make you an accomplice."

His jaw contracted.

"Face it, Jack, you're screwed. Either way."

It occurred to me then, as I stood staring at Jack, exactly how much of a risk he took to be here. He really was a hero.

Which was something that drew me like gravity. Probably because it was the exact opposite of what I was. I might have been many things, but who would ever have mistaken me for a hero? A dark, ugly thought whispered in my ear: *what sort of hero lets her baby sister die?*

Jack was thinking hard, as we stood close together in the club car. The train rattled over the tracks, cocktail glasses clinked inside the car. A white-jacketed attendant bustled by. "I can cover. I'll be able to explain," Jack said.

I looked at him uncertainly. "Explaining might mean turning me in."

He hesitated. During which time my stomach clenched in terror. "No. I won't have to do that," he said firmly.

I quietly exhaled. "Listen, that guard didn't get a good look at our faces," I pressed on. "He was too embarrassed. He probably won't be able to identify us—but only if we disappear. Your only chance is to get off this train with me now."

He paused and a few more seconds passed. "Fuck," he said, at last. "Fine."

We squeezed ourselves through the door and into the space between the cars, wind whipping and tearing at our clothes and hair. The rhythmic chugging of the train thundered in my ears. I pulled on my night-vision goggles and checked my watch. We were due to arrive at the bridge in about seven minutes, so we were going to have to book it.

"Just so you know, this is *not* what I intended when I got on this damn train," Jack said, looking severely pissed off but resigned, as we climbed up to the roof of the train car. We gripped the cold iron bars of the ladder and hoped that eighteenth-century metalworkers took pride in their work.

"Hey, me neither," I said through my teeth. "This job would have gone perfectly fine if it weren't for your meddling. And now we're going to be lucky to get out of here."

"Meddling? I was trying to save your ass!"

"Who asked you?" I hurled. "For Christ's sake . . . let's get going. This isn't going to be easy."

I handed Jack my backup harness and we strapped ourselves in. I knew that Jack had never done this before, so we'd have to do a tandem jump. I fastened the back of his harness to the front of mine at four points, then attached the parachute pack to my back. The straps dug into my thighs. The cold, rushing air made my eyes water.

Okay, there it was. A deep canyon. This was our one chance. It was the only spot high enough for a BASE jump. The train hurtled toward the bridge. I steadied myself and made sure all straps were pulled tight.

"Ready?" I yelled into the wind. A grunt was all I received by way of a response.

We pitched ourselves out and away, off the top of the train.

Chapter 22

We hurtled down through the black sky. But there was no time for free fall. With a jump this low, we wouldn't make it. The static line I'd set deployed the chute instantly, the drogue released, and then the parachute unfurled, snapping us up. We sailed down through frosty air. The wind was a torrent in my ears. My stomach was doing back-handsprings as we fell toward the earth. It was exhilarating. But beneath the exhilaration lurked a core of terror. Many of the things I did in this job brought me close to death. And I would have liked to say I wasn't afraid. But I was.

For a moment, sailing through the night sky gripping tightly to the parachute handles, I imagined a life without this stuff—without the proximity to death. A life of peace. And I had to admit, there was something deeply appealing about that. But I automatically forced myself to stop thinking about it. Truth was, I didn't particularly deserve a life of peace.

As an undergraduate, I had taken a class on ancient Greek mythology. One day the professor was lecturing on the underworld and the souls being punished there. For his sins, Sisyphus was forced to push a boulder uphill and once he got it to the top it would roll back down again. For eternity he would do this. I remember sitting in the back of the darkened lecture room, staring at the illustration of Sisyphus illuminated on the screen. I'd been rooted to my seat.

Is that what I was doing? Endlessly repeating the same task—stealing—in hopes of someday receiving forgiveness for what happened to Penny? But was it all in vain?

The ground was growing closer. I steered the ram-air parachute with hand toggles, and we landed on the hard rock of the canyon.

When we touched down, Jack was breathing heavily. With the terror removed, the adrenaline rushed through me unconstrained and gave me a supreme feeling of victory. Dark thoughts of the underworld crumbled away like ancient pottery turning to dust. I detached our harnesses. Jack struggled away from me and flopped down on the ground. He looked up at me, face flushed and hair windblown.

"Okay, that was wrong," he said. "Very wrong."

"But fun, no?" I said, with a huge smile.

His face cracked into a grin bigger than mine. "Hell, yes."

I briefly struggled with one of the straps. Jack reached over to help me. He was very close, intoxicatingly so. The palm of his hand—rough and warm—brushed mine as we grappled with the straps. I could feel myself reaching the approximate temperature of a volcano. In an instant, I was back in the baggage cart, pressed up against Jack, clawing at his shoulders and tasting his mouth. . . .

Standing in the canyon, I noticed that Jack's eyes were slightly out of focus. I wondered if he was thinking about the same thing I was. At once, abstract, fairy-tale visions of a future with Jack sprang involuntarily to mind. Fantasies I'd stupidly indulged in when we were a couple. Those ideas had been squashed months ago. But at that moment—there was something about the way Jack was looking at me that made all those gauzy images come into sharper focus.

"Cat," he said gently.

"Yes?" My voice came out Marilyn-Monroe-breathless.

There was a long pause. He raked his hand through his hair and seemed to be struggling over something. Then he looked down and started packing up the parachute. "So, anyway. Did you get the invitation to the golf tournament Nicole is hosting?" he asked briskly.

The string section that had previously been performing in my head came to a screeching halt.

"It's just . . ." he continued, avoiding eye contact. "I know she wants you to come. It would be fun. You should come. . . ."

I blinked, at a loss for words.

* * *

The stone room beneath the masquerade mansion flickered with wall sconces. I was seated at a table with Sandor and his people. All eyes were on me and despite the damp chill in the room, I was sweating under the scrutiny. I shifted in my seat to improve my comfort level. Not effective.

"Miss Montgomery," Sandor said, "we need you to tell us how the job is coming along." Okay, so they needed an update. Probably some reassurance. Fine. I could do that.

It was peculiar—this evening Sandor looked much less like the benign schoolboy I met in the diner that night. Somehow he looked like a much older man, much harder. I swallowed. "Well, I've got all the information I need about the security," I said.

"Good. Go on." Sandor's gaze was unwavering.

I tried to keep my tone confident. "Of course there's some equipment I need to gather. There's a particular piece that needs to come in through my supplier."

When I'd gone home after my little expedition with Ethan, I'd pored over all the information. After reading everything, I felt comfortable about my ability to deal with most of the security technology. With one exception.

That noxious gas. I'd researched Kolokol-1. It was designed to only render its victims unconscious, but still, I was not fond of the possibility of being gassed to death. So I called my tech guy, Lucas, yesterday, to get a gas mask.

"Nope," he'd said. "Regular gas mask won't do the trick."

"Why not?"

"It's this pesky Kolokol-1 stuff. Very rare. Very noxious."

"Is it true they used it in that hostage thing in Moscow?" This was what Ethan had told me.

"Yep—believed to be."

"And," I said, "what about the rumor that a lot of hostages were killed by the stuff? That's not true, is it?" I gave a light, nervous laugh.

"Totally true."

I stopped laughing.

"Of course," Lucas continued, "that was probably because the dose was way too large. In your situation, the dose won't be as large.

Most likely. It's fascinating, actually. Some sources believe it to be carfentanil, an aerosolized narcotic, but it's difficult to manufacture, a very secret chemical composition—"

"*Lucas,*" I said firmly. "Focus, please?"

"Right," he said, clearing his throat. "Point is, we need a mask with a very specific filter that will protect against Kolokol-1."

"Can you get it?"

"Sure can. But . . . it's gonna take a little time."

"How much time?" I winced, waiting for the answer.

"Well, we need to order it in from Minsk."

"*Minsk?*"

"Minsk."

I closed my eyes and rubbed them with my hand. "And that's going to take how long?"

"Few days, hopefully. Maybe more. Hard to say."

In the stone room beneath the masquerade mansion, I smoothed my skirt and looked around at Sandor's people. "Don't worry, it's completely in hand," I said with a serene smile.

At this point, Sandor's assistant, Gilda, a wiry woman in her sixties with short, steel gray hair, walked in and said, "Sir, they're here, asking to talk to you." I noted a slight emphasis on the word *they're.*

"Where are they?" asked Sandor.

"Across the hall in your office."

Abruptly, our meeting ended, and I was left to see myself out. Which I started to do. And then, I reconsidered.

A hook of curiosity snagged the back of my brain. Who were *they*? Who was here to talk to Sandor? I bit my lip. Was it another thief? My potential replacement?

The truth was, there was a host of other possibilities. And when it came right down to it, I didn't know a lot about Sandor and his people. What else were they up to? Who else did they deal with? If it had anything to do with the Fabergé, shouldn't I know about it? And if it didn't . . . well, maybe there were other things I should know about.

It was clear to me this curiosity was not going to go away. Only one thing to do. I glanced furtively in all directions, then doubled back. There was an unoccupied room beside the one where Sandor was meeting the mystery people; I tucked in to it.

It was dark and smelled musty and damp. The room appeared to be disused, empty apart from a few boxes collecting dust in the corner. There was a heavy oak door on the inside wall that connected this room with Sandor's. I soundlessly moved across the floor and pressed myself against the warm oak.

I could hear voices. But not well enough to make out words.

There was a small gap beneath the door. Perfect. It would be just enough. I opened my backpack and fished out my fiber-optic bendy wire. This was the best invention ever. Better than self-tanning moisturizer, even.

With this I would be able to see, and hear—through the micro-microphone—the other room. I slipped the wire under the door, allowing it to point upward. With a little wriggling and adjustment, I managed to train it on the people in the room.

The moment I did, I almost lost my grip on the fiber optic. Because sitting there talking to Sandor across his broad desk were the two men dressed like monks who had been following me the other day.

". . . but that's just it, we came here to request that you call off your search for the Aurora Egg," the tall monk with mushroom ears was saying. His voice cracked as he spoke.

"Why would I do that?" Sandor asked, looking somewhat bored.

"Because it's the right thing to do." The darker, square-jawed monk's chair creaked as he leaned forward. "Surely you must know what is contained in the Egg. You know it's the rightful property of the church."

My eyebrows went up. So these two really *were* monks—it wasn't just a disguise.

"What?" Sandor said, laughing with surprise. "What are you talking about?"

"We entreat you," said the tall one. "If you do locate or acquire the Egg, please—whatever you do, do not open it. There will be great danger. Instead, please contact us immediately."

"I'll think about it," Sandor said, nodding noncommittally. "Good day, gentlemen." He stood and the monks followed suit, quickly scurrying out like brown rabbits. Sandor and his entourage shortly exited, flicking off the lights behind them. I sat back on my heels in the musty darkness with mind whirring. I *knew* it. I knew there was something important inside the Egg. But what? And why was the church interested? Did Sandor know what it was? He wasn't letting on that he did. And clearly, even if he did know, he had no plans to tell me.

Only one way to find out. I'd just have to get the Egg and see for myself.

Chapter 23

As the car rolled to a stop in the clubhouse parking lot—my brain spinning with thoughts of Fabergé Eggs and what they could possibly contain and when was that damn gas mask going to arrive anyway— I experienced a tweak of anxiety about the immediate task at hand. But how difficult could golfing possibly be? I'll admit that, *technically,* I'd never golfed before. But that didn't mean I couldn't do it. Just look at those guys playing golf on TV—their median age must be, what, seventy? If they could do it, I could do it. Anyway, I just needed to make an appearance and, ideally, make Jack *chartreuse* with jealousy and impressed by my sportswomanship and then make a fabulous exit. Besides, it would be a nice distraction; there was little I could do about the Fabergé job until my mask was delivered.

I had been firmly against attending Nicole's golf tournament. But when Jack had asked me about it after our train escape, I'd lashed out. "Yes, of course I'm coming," I'd said, angrily stuffing my parachute back in its sack. "And I'm bringing a *date.* I hope that's okay."

I'd glared at him defiantly, daring him to object. He'd blustered a little and then said, "Yes, of course . . . Why wouldn't it be?"

Naturally that left me with the small matter of recruiting said date. After several sweeps through my address book the only person I could come up with was Ethan. When I called him and extended the invitation there was a moment's silence, during which I clenched and unclenched my jaw.

"Wait a sec," Ethan said. "This is a golf tournament with a bunch of cops, right? FBI and such?"

"Yes," I said, employing a breezy and unperturbed tone to suggest that it was a perfectly normal occurrence for criminals and law enforcement to mingle in a social-slash-recreational forum particularly when charity was involved. "Is that a problem?"

There was another pause. And then, with a mischievous laugh, he said, "Not a bit. Sounds like a blast."

In preparation for this torture I decided it was mandatory to look absolutely fabulous. So I bought a marvelous outfit for the occasion: cute golf skirt, two-tone shoes, Nike visor, the whole works. And I borrowed a top-of-the line set of clubs from Mel, who golfed religiously.

For the finishing touch I popped over to the local mall to get an airbrush tan. It was something I'd never done before. But what looks better than a healthy, tropical glow? When I got home I thought it looked a little peculiar but I didn't have great lighting in my bathroom. Memo to self: Remember to get lightbulbs.

Ethan and I crunched across the gravel of the parking lot and strolled into the clubhouse. And then I did something I promised myself I wouldn't do: I immediately started scanning the room for Jack. I couldn't help myself.

It didn't take long. He was standing in a small clutch of people. As if sensing my arrival, he looked up. When he spotted me he broke into a great smile. My heart twanged like a giant bowstring and I couldn't help smiling back. Then Jack's gaze shifted to the man standing beside me. His eyebrows lifted in surprise.

And this—well, this angered me greatly. Did he think I'd been bluffing? Okay, so *yes,* at the time I was bluffing, but that wasn't the salient point.

Jack had more nerve than a broken tooth. Break up with *me,* crush my heart, then start dating the perfect woman, invite me to this ridiculous event . . . and I wasn't supposed to bring anyone?

Nicole appeared at my side. She grabbed my hand. "Cat, I'm glad you could come," she said with a warm smile. This statement had the effect of making me extremely grouchy. She drew me and Ethan over to the group.

I noted that none of the other women were dressed quite the way

I was. They were all much more casual, in shorts or pants and simple T-shirts and sweaters. Nothing quite so, um, flashy as my outfit. Or so bare. It was mid-September, after all. But it was fine, I told myself. Nobody ever said that FBI agents, or golfers for that matter, had much fashion sense.

I flicked a glance at Jack. His expression had been smoothly replaced with a mask of cordiality.

"Nice clubs," he said to me, nodding toward Mel's golf bag. "They're yours?"

"Of course."

He looked momentarily confused. Like he thought he knew me. Like he thought he knew I don't golf, that we'd had conversations to this effect in the past. Well, *ha,* Mr. Barlow. Guess you didn't know me as well as you thought. (Okay. So maybe we did have those conversations. Still. It didn't mean he knew me.)

We had another minute to wait for free tee decks. Jack turned to my date. "So what do you do, Ethan?" he asked, with barely re-strained hostility. His hands were gripped firmly around a golf club and I could see his forearm muscles flexing.

Ethan, on the other hand, was enjoying himself greatly. "Oh, I'm a professional thief," he said.

Next came a stunned silence in the group. Followed by hearty laughter, as everyone got the joke. Jack's face darkened.

As someone else engaged Ethan in small talk, Jack stood next to me and I could feel his eyes on me. I ignored him, focusing instead on the conversation between Ethan and the others in the group.

"What's wrong with your skin?" Jack whispered to me.

"What do you mean?" I asked uneasily.

"You look a bit . . . weird."

I shrugged, but when he turned away I immediately dashed to the washroom. I stared at my face in the well-lit bathroom. As I did so my head swam. Unfortunately, I looked precisely like an Oompa-Loompa. My skin was a lovely burnished orange, a shade generally reserved for shag carpet circa 1972.

Okay, no need to panic. I ripped out a compact from my handbag and vigorously rubbed on more blush to try to take the orange out.

I'd come this far and I was not backing down now, *dammit.* Besides, I needed to look at the positives. I had a great outfit, and my hair, thank God, looked excellent in my adorable visor.

When I returned from the washroom I caught a snatch of conversation as I approached the group.

"She's really making her mark on the department, isn't she?" a man was saying to Jack. They were both looking in Nicole's direction, who stood by the desk signing our group in. Ridiculously, I tucked myself behind a large potted ficus tree to hear what would come next.

"Yes, she is," Jack said, matter-of-fact. "You know she wrapped up that Phillips case this week?"

"The bane of the department for three years?"

"That's the one," Jack said. He smiled warmly.

And that small thing—well, it just about killed me. He'd *never* looked like that when talking about me. I'd never heard that tone of voice, not when it came to me. And certainly not when it came to my line of work.

Nicole returned and began herding everyone out to the practice range. I was tempted to bolt right then and there but *no.* I was not going to do that. I rejoined the group and walked outside. My skin broke out in gooseflesh as the chilly wind whipped my bare legs. In retrospect, I really should have consulted a weather forecast before selecting my outfit.

Everyone in our group took a position at the driving range for a warm-up bucket of balls while we waited for our tee-off times. I did the same. Jack lined up on my right, Ethan on my left.

As I was getting myself set up on my little square of AstroTurf I snuck a glance at Jack. He looked amazing as he swung his driver. So masculine, so smooth. He hit the ball professionally, with a lovely *schuck* sound, and it went far. Who knew golf could be so sexy?

On Jack's far side was Nicole. She swung and her ball sailed up and away. Unreasonably far, if you ask me. And straight. What was she, the Bionic Woman?

No problem. I could do that. What was so difficult? You swing the club, you hit the ball. I copied the way Nicole lined up in front of the tee. *Here goes.*

First swing, I missed the ball entirely.

I looked around furtively. Nobody appeared to have noticed. *Fine.* I'd chalk it up to a practice swing.

I swung again and . . . missed. I looked down at the stupid white ball sitting there, mocking me, looking all innocent perched there on its miniature pedestal. "What are you looking at?" I hissed to the smug little ball. I tugged my skirt down, which now felt somewhat idiotic, lined up and swung again. Nothing but air. Quite possibly I might have cried.

I became acutely aware of how absurd I looked. Skirt and visor and everything, like I was on the PGA tour or something. I wanted to tear off the visor, given that there wasn't actually any sun out at the moment, but I knew my hair would look horrible if I did. And I would have loved to change into a nice comfy pair of sweats.

But what I really wanted was to hit the goddamn ball. Ten swings later, I still hadn't made contact. I glanced over at Nicole. She swung. *Schuck* went the ball, as she made contact and the ball flew up and away. Perfection, again.

I clenched my teeth and swung hard. I made contact with a loud clunk. Hurrah!

The ball shanked off at a ridiculous angle and hit a guy in the shin.

"I'm *so* sorry!" I hollered, cringing. I lined up again.

"Just stay loose, Cat," said Jack next to me, in a low voice.

Loose. Okay. I could do that. I swung again, thinking loose . . . *loose.* . . . The club went flying from my hands, out onto the range.

"Fuck," I said—aloud, I'm pretty sure. The good news was the club flew a pretty respectable distance. Was it wrong for me to be proud of that? I darted down the hill to retrieve the club.

"Attention!" a voice boomed over the PA. "Would the golfer *in the skirt* get off the range . . . immediately!"

So apparently it wasn't "okay" to go onto the range. How was I to know that?

The marshall strolled over to inform us that our tee-off time had arrived. Everyone started moving away to the course. The thought of continuing on this way made me feel ill. I wanted to disappear. To scream. And mostly, to cry.

But how could I back out now? Making up some lame excuse would make me look—and feel—even more pathetic.

At that moment, Ethan appeared at my side. "You okay, Montgomery?" he said in a low voice, looking closely at me with concern.

I returned his gaze and everything he needed to know was written all over my face. He nodded, mouth set in a line.

At that moment, Ethan's cell phone slipped out of his pocket and bounced on the square of Astroturf. He bent down to retrieve it, and suddenly grabbed at his low back, letting out a yelp of pain. He remained frozen there, hunched over in an awkward posture.

"Ethan, are you okay?"

An attempt to straighten triggered another moan of pain. I stooped to help support him. "I'll be fine," he said. "It's this old injury—"

I looked up and saw that everyone had stopped, watching us uneasily. "Can I help?" asked Jack.

"We'll be okay. You guys just go ahead," I said.

Ethan was not moving. His breathing was heavy and his eyes were squeezed shut.

I hunched over further, supporting him from underneath his left side. I looked up into his face, hidden as it was from everyone else. And he winked at me.

He was faking it. *Of course* he was faking it.

I bit my lip to keep from smiling, as a warm crest of relief and gratitude broke over me. He'd provided me with parole. And more than that: he was willing to make himself look ridiculous for my sake.

"This is so embarrassing," Ethan muttered, loud enough for those closest to us to hear. We made an attempt at hobbling to a bench inside the clubhouse, assisted by one of the golf pros. Moans and groans punctuated the journey. By this time, everyone else had packed up their things, ready to move off to the golf course.

I left Ethan sprawled awkwardly on the bench and found Nicole. "You know, I think I should just take him home. He doesn't seem to be doing very well."

Jack was standing beside her. A peculiar look played on his face.

Did he know Ethan was liberating me from my torture by faking his own? I couldn't be sure. He certainly wasn't saying anything to dissuade me.

"Of course," Nicole said. "I completely understand."

The golf shop staff put our clubs in Ethan's car and I helped him climb into the passenger's seat.

I flopped myself down in the driver's seat, ripped off my ridiculous visor and stared out the window. I watched as our group moved away to the course. Jack and Nicole were walking side by side, the gently rolling green ahead of them. Nicole inclined her head to him and said something. A horrible ache crushed my chest. And with that, I realized the truth. It was *right* that they were together. It made sense.

"Let's get out of here, shall we?" Ethan said. "I think that's more than enough golf for today."

I turned to him. "Ethan, how can I thank you enough for getting me out of there?"

He shrugged. "Forget it, Montgomery. You'd do the same for me."

We went back to his place, picking up Thai food on the way. It was just what I needed: a nice warm meal and then I'd be off home to soak my miseries in a hot bath. Outside, the sky had grown thick and gray; the wind carried the scent of rain.

Ethan cracked open a frosty beer for each of us. "So you used to date that guy, huh?" he asked casually, as I broke my chopsticks apart.

I looked at him with surprise. "Which guy?"

"You know. Mr. Tall, Dark, and Handsome. The hero guy. The FBI."

"You could tell?"

"Painfully obvious."

He peeled the lid off the pad Thai container and a spicy aroma of peanut and lime curled upward. "He was the heartbreak, wasn't he? The one you were talking about at the conference." I nodded, dipping a spring roll into chili sauce and biting down with a loud crunch. "You know," he continued, "if you don't mind me saying, he's just not your type."

I raised my chin defensively. "Excuse me?"

"Montgomery, he's a good guy. You, my dear, are a bad guy. And bad and good don't mix. It's like roller coasters and egg salad."

I took a sip of my ice-cold Stella Artois. "What about 'opposites attract'?"

"Sorry, babe, I don't buy that."

I became aware of Ethan's proximity to me, beside me on the sofa, and the way he was looking at me. I was not getting involved with him. Absolutely not. I did not need more heartache.

"Tell me, Montgomery, why do you do this? What keeps you in the criminal game?"

"Well, it's complicated," I said. I dug into a container of shrimp and spinach curry. I sipped more beer and felt a distinct tingling in my legs.

"I've got nowhere to be," he said.

And then—maybe because of the alcohol—maybe because I needed catharsis after my awful day, or maybe because I felt like I could trust Ethan, after what he'd done for me today, I found myself telling Ethan all about my sister, Penny. He watched me thoughtfully as I told him.

"And that's why I keep doing it," I said at last. "That's why I can't get out—not until I finally make amends."

"Okay, Montgomery, but you don't seriously think you would quit, then, do you?"

"Yes. I have to." *How am I supposed to get my fairy-tale ending otherwise?*

"Montgomery, there's no way. You wouldn't do it. You wouldn't choose to be ordinary any more than I would."

I frowned at him. "And what makes you think you know me?"

He smiled mischievously. "Well, I admit, I don't know you as well as I'd like to, right now"—at this point, his look took on a smoldering quality—"but I'm pretty sure I'm right about this."

I realized, belatedly, that I'd probably had too much to drink. Right. Focus, Cat. Do not give in to temptation.

"Think about it, Montgomery," he continued. "What was your life like before you discovered your skills?"

I nodded, chewing noodles. "Pretty bad, actually. I mean I was just a kid. But I was always mediocre at everything I did. So garden variety. Nothing special." I bit my lip; it wasn't easy to admit this. "I hated it." My insides twisted, remembering how I felt when I was young. And I wondered just how far I would go to avoid feeling that way again.

"Right. So when you discovered your hidden talents—how did you feel then?"

Alive. I didn't say this, though.

"Like, all of a sudden, you had a place in the world, right?" he said. "A purpose. There aren't many truly great thieves in this world . . . but there are a whole lot of accountants, sales reps, and middle managers out there. All living lives of quiet desperation."

I flashed him a wry smile. "Oh, so you're quoting Thoreau now?"

"I'm serious. Do you really want to be one of those people? I'm sure you've got people like that in your life right now. Think about it—do you really want to turn out like them?"

I looked down, frowning. I instantly thought of my parents. As much as I loved my mom and dad, I could see how their choices left them vaguely unfulfilled and unsatisfied. And, ultimately, insignificant in the world. My heart crushed with a desperate desire to avoid that fate.

"There was a girl in school when I was a kid," I heard myself saying, "and she was going places. She was a singer—truly talented. Everyone could tell she was destined for greater things. And she was. Early on, she left, to have a spectacular career and glamorous life. Kelly Bishop—you might have heard of her?" Ethan's eyebrows rose in recognition of the name. I nodded. "I longed for that. Not singing—I knew I couldn't sing well enough to be a star. Or dancing, for that matter. Or sports, or music. And believe me, I tried it all, desperate to find my one special thing."

"Well, Montgomery, being a thief is your stardom. And yeah, maybe it means you're the villain. But better *that* than nothing."

The rain had started; it poured down the windows in sheets.

"You know what?" I said. "You're right. I *am* the bad guy. And like you said—what's wrong with that? I'm *good* at it."

"That's my girl."

My head was wheeling with a new feeling of empowerment. It felt good. Possibly the Stella Artois was contributing but I didn't care. Ethan stretched an arm out and touched the back of my neck with his warm hand. It was like his fingertips were electric.

To hell with caution. I turned toward him and gazed at him from under lowered lashes. He was no novice; he knew exactly what I meant by that look.

Suddenly we were in his bedroom, tearing at each others' clothes, groping and rolling together, half naked. Then a lucid thought pushed itself into my fuzzy brain. *Oh my God, did I have spinach in my teeth from that shrimp curry?* I tried to forget about it. But dammit, now the thought was in my head, I couldn't get it out.

I mumbled something vague to Ethan about needing the washroom, disentangled myself, and darted into the en suite.

I quickly checked my reflection, and sure enough, an enormous piece of spinach adorned the space between my left front incisors. A frantic, semidrunk scramble through Ethan's medicine cabinet searching for dental floss came up empty. Desperate to get back to that warm, strong embrace in those tangled sheets, I savagely picked at my teeth with my fingernail, and the most stubborn piece of spinach ever finally relented its hold.

Of course my gum was now bleeding.

I stopped that with a cold cloth and perhaps more pressure than strictly required, and at last I emerged from the bathroom. I noted that the delay had the effect of heightening my anticipation even more. My legs quivered with nervous excitement.

Ethan was lying bare chested on the bed, propped up on one well-carved, tanned arm. "Everything all sorted out, Montgomery?" he said. One eyebrow was raised, and he was wearing his signature smile of mischief.

"Yes, thank you," I said primly.

"Good. Then come here." His voice was suddenly low, velvet, with a raw edge.

What came next was a hot blur.

Chapter 24

The old stone monastery, tucked into the hills, was surrounded by masonry walls and a black iron gate. The night sky swirled chalky black and gray, heavy with the impending storm. A strong wind flipped the leaves on the trees and showed their pale underbellies. Jack glanced up at the starless, moonless sky. He hoped the monks would arrive before the rain did. He adjusted his night-vision goggles and trained his sight line on the monastery gate.

He shifted for comfort. A futile endeavor, when hiding in bushes. A cluster of sharp sticks poked him in the side.

This had better be worth it. They were badly in need of information. Ever since losing the two monks that day of the stakeout, Wesley had been struggling to ferret them out. He had, interestingly, learned that they were indeed men of the cloth. But that was the only solid bit of information he could find. Jack's job tonight was to observe and glean a few more details.

Jack knew, of course, that the mere fact they were monks was no guarantee of benevolence. Corruption within the church was rampant. On the other hand, what if their motives were good ones? Could they possibly all be on the same side? It was up to Jack to find out. Jack felt a stirring, the feeling of being on the cusp of something very big. Maybe they were actually going to succeed this time.

Success, at last—after so many generations of failure.

Jack's mind flashed with a memory of his father. It was a time when John Robie had come home after a long trip overseas. He'd arrived home late at night and crept into Jack's room to check on him.

Things were bad between them at this point. Jack knew his father was a thief. Yet he wasn't old enough to leave and be independent. He was a prisoner in a criminal household and he hated it.

But they did have moments of civility.

"What's wrong?" Jack asked, still awake, when he saw the deep lines and dark shadows in his father's face.

John Robie sighed, and sat on the edge of the bed. The mattress creaked softly. "We lost it. Again." His voice was flat and quiet.

Jack knew about his father's quest. He knew that it involved several other people all around the world. The object of the quest was something ancient, called the Gifts, which had been lost long ago. Beyond that, he knew little. Far less than he knew now.

It was the only thing Jack admired his father for. But something had been bothering Jack lately. "Dad—when you finally do locate the Gifts—will you have to steal them?"

"Yes, Jack. We will have to steal them back. That's what we've been training for. That is the legacy of the thieves. It's the quest that has been handed down through generations."

Jack rolled over, turning his back to his father. It was not what he wanted to hear. Stealing was wrong.

And yet—here in the bushes at the monastery—here Jack was, part of the plan that would do exactly that. Jack had taken up the mantle from his father. And the strange thing? It felt like the right thing to do.

Just then Jack saw movement within the magnolia bushes next to the monastery gate. A subtle movement, but unmistakably unnatural. Someone else was there, hidden. He sharpened the focus on his binoculars, training them on that area. Who was there? Were they waiting for the monks like Jack was? Their position was too close for observation. It was the sort of position one would choose for an ambush.

Before Jack could do anything more, headlights shone and a taxi pulled slowly up the driveway. Wesley's intel had said the monks would be arriving in a cab. Jack immediately began to shift closer to the gate, positioning and preparing himself for whatever came next.

The two monks clambered from the taxi just as the rain began to fall in its first delicate drops. Standing next to the cab, they fussed with their bags and cloaks and finally located a yellow umbrella. Jack watched the taxi drive away. The monks turned toward the gates, walking ever closer to the row of magnolia bushes. Jack gritted his teeth. What was he going to do now? It was like watching two little antelope innocently springing toward lions crouched in the grass.

As the cab's headlights disappeared down the hill, two men emerged from the bushes, moving with the coiled danger of cobras. One was a muscle-bound steroid monster, the other a wiry man with the physique of a hard laborer, older than the other and although smaller, clearly much more dangerous. Jack spotted a dragon tattoo on the man's forearm; he recognized it from the attack in the parking garage. They positioned themselves between the monks and the monastery gate.

The monks, however, hadn't noticed a thing yet as they struggled to open their umbrella. In a moment they gave up on it and turned to dash into the monastery. They froze when they saw the two men.

"Who are you? What do you want?" demanded one of the monks bravely, the tall one with ears like doorknobs.

"Just to chat," said the wiry, more dangerous man. Both thugs loomed closer, menacing, intimidating. "You two need to stop meddling in things that are bigger than you."

"What are you talking about?" The monks exchanged a quick, panicked glance. Jack could see the Adam's apple of the tall man bob as he swallowed. They blinked against the falling raindrops that splattered on their hair and faces. "We don't know what you mean."

The wiry thug closed his eyes with a pained expression.

"Sure you do," said the steroid monster. "And as long as you mind your own business, you won't have any trouble." Rain was now splashing down in small puddles on the gravel.

Jack stayed hidden, for the moment, holding his breath. *Just agree,* he silently willed the monks. Just tell them what they want to hear. *Okay, no problem . . . sorry to bother you—*

"We can't do that," said the shorter, darker monk. He held his chin defiantly but his voice was tight and pitched high. "This is too important."

Jack winced. He knew in the next moment he'd be forced to cross the line, knew that he wouldn't be able to sit and watch. His muscles tightened in readiness. He pulled out his handgun. The two thugs looked at each other. With no further comment they withdrew their weapons—a crowbar and a knife—and began to close the gap between themselves and the monks.

And that was enough. Jack leaped down, kicking the crowbar from the wiry man's hands. Everything after that became a pinpoint focus of physical movement. With the advantage of surprise, Jack had a shaved second in which he brought the butt end of his gun around to smash the back of the guy's head, knocking him out cold. Jack spun, just as the second guy was coming at him with his knife. It was too fast to get a clear shot—he knew he might hit a monk. Jack managed to dodge the thrust of the blade—steroids gave the guy strength but not speed or agility. But Jack couldn't avoid being brought down by the sheer mass of the man. The full force hit Jack like a train as they slammed into the mud. A searing pain fired into Jack's leg like a hot needle—he looked wildly downward at the knife plunged into his lower leg.

The thug ripped it loose, ready to strike again.

Jack gasped for air and struggled away on the muddy ground. He flipped himself over and aimed the gun at the man who was bearing down on him.

A loud crack echoed against the stone walls. The man crumpled in a giant heap, bleeding from a chest wound. Jack rose, heart pounding. Then, he heard a strangled sound directly behind him. He spiraled, raising his gun automatically, to see the wiry man, consciousness regained, holding a knife against the throat of a monk.

Jack froze, arms raised, gun pointing forward, leveled on the attacker. He rasped for breath. The other monk was several steps away and cowering by the magnolia bush.

"You don't have a shot, Barlow," the thug growled. "It's too dark. And I'm pretty sure you're not the type to risk killing a monk."

He was right. On both counts. Jack knew his night-vision goggles lay on the ground back in the shrubs, of no use to him now. There was too much chance of missing the shot. And if he missed, Jack had no doubt the guy would cut the monk's throat. The thug backed up slowly toward the monastery gates, pressing the knife to the monk's throat. He had to stop him getting into the monastery. He couldn't allow a hostage situation.

Jack then noticed a dim lantern above the monastery gates. That could do it—just a little more light. The rain was heavy now, streaming down all their faces in ribbons.

"Where are you going to go?" he challenged the thug. "You've got nowhere to go. Why don't you just back off, put down the knife, and we can talk about it."

The thug took another step backward, dragging the monk with him.

Jack's eyes were riveted to the two men. He didn't blink. His breathing slowed, everything moved in crisp, slow motion. Raindrops fell from the sky, stretched out in time like a nature documentary. Just a few more steps . . .

Bang.

A sharp red circle appeared on the thug's forehead. He buckled and landed in an unmoving pile. Jack lowered his gun, exhaling, satisfied with his aim. The monk fell away, gasping. Jack was by his side in two strides. The monk was not badly hurt, the only visible wound a thin line of red on his white throat. The other monk staggered over. Jack inspected them; overall, no major injuries. Just bruised and scared.

They sheltered beneath the overhang of the gate. Rain streamed down in a waterfall over the ledge, hammering on the ground and creating a deep channel in the mud. Jack took out his cell phone.

He hesitated before dialing Wesley's number—but what choice did he have? There were two bodies and he needed them taken care of, ASAP. And he couldn't make an official call. Too difficult to explain.

He felt a tug across the line between right and wrong. Admittedly, there was a certain comfort in aligning with the "other" side—the side that did not question, that accepted that certain things simply needed to be done. Did he like that his mind was raking in this direction?

The rain sounded snare-drum beats on the stone ledge above them. Jack punched in Wesley's phone number.

"Don't do anything," Wesley said flatly after Jack described the situation. "We can handle it." Jack pressed the phone to his ear so hard it almost hurt, but he could barely hear over the rain.

He looked at the two dead bodies, at the water drops falling into their open, upwardly staring eyes. He was too far in now. He shivered, and uttered a curt "Fine." He disconnected the call and stared out into the rain.

The reedy voice of one of the monks pushed through his awareness. "We can't thank you enough, Jack."

Jack turned and regarded them carefully. "How do you know my name?" he asked, narrowing his eyes. The monks exchanged an uncertain glance. Their robes hung off them now in sopping drapes.

Jack crossed his arms over his chest. "I'm going to need an explanation and I'm going to need it fast. Who are you? And what are you up to?"

The Latin-looking monk gave the taller one a brief nod. "I'm Brother Anthony and this is Brother Franco. We're seeking the Aurora Egg," he said. "Just like you."

This did not come as a huge surprise. Jack had already pieced together as much. What he wanted to know was why. Jack leaned back against a cold stone post and scrubbed his face. "Fine. The church is involved. Why—after all this time?"

Brother Franco coughed and looked vaguely uncomfortable. "Actually the church isn't involved. Not officially. It's just us. Technically, we're not supposed to be here."

Jack frowned and rolled his hand in an onward motion. "Go on."

"We've been trying to make our case for a long time, but our superiors have totally dismissed the evidence that we've put forward."

Also not a surprise. The church often denied the existence of biblical artifacts. Until they were pressed beneath its nose, that is.

"But soon, there will be no disputing things," Brother Anthony said, with a gleam in his eyes. "Because we know where the Egg is now. Without a doubt. Its precise location."

Jack raised an eyebrow. Now this, this *was* a surprise. "Its precise location?"

They nodded, heads bouncing like bobble-head dolls. "I'm sure that's the reason behind this attack," Brother Franco said, sparing a brief, grim glance toward the bodies in the mud. The rain had lightened now; drops fell in gentle threads.

"Okay, so where is it?" Jack asked.

"The Gorlovich family has it in their possession."

"Not helpful—already knew that. Besides, that family has a million places they could be keeping it. Tell me something I don't know."

"Okay. It's in the Starlight Casino. In the vault named Bagreef. An anagram for Fabergé."

Jack's mouth opened slightly and he froze. "You're sure?"

"Positive."

Jack frowned, considering all of this. He looked at the monks carefully. Jack was wary—he didn't want to reveal too much, in case there were pieces they didn't know. But he had to get to the bottom of things. "Just so we have this straight—you believe the legend is true?"

Both monks nodded solemnly. "Yes, Mr. Barlow," Brother Franco said. "We know, just as you do, that the Fabergé Egg contains the long-lost Gifts of the Magi."

Chapter 25

I was pulled out of a deep sleep by an odd, loud noise. My eyes opened and slowly focused. I saw Ethan's face. Memory came surging back. My face heated up and my heart sang *hallelujah*! I didn't remember every detail but I was quite confident that it involved some rather marvelous sex.

"Mmmm . . ." I said. I tousled my hair and stretched kittenishly. "Hi, you . . . What was that sound, just now?"

Ethan was propped up on pillows, looking bemused. "You, my dear. You were snoring."

I froze. "You're kidding." I could feel the flush of mortification rise up my bare neck.

"Nope," he said. "I was just considering flipping you over to make you stop."

Which is exactly what one hopes a new lover says the morning after. Snoring? Excellent, Cat.

But I wasn't going to let the humiliation ruin my afterglow.

Unfortunately, I noticed something else was threatening that. A subtle undertow: there was a small part of me that wished it had been Jack's bed I'd woken up in.

I scolded myself. That could never be.

When I got home from Ethan's apartment there was a large padded envelope waiting for me. More specifically, my neighbor Bradley was waiting for me, holding the envelope. At the precise moment I'd arrived at my apartment door, fumbling with my keys, his door had flung open and there he stood. The guy needed a hobby.

"Thanks, Bradley. You're such a help," I said tonelessly.

"No problem," he said, with a condescending smile. "I noticed you didn't come home last night, so I wanted to be sure you got this first thing. It's not from the IRS, like the last one, though—"

Slam. (My door, closing in his face.)

I glanced at the return address—my tech lab—and beelined for my bedroom. I opened my closet and pushed aside stacks of shoe boxes, scarves, and clothes, and burrowed my way to the very back of the closet. There was a small camouflaged touch pad here. It illuminated as I pressed my fingertip to it and the back of the closet slid open, revealing a hidden room. The lights clicked on automatically as I stepped through.

Creating this room involved sacrificing precious closet space, which had been a struggle. In the end I'd decided that staying out of prison would be worth it.

My room contained various tools, weapons, disguises, and a top-of-the-line safe. There was also a secret exit: a hole in the ceiling that connected with the building's air vents. In the event of a raid I could lock myself in here and escape.

I shredded into the package and tossed the lab report aside; the scientific details were not what I was looking for. It was the product I was concerned with. From the envelope I carefully pulled out a pair of very special gloves. A small pouch was built into the index finger of each glove, containing a drop of fake blood. This was what, if all went to plan, would fool the biometric sensors.

I held the gloves gingerly and my skin tingled. I was almost ready. Now all I needed was the gas mask. I frowned, picked up my phone and called my tech guy.

"Sorry, Cat. Still not here," said Lucas. "Something went screwy with the shipping people, and it looks like it won't be here for another week, possibly."

I closed my eyes. "I don't have a week." I only had three days to go before Sandor's deadline.

"Sorry. There's nothing I can do," Lucas said.

I flopped down on my chair after hanging up. I had a decision to make. Option A: I could wait the week for the mask to arrive. But then it would be too late. I'd lose the job. All my work, all the risk, for nothing. Option B: do the job anyway.

I compressed my jaw. "Well," I said quietly to myself, "I'll just have to be perfect, and not trigger the alarm."

When I exited my secret room into my closet, I immediately stopped. All the hairs on my arms stood up. There was someone in my apartment. It was a sixth sense, I was sure—it was something about the sound, the feel in the air. Either way, there was someone there, and I didn't know who.

I stayed motionless, allowing my eyes to adjust to the darkness of the closet, considering my options. I then peered through a crack in the doorframe.

Sitting on the end of my bed, facing the closet expectantly, was Brooke.

I stepped out angrily. "Brooke, what the hell?"

"Ah, there you are," she said. Her tone suggested I was a few minutes late meeting her for coffee. "You know, I've been admiring this piece of equipment of yours." She picked up my fiber-optic bendy-wire from beside her on the bed. "I love this little thing— where did you get it? I really should get one myself. Although I must say, Cat, it's a little sloppy leaving it lying around."

My face burned with irritation. "Give me that," I said. "Seriously, Brooke, do you mind? Also—what do you think you're doing in here?"

Brooke shrugged and handed me the bendy-wire, ignoring my question. "So, Cat, what job are you prepping for, anyway? What are you cooking up?" She craned her neck to try to look past me, into my closet and the secret room behind. "I must say, it doesn't seem like an AB&T-sanctioned job. In fact, I'm not sure they've got you on assignment right now. So what are you up to?" She applied an expression of mock concern to her face. "Would they be happy to learn you're moonlighting?"

I panicked—was there any way she could have seen my special-order glove? No. Impossible. Still, this was a bad line of questioning. I could not have Brooke finding out about the Fabergé job.

But then something else occurred to me. I narrowed my eyes. "Brooke, how are you so in tune with what's going on at AB&T anyway? Are you sleeping with someone there, or something?" The look on her face told me that was exactly what was going on. "Oh, Christ, Brooke, you are. Do you have any principles at all?" She gazed at her fingernails with boredom.

It took me less than five minutes to eject her from my apartment. She grinned the whole way out, however. I suppose it was mission accomplished for her. She'd rattled me.

Locked inside my apartment again, I sent an urgent message to Templeton warning him that Brooke Sinclair was having inappropriate contact and communication with someone at AB&T. He needed to screen all his people carefully and give strict hush orders. I wished I could tell him more, but that was impossible. I could only hope Brooke would learn nothing else, until I'd finished the job.

One more day. Just one more day, and it would all be over.

The next morning I clipped along the sidewalk in the financial district of downtown Seattle in sensible pumps and a navy pencil skirt, my hair pulled back into a sleek ponytail. It was a bright Indian summer day with a warm wind and an apple-crisp sky. And I was trying hard to be positive about the task at hand. I was going to this interview solely for my dad, but I had to make a good show of it. Part of me said this was a completely ridiculous waste of time. But I was hoping that if I could just make this show of good faith for my father, it could be the first step to mending our relationship. I had to try. So I needed to get my head in the game. I needed to think: balance sheets, accounts receivable, taxes. . . .

Nice building, I thought, as my eyes were drawn up the sleek lines of a steel and glass tower that I was striding past. Reflexively, I started mapping out a way to scale it.

Stop, Cat. Focus. I clenched my teeth.

A massive helmet of single-process blond sat atop the head of the receptionist at the accounting firm's suite. She smiled pleasantly as the telephone bleeped insistently on her desk; several lines were flashing on hold as I introduced myself.

I sat on a fabric-covered chair in the waiting room that smelled of carpet cleaner and thumbed through an old copy of *Reader's Digest*. I was eventually shown into another room, to stand in front of a panel of two men and a woman. They were all dressed in virtually identical gray flannel suits. After the initial polite introductions and firm handshakes, they offered me a seat.

"So, Catherine. We must tell you: before he retired, your father was one of the best. And now he tells us you're interested in the accounting world."

"Oh yes," I said. "Very interested. I like money, anyway!" My attempt at levity fell flat. All I received were expressionless gazes peering over reading glasses.

Memo to self: Tax accountants and jokes are not a natural fit.

"Listen, we want you to know that this is a very dynamic place to work," said the older gentleman. His jowls jiggled slightly as he spoke. "We pride ourselves on being a fun workplace. This isn't your regular nine-to-fiver!" he indicated vaguely, sweeping around the office with a gesture.

"Mmm. Yes, I can see that," I said, unable to resist shifting my eyes right and left, to see if I could make out what he was referring to. I had no idea.

No matter. All I had to do was get through the interview so they could provide a good report to my dad.

They began asking me questions about myself. Standard interview stuff about my strengths, my weaknesses, what I typically ate for breakfast, that sort of thing. And I must say, things were going very well. I caught an exchanged glance between the two men that consisted of pleasantly surprised smiles and a briefly raised eyebrow. I made no further joke attempts, and answered their questions pleasantly.

And then the woman on the panel asked me, "So, Catherine, tell us *why* you want this job. What is it that fascinates you about being an accountant, exactly?"

All three were smiling at me, expectantly. I got the feeling the job was mine if I wanted it. Silence was stretching out. The woman's smile twitched ever so slightly. And I was staring at a stapler that sat atop the desk before me. It was a perfectly ordinary stapler.

Heavy black metal, chrome trim, *Standard* engraved in script along the side. And that stapler, well, it belonged there. It made sense. It was fulfilling its destiny there. Doing exactly what it was best at doing; doing exactly what it was put on this earth to do.

At that moment, the reality of the situation hit me, square between the eyes like one of those toy arrows with suction cups on the end. This—me sitting here, wearing Clarks and panty hose and feigning interest in the responsible world of grown-up work—was all wrong.

"You know," I said, looking at all three panel members, "I have to go, actually."

More silence followed. All I could hear was the buzz of the fluorescent lights overhead and the faint rhythmic chugging of a photocopier in the next office.

The woman tilted her head like a bird, observing me quizzically. "Um, I beg your pardon—"

"Yes. Ah, I'm terribly sorry," I mumbled. I grabbed my purse and briefcase and umbrella and hurried out of the room. As I closed the door behind me I caught a few confused murmurs following me out.

I burst from that office feeling like I could breathe again, like everything had bloomed into color, like I could fly into the sky if I wanted to.

And then a pinprick deflated it all. I had no idea how I was going to explain this to my father. I forcefully pushed the thought away. I couldn't worry about that right now. Because I had something more pressing on my schedule at the moment. I had a casino to bust into.

Chapter 26

Jack and Wesley strolled into the Starlight Casino. The warehouse-sized space was a writhing mass of flashing neon, bleating machines, and continuously chinking coins. Jack allowed a small smile and breathed deeply. The Fabergé was here somewhere.

But this was no leisurely treasure hunt. If those monks knew the location of the Egg, Jack was certain the Caliga did, too. And if they hadn't already, they would soon be hiring a thief to carry out the job. Jack knew that the Caliga had lost the old art of thievery a long time ago.

He glanced around the casino floor—at the rows of permed hair at slot machines, the students gathered around the roulette wheel. Was the Caliga's thief here somewhere? Staking things out, just as they were? He shuddered slightly. He hoped the contracted thief was valuable to the Caliga—otherwise he'd be dead the moment he turned the Fabergé over to them.

"So? What do you think?" Wesley asked.

Jack scanned the room. They needed somewhere to sit and discreetly watch. "I think we need to get a drink."

The two men ordered whiskey at the bar.

"Okay, so where do we start?" Wesley said.

"Security center, control room, I'd say." Jack sipped his drink and gazed out over the casino floor. "We're going to need to know everything about their systems. That'll be the quickest way."

"How are we going to get in?"

"Good question."

"Well, you're not an FBI agent for nothing," Wesley said, shrugging. "You don't have that badge *for decoration,* do you?"

Jack turned to Wesley's smiling face. He closed his eyes. "No. No way."

"Come on, Jack, we need that info. It's the best way. We can go in for some official reason or other, poke around, scope out the system, ask a few questions. . . ."

Shit. Jack could envision a million ways this plan would end badly.

"You know what I'd like to know?" Jack said irritably. "I'd like to know how I ended up in this spot, exactly. Who was the genius, all those goddamn generations ago, who chose this nice little quest to pass on to his unsuspecting descendants?" He looked away, toward the endless rows of slot machines. A middle-aged couple in jeans and sweatshirts sat in front of "Pot of Gold" machines sipping draft beer from plastic cups. "But I guess nobody will ever know, will they?" He took a slug of his whiskey.

He felt Wesley's eyes on him. He turned to see the man staring at him with surprise. "You don't know? Your father didn't explain this to you?"

"Explain what?"

"Jack, the lost Gifts of the Magi is the legacy of thieves. And we know exactly how it happened."

"What are you talking about?"

Wesley put his drink on the bar. He lowered his voice. "The Bible doesn't say what happened to the gold, frankincense, and myrrh that the Magi brought. But there's a strong folk legend that it was stolen by two thieves. You've heard that there were two thieves crucified beside Jesus himself?"

Jack struggled to remember his Sunday-school days. "Yes, okay, that sounds familiar."

"So after the thieves stole the Gifts, they argued and fought, because one thief began to regret what they'd done. He also didn't believe what the other thief believed: that the Magi were Zoroastrian priests and astrologers, and they had charged their Gifts with great magical power."

"Power?" Jack said, not bothering to hide the disdain in his voice.

Of course he'd heard the idea that the Gifts had mystical power. It was something the Caliga believed. Jack hadn't believed it the first time he'd heard it; he wasn't about to be converted now.

Wesley shrugged. "Yeah, I know, cheesy right? Well, the unremorseful thief believed it—and it was one of those take over the world, total domination type scenarios. Anyway, the thieves betrayed each other. They tried to swindle each other and smuggle the Gifts away. They roped some of their shady colleagues into things—everyone's lying to everyone else. But before you know it, people lose track of the Gifts in all that shuffle. Nobody knows who's got them."

Jack narrowed his eyes. "So you're saying—that's how they became lost?" He shifted on his bar stool and leaned forward slightly.

Wesley nodded. "In trying to screw the other guy, both thieves ended up screwed. And then, *ba-da-boom,* they're both up for execution. Before his crucifixion, the remorseful thief made his family promise that they would retrieve the Gifts, and return them to the church. That group flourished. Honed the skills of thievery, ready for the opportunity to take the Gifts back."

Jack was fascinated now. His whiskey sat forgotten on the bar. "And the bad guy?"

"Yeah, well, he gave his sons a mission also."

Jack nodded. "To retrieve the Gifts."

"You got it. And, by doing that, he gave rise to some real nasty pieces of work."

"Ah. Caliga Rapio." So that's where they came from. It explained the Caliga's crazed obsession with unlocking the Gifts' power. Jack shuddered. He knew the Caliga's plans to complete this task involved a ritual human sacrifice. His father had told him that much. That had been one reason to find the Gifts before the Caliga did.

"So how did they end up concealed in a Fabergé Egg, exactly?"

"It was your father's generation that pieced this together, I believe," Wesley said. "They'd managed to uncover the true path of the Gifts. They'd been smuggled, stolen, and traded on the black market, and finally made their way to imperial Russia. There, Fabergé himself transformed them into the Aurora Egg. After the Russian Revolution, of course, the Gifts were once again lost, underground, to resurface here."

Jack was motionless, now, staring down at the rings of condensation on the bar's surface. At once he felt aware of his own insignificance in the face of such a monumental concern. The gears of his mind began to turn. And he came up with an idea to get them into the casino security room. Nicole had been doing an investigation involving several casinos about a month ago. The Starlight was one of them, if memory served. He could use that information as a pretext. And use his badge. Would he get away with it, though? But what other choice did they have? He rubbed his face. "All right," Jack said with resignation. "Let's do it."

The moment I entered the casino I was thrown into a carnival of blinking lights and glittering colors, electronic bleeping, and choking clouds of cigarette smoke. A spontaneous burst of cheering erupted from a far corner. Three men in Armani and a woman in a Vivienne Westwood cocktail dress and diamonds strolled across the floor toward the high-stakes room, martinis in hand.

And me? I walked in wearing mom jeans. You know—the high-waisted, pleated kind that make your butt look enormous and your legs like stumps? My white aerobics shoes squeaked on the marble floor of the lobby. My hair was buried beneath a mousy brown wig and my face was concealed behind oversize glasses circa 1983.

My first choice of disguise for tonight had been a hot, sequined minidress and glossy black china-doll wig: high-roller style. Or— better still—the arm candy of a high roller. On further reflection I had decided that such an appearance would be too conspicuous. Extra attention was not what I wanted tonight.

Which is why I was walking into the casino wearing a shapeless, silk-screened sweatshirt that read *Life is a beach in St. Petersburg, Florida!* Tonight I was the housewife escapee. A night out playing the slots. I must say, my strategy appeared to be working perfectly. Nobody spared me a second glance.

My heart pumped with excitement. This was the moment I'd been waiting for—the culmination of all my preparation and planning. Of course I'd have felt a little better if I had that damn gas mask, but I did not want to get into that again. For that, and many reasons, failure was not an option tonight. I would leave the casino tonight with the Fabergé or die trying.

I wound my way through the bonging, blinking slot machines, heading to the far end of the casino.

Then, turning a corner, I spotted someone who did not belong. Seated at a twenty-five-cent slot machine—Action Stacked Diamonds, to be exact—was Brooke.

I slipped back behind the row of machines. My mind raced: had she seen me just then? Then my shoulders dropped. Did it matter? Clearly, she was here because she knew I was here. Whether she'd seen me just now, or five minutes ago, made no difference.

My only hope—that she didn't know exactly what job I was doing here. If she knew I was headed to the basement vault, wouldn't she already be there, to catch me in the act?

If I was still going to do this job, I had to ditch her somehow. I immediately thought of the woman in the Vivienne Westwood and the men in Armani—who were, let's face it, examples of much more logical targets for me.

A plan formulated in my brain.

I circuited back and strolled near where Brooke had been. I stayed visible, allowing her to see me, but not being too obvious about it.

Then I made my way to the high-stakes poker room, knowing that Brooke would follow and watch my every move.

I just needed one chance. I observed the sparkly people strolling in and out of the room, gauging who was likely to be a guest of the hotel, who'd had a few too many martinis. . . .

And then I found a perfect mark. A woman, blowsy and rich, lots of hairspray, fumbling with her purse as she teetered toward the restroom. I made my move and bumped into her on a cross-path.

"Oh, pardon me!" I said, bending to help her pick up the sprawled contents of her purse.

She took in my outfit and glared at me with a pickled glower of contempt. I smiled into her heavily mascara-smudged eyes and pocketed the key card for her hotel suite.

I melted away into the depths of the slot machines and headed in the general direction of the elevators that went up to the hotel. That should do it. Brooke would think I was going to hit the woman's suite. It would be a tidy little job, actually, the sort of thing I'd done a hundred times. I snaked my way through the casino, losing myself—and Brooke—through the labyrinth of slot machines. I doubled back, again, and returned just outside the elevator lobby. I peered around a slot machine. Yes, there was Brooke, waiting for an elevator going up. She'd taken the bait.

Smiling, I slipped away to the far end of the casino, to the infrequently used elevators. Including the one that went to the basement. By the time Brooke figured out I wasn't breaking into any of the suites upstairs, I'd be gone without a trace.

I pressed the call button. The elevator arrived. The instant before walking inside, I flicked a switch in my pocket, which activated my anti-CCTV sensor. A variant on my usual gadget, this one blocked the feed of cameras within range. Too many cameras in the casino—I couldn't possibly deactivate them all manually. Would be too obvious, anyway.

I knew there was a camera inside the elevator car. It would now show a picture of an empty elevator. I casually strolled inside. These elevators weren't used often, so I was alone.

Of course if anyone had really been paying attention in the control room and bothered to match up the two feeds of the elevator lobby and the interior of this elevator, they would have seen a housewife disappear into an elevator. But I was counting on my utterly dishwater appearance to cause the security staff to ignore me on the video feeds.

I attached my earpiece and clicked it on.

"Okay, ready to go, Gladys?" I said in a low voice.

"Ready, dear." At that point, Gladys took over control of the elevator. She'd hacked in from her bungalow. I knew she'd disabled the car when it stopped, hovering in midair.

Which was my cue to move. I only had a few minutes before somebody made the call to the elevator company to fix the broken lift and I had things to do before then. I unpacked the climbing gear that had been concealed beneath my shapeless sweatshirt, wrapped around my body.

I used the railing of the elevator to hoist myself up toward the ceiling of the car; I stretched upward and clung on to the tiles, pushed the escape hatch up and away, then pulled myself up with all my strength, triceps and shoulders burning. I levered out and twisted, to sit on the roof of the elevator car.

My eyes adjusted to the darkness and I sat, surrounded by cables and the smell of pulley grease and brake smoke. I paused a moment, slowing my breath.

Jack folded his arms and squinted at the camera feed in the control room, but the screens were too far away—the staff in there wouldn't let him anywhere near them. He probably could have pushed it, made a big issue out of it, but he didn't want to draw attention to himself.

After a few minutes in this room Jack felt hollow with discouragement. There was nothing that was going to be easy about this job. How the hell were they going to get into the vault? This casino had rock-solid, tight security. And nasty aspects, too. Not that he'd gleaned much detail so far, just a hint of biometrics and booby traps.

Wesley had remained well away from the control room, continuing to scout the situation on the floor. Jack wondered about Wesley's skill as a thief. Was he up to the job? His mind flashed to Cat. This would be the sort of challenge she would love. But there was no way he would ever call on her; no way he would want to get her wrapped up in this.

Jack strained again to see the CCTV screen. This was ridiculous. He wasn't getting anywhere this way. He was going to have to probe deeper, which meant he was going to have to carry his bluff a little further.

A bulky supervisor with doughnut powder on his upper lip strode past Jack to stand beside a young man in shirtsleeves at a small workstation. "Elevator nine is out," said the supervisor, snapping his fingers to get the man's attention. "Call the repair company."

* * *

I intercepted the call intended for the elevator company with my iPhone. This was a little coup that came courtesy of Gladys and her fabulous ability to tap into the telephone network and redirect certain calls. I answered the call. "HR Elevators. Twenty-four-hour service. How can I help you?" I used the automaton tone that answering services typically employ. I listened as the security guy at Starlight Casino reported the problem. I told him we'd have someone out there right away. I figured this bought me at least thirty minutes.

I crouched on top of the elevator and connected my rappelling harness, moving quickly but carefully. I silently descended the elevator shaft after squeezing past the car. It didn't take me long, largely because I knew there were no security cameras in the elevator shaft—one reason I'd selected this particular route. I was in full flow of the job. My breathing was fast and regular and my focus was supercharged.

When I reached the bottom of the shaft, I pulled out my perfect little folding titanium crowbar that would take care of my next task—levering open the doors. I checked to make sure my anti-CCTV sweeper was still functioning.

I slipped it into the joint and inched the doors open, bit by bit, feeling the strain in my shoulders and forearms. I licked my lip and tasted the sweat that was there, partly from labor, partly from nerves.

When I made a small crack, I pulled out my fiber-optic bendy wire to check the corridor outside. I flicked it on and . . .

Nothing. It wasn't working. What the hell? I'd just used it a couple of days ago and it had been fine then. Maybe the battery needed jiggling. I twisted open the compartment. Inside was a small, rolled-up piece of paper. No battery. I stared in bewilderment. Then, I pulled out the tiny paper roll, unfurled it, and read: *Needed a battery for my heated eyelash curler, so sorry! Love, Brooke.*

No. This was not happening.

I flashed back to Brooke, sitting on my bed, holding the fiber-optic wire. She must have done this then. How could I have been so stupid?

A terrifying thought then occurred to me. Panicking, I checked all my other pieces of equipment. . . .

No, they were all fine. But still—*my bendy wire.* I didn't have any spare batteries for it. How was I going to do the job now? I considered aborting. Instantly, all the reasons why I couldn't abort crammed into my head. Okay, I could do this. The wire was good, but not a crucial part of my kit, right?

Think, Cat. I needed to know that this hallway was clear—that was the main reason for the scope. So, I could go old school. That meant first, listening. Guards weren't usually as silent as thieves. They had no need to be. Even if a guard was standing still, he would eventually shift, or cough, or something. I stilled myself to utter silence and listened.

Nothing.

Next, I let my head peek through the very bottom of the gap, just enough for one eye to be exposed, doing a visual check of the corridor.

Clear.

Now I moved fast. I prized the doors open the rest of the way and crawled out of the shaft. A long, shiny hallway stretched in front of me, dimly lit. A series of plain steel doors punctuated the concrete walls. It didn't matter that they were unlabeled because I knew the exact one I was looking for. I'd memorized the blueprint.

I crept cautiously and quickly down the hallway until I reached the vault room door. Access to this room was controlled by a magnetic key card lock. I made swift work of this using a magnetic dummy card and just the right touch. The door's seal released with a hiss and slid open.

My heart did a triple beat of excitement: another step closer. Now that the door was open I saw a great web of laser beams. There are many ways of bypassing such a thing. Acrobatics come to mind. Target-shooting the emitting mechanism on the far wall is another option. Tonight, I was going to skip those theatrics in favor of simply punching in the disabling code, courtesy of the security file from York. Cheating? Maybe. But all's fair in love and war. And burglary.

I punched in the series of six numbers. I held my breath; the sweat on the back of my neck was cold. And then, the lasers flickered and turned off. I exhaled.

I needed to be swift. This was a risky stage—if people in the security room felt so inclined, they could pull up the current status of the vault on their computers. But I knew, from the security file, that rarely happened. I knew they were highly reliant on their automated systems. And this area was checked as part of a scheduled sweep of the system every twenty-seven minutes. I checked my watch. Twenty-three minutes away.

The room was dark with only a scattering of recessed lights shining down from the ceiling. The marble floor tiles made a black-and-white checkerboard. In the silence, my breathing roared in my ears. The walls were lined with rows of steel compartments—security boxes. Each box contained its own lock and electronic security system. In the schematics there'd been mention made of many artifacts and Romanov treasures contained within the vault room. These guys had really gone to town when they looted the Winter Palace.

But I didn't want any of that. I turned my attention to the huge round vault door on the far wall surrounded by a massive, riveted ring. It led into an inner chamber: the Bagreef Vault. The hairs on my arms rose up. I took a deep breath. *Here we go.*

I swapped my leather gloves for the pair from the lab. I put my hand on the biometric sensor pad that resided in the wall beside the vault door. Now, there are painless, noninvasive biometrics that measure things like fingerprints and iris scans. And then there's the kind of biometrics these guys employ.

With a snap, a needle popped up to pierce my finger and take a fresh blood sample. Instead of my skin, of course, the needle punctured the small pocket that was built into the glove. In this pocket was a reservoir of artificial blood—blood whose DNA perfectly matched Gorlovich's.

I held my breath as the computer analyzed the blood sample and my brain crowded with doubt about whether this would work. My heart was racing and my muscles were taut, ready to enact a very quick escape if this failed.

* * *

Jack watched the man stroll across the blue-carpeted control room directly toward him. He steeled himself for the torrent of lies that would soon be exiting his own mouth.

"You are Jack Barlow?" said the craggy-faced head of security. He wore a tie and shirtsleeves.

"Yes." Jack pulled out his badge again, inwardly cringing. He hoped the man had a poor memory for names; he did not want to be memorable here.

"My staff tells me you have questions."

Jack nodded. "I'm involved in the investigation about the recent attempted theft."

There was a pause, during which Jack sweated it out. He was completely bullshitting on this. He had no definite knowledge about an attempted theft, had no idea if that's what Nicole had actually been investigating, but he was banking on the fact that people were always trying to break into casinos.

"Recent?" the supervisor bristled. "That investigation was months ago, and your people were already through here poking about. Why are you here asking questions about that now?"

Damn, thought Jack. This guy was not going to make this easy. Which, Jack supposed, was probably what made him good at his job, and head of security. "Yes, well," Jack said, "we've reopened that case in connection with some others."

The man's eyes tightened as he scrutinized Jack. After several seconds of this Jack was on the verge of pulling out.

"All right, fine," the man said slowly. "The attempted theft was in our inner layer of vaults. Come with me, I'll pull up the data. We can see what's going on in there right now."

Jack followed as the head of security strode through to another, smaller room, filled with computers and CCTV screens. Jack felt a lightening in the tension centered at the base of his skull. This was good. He could get the information, and then get out of there.

When they entered the room Jack knew that his relief had been premature. Sitting in front of one of the computer screens was Nicole.

"Jack? What are you doing here?"

"Nicole. I——" *Shit.* Now he was going to have to come up with an explanation, and one that wouldn't contradict what he just told Mr. Friendly here. "—was just investigating a case."

"Oh?" Her brows knitted together in confusion. "I didn't know your department was involved." She shrugged and turned back to the computer screen. "Fine. I was just about to take a look at the inner vault. We can do that together, and you can catch me up to speed on what you know."

"Great," he said faintly. This was flatly not going to work. She would be asking questions that required detailed knowledge of the case, so it wouldn't take long before it was obvious that Jack was bluffing. It was time to abort this. But he couldn't leave Nicole in there with the head of security. If they talked or compared notes in any way it could become just as obvious that Jack had been full of shit.

"Nicole, actually, since you're here, there's something I need to brief you on. An unrelated case that my department wants to consult yours on."

"Oh? Okay, then."

Jack glanced at the head of security apologetically. "Sorry, it needs to be confidential." He looked at Nicole. "Would you come with me a moment?"

Her face clouded with puzzlement but she obliged and allowed Jack to lead her out. Just what, exactly, Jack was going to tell her once they were out of the control room he had no clue. But it would have to be something to get her right out of the casino with him. He'd have to bring her in on another case, tell her he needed her expertise, something like that.

"I hope this is important, Jack, I have a lot of work to do," Nicole said, irritation in her voice.

"It is, Nicole. Very important."

The biometric sensor, containing my sample of fake blood, suddenly flashed green. The vault door unlocked with a loud *chunk* and began to open. *Ah, beloved tech lab, how could I have doubted you?*

I shivered with delight as the heavy steel door swung smoothly open on an automatic hinge. Dead center of the vault, on display in a clear glass case, was the Fabergé Egg. The Aurora. The only lighting in there was from the pinprick halogen lights within the display case; they set the jeweled Egg sparkling.

"Okay, Gladys," I said quietly, "I'm going in." There would be no signal within the vault itself. I'd be on my own.

"Good luck, dear," came the warm, crinkly voice.

I stepped through into the vault. The air in there was stale and silent, like a tomb.

The final obstacle was a touch pad for entering an intricate series of codes embedded in the base. Once again, I pulled up the codes from York Security on my iPhone and meticulously entered them. The case glided open like an unfolding piece of glass origami.

I reached out and picked up the heavy, bejeweled Egg. At last, I was holding the Fabergé in my hands. I was dazzled by its beauty. The metalwork was so intricate and the jewels and pearls were flawless. It was obviously the pinnacle of the jeweler's art. It was as heavy as a melon, and the sharp scrolls of metalwork pressed through my gloves into my fingertips.

As I turned the Egg in my hands I found myself suffused with a feeling of well-being. It was like the feeling that comes sometimes upon awakening, when you know that something good happened yesterday but you're not quite awake enough to remember. I shook my head slightly. I must have been imagining things. Perhaps the low level of oxygen in the vault was getting to me; I was surprised the effect the piece was having. I'd held plenty of beautiful jewels in my day, but this seemed different. Could this be what I'd been waiting for all this time? An image of Penny glimmered in my mind.

I suppose it was that slight distraction—that infinitesimal loss of focus—that caused me to make my error.

I tucked the Fabergé into my black nylon bag and reached forward to gently close the glass case. But I did it without recalibrating the alarm.

Sirens screamed. The vault went into immediate lockdown. Lights on every wall flared and the enormous round door flung shut with a deafening thud; my ears throbbed with the pressure of being sealed inside.

Oh God. What had I done? The next thing I saw was gas spilling out, smokelike, from a vent near the floor. *Kolokol-1.* My mouth went bone dry. My instinct was to flee from the gas but I had nowhere to go. My eyes swung wildly to the only exit: the enormous vault door, locked tight. Surely guards were descending right then into the vault room outside. They'd simply wait until enough time had elapsed to have rendered me unconscious—*or worse*—and then they'd come in.

Panic surged through my bones. I had to get out. I experienced an irrational hope that time might rewind, that I could go back and do that moment over again and do it differently. I struggled to keep from flying apart. Why did I take this job? A mistake. My gut twisted. I was going to live to regret it . . . if I lived, that was.

I had to get out. But it was impossible. Worse, there was nowhere to hide. The room was a sealed steel cylinder. And in a matter of seconds the whole place would be filled with gas.

Wait—the gas. Where was the gas coming from; was there a vent? A vent would be the only seam in the otherwise seamless wall. And a seam might offer somewhere to hide. I clung to that gossamer thread of hope with fierce desperation. With stinging eyes I moved toward the cloud of gas. The only mercy here was that it wasn't a terribly quick-acting gas, so I had a few seconds. I hoped.

I crouched down, squinting at the vent. Was it big enough for me to crawl inside and hide? A very tight fit, but it was my only chance. I ripped off the vent door and hurled the bag containing the Fabergé inside. I'd have to back in, so I could close the vent behind me. I hooked my feet onto the edge and wriggled back in. My heart was squeezing tight: *please let this work.* A panicky thought occurred. Being so close to the source of the gas—might this cause an overdose?

Things were beginning to get fuzzy, blurry. I needed to stay awake long enough to get inside, just long enough to close the vent door after myself. I wriggled, gripping the cold metal door. At last

I was in. With arms outstretched, I pulled the grate home. It clunked into place. The next moment I heard a loud thud from outside the vent, in the vault itself. There was shouting, and loud footsteps. The guards had arrived.

The world went black.

Chapter 27

"Okay, Jack, what is it?" Nicole said, arms crossed, as they stood in the hallway just outside the security control room. "What did you drag me out here for?"

Jack was just at the point of having to make something up—dammit, he was not good at this—when the alarm sounded.

Sirens wailed from within the security offices. Jack and Nicole heard it, muffled, through the doors. They looked at each other, stunned a moment, then bolted back into the control room.

Commotion and turmoil greeted them. People were shouting at each other, frantically pulling up every possible CCTV feed onto the bank of screens. A team of security personnel rushed past them, out the door.

Jack and Nicole located the head of security. "What happened?" Jack demanded.

The head man was barking orders at everyone, but spared them a glance. "Vault breach," he snarled.

"Which one?" Jack asked. But he already knew. He heard the word Bagreef mentioned. His stomach promptly curdled.

Jack and Nicole turned to join the security team going down to the vault. The head of security stepped in their path, stopping them. "Hold up. Where do you think you're going?"

"To the vault. Like you."

"No. You have no jurisdiction here. This is private property. If we want your involvement we'll let you know."

"There's an obvious crime in progress here." Jack swept an arm to indicate the pandemonium. "And that *makes* it our jurisdiction." The head of security's jaw clamped shut. Jack could see he knew this was true.

When Jack and Nicole arrived outside the vault with the casino security team, they were forced to wait with everyone else while the gas cleared.

He turned to Nicole and hissed, "What did you see, back in the control room? You were pulling up the feeds in those inner vaults—did you notice anything?"

Nicole shook her head. "I didn't have a chance to look before you dragged me away. I didn't see a thing."

The vault door swung open then, and the team poured in. Jack saw what everyone else did: an empty glass case. And no sign of a thief anywhere.

As the team quickly dispatched to search the casino and surrounding area, Jack stood rooted to the spot in front of the case. The truth hit him like a punch in the solar plexus. He was, at least in part, responsible for the Fabergé disappearing into thin air again. He'd pulled Nicole away from the screens because of his own paranoia. Nobody else had been monitoring that feed because the FBI had commandeered that work station.

If it wasn't for him, would the thief have been caught in the act?

I became aware of my arms stretched out above my head, saw my hands in front of me if I turned my neck, which sent shards of pain down my spine. I was lying on my stomach. My face felt numb where it had been squashed against a cold metal floor.

In front of my hands I could see thin strips of light marking out a small square. And then the memory came flooding back. The vent door! A warm rush of relief poured through me. It actually worked. I was still in the ventilation shaft. And I was still alive. I could breathe. And the air smelled sweet and normal. No more burning.

I strained to hear outside. There was absolute silence.

The gears of my mind accelerated as I processed the clues. The guards must have come in—I remembered that happening—and found an empty vault. They would have had gas masks on, I was sure of that. They would have seen the Fabergé missing, so they wouldn't have thought it was a false alarm. They might have decided that the intruder escaped before the vault door closed, in which case they would have cleared the air and vacated. I shifted my feet slightly and felt something heavy bounce against them. The Fabergé.

I had no idea how much time had elapsed. Minutes? Hours? I waited a little longer for consciousness to fully return. And then began my escape. Again.

I crawled out, gingerly. Moving quickly was not an option just yet, given the blinding headache I was dealing with. And the massive cramp in my left thigh. But I pushed through all that.

I shoved the vent out and it landed with a clang. I pushed myself forward with my toes, then hooked my fingers around the sharp metal edge and heaved with all my strength. Bit by bit I wriggled free of the shaft and found myself standing, once again, in the empty vault. I reached back in and retrieved the bag that contained the Fabergé. I quickly checked the time. Five a.m. I'd been in the vent for about six hours.

The vault looked the same—apart from a blatantly empty case where the Fabergé once resided. I imagined the cascade of reactions to *that*. I wondered who would be given the task of advising Gorlovich himself. I shuddered, and felt a fierce urge to get far, far away from there, posthaste.

I took care to not repeat my previous mistake. I recalibrated the vault with the security codes and strapped on my gear, ready to leave. I double-checked my anti-CCTV gadget. Functioning. But wait. What if there were guards posted outside the vault? No, that wasn't likely. What would be the purpose in hanging around the site where the thief—not to mention the booty—so clearly were not?

But how could I be sure? The answer was, I couldn't. I couldn't stay in here any longer. I didn't possess the ability to see through metal. I was just going to have to take the chance, and ready myself for conflict. My heart was pounding out of my rib cage as I opened the vault door.

But nobody was there.

The rest of my escape through the vault room and the corridors was uneventful.

As I made my way to the elevator a thought occurred to me, accompanied by a sinking feeling. How was I going to climb back up the elevator shaft? Surely they'd have repaired the elevator by then.

I thought for a moment, then flicked on my earpiece and pressed redial on my phone.

I held my breath and closed my eyes. If I could just get Gladys, I could sit tight until she locked the elevator—just long enough to climb out again.

There was a lengthy pause.

And then there was a click on the line. "*Cat?* Is that you, dear?" I pressed my fingertips to my closed eyelids and breathed again. Everything was going to be okay.

"Yes, Gladys, it's me."

"Oh heavens," she said, "I thought you'd died."

"To be honest, Gladys, it feels like I did."

A few hours later, after a purposefully long and snaking route, I returned to my apartment.

First things first. I poured myself a generous drink and took a large gulp, sending two extra-strength aspirin down my throat. I then tucked myself safely in my secret room, and sent a text message to Sandor: **The birthday gift is in pocket.**

This was the code he insisted on. I assured him that the communication channels I used were entirely encrypted and secure, but he was resolute.

He swiftly texted me back, and we arranged a meeting time and place: nine p.m. tonight, Seattle pier. I wondered why he wanted to wait until nighttime. But it was fine. It gave me some time alone with the Aurora Egg. I removed it from my black nylon bag and placed it carefully on my desk.

Behind the desk, pinned up on a bulletin board, was an old photograph of me and my sister. The grainy image glowed with sunshine; we were caught, suspended in the air on playground swings, limbs summer-brown.

I was so near to completing the assignment, to closing the circle. Soon the Fabergé would be back to its rightful owners. I wondered: would I be able to look at that photograph without the familiar empty ache, then?

I picked up the Fabergé and held it in my hands, turning it this way and that. *Now. What are your secrets?* I whispered to the object in my palms. I found myself asking: what was to stop me from opening it and looking at what was inside? The answer I came up with: nothing.

I toyed with the gold clasp between my thumb and forefinger and then I recalled the conversation I'd overheard between Sandor and the monks. *Do not open it,* they'd said. *There will be great danger.* What did they mean by *danger?* Was I going to unleash some kind of curse? I smirked at this idea, but even so, I found myself hesitating. Briefly.

The tiny, intricate gold latch yielded with no trouble. I peered inside eagerly as the hinge opened. The entire interior surface was lined with gold, and a tiny gold statue of a pelican rested within. Two small glass vials with ornate gold stoppers were embedded in the statue. They each held pieces of waxy, rocklike stuff; one was yellowish and the other was red-brown.

I stared. The significance of what I was looking at remained completely obscure.

But I had an idea. I opened the stopper of the milky yellow stuff. I took a sniff. Warm, sweet, resinous fragrance curled up my nose. Pleasant, but not familiar. Using a pocket knife I shaved a miniscule sample and placed it gingerly in a Ziploc bag. The second vial contained the dark reddish brown chunks. It smelled sharper, slightly bitter, but still quite agreeable.

I tucked my samples inside a padded envelope and addressed it to Lucas at my trusty lab for analysis. I'd drop it off at the courier today, on my way.

As I extinguished the lights to my secret room and rekeyed the security pad, I couldn't help a slight twinge of disappointment. I guess I'd hoped the "surprise" inside the Egg would be something a little more interesting.

* * *

Jack entered the barbershop with a feeling of dread.

Mr. Cole was seated in a burgundy leather and chrome barber's chair. A bald man in a crisp white barber's jacket stood behind him, pinning a black vinyl cape around his throat. A bowl of steaming water and a tall cylinder of blue Barbicide rested on the counter. The astringent smell of aftershave filled the air.

Wesley perched on a stool beside Mr. Cole. Jack leaned and sat down on the ledge of the front window.

"So?" Jack asked. When Cole had called him for this meeting, he had not sounded happy. Jack knew exactly why.

"Wesley tells me the Aurora Egg was stolen last night."

Jack nodded, face dour. The barber began combing through Oliver Cole's thick hair.

"Do you have any leads on who did it?" Jack asked. "Because the casino has nothing. And the FBI are coming up empty, too."

"Well, there's one obvious possibility."

Jack tightened his jaw. "Caliga."

Wesley nodded. "But we don't believe the Caliga could have pulled this off themselves—everyone knows they've lost the art of thievery. They must have hired someone else for the job."

Lost, again. What had felt so close was now floating away, dissolving within Jack's grasp. Was there any chance of finding it before the Caliga took it underground? Worse, was the thought of what they would do with it now.

Snip. Snip. Hair fell to the shiny, lacquered floor in a fuzzy snowfall. "We need to find the thief they hired," Mr. Cole said. "We need to talk to that person."

"*If* the thief is even still alive," added Wesley.

Jack nodded grimly. Whoever the thief was, that person was in big trouble. The Caliga were ruthless and would certainly eliminate any loose threads. "How are you going to find him?" Jack asked.

"We have a short list of possibilities. One of the names that kept coming up was Cat Montgomery." Mr. Cole turned his eyes toward Jack as the barber worked away on his sideburns. "What do you think?"

"No," Jack said firmly. "Impossible. She'd never work for the Caliga."

"Wesley advised me she was at the masquerade ball."

"So?"

"It's suggestive."

Jack shook his head. He didn't have a good explanation for her presence at the ball, but he was certain she wasn't involved. He frowned. Mostly certain.

"Wesley tells me you have a blind spot when it comes to her."

Jack glared at Wesley. The other man shrugged.

Mr. Cole continued. "Anyway, we need to question the thief, and learn the Caliga's plans."

A seed of doubt had now been placed in Jack's brain. And he didn't like it. "What makes you think the thief will tell you anything?" he asked.

Mr. Cole's eyes hardened into flinty shards. "We have techniques."

Jack rubbed his face and stared at the man. He had no illusions about Oliver Cole. He knew the man was accustomed to getting what he wanted and would use whatever means were available. Torture if necessary. Jack's tongue felt dry. In spite of their common goal, in spite of working together with these people, he knew they were different types.

When Jack left the barbershop he pulled his coat collar up. The late afternoon sun burned bright, but cold. It matched the chill in his chest. Jack was further than ever from completing his quest. The Fabergé was, essentially, lost again. But more than that, he now had to worry about Cat—and whether she was in a snake pit of danger.

The phone in his pocket bleeped. He glanced at the reminder. Dinner with Nicole tonight—new restaurant opening.

Damn. Not what he wanted to do right now. He climbed in his car.

On the other hand, dinner with Nicole would allow him to assess how much the FBI knew about the stolen Fabergé. That would be useful. He turned the engine and pulled his car smoothly away from the curb.

Still, the timing was bad. All he wanted to do right now was find Cat and make sure she was safe.

As Jack drove, he thought about what they'd discussed in the barbershop, just now. His grip tightened around the steering wheel. He hated that feeling of being one step behind the Caliga. Although, just before Jack left, Cole had provided one extremely useful piece of information. After working all this time to unearth the identity of the Caliga leader, Cole's people had finally come up with it.

The Caliga leader was a man by the name of Sandor.

Chapter 28

I walked to the pier in darkness, crisscrossing the deserted streets of Central Waterfront. The darkness tonight was a witchy variety, the sort that contained oddly shaped shadows. A brisk wind stirred dry leaves and litter, and this was throwing off my peripheral sense that detected movement. It made me feel strangely jumpy. Ribbons of hair flapped across my face. The nippy wind blew through me.

I wondered why Sandor wanted to meet at the pier. All part of his cloak-and-dagger routine? Well, it didn't matter. I was quite used to meeting in shadowy public places. This was how Templeton and I typically operated. With that thought I felt a wave of relief; soon I wouldn't have to lie to Templeton anymore.

I reached the pier and saw Sandor standing by the railing, waiting, just outside the dim circle of a lone lamplight's glow. Pier 46 was used as a container shipping port and was deserted by nightfall.

I exhaled. Good, I was almost done with this.

Sandor turned as I approached. We were hidden from street view by the darkness of the isolated pier. The career criminal in me liked that. The female in me gave a small shiver of discomfort.

"You have it?" he asked eagerly.

"Do you have the payment?"

He nodded toward a briefcase at his feet.

"Cash?" I said in surprise. "That's a bit old school, isn't it?"

He shrugged. He handed me the briefcase and I opened it with a *click*. I levered the lid open just a crack and peered inside at the bundles of crisp bills, neat in their rows. I slipped one thin bundle out and tucked it into my pocket. I closed the briefcase.

Wordlessly, I handed Sandor the Egg from my canvas backpack, wrapped in several layers of plain tissue. He unwrapped the layers, exposing a small glimmer of the Egg. Sandor's eyes glittered. "At long last," he said quietly. He traced a fingertip over a line of gold on the Egg's surface. The tissue paper rustled as he swaddled it again. "Miss Montgomery, our family has waited a very, very long time for this."

I smiled and exhaled. It was done. The circle was complete. This was my thing, truly the thing I did best.

And then, I found myself holding my breath. Waiting for . . . what? Some kind of feeling of completeness or wholeness, I suppose. I stood on the pier and twisted the ring on my finger. *Is it enough, Penny?* Had I done enough to make up for everything that had happened? I bit my lip. But just like the yacht job, I didn't feel any different.

I frowned. Why *not?* I'd been sure this would be the job to bring me closure. What was I doing wrong? I tightened my hand around the smooth leather of the briefcase handle. At least I could get the damn IRS off my back now. The rest I'd have to figure out later.

I looked at Sandor. "Well, I suppose that's it. It was good working with you." I glanced over my shoulder at my exit route.

Sandor turned to face me. His hand was in his right jacket pocket. There must have been something funny about the shadow cast by the dim lamplight, because the expression on his face was not one I'd seen on Sandor before.

All my spider-senses suddenly started firing. Something was not right here. A powerful urge to get away took hold.

At that moment, a group of drunk college kids stumbled onto the pier, loudly. There was a smash of glass as one broke a bottle on the concrete pier. An outburst of pickled laughter followed. They were mostly young men—large, football types—and there were at least a dozen of them.

Sandor's head snapped toward the newcomers, then his eyes swung back to mine. He melted wordlessly into the shadows. I disappeared in the opposite direction, sliding past the oblivious group of college kids, exhaling with relief.

As I lost myself in the populated part of the pier complex, I felt cold inside thinking about Sandor. What had happened back there? I strode out to the street, wondering if I'd just been imagining things. On my way I passed a homeless woman slumped against a building. I reached into my coat pocket, where I'd slipped one small bundle of bills. I pressed the money into her filthy hand and quickly disappeared around the corner. I scanned the street for the beacon light of a taxi. Abruptly, a car parked directly across the road pulled out and drove away. I caught a glimpse of the driver. I saw long, glossy, raven-colored hair.

I stiffened. No. It couldn't have been. Just my imagination. Or was it? Was that Brooke? And if it was—how much had she seen?

Argentinian music with a cool, strong beat surrounded us as we entered the restaurant. I was there with Mel and Sophie, and we were celebrating the completion of my job.

Besides, opening night at a new restaurant is always fun. The ultrachic space was all chocolate brown walls and glossy white leather booths, with halogen light reflecting off black lacquered tables. The hostess led us to a table near the open-concept kitchen, which smelled of charred ahi tuna and garlic and olive oil. I heard searing on the grill and the chink of plates. We slid into our seats and Mel looked around keenly, assessing the talent. Then her face plummeted.

"Oh. My. God," she said.

I turned abruptly, following her gaze. Seated at a table on the other side of the restaurant were Jack and Nicole.

My chest constricted. It was the first time I'd seen them together since my humiliating performance at the golf tournament. I know I shouldn't have cared. Besides, I'd been with Ethan since then.

"Okay, Cat, it's cool," said Mel. "Who cares? Nothing you can't handle."

Sophie looked at me uncertainly. "Do you want to leave?"

I considered this a moment. I hazarded a second glance at their table. Admittedly, neither Jack nor Nicole looked terribly happy, but that didn't mean anything. They were probably hungry and waiting for their food, or something. "No," I said firmly, shaking my head. Dammit, I didn't want to be running away from these two all the time. Sooner or later I was going to have to come to terms with it. And it might as well be sooner. "Just somebody get me a drink."

"That's my girl," Mel said.

Our table was soon filled with frosty caipirinhas and tapas: calamari and spicy green beans. After some therapeutic gossip, I found myself forgetting about Jack and Nicole's presence. I stood and made my way to the restroom.

My shoes clipped on the Brazilian cherry hardwood floor as I walked, slightly wobbily, along a dark narrow corridor. Suddenly a hand gripped my elbow and someone was at my side. Before I could protest, Jack pulled me to the side of the corridor. He looked at me with anger in his eyes, but beneath that was something else. Worry, maybe?

"Did you have anything to do with that Fabergé being stolen?" he demanded. "The Aurora Egg?"

My eyes flew open at the mention of the Aurora Egg. How did he know about that? My stomach tightened. Was this Jack as an FBI agent questioning me? Or Jack as a concerned ex-boyfriend, needing to be the hero at all times?

I attempted to erase emotion from my face and deliberately removed his hand from my forearm. "I'm sorry, Jack, but what are you talking about?"

"Tell me the truth, for Christ's sake, Cat. It's important. You don't understand."

I crossed my arms over my chest. "No, *you* don't understand. You don't have a vote in what I do anymore—got it?" I glanced around to see who was in earshot. There was no immediate company but this corridor was not exactly private.

"Listen, Cat—"

"Do you mind?" I spat between clenched teeth, interrupting him. "Your girlfriend over there has the ability to ruin my life, so I would appreciate it if you weren't so obvious."

"She's not my—" he started, then stopped abruptly. "It doesn't matter. Come here." He dragged me out of the corridor, lifting up the coat check counter and pushing me into the muffled darkness of the cloakroom.

He relatched the counter and turned to face me. I stood there deliberately examining my fingernails, a move designed to piss him off. "You have something more to say to me?"

"Listen, Cat. Whoever did this job is in danger. If it was you, you have to go into hiding."

"I swear. It wasn't me." I held up three fingers, Girl Scout-like. Not that I was ever a Girl Scout, but I was pretty sure this was how they did it.

He narrowed his eyes and folded his arms over his broad chest, regarding me closely. At last, he nodded. "Fine."

Apart from muffled sounds from the restaurant, it was very quiet in here as we faced each other in standoff.

"Good. So we're all done here," I said. "Or do you have something more to say to me?"

"As a matter of fact, I do," he said. "I want to know why you're with that Ethan guy."

Again, *not* what I was expecting. I struggled a moment, not knowing how to respond to this, and finally said, "Well, he happens to be a lot of fun."

"He's a thief, Cat."

I uttered a short laugh. "Umm, Jack, in case you hadn't noticed—"

"He is not a good person. You should stay away from him."

And then, I felt my blood simmering once more. "Excuse me? You think you've got some sort of right to tell me who I can and cannot associate with?"

"I'm concerned."

I planted my hands on my hips. "*You* relinquished your right to be concerned when you broke up with me."

He flung his hands up with exasperation. "Cat, that doesn't make any sense. Just because we can't be together as a couple, doesn't mean I don't care about you as a person."

"Fine. Whatever. Concern noted."

At that point, we heard someone unlatch the cloakroom counter and enter.

In retrospect, it would have made sense for one of us to hide and the other to make an appearance, an excuse, and an escape. Alas. This we did not do. We both dove deeper into the closet of coats to hide. All I can assume is that we were both just too accustomed to furtive-type behavior. Which was ridiculous because I then saw, between coats, that the intruder was none other than the coat-check attendant. Still, we couldn't come out now.

While we waited for the attendant to finish we stayed silent. Unfortunately, the snug proximity to Jack, in combination with the four caipirinhas I'd recently consumed, was doing naughty things to critical parts of my anatomy. I could smell the musk of his aftershave. I could feel the heat from his body.

The attendant clicked her pen and exited. I had the better vantage point of the two of us, so I turned to Jack to tell him it was safe to come out.

But as I turned, and before I had a chance to speak, he pulled me very close and pressed his mouth to mine in a hot, hungry kiss.

Chapter 29

The world tilted. Jack's hands twisted in my hair and I felt every nerve tingle. I returned his urgent kisses, and gripped tightly to his broad shoulders. He slid his hand roughly up my side, along my bare skin that prickled with goose bumps. He fumbled with my top and bra straps as I clawed at his shirt. We tumbled down to the floor, bringing several plush coats down with us as we fell. We rolled around in cushiony fleece and fur, pressing our bodies together. He murmured my name and my heart soared.

I was filled with ripples of excitement and happiness. Was this actually happening?

And then my iPhone bleeped: a text message. The beeping was urgent and loud and it was not the sort of thing that would be quiet unless I did something. So I fumbled with one hand to turn it off. As I grabbed the case I glimpsed the message. It was from Templeton. And it said: We know.

Ice-cold water poured down my back.

Jack looked down. "Who is it?"

"Um—" My mind was whirling. There was only one thing I could think: Templeton, and AB&T, must know about the Fabergé job. Panic clawed up my throat.

"Cat—what's wrong?" Jack said, eyes full of concern. "Who was it?"

"Templeton," I said breathlessly.

"Who?"

I stared into space, trying to think clearly. How could they have found out? "You know, my handler . . . at AB&T . . ."

When I said that, Jack sat up. His eyebrows furrowed and he gazed down at his hands. With that, I knew the spell was broken. "Oh. Right. Well, you'd better go," he said in a detached voice. He started buttoning his shirt. My brain was a maelstrom of conflicting needs. I was desperate to stay, but *goddammit*, I had to deal with this situation. Posthaste.

"Okay, yes, I have to go . . . but, um, maybe we can continue this later. . . ." I tried for a playful nuzzle on his ear.

He pulled away and shook his head. "I'm sorry, Cat. I can't do this. I don't know what I was thinking."

My chest pinched. "Wait, Jack—"

"Nothing's changed, Cat. You're still in the same line of work. In fact, it's never going to change. You and me—we just can't be together." He stood. "I'm sorry if that was confusing." With a torn expression, he left the cloakroom.

I was lost at sea, tossed about by bewildering waves of emotion. I sat there for a second, then stood up and clambered out of the cloakroom. And steeled myself for what I expected would be a very ugly conversation with Templeton.

As I hailed a cab, I reread the second part of Templeton's message. Meet me in the grocery store. Tomatoes.

I arrived at Whole Foods and beelined to the produce section. The intermingled smells of onions and melons and cabbage, normally pleasant to me, was overpowering just then and made me feel like gagging. I stood rigidly inspecting and squeezing tomatoes. After placing a third tomato in a canvas bag, I sensed movement and looked up. Templeton stood on the other side of the tomato pyramid, solemnly filling his basket. I glanced at his face.

A voice announced in my head: "Ladies and gentlemen, the role of Templeton will be played tonight by our understudy . . ."

Templeton's normally good-humored expression had been replaced by something much more grave. I felt a whorl of nausea. Any residual hope I'd been clinging to that perhaps Templeton's ominous *"We Know"* was referring to something else was squashed when I saw his face. I shuffled around the produce pyramid and stood beside him, continuing to select tomatoes.

"Cat, we know about the Fabergé Egg job."

I closed my eyes and nodded. Templeton continued. "The AB&T board are not happy. And, to tell you the truth, neither am I."

"Listen, Templeton, I can explain—"

He held up a hand to stop me, and looked at me from hooded, tired eyes.

I thought about lying. I thought about giving Templeton some kind of story about being forced into doing the job. I could tell him Sandor threatened my family, perhaps.

But I couldn't do it. Guilt demons occupied too many shadowy places in my heart as it was. I didn't need to complicate things by lying even further to Templeton. No, it was time to face up to my misdeeds.

"I've already begun damage control. I'll do what I can to fix this," Templeton said. "But I have to tell you, there's no way promotion to Elite status is a possibility now."

"Right. Of course." I bit the inside of my lower lip.

"You may even be out of AB&T forever. We'll have to see."

Templeton was cutting my heart out with a spoon, with those words. Not work for AB&T? Where would that leave me? No other agency would touch me with that sort of history. Did that mean I would have to retire? That all my aspirations and dreams would have to be abandoned—forever unfulfilled? It was something I could barely stand thinking about.

There was silence between us. A female shopper glided by behind Templeton, down the aisles of produce pyramids, pushing a cart; a cloud of Chanel perfume wafted after her. The PA system crackled and announced a sale on Nature's Path breakfast cereal, aisle 9.

"How did you find out?" I asked quietly.

Templeton pressed his lips together and shrugged. "Not that it matters now. But we received a tip, then checked it out ourselves."

Dark, ominous storm clouds gathered in my brain at that answer. "Who provided the tip?" I barely whispered the words. I cringed, waiting for the response I knew was surely coming.

"Actually, Catherine, it was Brooke Sinclair."

* * *

First thing next morning I marched straight into the spa, past the receptionist with her flawlessly made-up face. I stormed right through the peaceful waiting room with its bubbling fountain and whale music that, given my current state of mind, gave me stabby rage. I thundered directly into the pedicure room. This was where Brooke was receiving a simultaneous manicure and pedicure, like the Queen of freaking Sheba.

"Brooke. Three words: What. The. Fuck."

I didn't care that I was making a scene. I didn't care that I looked like a lunatic. And I certainly didn't care that I was using coarse profanity in an institution that favored euphemisms such as "Brazilian" in place of more accurate and truthful descriptions, i.e., "ripping every last pubic hair out of your body using hot wax." I had one thing I cared about right then: stopping Brooke from further ruining my life. And I had an idea how I could do that.

Everyone in the room startled at my intrusion. Everyone except Brooke, of course, who remained as serene and unflappable as ever.

"I'm sorry, Cat. You're going to have to be a little more specific."

"You know what I'm talking about," I said through gritted teeth.

Brooke's estheticians suddenly found themselves running dangerously low on cuticle softener. They beat a hasty exit.

I clenched my fists. "Jesus, Brooke. Don't you have something better to do with your free time?"

She paused, putting a finger to her mouth in a thoughtful posture. She glanced down at her half-painted toenails and shrugged. "Not really, actually."

I felt an irresistible urge to scratch her eyes out. But then it occurred to me: what *was* Brooke doing, anyway? Was she still working? Now that she'd been in prison, and come out publicly, I wondered—was it possible she'd never work again?

And that, I realized, played in perfectly with my idea.

"Brooke, how much do you need, to leave me alone?"

She looked at me with narrowed eyes. "Meaning?"

"Meaning, I'm prepared to buy you off. If it will make you go away."

It was a desperate plan, I know. Mostly because I had no money.

Everything I'd just made had gone to the IRS. But I could earmark the next few jobs to her, if I had to. It would be worth it.

She blew on her shiny wet nails. "Seriously? That's the best you can come up with?" Her mouth twisted with scorn. "There's something you don't get, Cat. No amount of money will change this fact: *you don't belong in this line of work.* I trained you. And I can ruin you. That's just the way it is. The world of thieves is a small one, and there's only room for one of us at the top. And it's not going to be you."

"And how can you be so sure?" I asked, crossing my arms.

A strange expression crossed her face—something I couldn't quite read. "Because people like *you* are not supposed to have things *I* want."

I stared at her, surprised. "You envy me," I said slowly.

She rolled her eyes. "Please, Cat. We both know the truth here. You've always been envious of me. Besides, who trained whom? Who turned you from a common pickpocket into a professional thief? Answer me this: when you're doing a job, and in a tight spot, how often do you think: *how would Brooke do this?*"

I cringed. Because she was right.

"You know, I hope you'll see someday that I'm actually doing you a favor," she said.

"You're completely delusional. What is your problem? Seriously."

"You should try asking yourself the same thing."

"What are you talking about?"

She looked at me squarely. "Why do you do all this, Cat? Why do you continue in this line of work? You have a chance at a normal life. You could have an academic career, and you've got a man who would be with you in a heartbeat if you gave up your criminal tendencies. So I'm asking you: what's *your* problem?"

I felt a slicing pain as that arrow hit too close to the mark. I gritted my teeth and told myself to ignore her. She was just trying to mess with my head.

Besides, I knew exactly why I couldn't give it up, not just yet.

"I assume you know why you're here," said the man with the comb-over and the gaps between his Chiclets teeth. He was seated behind a large mahogany desk, tapping a pencil irritably. Mr. Frank was Templeton's boss at the Agency, head of the HR Department. Templeton stood to Mr. Frank's left, looking grim. To complete the triangle I sat in front of the desk, knees together, eyes lowered like an admonished teenager.

"Yes, sir," I said.

I was in the principal's office—but a thousand times worse. And, as a further distinction, surrounded by dental equipment. The waiting room was filled with catalogs and samples of drills and dentures and X-ray machines. AB&T headquarters was disguised as a dental supply company. That was our cover.

It was hot and stuffy in there; my palms felt slick and the backs of my knees were prickling. Of course I knew why I was in trouble. What I didn't know was what they were going to do about it. My stomach corkscrewed.

"Part of your contract with AB&T," Mr. Frank continued gravely, "is that you are *not* to take outside jobs. When people hire thieves independently that undermines the entire fabric of this agency. This is a business we're running here."

"Yes, sir."

"It's also a security issue. Every time you engage with an un-screened party, there could be risks."

I knew all that, of course. I steeled myself for what was coming next. Mr. Frank paused, breathing loudly through his nose. "You're an excellent thief, Miss Montgomery," he said, clenching his jaw. "You have done some superb work for us."

"Thank you, sir."

Mr. Frank reclined in his chair and squinted his eyes into tight slits. I suspended my breathing. I waited for the blow to come. *And, by the way, don't expect a reference. . . .*

"In short," he said, "we have decided to overlook this trans-gression."

My jaw hung open. "What? You have?" I started to smile, but neither of them were smiling so I wrenched my face straight.

"This must absolutely never happen again," Mr. Frank said. "I cannot stress this enough. Let's be clear on the terms, shall we?"

I nodded rapidly. He held up a hand and counted off rules on his fingers. "No more assignments outside AB&T. No more freelance. No more interactions with these people—this Sandor—or anything to do with this Fabergé. Am I clear?"

"Yes, sir. I understand."

My head felt light with disbelief. I was off the hook. There was only one way this could have happened: Templeton must have really gone to bat for me. I glanced at him. His expression was mixed. He was relieved, that was certain. But I could also see his disappointment in me. He couldn't quite meet my eye.

I knew it would be a long time before he forgave me for deceiving AB&T—and him. So when I swore to them that it would never happen again, I really meant it. Firstly, because I knew there wouldn't be any more chances. But mostly because there was no way I was going to betray Templeton again.

Absolutely no way.

Unfortunately, that very afternoon I realized, to my horror, that I was going to do exactly that.

It was a day of torrential rain and I was going with Ethan to an art gallery. I was expecting a reasonably pleasant couple of hours gazing at paintings while Ethan scoped out the security system for his next job.

I'd been a little hesitant when he'd first invited me. I hadn't actually seen Ethan since our—*ahem*—night together at his apartment.

"Come on, Cat, it'll be a great distraction for you," he'd said earlier today, cajoling me to come along. "And I know you need a little of that." He was well aware of my recent offense and near-firing from AB&T. I had been pretty hot gossip at Agency watercoolers.

The residual awkwardness when he'd first picked me up quickly dissolved, then we simply became two regular thieves out for a pleasant afternoon at an art gallery.

We entered the main foyer. A grand vaulted ceiling soared away from us, high above the intricate mosaic floor. Sounds echoed, cathedral-like. The poster in the foyer announced a visiting exhibit on Russian portraits.

Ethan turned to me. "Okay, I'm going to take stock of the camera locations and get a fix on their infrared system," he said in a low voice. "You look around and enjoy yourself. Then we'll get some lunch, okay? The gallery café is excellent." He winked and walked away.

As I made my way to the Russian portraits I couldn't help wondering why I was here with Ethan. The thought nagged at me and got tangled up in my brain like a loose thread in a washing machine. Was this a date? Did I even want it to be? I was attracted to Ethan, of course, but that begged the question: what was I doing in the cloakroom with Jack?

I had to forget Jack. Ethan—this was the guy I should have been with. Even on paper he was perfect: Cute, charming, criminal.

I passed beneath a marble archway and entered a small room with burgundy walls and parquet floor and carved golden frames. I strolled to one end and stood before a large portrait of a man, a royal portrait it seemed, based on the uniform, the decoration, the imperial pose. I should admire the brushwork, I thought. Not that I knew anything about brushwork, but that shouldn't stop me from admiring it, should it? I peered closer, gazing at the portrait's face.

Every molecule inside me froze, instantly. My eyes darted down, panicking, to read the brass plaque on the frame. *Oh no.* No, no, no. This couldn't be happening.

And just like that, I knew that I was going to have to do the exact thing I just promised AB&T, and Templeton, that I wouldn't. The plaque read: Czar Nicholas II: 1915. It was a portrait of the last monarch of the House of Romanov.

Who just so happened to be a dead ringer for Gorlovich, the owner of the Starlight Casino. I could see it in the slant of his eyes, the high forehead, the angle of his cheekbones. Gorlovich, the former possessor of the Aurora Egg, and recent victim of a major theft. I stared hard at the painting, desperate to see Sandor's features in the face. But there was nothing. No resemblance whatsoever. Someone had pulled the bath plug, and I was being sucked down as everything I'd believed drained away. There was only one obvious explanation here: I'd been tricked.

Chapter 30

The Gorlovich family were the rightful owners of the Aurora Egg. That was the only explanation that made sense. *They* were the Romanov descendants, not Sandor and his group. And the truth of what I'd just done? I hadn't stolen the Egg back for the good guys. I'd just stolen it. Outright.

I quickly found Ethan. "I have to go," I said abruptly. My teeth were gnashing at the thought of being used so brazenly. I savagely twisted the ring on my finger. One of my reasons for taking this job had been to correct an old wrong. But I hadn't corrected a thing. In fact I'd made it all so much worse. I felt sick with betrayal. But before I started tearing the city apart, I needed to confirm this somehow.

"What's wrong?" he asked, staring at me with concern. "You look angry . . . or something. . . ."

"I—I have to go sort something out. Right now. Sorry," I said, and dashed from the gallery.

I flew home and immediately locked myself in my secret room. I flung open drawers and threw papers off shelves and finally found the envelope that my gloves had arrived in. The one that held the report on Gorlovich's hair specimen that I'd tossed aside without reading. I gripped onto the report, and read it.

Specimen: Hair.
Duplication Protocol: PCR
DNA Analysis & Identification: Identity confirmed to be
Alexei Mikhail Nicholas Romanov, male, born 1968.

I crumpled the paper and slammed it onto my desk. God, I couldn't believe it. I'd been completely and entirely duped. I dug my fingers into my hair and pulled at the roots. *Damn it.* The people I'd thought were the good guys were actually the bad. And here I thought I was doing something *honorable.* But in spite of all that, I ended up being the bad guy after all. In trying to fix the past I only managed to make it worse. I wiped at an angry tear and then stopped, frowning. Why was this affecting me so much? And then I wondered—was this why I hadn't felt any different after handing the Fabergé to Sandor? Because I hadn't truly righted anything, in a universal sense?

I shook my head and tried to rattle the pieces back in place. Several questions pushed forward. For one thing, if not a Romanov, who the hell was Sandor? Who were all his people? Why go through such an elaborate ruse to steal a single piece?

The most important question, though, elbowed its way forward in my consciousness: what was I prepared to do about it?

Two hours later I was hiding in the darkness, deep within the labyrinth of rooms beneath the masquerade mansion. I'd tucked myself into an antique wardrobe that held old clothing and linens and I was trying to breathe through the odor of musty fabric and mothballs.

I'd had a vague, unformed plan to break in here and hunt for information. But within minutes of arriving in the old stone conference room I'd heard voices approaching from the corridor just outside. So I hid—flinging myself into the nearest place, which turned out to be this dusty old wardrobe—and held my breath, waiting to see who would appear in my sight lines. I was sweating with the desperate hope that I wouldn't sneeze.

Of course I now had to admit that my friends had been right. I'd consulted them before coming here. And they, in the nicest possible way, had told me I was insane.

"So, explain this again, Cat, because I don't get it," Mel said. "Why do you need to return the Aurora Egg to the original family? You've stolen loads of things from original owners."

We were at her apartment. After reading the DNA report, I'd gone directly to Mel's place. Sophie had arrived shortly thereafter. "I know. But I don't like being deceived and tricked," I said. "I was used."

"So it's an *ego* thing?"

"No . . . not exactly . . ." I said, searching for the right words. "It's more like, what I did . . . is just not right. I thought I could fix an old wrong. Fix the past."

"Cat, you can't fix the past," Mel said.

"Yes, you can. Sometimes you can."

"Cat? No you can't," Mel said firmly. "You have to let the past go. You have to move forward. This is your life." She sighed and her face softened then. She came and sat next to me on the sofa. "Learning from past mistakes is one thing, but a person can become consumed by it. An obsessive quest for atonement can only lead to one thing: self-destruction."

There was silence. And then Sophie said, "We—we're not talking about the Fabergé Egg anymore, are we?"

I looked away, out the window.

"It's too dangerous, Cat. Just take care of yourself," Mel said.

"And what about Templeton? You'll be betraying him again," Sophie said.

Everything they'd said was true. But this thing had grabbed on to me and refused to let go. So here I was, in the wardrobe.

I waited, slowing my breathing. Then, I heard the door open and shadows moved across my line of sight. Somebody began lighting wall sconces; I could smell burning candle wax and the sulfur of the matches. Despite the flickering light, I couldn't see very well, so I opened the wardrobe door a crack further, heart pounding. I made out Sandor, and other faces I recognized from previous meetings: Hugo, Mikhail, Gilda. And then two other men came into view: the monks. They remained standing at the end of the table.

"Well? What do you want?" Sandor said to the monks. His voice sounded different. Sharper and pointed, like an ice pick. He even looked different to me then—harder, older, and more unpleasant. Was it my imagination, now I knew he was a liar?

"We know you have the Aurora Egg," said the handsome, Latin-looking monk, his voice shaky and cutting off at the end in a nervous, involuntary stop. His temples, beaded with sweat, glistened in the candlelight. "We're offering to purchase it from you." Sandor looked indifferent. "I'm listening," he said.

"We're prepared to offer you six point three million dollars." My eyes sprang wide. Sandor stared at the monks without reaction. "That is not an acceptable offer," he said. The monks protested and blustered.

Sandor held up a hand to stop them. "You know, I find myself wondering something. Why would the church be so interested in a simple, albeit beautiful, piece of Russian decorative art?" He stood and began to walk the length of the table, growing slowly closer to the monks. The tall monk took a step backward. "Now, you've come to me before. And judging from your persistence, I would say the church is very interested. But I'm curious what it is, exactly, that has you so intrigued."

Yes, I thought. *That is a good question. Let's hear the answer to that.* But the monks said nothing. The tall one had developed a bright, blotchy flush up his neck.

"Now. How stupid do you think *I* am?" Sandor said. His lips curled back into a nasty, toothy smile.

The monks blanched. "Listen, we know what you have planned with the Aurora," the handsome one said, glancing at his partner. "And we're here to beg you not to do it. It's monstrous."

Sandor folded his arms; he looked unmoved. The monks conferred, whispering urgently. "All right," said the tall one. "We're prepared to offer you double our first amount."

I tried not to choke. Sandor looked bored. He sighed and then glanced—just the slightest flicker of a look—at Hugo on his left.

Two deafening gunshots rang out as Hugo shot both monks, point-blank, in the head. The monks crumpled to the ground and lay there, unmoving, in blooming pools of blood.

My vision narrowed to a tunnel and I could hear blood thundering in my ears. It took every ounce of self-control to not scream out. I tore my eyes away from the monks' bodies and watched as Sandor and his group prepared to depart, briskly gathering papers. I was breathing so loudly I was sure they'd be able to hear me, hidden, so vulnerable in this wardrobe. An icy chill curled around my throat. I forced myself to focus on what was being said.

Sandor ordered his men to pack everything. "We're leaving for London first thing tomorrow morning."

"Yes, sir," one of the men replied.

"Has our prism landed in London yet?" Sandor asked.

"It appears so," Gilda said, flipping through a file.

Sandor's lips curled back. "I don't want appearances. I want confirmation."

They might as well have been speaking in Sanskrit—what were they talking about? *Prism?* It was all a blur. "Is someone going to clean this up?" Sandor demanded, waving a hand vaguely in the direction of the monks' bodies. He exited the room.

Two large men bundled up the bodies in heavy plastic with frightening efficiency. The wall sconces were extinguished and the room emptied, leaving me alone again in the darkness, trembling. But there was something bigger than fear for me, now. And that was the knowledge that, more than ever, it was going to be impossible to let this go.

But one lucid thought pushed through: I was going to need some help.

Chapter 31

The sky was painted the cold blue gray of dawn. Streetlights glowed their sodium vapor, not yet acknowledging the coming day. Jack parked his car in front of the masquerade mansion and climbed out. Sandor had agreed to the meeting, but he'd said it had to be early. He had a flight to catch.

I bet you do, Jack thought. Jack knew Sandor had the Fabergé Egg now, and would be planning his next steps without delay.

The curved driveway glistened darkly—it had rained last night. The air was crisp and fresh from it. Dawn was a time of duels, Jack thought. Of foggy moors, first light, the smell of gunpowder.

What the hell was he doing here?

It had been his idea, of course, so he had no one to blame but himself. The day after his cloakroom incident with Cat—what a mistake that was—he'd gone to Wesley and Oliver Cole. He'd met them at the private room in the restaurant in Delridge neighborhood, the place of their first meeting. He told them that Cat had denied any involvement in the Fabergé theft. And that he believed her.

They'd listened. And then they'd promptly advised him that he was wrong.

"Cat Montgomery is the confirmed thief on this job," Cole said, reclining in his smooth leather armchair. "Her agency superiors just disciplined her for the conflict of interest. We have corroborating information to back this up."

Jack stood before them both, arms crossed. He silently cursed Cat for turning him into a fool. And then, the gnawing worry began again.

"So what next?" he asked.

"We're going to contact Montgomery," Cole said, drawing on his cigar. "We're going to recruit her to help us go in and retrieve the Egg from the Caliga. She's done it once, she can do it again. She's got insider knowledge of how they operate, presumably."

"No," Jack blurted. "Not Cat. Keep her out of it." She was in enough danger as it was, already having worked for Sandor. If she now became tangled in a double-cross operation? Cold fear touched Jack's bones. He had an impulse to rush out and sweep her away somewhere safe.

"Impossible, Jack," Cole said.

"Listen, I'll do whatever you need."

"Jack, you're not a thief. The job is too difficult. Fact is, we probably should have involved Cat Montgomery right from the beginning. But we can learn from our mistake."

Wesley leaned forward. "We know where the Fabergé is—more or less. It's being kept somewhere in the underground caverns of the masquerade ball house. Until they can smuggle it out of the country, Sandor is not letting it out of his sight."

Then Jack got an idea. "He will, if it's to meet me."

"What?" Wesley said.

Jack was thinking fast. "I'll go and talk to Sandor myself. They won't be able to resist my request for a meeting. They must know who my father was. So during that distraction, you"—he looked at Wesley—"can get the Egg."

"Jack, that's crazy," Wesley protested. "You'll be a sacrificial lamb."

He shook his head. "They won't hurt me, I'll be fine." Jack was not at all certain, but he didn't have a lot of choice.

Cole, who had been silent, nodded his head. "I like the idea," he said. "Let's do it. But it can be Wesley and Cat who get the Egg while you're doing the distracting."

"No," Jack said firmly. "No deal. I only do it if Cat is out."

Cole sat back and rubbed his chin, mulling it over. "Okay. It's a deal, Jack."

Jack and Wesley left together. As they strode through Delridge's shifty alleys and shadowy streets, Wesley said, "That was quite an act of chivalry, Barlow."

Jack said nothing, but shrugged and shoved his hands in the pockets of his wool coat.

"Although I'm not surprised," Wesley continued.

"If you have a point, you should get to it."

"It's just obvious, that's all."

Jack stopped and gave him a level look. "What are you talking about?" he said between clenched teeth.

"Jack, give me a break. You're still in love with her. Cat."

"Oh fuck off, Smith," Jack spat. "That's ridiculous. Cat and I could never be together again." He turned and began striding away.

Wesley shrugged and fell in step beside him. "Maybe," he said. "But I didn't say you were going to *be together*. I just said you still love her."

Jack stopped again and turned to look at Wesley, ready to tear another strip. He opened his mouth to say something, then hesitated.

This conversation was still bothering Jack as he climbed the steps to the masquerade mansion. But he had more critical things to deal with now.

Jack was quickly granted entrance to the house. He experienced flashbacks to the masquerade ball—the ice sculptures, the chamber music—as he was led by a butler to an enormous parlor. He was frisked for weapons and wires. Then, as he waited, he shifted back and forth. He tugged his collar to give a little breathing room. He knew that, in one minute, Wesley would be gaining access to the underground passages from the exterior hatch.

"Jack Barlow," said Sandor, striding into the room. Jack had only seen photographs of the man. It was unnerving, the apparent age of Sandor. He looked barely old enough to be shaving. But Jack was wary enough not to be disarmed by this appearance.

Four other men slipped into the room behind Sandor, taking up positions by the door. They had no visible weapons. But Jack knew better.

Sandor shook Jack's hand and they both sat down in velvet-upholstered armchairs. The room was sumptuously decorated with long swags of silk curtains and hand-woven rugs covering the marble floor. Jack imagined Wesley, now, slipping along the stone corridors below, homing in on the target.

"Well, Mr. Barlow, I must tell you I was surprised when I was advised that you wanted to meet with me," Sandor said in a genteel voice. *So that's how he was going to play it,* Jack thought. "Please don't leave me in suspense any longer. What can I do for you?"

"I don't want to waste my time or yours," Jack said. "So I'll just get right to it. I know you have the Aurora Egg. And you know that I know. But the fact is, I'm here because I want to join you."

Sandor did not immediately respond. But his eyelids lowered a little, his expression turned fractionally more dangerous as he waited for Jack to continue.

"I want to be involved in what happens next with the Fabergé," Jack said.

Sandor watched him carefully. He tapped his front teeth with a fingernail. "And what makes you think I'll believe this little piece of fiction?"

Jack shrugged. "Quite simply, I like to be on the winning team." Jack's breathing was fast and shallow now and he forced himself to not move his eyes to the men standing by the door. His mind spun away to Wesley, down below. Was he encountering obstacles? Sandor's core guards were here in this room, which he hoped meant the chambers below had been left minimally attended. "My father taught me a lot about the Gifts of the Magi," Jack continued. "And it seems apparent to me that the Caliga are the ones to take it to the next step."

Was Sandor buying it? Jack couldn't be sure. He searched the man's face for clues.

Jack continued speaking when Sandor said nothing. "I'm concerned, however, about your loose threads. People who know about this project but are walking around freely." This was his riskiest statement. But he had to know what their plans were.

"Such as?"

"Cat Montgomery."

Sandor nodded. "Yes, our original plan had been to eliminate her—but I was . . . interrupted." Jack's mouth went dry. But—at least Sandor was being candid with him. Sandor then shrugged. "There is no need for us to eliminate Cat Montgomery now, because she doesn't know anything."

Jack nodded. Sandor's eyes narrowed. "Now, this line of conversation reminds me of something," Sandor said. "Ah yes. Wasn't Miss Montgomery a girlfriend of yours?"

Jack's stomach tightened. "Yes. Emphasis on the *was*."

"And this line of questioning isn't meant to protect her in some way?"

"No, like I said, we're no longer together. I'm with someone else now."

Sandor's face turned unpleasant. "Now here I know you're lying. I know that you ended your relationship with the FBI agent."

Jack struggled to conceal his surprise. How could Sandor know this? They had only broken up last night, at that damned restaurant opening. Jack had finally decided it had to end with Nicole, especially after that thing—whatever it was—with Cat in the cloakroom. But how could Sandor know about this? His sources were good. Frighteningly so.

Maybe this was a bad idea. Jack flicked a glance at his watch and wondered how much longer Wesley would be. How long could he keep this up?

At that moment an intruder alarm sounded, piercing the air with sirens. The parlor door flung open and a woman darted in. "Sir— someone is in the vault." Two of the four henchmen immediately rushed from the room.

Sandor's eyes sprang open. His head spun to face Jack. "How stupid do you think I am?" Sandor snarled.

Jack's heart seized. He had to get out of there. Now.

The billiards hall cracked with the sound of a break shot; Ethan straightened from his position over the pool table, scrutinizing the results of his shot as billiard balls rolled and clicked across the green felt.

"Ethan, I need your help," I said, standing beside him, shifting between my feet.

Ethan picked up his lowball drink from the edge of the table. The sleeves of his crisp button-down shirt were rolled up to the elbows. Ice cubes clicked as he took a sip. Then he smiled. "Well, I like the sound of that. What's up, Montgomery?"

Before I could speak, he offered me his pool cue and indicated the table. "Want in? We could play for something interesting—"

I shook my head vigorously. "No, Ethan, I really don't have time. This is important. . . ."

I glanced around. The billiards hall was scantily inhabited this morning: a smattering of retired men in golf shirts, and a pair of university students in the corner, drinking beer, clearly recovering from the night before.

"Listen," I said, "you know the job you helped me with, when we broke into York Security?"

"Of course," he said, strolling to the other side of the table and lining up his next shot.

"Well, I think I need some help. Things are . . . a lot more complicated than I thought. I thought I could handle this by myself. But I was wrong."

He watched me carefully and rolled the pool cue between his hands. "Tell me, Montgomery. I'm all ears."

Over the background sounds of clacking billiard balls and the occasional triumphant cheer from distant tables, I told Ethan all about the Fabergé job. I told him everything I knew about Sandor. And how I knew, now, that Sandor wasn't actually a Romanov descendant.

"Ah, that's what you were freaking out about in the art gallery," he said, understanding dawning on his face.

I nodded. Then I told him what I'd seen in the masquerade mansion.

He froze, midshot, as I described the monks' murder. He straightened, face darkening.

"Do you have any idea who these people might really be?" I asked him, nibbling a fingernail.

Ethan picked up his glass and slid onto a bar stool beside the pool table. He thought about it for a while. "I can't be sure, obviously.

But I know who this sounds like. Have you heard of a group called the Caliga Rapio?"

My eyes opened wide. "That's real? I thought it was just an urban myth."

"Most people would say people like *you* are an urban myth."

"Good point," I said, nodding. "So tell me. What's the truth?"

"The Caliga are extremely secretive. But we know a few things." Ethan began describing an international, underground circle of criminals. But the sort that operated without conscience, and without a code. According to rumor, they'd even lost the old skills, the art of burglary. What was worse, they were the kind who did not hesitate to kill people in their way.

Sandor's face blazed in my mind, cold and detached, stepping around the dead bodies of the monks. I shivered.

"How long have they been around?" I asked.

"I don't know. But from what I've heard, a long time." Ethan stared into his drink, swirling the ice cubes. "You know what I think you should do?" he continued. I waited expectantly. "I think you should stay out of it. You were involved, and now you're not. I say just drop it. Forget you ever knew about it."

I nodded. It sounded like good advice. There was just one problem.

"I can't do that," I said. "The Aurora is clearly more than just another Fabergé Egg. There's something special about it. I just don't know what. They've obviously got unpleasant plans for it." I paused and looked down, rotating the ring on my finger. "I took this job because I thought I was correcting something that had happened in the past. I thought I was returning a Fabergé Egg to its original family. But I was tricked, and used. Instead of feeling better now, I actually feel worse. I'm not sure I can live with that. And to be honest, Ethan, I don't need any more regrets."

Jack gave Sandor a swift, mighty kick in the chest, knocking the smaller man down. He hurled a chair—his only weapon—at the henchmen pulling their guns.

The chair flew through the air and both men scattered. One crashed into a glass coffee table, smashing it. Shards of glass flew everywhere. Jack grabbed a fractured table leg and sprinted for the door, smashing the knees of the henchman standing in his way. He had to get out of this house. As he ran, his hip slammed into a chair and his shoulder thudded into the door frame, but he kept going. He heard a bullet ping into the joinery around the door, splintering wood. Then the crash of more breaking glass as bullets plowed into a nearby mirror. Sandor was not a good shot.

Jack's vision narrowed to a mine shaft. His heart beat at an uncountable rate. It would be sheer luck if he got out of here without being shot. His muscles strained as he sprinted through the hallway toward the front entrance. There were shouts and thundering footsteps right behind him.

Panicky questions crowded into his head: Where was Wesley? Was he alive? Did he have the Egg?

He had to stick to the plan. Wesley had his own getaway route and they had agreed that it would be every man for himself if something went wrong.

He reached the main foyer where a butler stood, startled and frozen in the path of the locomotive. Jack shoved him aside and lunged for the front door, keeping low. Another bullet zinged by his head, then one smashed into a vase standing beside the door. The vase exploded in ceramic fireworks. A jagged fragment flew up and caught Jack just above the eye.

Jack flung open the front door and hurled himself out into the morning light, thrilled to be still gulping air. The sun was bursting over the horizon now. A flock of birds flew up from a nearby tree in alarm at the sudden sounds emerging from the house.

Jack lunged desperately for his car—why the hell hadn't he parked closer?—and ripped open the closest door, the passenger's side, when he reached it. He dove straight in. At least he had the sense to leave the keys in the ignition for a fast getaway. He threw the car into gear. A bullet smashed the rear window into a glass spiderweb. Jack peeled away, the tires squealing on the driveway. His rear end fishtailed and the side of the car scraped along the iron gate as he burst through it, and onto the road.

* * *

Jack sat on the cold edge of his bathtub, wiping blood from the laceration above his eye and holding a pack of ice to his lower lip. He was back at home. He turned on the fan to clear the rubbing alcohol smell. His cuts stung and he felt the dull ache of bruised muscles. A minute ago he'd received a message from Wesley: he was fine, he'd escaped, but he hadn't been able to get the Egg.

Well, at least this way Jack knew the Caliga wouldn't come hunting him down. If they still had the Fabergé they would be concentrating their efforts on getting out of the country. They wouldn't bother coming after him now. Or so he hoped, anyway.

Jack had placed a call: the airports would be on the lookout for Caliga members, using the descriptions he'd faxed. But Jack knew that wouldn't prevent their escape. The Caliga would use private jets and private airports. If there was more time or if this were an official criminal case, he could do something about those, too. But there was nothing official about this. And Jack couldn't make a case of it without having to explain things he was not willing to explain.

Jack opened the medicine cabinet to look for some aspirin and a Band-Aid. He turned the aspirin bottle upside down in his hand. Empty. He shoved aside a crusted bottle of Pepto-Bismol to get the Band-Aids behind. He grabbed it and stared at the box. The Band-Aids were cotton-candy pink. Cartooned with miniature martini glasses.

Jack stood there holding the package. They were Cat's Band-Aids. He looked up at his reflection in the medicine cabinet mirror. His face was bruised and cut. He'd removed his shirt; an ugly purple swelling was developing on his right shoulder.

All of this, every wound and abrasion, had been sustained to protect Cat. To keep her out of the fray. Wesley's words echoed in his mind: *quite an act of chivalry, Jack.*

Was it just chivalry? Was he simply doing the decent thing? Or was it something more? Jack had protected a crook. How had things become so twisted? He was FBI. His job was not about protecting crooks.

He studied his reflection. The truth was, he no longer saw things in black and white anymore. The world was not divided between crooks and noncrooks. The world was in various shades of gray for him now. When had that happened? The man he was looking at in the mirror was no longer the same man who'd disowned his father. Jack felt a knife-twist of guilt. His father had died alone, with a broken heart. Was that why Jack had been compelled to join the Fabergé hunt? So he could forgive—not his father, for being a crook, but himself, for breaking his father's heart?

He sat back down on the bathtub's edge, still holding the small box of pink Band-Aids. He stared at the hand clutching the box. The bruises and scrapes there, the aching in his shoulders—all of it was evidence of his feelings for Cat.

Images of Cat flashed in his mind: the concentration on her face as she cracked the safe on the train, her ridiculous performance at the golf tournament. Jack smiled at that one. Cat was spirited, brave, and resourceful. She was a firecracker; she was a tempest at sea.

It would be easier to be in love with Nicole and be happy. But life wasn't about choosing the easy path. And, more than that—falling in love wasn't a voluntary, logical decision. At that moment, he realized leaving Cat had been a huge mistake. Because he knew, now, that his heart belonged to her.

A single question remained: was he too late?

Chapter 32

When I arrived home after meeting with Ethan there was an urgent message from Lucas on my encrypted voice mail. I called the lab and was put through on a secure line. On hold, I opened the fridge and scanned for something edible. I was starving.

Lucas picked up just as I found a package of processed cheese, in which only two slices remained, and a three-quarters empty jar of marmalade. "Okay, we processed those samples you sent us, Cat."

Ah, the samples from the Egg. Excellent. I began unwrapping the cheese while Lucas continued.

"I gotta tell you, we received some very intriguing results," he said.

"Oh?" I opened the freezer and frost spilled out. I peered through the clouds and came up with a crumpled box of Eggos with exactly one freezer-burned waffle inside.

There was a pause on the line. "Where did you find this stuff you sent us, exactly?" he asked.

"You know I can't tell you that." I cradled the receiver between my shoulder and ear and popped the waffle in the toaster. I wrestled with the marmalade lid. I didn't know where I was going with this little buffet but I needed to eat and that was all that mattered.

He sighed. "I know. Just thought I'd check. Also, I'm wondering: was there anything gold, perchance, that accompanied these two substances?"

I paused, frowning. "In fact there was," I said slowly. The pelican sculpture was gold. "How did you know there would be?"

"Just bear with me a sec. I'll get to that." His speech was speeding up and I recognized the excitement in his voice.

The marmalade lid was firmly crusted shut. I twisted on the hot water tap and held it under.

"The yellowish stuff was an aromatic resin," Lucas said. "Otherwise known as frankincense."

"Oh. Weird." The water pouring over my hand was growing hotter.

"Yeah, well, it gets weirder," he said. "The reddish-brown stuff turned out to be, if you can believe it, *myrrh*."

Scalding heat seared onto my hand and I realized that I was still holding the jar under the tap. I pulled my hand out and clunked the dripping jar onto the counter. "Wait a second, Lucas. *Gold, frankincense*, and *myrrh*. Are you joking?"

"Nope," he said gleefully. "Wanna hear the most interesting part? We tested the samples for age, and they're both roughly two thousand years old."

At this I froze, holding on to the kitchen counter with a sopping wet hand. My eyes were wide as my brain spun it through. "Are you saying . . ." I said slowly, in disbelief, dropping down into a chair at my kitchen table. "Are you telling me what I *think* you're trying to tell me?"

"I think so."

At that moment the smoke detector pealed and I could see out of my peripheral vision puffs of gray and white pouring out of the toaster; I was dimly aware of the smell of burning waffle. I didn't move.

My tires squealed as I took a tight turn. I was on my way to meet Ethan at the Governor Hotel lobby, and I was late. My stomach fluttered. Would he believe me? More importantly: would he help me?

My brain felt like it was going to explode. After hanging up with Lucas I had immediately called Gladys. I needed her help; I needed information. I told her what the lab suspected. Gladys immediately set to work. There was nobody as good when it came to ferreting out the truth. After talking to Gladys I'd called Ethan, then raced out the door once he agreed to meet me.

Speeding down State Avenue, my phone rang. It was Gladys calling me back. I flicked on my hands-free.

"The Gifts of the Magi," Gladys said firmly, her voice coming through on my earpiece. "Your lab fellow is right, my dear. That's what's inside the Aurora Egg."

I slammed on the brakes for a red light. "This is for real? It's not a coincidence?"

"It most definitely is for real." I processed that a moment, chewing the inside of my cheek.

"Are you religious, my dear?" Gladys asked.

"Not a bit."

"Well, fortunately that's not necessary. Because none of these affairs are in the Bible."

Gladys told me, then, how she'd hacked on to the encrypted files of the Catholic Church. There were very old papers that had been scanned into their systems for preservation and then locked away, virtually, under heavy firewalls and online security. Nothing that a little ingenuity couldn't bypass, however.

She told me a story about two thieves who had lived long ago. They'd been the ones to first steal the Gifts of the Magi.

My eyes widened as she told the whole tale of betrayal, remorse, crucifixion, and finally the loss of the Gifts. It would become the legacy of thieves. It would also give rise to the Caliga.

I flew down Laurel Street toward the Governor Hotel. Gladys told me what the Caliga believed about the gifts: that they contained a mystical power endowed by the Zoroastrian priests and astrologers who were the Magi.

To unlock the powers they needed to perform bizarre rituals that would end up destroying the Fabergé, and the Gifts, in the process.

I couldn't let that happen. If it did, I'd never be able to reverse the damage I'd done.

Did I believe all that stuff about magical powers? No. But that didn't matter. What I did know was *they* believed it. I had to stop them. But I was going to need some help.

Mostly because those bad guys were really bad. And dangerous. But worse, they knew all about me.

I knew they had taken the Fabergé to London. Guaranteed, they'd have it under rock-solid security. It was going to be virtually impossible for one person to do this job. I was going to need another thief. I needed someone good, with lots of experience. More than ever, I needed Ethan to agree to help me. I hoped I could convince him.

I squealed up to the Governor Hotel and dashed through the first few drops of rain—practically flinging my keys at the valet and racing inside—hoping Ethan hadn't been waiting long.

"There's one more thing you need to know," Gladys said in my ear as I strode into the lobby among the leather club chairs, gleaming marble, and piano jazz. "And this is where things get ugly."

"Okay," I said reluctantly, scanning the lounge for Ethan.

"There's an elaborate ritual involved in unlocking the powers of the Gifts. And the ritual involves the use of a prism."

Prism—they'd used that word. Sandor was talking about it just after murdering the monks.

"So what's a prism?"

"A prism, in this situation, is a person." Gladys's voice was grim. "And that person is to be killed in the ritual."

I choked. "A human sacrifice?"

I squeezed my eyes shut. I had to stop this. Because now, if someone died, it would definitely and directly be my fault.

Chapter 33

Jack was running now, barely feeling the rain drizzling on his uncovered head. He spotted the hotel on the next block: the Governor Hotel. Silvery waterfalls dripped over the edge of the black awnings. The hotel was a grand dame, all brass doors, lanterns on cutstone walls, potted topiaries flanking the entrance. A red-uniformed doorman peered out from underneath the awning, examining the sky, feet planted on a thick outdoor carpet.

Jack had been scouring the city for Cat for the past two hours. Thanks to his network of FBI agents, he had finally located her. His heart was beating fast and it wasn't from the sprint over here. He was filled with apprehension, and the desperate hope that she would listen, that she didn't hate him. His insides writhed and squirmed. He hoped he hadn't waited too long.

The doorman gave a small cough, and Jack realized he was standing immobile before an open door. "Can I help you with anything, sir?" the doorman asked, his tone bemused.

Now that he was here, Jack hesitated. He flexed his jaw. He took a few steps away and peered through a window beside the front shelter. Maybe if he just caught a glimpse of her first.

And he did. She was seated in an armchair in the hotel lounge, sipping a drink from a highball glass. She jiggled her ankle impatiently and wore a look of anxiety. Jack wondered what she was waiting for. He took a step closer to the window. Rain dripped on his head but he wasn't concerned. Cat's caramel hair traced a path over one eyebrow. A black trench coat covered her petite frame. Her eyes, which were so often smiling, looked troubled now, and Jack wanted to sweep that away.

Then someone else arrived at the front of the hotel. Jack flicked his gaze briefly, seeing a man's suit beneath a black-and-white houndstooth umbrella. The doorman admitted him and he walked in. *See how easy that was?* Jack chided himself. Enough. It was time to go in.

But just as he was about to turn for the door, he saw somebody approach Cat's chair. The man with the houndstooth umbrella. With the umbrella now closed, he recognized the man immediately. Ethan Jones.

Jack froze. Cat stood and embraced Ethan. She was smiling at him; she appeared to be genuinely happy to see him. They stood close together and Cat began eagerly talking to him. Her hands were animated. She was telling him something that was clearly important to her.

Then they turned and walked together toward the elevators for guest rooms. Ethan's hand was on Cat's lower back, guiding her.

Jack's chest caved in with a sudden agonizing emptiness. Then anger flared, briefly, and he felt a great impulse to rush in and drag Cat away.

Rage soon subsided into numbness. Icy raindrops slid down the back of his neck, under his collar. And then, Jack saw the truth.

It didn't matter how he felt. Cat deserved to be happy. And she could be happy with a man like Ethan. Someone from her world. Someone she didn't have to keep secrets from. Someone who was not going to judge her.

Just then the doorman coughed again. "Sir? Are you certain there isn't something I can do for you? Can I call you a cab, perhaps?"

Jack stared at him a moment. Tires hissed on the wet roads in front of the hotel and streetlights flicked on, pushing their golden halos against the gray drizzle.

"No, thank you. I'm fine." He turned and walked away along the rain-slick sidewalk.

"Gold, frankincense, and myrrh," I said in a low voice to Ethan in the elevator. "The real deal. Can you believe it?" Ethan looked surprised but said nothing, standing very close to me in the elevator. We were alone in there. I could smell his aftershave. He had arranged for a room before he met me here at the hotel. It had been a good idea since this conversation really needed to be private. Of course, that hadn't stopped me from telling him most of the story before we even got to the room, however.

Ethan had listened carefully as I explained how I discovered what the Fabergé Egg had really contained. Now, as I told him that Sandor had spirited the Egg away to London with plans involving a human sacrifice, Ethan frowned with concern. But instead of speaking, he moved closer and slid an arm around my waist. His other hand played with a strand of hair beside my face.

Ignoring him, I continued my story. I told him I meant to follow Sandor to London and get the Egg back.

The insipid elevator music was only serving to increase my agitation. I needed Ethan to agree to help me. I didn't want to come off as desperate, but that's exactly what I was.

"Well, what do you think?" I asked, wringing my hands.

Ethan's warm body was very close to mine now, and he brushed his thumb across my lips.

"Ethan, stop. I need you to listen to me. Did you hear what I've been saying?"

"Yes, I heard. But do we have to talk shop right now? Let's just leave it for a moment. . . ." He nudged my hair aside and bent his face to my neck.

I stopped him, pushing back gently but firmly. "No. I need to know now. Will you help me?"

He paused. He looked up into my eyes, then straightened, face serious for once, with a hint of regret. "No," he said. The elevator doors opened. We both exited.

"What—what do you mean, *no*? Just no? That's it?" I stared at him with bewilderment.

"Yep. That's it." He checked the number on the key card and walked down the hall noting room numbers.

"Maybe you didn't hear what I was telling you," I said, following behind him. I needed to make him understand. I leaned against the wall beside the door Ethan was opening. "These guys are really bad. You know that—this is Caliga we're talking about. And this is really important. Somebody's life is at stake."

"Listen, Montgomery, I told you before, I think you should leave this one alone. There's nothing to be gained by it. Why would you risk your neck for a bunch of Bible relics?" The room key card clicked and he opened the door.

"Ethan, that's not the point." I looked down, shaking my head, following him into the room. It smelled of starched sheets and shower gel and the air was cold—the heat hadn't been turned on yet. "What matters is that it's wrong. And, more importantly, someone's life is at stake. And all of that is my fault. I need to make it right—"

"Stop." He smiled and took my chin and gently turned my face up to his. "Listen to what I'm telling you, Montgomery. Not only do *I* not want to do it, I don't think *you* should do it, either."

I frowned, searching his face. This was not going the direction I needed it to. I flopped my handbag down on the mahogany desk. "I don't understand. You helped me when I needed you to break into York Security. Why did you do that?"

He shrugged. "Because it was fun. And because I knew it could be done. It wasn't about being a hero, it was just about getting a job done. Plus, let's face it, Montgomery, I was interested in spending time with you." He flashed a raffish smile. "I don't do things without a good reason."

"And helping people isn't a good reason?"

He shrugged, saying nothing.

I sat down on the end of the bed. "Ethan, this is really important. If you're a good person, you'll help me with this."

There was a very long pause. Ethan looked slightly confused. "Whoever said I was a good person, Montgomery?"

I blinked, staring at him. *Oh. Right.* Suddenly, everything was clear to me about Ethan.

He sat on the bed next to me and began kissing my neck again. "Now," he said in a low voice, "let's see if we can get you to forget about all that stuff." His warm, rough hand slid under my shirt, up the small of my back. "Or maybe, you can try to convince me a little more. . . ."

I stood then, peeling his hands away. "No, Ethan. I don't think so." I reached for my handbag.

"Montgomery, come on," he said, an edge of impatience in his voice.

"See you around, Ethan." I swung my handbag over my shoulder, walked out to the hallway and pushed the elevator button. It bonged and illuminated. I frowned with confusion as I waited for the elevator car. Had I been mistaken about Ethan? Despite his smoldering eyes and swagger and criminal tendencies, was he all wrong for me? I felt a surprising pinch of disappointment in my chest at that thought.

Not that it mattered now. I was still in a pickle.

And I still needed help. However, now there was only one other person I knew with the skills to pull this off. I swallowed and felt a wave of nausea. This was not going to be good.

An hour later I climbed out of a cab and stood on the sidewalk, beneath my umbrella, peering into the coffee shop. There she was, right on time. *Well, this was going to be agonizing.* But I had no other options, so I took a deep breath and walked in.

"Hi, Brooke," I said grimly, walking over and standing next to her table.

Brooke looked up from her latte and *Vanity Fair* magazine. "Hello, Cat," she said. There was a mischievous twinkle in her eye, and her face was full of curiosity. "Have a seat."

The coffee shop was small and smelled of newspapers and freshly roasted coffee beans. I wished, now, I'd selected a venue that was licensed. This conversation would be much better with something stiffer than a cappuccino. I took a seat and decided to dive right in. "Listen, Brooke, I called you because I've got a problem."

"Just the one?"

"Ha. Funny. Anyway, listen. I know your mission in life these days is to screw me. But I'm hoping you can put that aside for a moment, in the name of a much more important pursuit." She rolled her eyes and deliberately flicked a page in her magazine. I wasn't deterred.

"There's a job in London. It's a really big job. And—well, I can't do it alone. You're the only person with the skills to pull it off."

She blinked. And then her face spread into a Cheshire cat grin. "Wait. Wait. You want *my* help?"

My skin crawled at the smug look on her face. "Okay, forget it. You're right. It was a stupid idea. This was a total mistake." Honestly, what had I been thinking? I rose abruptly to leave.

She watched me gather my things and then said, "Wait." She grasped my wrist and motioned me to sit again. She looked thoughtful. "Why don't you tell me a little more."

I screwed my eyes tight and war waged in my head. But I had no real choice here. I sat back down. Looking Brooke directly in the eye, I told her about the Aurora Egg and the Caliga Rapio. I kept things vague, reluctant to tell her too much.

And then I paused, cringing inside, waiting for her response. Here, I expected Brooke to laugh and be on her way.

Instead, she licked her bottom lip, nodded, and said this: "All right, Cat. I'll help you." And she wasn't joking.

Chapter 34

Naturally, I was immediately suspicious. "Why?" I asked Brooke, my eyes becoming slits.

Brooke shrugged. "Truthfully, I've been getting bored." She fiddled with her coffee spoon. "I'd love an assignment, I've been itching for a challenge. Dabbling with this FBI work is diverting . . . but it's just not the same. Of course no agencies will work with me now. I don't have many options."

She stated this flatly, like she didn't care. But I could tell by the tightness in her mouth that this was a difficult admission.

So, it was as I suspected. Her career had been left in shreds. And I could see in her face exactly how much that had broken her. How much it had left her an empty shell of a person. And I got that. Because it was exactly how I would feel.

I didn't know if I could trust Brooke. Actually, let's be honest. I was quite confident that I *couldn't* trust her. However, one thing I did know about Brooke was that she was an excellent thief. And she aimed to succeed, whatever the job. The reasonable part of me was whispering in my ear that it was a mistake trusting her and working with her. The other part knew I didn't have a choice.

Once we'd agreed, we wasted no further time. Brooke used her cell phone to book seats on the next direct flight to London. Which happened to be leaving late that evening.

My mind whirred. I had a lot of work to do before departure. And so did Brooke. She pulled out a pen and was busy scribbling notes and lists.

"Okay. Meet you at the airport?" I said, gathering up my handbag and rising.

She looked up. "You're on. Meet you there."

Back in my secret room I ransacked drawers and cupboards, packing quickly. As I rummaged in my closet I dialed Lucas, my tech guy, and flicked my phone to hands-free.

"Lucas, I'm going on a trip overseas," I said when he answered the phone. "And there are a couple of items I'm going to need on the other side—things I can't bring with me on an airplane. Grappling hooks and glass cutters and such. Can you help me?" Lucas was stationed in Minneapolis, the tech lab headquarters. The lab had branches and contacts all over the world.

"Sure thing, Cat. Got a list?"

I rattled off a menu of bits and pieces I would need for this job—the sorts of things that would trigger severe eye twitching in the first airport security agent to spot them on the CTX scanner screens. And would have me facing some rather awkward questions.

Lucas said he would do his best to have them all waiting for me at our hotel.

I hung up the phone and continued packing and planning. I worked away steadily, partly because there was precious little time. Mostly because I was afraid that if I stopped to think about what I was doing the tendrils of fear that I could feel curling around the edges of my consciousness would gain strength, coil and crumble the fragile stone house of my determination.

But there was something else nagging at me. When I finished gathering my equipment I glanced at the clock on the microwave. Thirteen minutes past three. I had just enough time. I decided to deal with it, head on.

I drove to the yacht club. Ever since my disastrous interview, my father had refused to talk to me. I found him waxing the sailboat; it was hauled up in the boatyard and he was preparing it for winter. It had stopped raining a couple of hours ago but the air was still fresh with it. Light was fading and growing streaky, and it was cold.

I pulled my sweater tightly around me. The boatyard smelled of dirt and wind and wax.

My dad rubbed the hull with a soft cloth, using long, measured strokes. His face was peaceful as he performed his meditative task. I breathed out slowly and quietly. "Hi, Dad," I said, walking up beside him.

He raised his head. "Oh hi, Cat." His eyebrows lifted slightly with surprise. He then chewed the inside of his cheek. His tranquil expression took on a shadow. "I wasn't expecting you tonight."

I nodded. "Can I talk to you, for a minute?"

"Sure. I need a break anyway." He smiled, faintly, and my heart tightened. He was trying.

I hopped up on a nearby stool. My legs dangled like a kid's. He dragged a wooden crate across the ground and sat on it. "I really need another chance to explain, Dad."

His eyebrows knitted together and he looked down at his hands. My dad's hands were big and strong, darkened by the sun and weathered from years of hauling sail rope and holding onto the backs of kids' bicycle seats. He didn't stop me, so I continued.

"Being a thief is what I do best. It's what I was made to do."

Two scornful lines deepened between his eyebrows. "That's ridiculous. It's illegal. It's not a way of life."

"For me, it is."

"Cat, you deserve a normal life, you deserve to be happy."

I looked down. "Actually, Dad, I don't." I made a fist and felt the edge of Penny's ring digging into the soft tissue of my finger.

My father, of course, balked. "Don't be ridiculous."

How could I even begin to explain this?

My stomach tightened like a reef knot. "Dad, it was my fault Penny died. And ever since then, I've been trying to make up for that."

"What are you talking about?"

"She was out there because of me. She needed me to steal something." My dad flinched. "It would have been so easy for me. But I wouldn't do it. I had decided that this thing I could do, stealing, was wrong. So she tried to do it instead. And the universe showed me my mistake.

"All she needed me to do, Dad, was be true to myself. There's one thing in this world I'm good at, and I have to honor that. Penny knew it. But I thought I knew better."

I bit my lip and kept going. "Ever since then I've honored Penny by not turning my back on my true calling. And I've been living with the hope that, one day, I will be able to atone for the fact that her death was my fault."

And then, I thought, maybe I'd be worthy of true happiness. The brief romance I'd had with Jack, the fact that it had failed and broke my heart was just proof that I did not deserve the fairy-tale ending. But . . . maybe someday.

I waited. My dad said nothing for a while.

"Cat—I don't know what to think. *Penny* knew about this? That's what she was trying to do when she—" His voice choked off. He shook his head. "I can't believe it."

I fiddled with the edge of my sweater. "If it reassures you in any way, I have rules for myself. I never steal anything that's not insured. I never steal from anyone who would go hungry. And I never steal frivolously. I'm still a good person, Dad. I'm just doing what I do best in this world. And isn't that what you always wanted for us? To do our best?"

He looked up at me. His eyes were creased with anguish, but he managed a small smile.

"But what's wrong with a fine, legitimate career? Maybe you don't want to be an accountant. But what about, say, becoming a teacher? That would be a good life for you, wouldn't it?"

"Dad—I don't want *fine*. I don't want *good*. That's not enough for me. I want to be *the best*. And being a thief—I could be the best." I twisted the edge of my sweater into my fists. "As long as I'm a thief, I'll never be ordinary. I don't want to have a mediocre life. I don't want to be an average person, with average accomplishments, and a so-so life."

The tissues around his eyes were pinched and taught; he looked tired. He was trying hard to understand, I could see that.

I pressed on, because I had one more thing I needed to tell him. "I'm going away on a trip, Dad. I'm leaving tonight. It's for a job,"

I said gently. He recoiled as if struck; he knew what *job* referred to. "This one is different, though. I'm not actually getting paid for this one. I'm just trying to make something right. If I succeed I'll be correcting a very old wrong."

He rubbed his jaw, but still said nothing. I slid down from my stool and walked to stand beside him. I grasped his rough hand in mine.

"There are some truly evil people in this world, Dad, but I'm not one of them. I know I'm not exactly following the rules of society as they've been traditionally laid out but, I swear, I'm still a good person. Your approval has always meant the world to me. So I'm here today to ask you: can you find it, somewhere in your heart, to support me on this?"

I took a deep breath. I was finished. I felt wrung out, yet somehow, hopeful. I stood staring at my father, holding his hand. My final question hung in the air.

There was a long silence.

In those moments, in my mind, there was a heartfelt hug. Tears. And gruffly mumbled statements of unconditional love. *If that's what you really need to do to be happy . . .*

In the real world my father looked at me and he said, "No, Cat. I just can't."

My chest crushed inward and I closed my eyes.

"I'm sorry," he said, and his voice cracked. He released my hand. "It's just too much. I'm afraid for you, yes, for your safety. Of course. But more than that, I just can't understand your moral choice. I didn't think your mother and I had raised you like this."

I gazed into his face. His eyes were oceans of regret and disappointment. "Of course, you're an adult," he said. "And you can do whatever you choose. I'm not going to try to stop you."

I nodded, not trusting my voice.

"But I'm not giving you my blessing. And"—he paused here, briefly—"I really don't want to hear any more about it."

And that was all there was to it. As I left the boatyard, my eyes stung and I blinked against the low, cold October sun.

Chapter 35

Jack walked briskly toward the airport from his parked car, wondering what this meeting would hold. He checked his watch eagerly and sped up a little, breathing in the smell of jet fuel. God knows he needed some distraction after the afternoon he'd had. And, at this point, anything would be an improvement over standing in the pouring rain having your beating heart ripped out of your chest.

Oliver Cole and Wesley Smith had made it sound urgent that Jack come to them tonight. Maybe there was some news? A development with the Fabergé? Jack crossed the road in front of the terminal, cutting it very close between two oncoming cars. One of the drivers blared his horn and yelled something incomprehensible, but Jack didn't slow down. He passed through the gliding doors, out of the night air and into the fluorescent-lit world of the airport terminal. The terminal smelled of floor polish, carpet, and stale coffee.

They hadn't told him to pack a bag but he had, anyway. He was ready for anything. He found them quickly, where they said they'd be in the international departures lounge. His badge admitted him past the security checkpoint. Jack slowed his pace, strolled over to them and took a seat nearby. He waited, keenly.

"It's over, Jack," said Oliver Cole. "The Egg is gone——overseas. Sandor and the Caliga have taken it to London."

Jack blinked. "Oh."

"But the good news, here, is that you're off the hook. We don't need you anymore. The case is now in the hands of our team over there."

Jack listened and said nothing. Of course, he should have felt relieved. Should have been happy that he was free now. But he didn't. He felt a failure, and he felt incomplete—like walking away from a card game when there was money on the table.

Jack had started to believe in this quest—beyond his obligation. He glanced down at the small overnight bag he'd packed. It looked pathetic sitting there on the seat beside him. Like a girl waiting to be asked to dance.

"What happens now?" Jack asked. "What are your plans?"

"Well, we're going to London to meet up with the team. They're already doing the groundwork."

"So what's the story? Where is it in London? Do you know?" He looked at Wesley.

Wesley nodded. "We finally tracked down the old prophecy that the Caliga are following." He handed Jack a folded piece of paper. Jack read it.

The Gifts, twice taken, will at last release their Mysteries.
The Thief will sacrifice to unlock the Secrets, at the place of
Time's origin. A place named for Stephen, first martyr.

Jack looked up. "Where did you get this?"

"We hacked into FBI e-mail. Looks like this has officially become a case now. And the agent heading it is Nicole Johnson."

Jack's eyebrows shot up. But he shouldn't have been surprised. She had, after all, asked him about it a few times. "Okay, so what does it mean? Twice taken?"

"We figure that refers to the fact that it was stolen in the first place, long ago, and now it's been stolen again."

A muffled announcement came over the PA system, last boarding call for flight AF275 to Paris. "And the place of time's origin?" Jack asked.

"We know they've gone to London. The obvious connection is the international date line at Greenwich. And, to confirm that, there's an old church and school in Greenwich, just down the hill from the royal observatory, and it's called St. Stephen's."

"Ah. The last line of the prophecy." Jack looked between the two men. "Did you figure this out all by yourselves?"

Wesley looked slightly sheepish. "No."

"Nicole?"

He nodded. "She had a source who supplied the answers, apparently."

Jack frowned, wondering about Nicole's source. Could it be Brooke? There was something about this—the hacked-in e-mail, the prophecy—that bothered Jack, but he couldn't quite place it. Besides, he had other questions. "Won't the FBI be all over this, then?" he asked.

"No. Nicole's supervisor is ignoring it—he's not taking Nicole's source seriously." Jack nodded. That was how her department tended to operate.

Cole and Wesley told Jack, then, that to protect him they would sever their communication channel with him, wipe it clean. There would be no official record of their relationship. That was why they had called him for this one last meeting.

"You won't be able to contact us," Cole said. "Should a need ever arise in the future, we will contact you. But you're under no obligation. We appreciate what you have done for us thus far."

They were words Jack should have been happy and relieved to hear. But, somehow, they made him feel worse. After Jack left the departure lounge he carried his sorry little bag to the airport bar before heading home.

What was he going to do now? Jack wondered, watching the bartender pour his Scotch. He took a sip, feeling waves of open ocean swell around him. He was a man adrift, bobbing like a cork. And only mere hours ago he'd been so certain of his bearing. Now, his compass had dropped overboard.

He swallowed another burning sip and looked up. The LCD television hanging above the bar captured his drifting focus. It was the *BBC World News*. Headlines ran across the bottom in ticker-tape fashion. The sports anchor was reviewing highlights of the World Cup game between Brazil and England. The picture then flicked to politicians standing in front of Westminster, the parliamentary buildings.

Jack frowned at this. It tugged at his mind, as though he should be remembering something—but he couldn't quite think what. He took a final sip, placed money on the bar and left, lost in thought.

I arrived at the airport and immediately went to the check-in counter. In the terminal, sounds bounced off the polished floor and around the cavernous ceiling. Luggage cart wheels squeaked. Ribbon-bordered lineups of restless travelers snaked across the floor. The faint roar of jet engines rumbled outside.

I sipped a stale, horrible cup of coffee and scanned the area for Brooke. I began to panic—*she's not here, she changed her mind*—and I had to calm myself down. My insides were simmering and rumbling, like a pot of pasta sauce on a stove top when you hear it starting to seethe. You know any minute it's going to boil and let out a great splat all over your ceramic backsplash.

I took a deep breath.

Major nerves were not going to help me now. I had to focus. Then I saw Brooke, striding toward me down the long gleaming foyer, toting a Louis Vuitton Pullman.

I nodded to her and we moved to join the check-in line. But as I turned, my eyes popped wide. Standing beside a row of luggage carts, smiling at me with a crooked grin, was Ethan Jones.

I was too dumbfounded to move, so Ethan strolled over to me. He had a small carry-on bag with him.

"You—you changed your mind?" I asked.

He shrugged. "Looks that way."

There was a polite clearing of the throat behind my right shoulder. I turned. Brooke was waiting, expectantly, eyebrow raised. "Someone you know, Cat?"

"Um, yes, right—Brooke, Ethan," I said, introducing them. "Ethan is a . . . *colleague*, at AB&T."

Brooke inclined her head appreciatively. "You don't say."

"Brooke is going to be helping me with this, um, job," I said to Ethan. "I mean—helping *us*, I guess?"

Suddenly, what had felt like *Mission Impossible* now seemed a lot more possible. With three of us we had a fighting chance. I watched while Ethan spoke to Brooke, as she asked him about his experience and history with AB&T. He glanced at me and I mouthed "Thank you." He grinned and winked.

After checking in and going through the security checkpoints, we located seats in the waiting concourse of Gate 32. I took the opportunity to pop to the restroom. "I'll be right back," I said to them. On my return I passed a bar, partially tucked behind plate glass walls. Ice cubes chinked as they dropped in glasses, people lounged at tables with newspapers and drinks. Bottles filled the space behind the bar, jewel-like, filled with colored liquids like an old-fashioned apothecary. And there, sitting at the nickel-plated bar and clutching a glass of whiskey, was Jack.

I stopped dead. What was he doing here? Should I go in and talk to him?

No. Bad idea. I'd have to explain why I was at the airport. Besides, he did not look in the mood for company. I experienced an agitated, torn feeling.

If I wasn't going to talk to him I had to move. If he saw me standing here staring at him, that would be bad. I tucked in against the wall. I noticed a drinking fountain and bent down to it. As the cool water touched my lips I turned my eyes up. I could still see him. His hair was unkempt, clearly hadn't seen a comb that day, and he was showing slight stubble. He looked miserable and lost and I had no idea why. And this made me sad. Truth was, I didn't know what was going on with Jack anymore. I just wasn't a part of his life.

I experienced an urge to comfort him, to walk into the bar and tell him that I loved him. That I have always loved him. My left foot took a step forward. But then I hesitated.

I flashed back to the last time I'd seen Jack, in the cloakroom, when he'd pushed me away. The pain of that still stung. I couldn't stand the thought of being rejected by him. And, let's face it, why *wouldn't* he reject me?

A small voice inside said: *I don't deserve him.* Not yet, anyway.

I stood immobile for two further heartbeats, then tore myself away and walked to the departure gate. I didn't look back.

I forced myself to sit. Imaginary ropes held me down to the waiting room chair. I borrowed a magazine from Brooke, compelling myself to read about liposuction and eyelash extensions and celeb gossip and this season's boots. I tried my best to ignore the feelings that were hovering in my peripheral vision like a spider in the corner of the room.

"So listen, ladies," Ethan said, leaning in to us. "After you came to me about this job, Montgomery, I did some digging and made a few calls. Interested in hearing what I found out?"

Brooke looked up, an eyebrow raised. "By all means."

This was a great idea. Talking about the job would be a perfect distraction. Not to mention necessary to the task at hand.

Ethan nodded and removed a file from his carry-on bag. I blinked. A file? This was a whole new side of Ethan. "From the intelligence I could gather, they've secured themselves within Westminster Palace."

Brooke blinked. "The Parliament buildings themselves? *Big Ben?*"

"That's right."

"Well, that sounds easy enough to break into," I said flatly. "Nondescript. Unnoticeable."

Ethan ignored my sarcasm and pressed on. "Sandor has a minister in his pocket. So they're using a wing of Westminster Palace. They're in the Victoria Tower, which is where the parliamentary archives are kept. It's got the tightest security of the entire building. From the reports I could gather, they haven't set foot out of there since arriving in London, so the Aurora must be up there with them."

I was inclined to agree. "I'm sure Sandor wouldn't let it out of his sight, or his possession."

At that moment our flight was called. Brooke, Ethan, and I boarded the plane and slid into the plush leather seats of business class. On this size of aircraft, the middle section of business class had three seats together. I sat between Brooke and Ethan. It grew stuffy as we waited for takeoff—in spite of the deafening ventilation that drowned out the piped-in music. Flight attendants bustled up and down the aisles as passengers jockeyed for position in the stash-your-carry-on game.

Just as I was settling into my seat, my phone rang.

"Hello, darling." It was my mother. "Listen, I want you to come with me tomorrow to get Reiki done. This girl I've found is a genius."

"Sorry, Mom. Can't. I'm on a plane right now." I admit, it gave me a small pleasure to be able to brush my mother off with a bona fide excuse.

"*Are* you? Where are you going? And with whom?"

"London. I'm going with some . . . colleagues." I glanced at Brooke, seated to my right. Ever since the bookstore signing, my mother had been on my case to be more like the famous thief who clearly had her life together and always had fabulous hair. "Brooke Sinclair, actually, is one," I said.

"*Really?*"

"Listen, Mom—don't mention anything about this to Templeton, okay? If you're talking to him, that is. Which you *shouldn't* be, by the way."

"Certainly," she said.

Ethan leaned over to me. "Cat, put your tray up, we're taking off soon," he said. I nodded.

"Listen," said my mother. "I don't want you going anywhere near that Hackney neighborhood in London. I was just watching this program on television and it's a very dangerous place. . . ."

"Mom, I'm not going to Hackney. I'm going to a very safe neighborhood. Westminster, actually. You know, Big Ben? I'll be fine."

"Hmm. Well, more importantly, dear, did you take a Bonine? You know you get airsick sometimes."

I rolled my eyes. "Mom, I haven't been airsick since I was five."

"Did you remember to pack the new grappling hook I bought you? I read excellent reviews about it—"

"Yes. I packed it," I lied.

"Oh, and, darling, do you have an umbrella? It's terribly rainy in London this time of year."

"Mom, I'm hanging up now."

"Good luck, sweetheart!"

I turned off my phone just in time for takeoff. The lights were dimmed and we were jiggling and jostling as the plane lumbered down the runway. There was a pause and then the engines roared louder and I felt pressed back in the seat, like there was an invisible hand on my sternum. We lifted up then, and everything felt lighter. We were on our way. I took a deep breath. The seat belt sign eventually bonged and turned off.

Within short order dinner was served: steaming hot beef bourguignon, crusty rolls, salad, chocolate cake, wine . . . but my food sat uneaten. I picked at the roll, drank most of the wine. After the trays were cleared and coffee was served, the lights dimmed. I looked around to see that, besides the three of us, everyone was plugged into headphones, gaze glued to miniscreens watching movies. Which left us free to talk business again.

Brooke reached forward and pulled out a quilted Chanel makeup bag. "Okay," she said, touching up her lip gloss in a tiny mirror. "So, Ethan, what do we know about security at Westminster?"

Ethan grinned. "I was hoping you'd ask." He withdrew a sheaf of documents. I smiled to myself. Ethan was thoroughly enjoying this.

Brooke paused in her grooming. "What's all that?"

"Intel. Recon. Blueprints and building schematics."

"Really?" She looked at me. "Impressive."

We discreetly sifted through floor maps and blueprints and satellite images and lists of CCTV locations and security systems, intruder alarms. One thing was obvious: this was not going to be easy. After looking everything over and making notes, I reclined in my seat. A yawn escaped my lips.

"We should probably get some sleep," Ethan said. "Big job ahead of us."

Brooke nodded, but continued frowning at the documents. She pulled out a pencil.

"Oh, hang on," Ethan said, flipping through his folder. "One more thing. Here's the file on the intended sacrifice victim."

Brooke snapped her head up and looked over her reading glasses— the reading glasses I was confident she didn't actually need but I had to admit looked very stylish, with their square plastic frames and *Donna Karan* engraved on the arm. "Sacrifice?"

I nodded grimly. "The Caliga believe they need a human sacrifice in order to unlock the power of the Gifts," I explained.

"Oh. Well, naturally," Brooke said.

"She'll be a prisoner, when we get in there," Ethan said. "We'll have to find a way of getting her out, too."

"How, um, mythical. Is she a virgin?" asked Brooke.

"That I don't know," said Ethan. "But here's the file."

He handed it to me and I flipped it open. I looked at the picture stapled to the inside cover. And found myself staring at Nicole Johnson's face.

Chapter 36

Ethan related the details on where they were holding Nicole, but all I heard was the voice of Charlie Brown's teacher.

"Oh. My. God," I said quietly, staring at the photograph.

Ethan glanced at me sharply. "Do you *know* her?"

I nodded. Brooke snatched the file from my hand. "That's Nicole Johnson," she said, looking at the photograph.

Ethan studied it again. "Oh, you're right. I remember her from the golf tournament. I hadn't really looked closely at the face."

I scraped my teeth together and closed my eyes. *Really?* Did it really have to be her that I needed to save? How did this happen?

I puzzled things back into place. Sandor must have grabbed her because he knew she was following him. She was the enemy, working for the FBI, and she was getting close to finding out the truth. It had been a smart move on Sandor's part, I had to admit, in the tradition of killing two birds and all that. Getting rid of the FBI on your back and landing yourself a sacrifice candidate, all in one go.

And then I remembered it had been me who had drawn Sandor's attention to Nicole's presence at the convenience store, when she was staking him out. I closed my eyes. This was my fault, too.

Ethan studied me with concern. "No worries, Montgomery. We'll get her out. She'll be fine."

I liked Nicole. I did. I told myself firmly this didn't change a thing. But just to recap: I was about to put myself in extreme peril and make a potentially career-ending move that involved teaming up with my sworn enemy and saving the woman who stole the love of my life.

Perfect.

It was a bright, frosty day and Jack was ready for a fresh start. In the kitchen he snapped a crisp newspaper, scanning the headlines and drinking coffee.

Life would go back to normal, Jack told himself. He would go back to his regular job as an FBI agent. And this time, with no conflict. He would go back to a life free from criminal entanglement. No Wesley. No Cole. No Cat. He felt a twinge there, but firmly chalked it up to heartburn from the coffee he'd just gulped.

Standing before the hallway mirror, he straightened his tie and plucked off the piece of tissue from his freshly shaved neck. Ready to go.

And then, the phone rang. Jack picked up the receiver resting on the front hall table. "Hello?"

"Jack, is that you?" said a woman's voice. "Judy Montgomery here—Cat's mother."

There was silence for several seconds. Cat's mom? What was she calling for? "Um, hi, Judy." He rubbed his face and frowned. "How have you been?"

"Fine, fine. But listen, Jack. I need your help. Catherine is flying to London for a job. I spoke to her last night when she was on the plane. And the truth is, I'm worried. I've been stewing about it all night. It's something Templeton doesn't know about. I don't understand it. She told her father she's not getting paid for this job. And that she's trying to make something right—correct a very old wrong. Do you have any idea what she's talking about?"

Jack's bright-morning feeling began curling up at the edges and shriveling away. "I—I'm not sure, Judy. Was she by herself?"

"I heard a man's voice in the background. He said her name."

Ethan, Jack thought, with a kick to the stomach.

"Oh, and Brooke," Cat's mother added. "You know, Brooke Sinclair?"

Brooke? Alarm bells sounded. "Are you sure?"

"Yes, I'm sure. I don't know, Jack, I have a bad feeling. She made me promise not to tell Templeton. Which . . . is why I'm calling you. She didn't say anything about not telling *you*."

Damn. Cat had gone to London to get the Fabergé back. That's what she'd meant by correcting an old wrong. She must have found out the truth somehow. Jack wasn't surprised, really; it made perfect sense that Cat would do this. The girl had grit, that was certain.

"Do you have any idea where they're going? Could it be Greenwich, perhaps?" He cringed, waiting for the answer.

"No," Judy said.

Jack exhaled with relief.

"Westminster Palace, actually," she said. "You know, Big Ben and all that?"

Westminster, Jack thought, frowning. Something about that made him think—

Wait. Jack dashed down the hall, cradling the phone. He scrabbled on his desk and found the piece of paper Wesley had given him, the transcribed old prophecy about the Gifts. As he reread the words, his skin prickled and crawled. Something was wrong. *The origin of time.* That could be—

Oh no. He quickly pulled up a browser on his computer and Googled St. Stephen's, punching the keys. He sat back hard in his desk chair as he stared at the first search result: St. Stephen's chapel, on the site of Westminster. . . .

The *time* reference could be the great clock. Big Ben.

Jack ground his teeth. Wesley and Cole were in the wrong place. He heard a woman's voice, tinny in his ear, and realized that Cat's mother had been speaking the whole time.

"I suppose if she's with Brooke," Judy was saying, "she'll be fine. That girl is very capable. . . ."

Brooke. Jack's blood ran cold. It was a trap; it had to be. Brooke could easily have fed false information to Nicole about the prophecy and Greenwich. And because of that, Cole and Wesley, and the FBI for that matter, had been sent off to the wrong location. The final part of the plan would be to accompany Cat to the correct location, Westminster, where Sandor was waiting.

Cat was in great danger.

Jack felt a hot flush of fear and anger. It was stupid of Cat to do this. It was reckless and risky.

Cat's mother was still talking in Jack's ear. "There's something else I feel the need to say, Jack. And I know Cat is not going to be happy with me for this, and this may not be the best time to mention it, but the truth is: she has always loved you."

"That's, um, kind of you to say, Judy. But she seems quite happy in her new relationship now. I'm sure it was Ethan Jones's voice you heard on the airplane."

"Ethan?" Judy said. She laughed. "Oh goodness, she's not in a *relationship* with that fellow. I believe she had a little fling, but it was nothing serious."

Jack frowned, confused. "How do you know that?"

"I have ways," she said lightly.

Jack's stomach flip-flopped. Could this be true?

"You know," Judy said, "I'm ever so glad I decided to phone you, Jack. I feel much better. You've been very reassuring."

When Jack got off the phone with Cat's mother, he pressed back into his office chair. He tugged his tie to loosen it, and rubbed his face. So much for a fresh start.

Jack picked up the phone to send an urgent message to Wesley. But when he tried, the call was blocked. He stared at the phone a moment, frowning. And then he remembered. Total severing of communication. He had no way of contacting Wesley.

Jack leaned forward, buried his head in his hands, and scrubbed his hair. He sat back and gazed out the window. So. What was he going to do now?

Chapter 37

My leg muscles tightened as I gained purchase on a foothold and hoisted myself several inches upward. I was a hundred and fifty feet off the ground, midway to the top of Victoria Tower, the tallest tower in Westminster Palace. The Thames glittered in the street-lights, far below. I could see the great clock, the one everyone calls Big Ben, lustrous atop the tower opposite me. Double-decker buses rumbled across Westminster Bridge; a big black cab honked faintly in the night.

The cold stone was carved with ornate Gothic features like leaves, birds, and gargoyles, which made for excellent climbing. An English drizzle hung in the air, soaking into my black Lycra.

Brooke and I were climbing together, tucked into the shadowy side of the tower, hidden from street view. My heart beat a steady clip and my limbs moved rhythmically. I felt like I was full of electricity.

Mostly, this felt like an insane idea. Like we didn't stand a chance. But there was a faint, tiny hope—and that's what I was clinging to.

After we'd arrived at Heathrow Airport that afternoon, a London cab had carried us away from the airport and into the city itself. The cab dropped us off at our home base, the Savoy Hotel. That was where we made our plans.

When we checked in, a package was waiting for me at the front desk. A plain brown-wrapped box from Lucas, containing a full com-plement of all my favorite tools: a climbing harness, grappling hook,

Manolos with a tranquilizing dart in the stiletto . . . everything. Just as I requested.

"Okay, here's how we're going to do it," Brooke said, pulling out a blueprint from Ethan's file and a notebook jammed with written notes. "So first of all—"

"When did you come up with this?" I asked her. I stared at the notes, frowning with confusion.

"On the plane."

"What? In your sleep?"

"I stayed awake."

Ethan and I exchanged a glance. A smile curled my lips. This was the old Brooke. The Brooke without agenda or artifice. This was the reason I asked her to help me.

She continued. "You know about misdirection?" she asked, spreading sheets out on an old metal table. "The way a magician uses one hand to distract the audience while the other hand does the trick?"

I frowned slightly, wondering where this was going. "Sure."

"Well, that's going to be us," she said.

We listened and she described in detail how we were going to get in. She stood up and started pacing as she laid out the plan, and then she reached the point where we get to the safe.

"And, Cat," she said, turning to me, "you'll take it from there."

"Me? Why?"

"Because you're the best at safecracking," she said plainly, without looking up.

"I—am?" A thrill passed through my insides at the compliment.

"I mean, no *offense,* Ethan Jones," Brooke said, not looking particularly concerned whether she was offending anyone or not. "But I don't know enough about your skills. That's why I've got you positioned here, to start, as a lookout." She put a finger on the schematic.

Ethan smiled wryly. "No offense taken, Brooke. And you're quite right. Montgomery *is* the best at safecracking."

Brooke went on to outline the rest of the plan. My eyes widened as she laid out the details; I saw Ethan's do the same.

Now, the wind whipped all around us as we climbed Victoria Tower for the first stage.

"So, Cat," Brooke said, her voice coming in with a faint crackle through my earpiece. "We're about to save the life of the woman who stole your man. Interesting, isn't it?"

And there we had it. There was the other side of Brooke I knew and loved. I scraped my teeth together. "Brooke, shut up," I spat.

"What?" she said with mock innocence.

Ethan's voice came crackling through our earpieces. "Do you ladies think you could cut the chitchat and focus on the task at hand?" He was posted at the bottom of the tower, posing as a homeless guy on a nearby bench. We'd left him sipping cold coffee from a shelter-issue Styrofoam cup, buried under layers of grubby sweatshirts and a plaid blanket, clad in pink slippers and a deer hunter hat, face dirt smeared to the point of unrecognizability.

Actually, he was more than merely a lookout tonight. He had also sabotaged the nearby CCTV cameras with a precisely, yet surreptitiously, fired paintball gun.

There was silence for a stretch as we climbed higher. I glanced over at Brooke. For at least the fourteenth time, I questioned my judgment in bringing her with me. But could I have done this without her? A small voice, deep inside, answered *No*.

Anyway, the plan was already in motion. I just hoped I wouldn't live to regret the decision. I continued climbing; I reached my grip upward and found a handhold on a stone gargoyle.

Brooke cleared her throat. "So I can't help wondering, Cat, why you're taking this job so personally."

I rolled my eyes. "Brooke, do you mind? Maybe you could psychoanalyze me at another time?"

"Au contraire, I think this is the perfect time. Here we are, risking life and limb, to undo a job you already did. It just begs the question: *why?*"

"What do you mean, why? It just wasn't right, that's all. And you know that."

Brooke was quiet a moment. The only sounds were the groan of our ropes, my breathing, loud and rhythmic in my ears, and the wind.

"You know," Brooke said slowly, her tone pensive, "now that I think about it, you've always been a little obsessed with making things right, correcting the past, that sort of thing. What's that about, anyway?"

"Brooke, cut the Oprah babble please." A drop of sweat dripped into my eyes. It stung and blurred my vision. My leather gloves creaked as I gripped the rope.

"Wait a second," Brooke said. She stopped climbing and studied me. "It's Penny, isn't it? Your sister. I can't believe I didn't see it before. That's what this is all about. That's what it's *always* been about."

At the sound of Penny's name, storm clouds gathered in my chest. Once upon a time when Brooke and I had been partners, and friends, I told her all about Penny. I regretted that now, naturally.

"Brooke, stop. I do not want to discuss this. Especially not with you. And especially not right now."

But Brooke was on a roll. "Yes, I think that's it," she continued, with great excitement. "You always thought it was your fault that your sister died, I remember that now. So you think that by correcting other people's mistakes, you'll somehow be correcting your own mistakes." She continued scaling the wall and musing to herself. "What do you call that? It's like . . . redemption. Or, no—it's *atonement*. That's the word."

My left foot suddenly slipped off its hold. I let out a short grunt of surprise and gripped onto my handholds in panic, my heart in my throat.

"Montgomery? You okay?" Ethan said in the earpiece.

"I got it. No problem." But my blood felt icy.

I resumed climbing and cast a surreptitious glance at Brooke. She was looking at me with concern.

Without further talk we reached our destination—the twelfth floor of Victoria Tower. And we did it—miraculously—without killing each other. The twelfth floor was our destination because this was where, according to Ethan's intel, Nicole was being held. It was also the floor where the Fabergé was locked up.

I sliced into the window with a glass cutter, scraping a large circle. We climbed inside and found ourselves in a dark, dusty room. Moonlight filtered in through the windowpanes. This disused room didn't have any security per se, but once we got out to the hallway, we'd have to deal with CCTV security. We hooked ourselves up with anti-CCTV gadgets—with a twelve-foot radius, we wouldn't be seen as we moved. We reviewed the map one last time although, truth be told, it was already committed to both our memories.

First task: release Nicole.

We moved quickly and silently through the labyrinthine corridors, vigilant for patrolling guards. I flicked a glance at Brooke. Joke time was over now that we were inside. And Brooke was a professional, just as I remembered. Everything about her actions was slick and perfect and practiced. My tension reduced slightly. We were in complete sync.

At an access point we climbed up into the overhead vents. I gripped my fingers around the edge and pulled. My tendons tightened and shoulders burned as I pulled my weight up and into the ventilation shaft. I was in. Brooke followed. It was a dark, compact space and my knees pressed into the cold dusty metal of the shaft. We pulled down our night-vision goggles and begin clambering forward. I felt like a rat creeping through a science lab maze.

We slinked through the tunnel until we reached the room where Nicole should have been imprisoned. But the shaft stopped just outside the room.

We peered down through the grate. Two guards flanked the door. They wore flak jackets and carried submachine guns. One I was less worried about—the more muscular of the two. He wore a bored expression, his eyes moved little as he stared ahead. He wouldn't be much of a problem. The other was more of a concern: his eyes were brighter, he looked around constantly, and there was tension in his body like a coiled spring. His weight was forward—the other rested slightly back on his heels.

The smaller, more lethal one would need to be taken out first— the other could wait a few seconds. Brooke looked through the grate. "Dangerous one first?" she said.

"The one on the left?"

"Of course."

My heart omitted a beat as I levered the grate away. This was where a thief's ability to be truly silent was tested. We looked at each other, give a brisk nod, and dropped down together from above. We dropped first onto the dangerous one, executing a partner *shinobi* ambush maneuver to take him down and render him unconscious. The second, as predicted, had barely registered our presence at that point, and even then, was not able to move his muscle-clad frame fast enough to prevent our attack. He went out cold, quite easily.

I reached down and grabbed a key card from the guard's belt and slipped it into the reader. There was a *click,* a small light turned green, and I pushed open the heavy door.

Nicole sat in the middle of the tiny room on a wooden chair, tied up, gagged with a filthy rag, and blindfolded. She looked petrified, trembling in her chair. A quick scan of her face and body revealed no bruises or other visible injuries. Which was unexpected, but a relief.

The room was lit with a single garish fluorescent strip-light and it was cold. The space was mostly bare, apart from some shelving with ammonia and cleaning supplies. There was a smell of bleach, and mildew from an old mop in a bucket.

I pulled the rag from her eyes. She blinked and her gaze shifted between Brooke and me, her eyes wide with bewilderment. I untied the gag and Brooke put a finger to her mouth to indicate quiet. Nicole nodded.

As Brooke worked at the ropes that bound her arms, I crouched down at Nicole's feet to untie her. "Cat?" she whispered. "What are *you* doing here?"

"Cat is black ops," Brooke said smoothly. "She's been working with Jack. Top secret. That's why you didn't know anything about her." I flicked a glance at Brooke. That was actually good. Nicole looked satisfied.

We released her and she stood, rubbing her wrists. "What did you do about the guards? And how did you find me anyway? How did you get in here?"

"Okay, no more questions. You've got to get out of here," Brooke said.

"Here's a copy of the blueprint—can you make it to the Clock Tower? Right there?" I pointed to the map. Brooke was clipping an anti-CCTV mechanism to the back of Nicole's jeans.

"No, I want to help," Nicole said earnestly. "That Sandor guy is crazy, you know that? He keeps mumbling about making things right and correcting old wrongs. I heard him say something about being worthless unless he can fulfill his quest. He's completely fanatical."

I frowned.

"I want to help you stop him," Nicole said.

There were a lot of reasons why this would not work. Nicole's eyes were heavily shadowed; she was clearly exhausted. Not exactly the assistant I typically preferred. Besides, I generally did my best safecracking when I didn't have an FBI agent hanging over my shoulder.

"This is nonnegotiable, Nicole," Brooke said. "You'll meet us at the Clock Tower."

Nicole reluctantly agreed.

"If we're not there by three a.m.," I told her, "then you'll need to go without us. Here, this will help you escape." I handed her a small pack that contained a rappelling harness and rope.

"But wait until that time if you can," Brooke added. "If you try to escape too early, you might raise an alarm prematurely."

Nicole nodded, understanding. As she disappeared I watched her with a warm flush of relief, and pride. Whatever happened, she'd be safe now.

A tiny barb hooked itself onto my heart. She'd soon be back in Jack's arms. The truth was, he'd be a wonderful comfort. He always was to me.

Brooke and I dragged the guards into the utility closet. Each man measured roughly the weight of an adult mountain lion, so we had to do it together. I leaned back and pulled hard on one muscle-bound arm while Brooke pulled the other. Together we dragged them into the utility room and locked the door. We climbed back into the ventilation shaft, using a grappling hook and rope. The grate scraped lightly as we slid it closed. We were in darkness, once again.

The interminable crawl through the veins of the building began. After a short time my shoulders and thighs were cramping and I longed to stretch my back. Sweat clung to my neck and face, and I could taste the dust in my mouth.

At last we reached our destination. Below us was a large grate. I crawled up beside Brooke, we took off our night-vision goggles and peered down through the grid into the lobby of the vault.

We could see five security guards posted there, just outside the vault doorway. All five were fully armed, large as black bears, and ready to use whatever force necessary. I quailed; it would be impossible to take out five guards at once, without having one of them raise an alarm—or worse, fire up at us.

But this was where Ethan came in. I flicked my earpiece and spoke softly. "Okay, we're in place. Over to you."

There was a crackle and I heard Ethan's voice. "Check."

I held my breath and waited. Everything inside me was wriggling and jumping and sparking, but I had to hold it all back. Would this work? I wondered. Would we get caught?

And then, the silence was pierced by the high-pitched whine of an intruder alarm.

My heart leaped. *Perfect*. Right on cue. There was a cacophony beneath us—guards barking into walkie-talkies, orders being shouted, rapid boot steps. I hoped Ethan would be able to make a clean escape, as planned, after setting off the entry alarm, and make it up to the Clock Tower.

Brooke had the better vantage point. She signaled to me: three guards left. Okay. We could deal with that.

Brooke was the better shot. We agreed, using sign language, that she'd take out two guards and I'd do one. For this, we were using tranquilizer darts. They were microlight darts loaded with an ultra-fast tranquilizer. Virtually painless and unnoticeable by the target.

We aimed for the neck and fired. Brooke shot her two in rapid succession. I missed on my first try.

"Shit." I aimed again, and got him. But now there were going to be several seconds of time lag.

Brooke's two guards went down. Mine shouted in alarm. "Hey, what the—"

He glanced around urgently, then looked up, eyes wide, and

raised his gun. We backed off in panic. I cringed and squeezed my eyes shut. And then . . . *flump*. We peered over the edge. He was out cold on the marble tiles.

We dragged the grate away, and Brooke dropped silently down. I waited above, watching as she approached the massive steel vault door. The iris scanner was embedded in the wall beside the door. There were various ways of bypassing an iris scanner. A fake was naturally the best—a printed contact lenses. But a super-high-resolution photograph could do it, too.

Unfortunately we did not have the time nor the opportunity to make either of these things happen. So Brooke was going with an old-school method: disabling the control panel. She assured me she could do it.

I held my breath as she attempted it. It takes a watchmaker's touch to penetrate a control panel. She lifted the cover of the sensor. I could see her shoulders tense. She exhaled smoothly, controlling her breathing, and examined the exposed panel. My stomach tangled and twisted like a rope. But I watched with admiration as she manipulated the wires with a deft touch. She was doing a good job.

But good was suddenly not good enough.

A piercing alarm blared. A steel cage ripped up through the floor, surrounding Brooke. My heart choked as the bars of the cage rose straight up and crashed into the ceiling, plugging into steel receptacles, locking with a sickening clunk. Brooke was frozen. Her face was pale and turned upward, registering her utter entrapment.

Chapter 38

Boot steps thundered a rapid approach. I frantically replaced the grate that covered the air duct, concealing myself from view. I peered down through the thin slats and my breathing was shallow. I tasted coppery blood in my mouth; I must have bitten my tongue when the alarm went off. Half a dozen guards burst into the foyer and aimed a bristle of Heckler & Koch MP7s at Brooke. "Freeze! Hands up!"

My heart pummeled my rib cage as I watched, hidden, unable to do a thing. Brooke stood unmoving, facing the squadron. She held her hands up, face impassive. They all stayed like this for a minute in a horrible tableau. Then Sandor arrived. He strolled into the room with a face that was murderous and hard. He cast a disgusted glance at the unconscious guards and stepped over them. He approached the steel cage and fixed those hard eyes on Brooke. I could see his face clearly; I imagined that it was me he was looking at with that vicious gaze. It was the stare of a man who could snuff a life with a finger snap.

Sandor's nostrils flared as he crossed his arms. His posture was ramrod. He cast a completely different picture than when I'd first met him. My memory slid back to the loose-spined, round-shouldered, geeky and earnest boy-man I'd first met in the diner. How could one person be so elastic? It was like witnessing the metamorphosis of a soft, furry caterpillar—but not so much into a butterfly as a dragon.

Except it wasn't a transformation. The innocent Sandor had been a fake. And the fact that I hadn't seen that made me feel angry—and very stupid. I thought I was better than that. My guts twisted with fresh doubt about my capabilities.

"What the fuck is this?" Sandor said. His tone was quiet, seething. Like a tarp pulled taut over a writhing vat of scorpions.

Brooke stared at him without blinking. She folded her arms deliberately over her chest, then shrugged. It was a slow, deliberate movement. She was the picture of indifference, which was the polar opposite of how I felt at the moment. I noticed, however, that her fingers, tucked beneath her crossed arms, were stick straight. With this I knew she was as distressed as I was.

Sandor narrowed his eyes. They were locked like this a moment, then he placed a call. With curt instructions, biting off each word, he commanded the cage be released.

After a moment's pause the cage unhinged with several metallic clunks and sank down under the floor. He reset the security system by gazing into the biometric eyepieces. The vault was armed once again.

"Well, it was a nice try," he said to Brooke. He smiled, showing his teeth. I'd never noticed just how pointed his canine teeth were. The back of my neck prickled. "Bait and switch, was it?" he asked. "Too bad you weren't so adept at escape as your partner."

At this statement I felt a slight softening of the muscles in my shoulders and back. *Good.* Ethan hadn't been caught. That was something, at least.

The guards were shifting, murmuring. "What do you want to do with her?" one of them asked. I was desperate to know the very same thing. Panic rose in my chest as I wondered what was to stop them from killing her on the spot.

At that moment I heard a faint click in my ear, as Ethan returned to the line. "Stay calm, Montgomery," he said. He'd resumed a safe position, somewhere inside Westminster.

Sandor examined Brooke. "Tell me, Miss Sinclair—how did you decide who would be the decoy and who would do the job, between you two? I'm surprised Miss Montgomery didn't insist on being the one down here doing the dirty work."

Brooke said nothing, but she showed a flicker of a frown.

Sandor smiled. "Yes, Brooke, I know you're working with her. I

know the decoy was Cat Montgomery. Please do not deny it." He
paced a small, slow circle around Brooke. "Although I must say,
I'm surprised she recruited *you* for this job. I was under the impression you two were rivals."

Brooke shrugged. "You seem to have a lot of questions about Cat
Montgomery," she said. "Interested in her whereabouts, by any
chance?" Brooke loaded this question with meaning. She raised an
eyebrow.

Sandor stopped pacing. My heart was slamming itself up my
throat. Sandor stood still and rubbed his chin thoughtfully. "Are you
proposing a deal, Miss Sinclair?"

She examined her fingernails. "Maybe. It seems to me we have
some things to discuss." She looked at him. "Is there somewhere
we can go? This vault room is lovely, of course, but I've had a hard
night and I wouldn't mind a drink, someplace to put my feet up, perhaps. You must have somewhere more comfortable than this place.
Oh, and I'm starving."

The other men shifted, watching their boss for a signal. Sandor
scowled, apparently weighing his options. "All right," he said at last.
"Let's go."

Sandor turned and strode from the room. The guards handcuffed
Brooke and frog-marched her away through the steel double doors.
I watched, frozen in place, as the entire party exited, boots echoing
on the marble floor.

I allowed myself to breathe. And smile. Everything was going
exactly according to plan.

"No Sandor," I whispered as I gingerly lifted the grate away once
more. I heard Ethan chuckle softly in my earpiece. "Not the old bait
and switch. The bait, switch . . . and switch." I flicked on my anti-
CCTV device, lowered my rope and dropped silently to the floor.

Brooke's capture had been part of the plan. In the old warehouse,
she'd laid it all out. "They'll think I used a decoy to distract their attention. They'll think I then made a mistake, which triggered the
alarm. Once they've cleared me away they'll feel secure about having
foiled our plot. And in you go, Cat."

I chewed a fingernail as I listened to her plan. "You'll be putting yourself at major risk," I'd said.

"I can handle myself."

Brooke assured me she would be able to stay alive. "Sandor will want you dead, Cat," she'd said. "If he thinks I can help find you—it'll be worth keeping me alive."

Even now, as I approached the vault, this part of the plan felt shaky. How long could she sustain the bluff? I had to work fast; I didn't want to leave Brooke with them too long.

I faced the biometric lock and took a deep breath. Fortunately, I now had an ace in this department. While everyone had been standing beneath me, I'd been able to train a military-grade microcamera on Sandor's eyes and snap a high-resolution digital image of his irises.

I located that image within the memory of the camera. I zoomed in on the eyes. Brooke had been confident this would replicate an iris and I'd called my tech guy Lucas to corroborate that opinion. He'd agreed. The digital image would capture all the points and pigments of an iris's fibrous and vascular tissue, the pattern unique to each of us—much more detailed than a fingerprint.

Lucas and Brooke were both confident we could fool the sensor this way. As I held the screen in front of the scanner, my palms sweaty inside my gloves and my mouth dry, I wished I shared their confidence.

There was a second of silence. Everything seemed suspended. And then—*beep*. A pinpoint LED light on the sensor turned green and there was a sharp *click*. Steel slid over steel with a slick metallic sound and the door disappeared into a deep pocket. I exhaled with relief and slipped silently inside the vault.

The vault itself was a steel chamber, lit with spot halogens in the ceiling. It was empty except for a safe embedded in the far wall. The cold air carried a stale, metallic smell.

"I'm in," I whispered to Ethan.

I heard nothing through the earpiece. "Ethan? Can you hear me?" Still nothing.

Shit. I fiddled with my earpiece. Silence. What did that mean?

Had something happened to him? Or was it just a malfunctioning communication line? I squeezed my eyes tight. Not good. Could I go on? Or should I abort, right now? Indecision wrung my insides. How could I stop now? I was so close. Maybe he was just having trouble with his receiver. I couldn't scrap the whole thing because of that. I paused, thinking it out. Nothing had changed; we all knew the plan, we all knew what to do next.

I jammed my teeth together. *Do it, Cat.* I turned to my next task: cracking this safe.

And it was a mother. I stood in front of it, arms folded, surveying the lock mechanism. The technology of this safe was shiny and new. It matched the specs Ethan provided. A month ago I would have been tripped up by this safe, big time. However, thanks to a very helpful workshop, I was entirely up to speed. *Thank you,* Twelfth Annual Conference of the Museum Security Alliance.

I pulled my gloves taut about my fingers and cleared my mind. I had to forget about Sandor in his bloodlust, Brooke trapped with the Caliga, Nicole creeping along somewhere in the building, Ethan God knew where, and Jack . . . *no.* I shut it all out. All that existed was this safe. I heard blood pulsing in my ears and I breathed slowly, shutting out all other thoughts and images and focusing only on this safe.

I turned the wheel pack, feeling for the slightest amount of give. It would be a barely perceptible sensation. But this was just the first step.

Every safe can be cracked. You just needed to find the right rhythm, the right music. Safes are unique, each with its own resonance. Even factory-made, externally identical models.

Twenty minutes later pearls of sweat were materializing on my forehead. A prickly discomfort crept up my spine—what if I couldn't do this? I blocked out the doubt and keep going, head bent, eyes closed.

And then, everything gelled. It was like sensing that infinitesimal moment when the tide changes. I found the rhythm, and one by one, the tumblers fell into place. I had it. I'd crossed the Rubicon. Just one more connection—

There was a glorious *click* and the safe swung open. I was in.

And there was the Aurora Egg. Gold filigree shimmered across the surface of the perfect egg shape, winking with the secret within. I'd seen this Fabergé before, of course, but now I knew what it contained. A chill traced through my body.

At once, I felt whole. I didn't need to touch the ring on my finger, concealed beneath my glove, to know it was there. This Fabergé Egg, this one thing, was like the final shard of a shattered vase—the fragment that flew far and became trapped under the sofa, lost and forgotten, condemning the repaired vase to incompleteness.

But finally, I'd found my lost shard.

It must have been because this thing, this Fabergé, had been taken so many times—first, as the original Gifts, taken from their rightful owner. Then smuggled, stolen again, transformed and concealed. Now at last I could return it, bring things full circle and correct that old, ancient wrong. *You can't change the past,* they'd said. But here, looking at this, I knew that I could.

I reached out and cradled the Fabergé in my gloved hands. My fingers tingled where they touched the jeweled surface of the Egg. I felt the sharpness of the metal scrolls encrusted on the Egg's shell. My hands and arms felt the weight of the Egg—heavy, but not nearly heavy enough.

It was time to finish it, and get the Egg back to those who rightfully owned it. My original plan had been to return it to the true Romanovs. They did have a claim. But the rightful claim, knowing what was inside, was with the church. With the monks who were murdered. Later, we would need to contact their monastery and get the Gifts back in the right hands.

But for now, I had to get out of here.

I looked at my watch. Right about then, Ethan was making his way to the Clock Tower from his hiding place. As long as everything had gone according to plan.

Also, at that moment, Brooke was enacting her escape. This, as long as she got a sliver of a chance. It should be all she needed. Her special talent was performing Houdini-like escapes. But if she couldn't do it? "Go without me," she'd said when we were making the plan. "Don't wait. If I don't get my chance before you get the

Egg, I'll find a chance later. I hope to meet you up at the Clock Tower, but the most important thing is getting the Egg out of there."

I closed the safe door, exited the vault and reset the alarm. It was with great effort that I restrained the urge to race out of there. *Don't rush, Cat. Just get it done quickly and silently.*

Once inside the ventilation shaft I pulled up the rope and replaced the grate. I'd left everything exactly as I found it, spiriting the Egg away.

I crawled, holding the blueprint in mind. Rivets and metal edges pressed into my knees and elbows, which were bruised now and groaned at me with a sore, gnawing pain. The only light in the dark and dusty shaft came from periodic vents, and even then it was weak and filtered.

My emotions were under lock and key; I couldn't get too excited yet. But, even still, a small measure of satisfaction slipped through. I had the Egg. I'd almost done it.

The ventilation shaft narrowed. My pulse quickened because this meant I was getting close. The space was tighter now, confined, and my progress slowed. I gritted my teeth, trying to ignore the closeness of the walls. I pushed forward and thought eagerly of getting out to fresh air, to freedom, to the lights of the city from the top of Big Ben.

At last, I reached the end of the shaft. I pushed away the grate and dropped down. It was just one stairwell now between me and freedom. The limestone steps would take me up to the belfry of the Clock Tower, to Big Ben. At each turn I methodically paused to listen, to ensure nobody else was there.

I reached the door at the top of the stair. If everything had gone according to plan, Brooke, Ethan, and Nicole would be up here already. *If.*

If all the levers and gears of this clockwork plan came together, then it would all be worthwhile. But if someone was missing—what then? My chest constricted at the thought of leaving someone behind. Because it would be my fault. I had dragged everyone into this and it was my responsibility to get everyone out.

I took a deep breath and pushed open the door that led to the belfry. Cold, wet air misted my face. Up above the great clock, the walls of the tower ceased to be solid brick, becoming instead a framed spire of cast iron and stone.

I blinked. Three shadowy figures were silhouetted in the drizzle. I squinted to discern who was there, and made out Brooke, Ethan, and Nicole. My heart leaped. They'd all made it.

"Everybody okay?" I ran my eye over them all. None appeared to be exhibiting any major wounds. I exhaled with relief. My breath formed a frosty cloud in front of me.

"Did you get it?" asked Brooke, apprehension in her voice. I walked closer to them, tracing a path around the great bells. Fog seeped through the latticework like fingers.

"I did." My insides were bubbling and fizzing like champagne. Brooke's eyes went wide, and she smiled a genuine smile of relief.

Ethan was also grinning. "Good work, Montgomery."

I did it. I was on top of the world. We'd pulled off the impossible job.

But we still had an escape to complete. I turned to Nicole. "You okay?" I asked. She nodded with a smile. She appeared to have recovered from her ordeal.

The small bells chimed the quarter hour.

"Okay, let's get out of here," I said. We began preparing our equipment to descend the side of the Clock Tower. Nicole went to stand guard at the door.

As we worked, I caught sight of the bump underneath my glove, on my fourth finger. Penny's ring. I smiled. *It's over, Penny.*

But then a small shadow passed over me. I'd fulfilled my quest . . . what now? Did this mean I was free? I'd always longed for that freedom, when I no longer had to be a thief, when I could stop being the villain.

But—that would mean turning away from everything else that made me feel whole. Everything that made me feel special. Is that truly, deep down, what I wanted?

Ethan dispensed harnesses and ropes while I cut a large hole through the heavy metal mesh that filled the ornately carved stone window frames. Beyond the frame was a small ledge bordered by a stone railing. Over this was a straight drop two hundred feet to the ground. Brooke fastened the anchors. We worked quickly and quietly amid the mist.

And then, the belfry door opened.

I spun. Sandor stood framed in the doorway, flanked by three of his men. My eyes flew wide—I was frozen. All four of them had weapons drawn. We held nothing, bits of rope and carabiners.

"Drop everything," said Sandor, glaring.

But—*what happened to Nicole?*—the panicky thought pushed through. She was supposed to be standing guard. Then I saw her standing to the side, near Sandor, gazing at us. She looked unruffled and unsurprised. More than that—she looked satisfied.

In one horrible moment the truth hammered into me: Nicole was working with Sandor.

Chapter 39

Nicole was a double agent. A traitor. They must have planned this all along. She must have alerted Sandor to our getaway rendezvous after we rescued her. And the rescue? A total scam. I felt a tidal wave of nausea at the deception and betrayal. My mind spiraled back to all those coincidences, all those invitations. Had she been keeping an eye on me for Sandor?

"Well, Miss Montgomery," said Sandor, lips drawing back. "It was a valiant effort. Unfortunately I can't let you go any further." His face grew even nastier. "I have not spent my life searching for the Gifts to have you snatch them away. My father did not die in this hunt so I could fail him again."

A mental blueprint of the tower flashed into my mind. There must have been an escape from here. There had to be a way out of this. I calculated obstacles and trajectories as we stood immobile, hands raised.

Sandor extended a hand. "Miss Montgomery . . . the Egg please?"

I didn't move. "Sandor, I can't let you have it." After coming so close, and after feeling that monumental sense of completion—I just could not hand it over. At this moment, I would face death first.

Sandor's countenance flashed irritation, then boredom. He sighed and raised a signaling hand. It was this facial expression, this particular gesture, that gave me my shaved second of warning. Because I'd seen it before: just before he ordered the execution of the monks.

I screamed a warning to Ethan and Brooke and dove behind a platform, just as a thug's black Glock exploded with a sickening bang. Brooke screamed and I saw her fall. Blood poured from a gunshot wound in her right leg.

The quarter bells suddenly chimed again, reverberating in my ears. Ethan lunged from his rolled position on the ground. With terrifying efficiency he withdrew a knife and threw it. The blade caught a man square in the throat, killing him. Ethan's face bore an expression I'd never seen on him: cold, inhuman, detached. Like a panther, unemotional about a kill. Suddenly there was a gun in Ethan's hand. Where had that come from?

After that everything happened very fast. It was a blur, a fugue. Bullets slammed into the stone and iron of the belfry and crashed into the bells with a macabre musicality. I was pinned behind a post now, unable to do a thing, terrified of who was left standing out there. I frantically scanned for an escape route.

Then Sandor's face loomed out through the mist, moving fast toward me. Cold fury twisted his ghoulish face. A knife blade glinted. There was a fierce swish as he sliced it through the mist. I grunted and dodged the lethal arc. I thrust my leg up and knocked the knife away, sending it skittering out of range along the stone floor. I grabbed on to Sandor and attempted to take him down but he was surprisingly strong for such a slight man. We were locked. His hands came up to my throat and I felt the terrifying pressure of his fingers around my neck, squeezing, sending panic to my brain. Stars exploded in my vision and I scrabbled at his hands with my fingers but he had an iron grip. I frantically scissored my legs up and wrapped around his head. With desperate strength I twisted and peeled him from me, wrenching his arms from my throat. I kicked, hard, catching him under the jaw; his head snapped back. He crumpled down, unconscious. I gulped oxygen.

I raced to Sandor's knife on the ground and grabbed it, then swung my eyes wildly back to Ethan. He stood above three dead men. Two had perfectly centered gunshot wounds in their foreheads and one seeped blood from the large gash in his throat.

The fog was thickening now, rolling in like cotton puffs around the iron staircases and girders. The haunting bells chimed the hour and Big Ben tolled three times. The sound was deafening.

Where is Nicole? I thought in a panic, gaze sweeping the belfry. There was no sign of her. The door to the belfry was ajar, swinging slightly. She must have run away when the Caliga began to fall.

I looked back at Ethan and saw, then, that blood was pouring from his shoulder. And his face was pale. He no longer appeared cold and detached.

"Ethan, your shoulder! Are you okay?" I shouted. He looked down, and I saw his face go slack. I lunged toward him just as he stumbled and fell. His head cracked on a stone ledge and he went out, cold.

I raced to Ethan's immobile body on the ground, by a stone post. He was breathing—his chest was rising in shallow, ragged breaths. But he couldn't be roused. The shoulder gunshot wound wasn't as bad as it had first appeared—the head injury was the greater problem now.

My eyes darted to where Brooke was. I spotted her, where she'd dragged herself behind a stone bench. She sat on the ground, breathing heavily. The good news was that her only gunshot wound appeared to be in her lower leg. The bad was that it was bleeding heartily. Blood soaked her Lycra leggings.

"Brooke! Can you hear me?"

Brooke's eyes were cloudy, unfocused, and her face was flat.

Fighting down emotions, I ripped off my shirt. The fabric tore loudly. I cinched a tourniquet around her leg, then ripped off my blood-soaked gloves. My eyes veered to the belfry door. I yanked a crowbar from Ethan's pack and darted to the door. I shoved the crowbar through the door handles. This should buy us a few seconds, anyway, when the rest of Sandor's people arrived.

"Brooke, we have to go. Now." My voice was ragged. Brooke, however, was fixed to the spot. I glanced back at Ethan, still unconscious.

"Brooke—I need help with Ethan." No response. I didn't think she'd lost enough blood to cause this catatonic state. She must have been in shock, stupefied by the trauma. Although there was always potential danger to our line of work, it was rare to have things get quite this grim. She had to snap out of it. Now.

The urgency to get off this tower was squeezing me like a hydraulic crusher. We had to get out of there. I dropped Brooke's harness next to her, then raced to Ethan. I hauled him up from the ground, dragged him closer to the edge, and struggled him into a harness. We'd have to do a tandem rappel. I turned my head and saw that Brooke was making no attempt to get into her own harness. Her eyes were distant, lost at sea.

I finished fastening Ethan's harness. "Brooke, you have to move. *Now.*" But she sat there, stunned. "Brooke. Go!"

She wasn't going. Ethan was still bleeding from his shoulder. And he was heavy. I closed my eyes and clenched my teeth. How was I going to do this? I left Ethan resting on the ground, and raced to Brooke. I lifted her up, slipped the straps around her catatonic frame, cinched the belt, attached the carabiners, and attached her rope to an anchor.

"Okay, *there.* Go." I led her limping through the open Gothic window frame, to the railing, and all but pushed her over the edge. She looked down, a shell of a human. With indifference, she clambered slowly over, woodenly lowering herself like a marionette.

I pulled my own harness straps tight, the nylon webbing taut around my thighs. I cinched the straps of the sack that contained the Fabergé. I then linked Ethan's harness to mine and climbed over the edge with him attached to me. As I leaned back I felt the straps tighten, cutting firmly into my legs. My stomach flipped up into my chest as we took the first drop. I couldn't see the ground through the heavy fog but I could make out the shadowy form of Brooke, farther down. We descended in front of the enormous, illuminated clock face. My heart surged: *we were going to make it.* We were going to be okay—

I felt a tug on the rope. I looked up. Seven feet up, Sandor's face appeared over the banister's edge. A dark bruise had blossomed on his jaw. And that cold fury he had before? Replaced now with good old-fashioned hot fury. His teeth were bared like an animal's and his eyes were wide, crazed.

"You're not going anywhere with that Fabergé," he growled.

He gripped the rope and vigorously launched himself over the ledge as I dangled, helplessly. He descended hand over hand and he was upon me in a second. He slammed into me and clutched at the sack where the Egg was tucked.

"Sandor, stop!" I gasped. "You're going to kill us all."

"You stupid bitch. You have no idea what you're doing. You have no right." He was pulling, dragging, clawing. "I lost everything in this search. I'm not going to lose the prize."

I felt the sack loosen as Sandor grappled at it. I twisted away. But he was in a better position, just above me. One more grab and he'd probably be able to wrench it away from me. I couldn't get Sandor off me. I couldn't do it alone. But Ethan was still unconscious.

"Brooke!" I screamed, looking down in a dizzy panic. "Help!" But she didn't respond.

Sandor groped at my harness, trying to unhook it. I'd tied my harness last, hastily, and the connections were poor. I could feel it shredding. I kicked at him, trying to push him away, but I couldn't get good leverage, and he was like a man possessed.

Suddenly I could tell the harness was not going to hold me. Ethan's weight was dragging me down. I twisted and scrabbled at the glass panes and the iron numbers of the clock face, desperate for a foothold. My foot smashed through one of the panes. I could feel myself losing my grip. My mind raced to the rappel anchors—they couldn't possibly support the weight of three.

Oh God. I'm not going to make it here. A crushing, hopeless darkness pushed through the panic.

"It's mine," hissed Sandor.

He had a firm grip on the straps of my bag at last. He loosened the opening and reached inside. I felt a lightening, but I twisted away and Sandor's hand wobbled. The Egg rolled out of my bag and rested, miraculously, cradled between the hands of the great clock. Time momentarily stopped as we stared at it, unbelieving.

We both reached for it but it was just beyond our fingertips. Sandor stretched, pushing me back. He almost had it. It was all I could do to hang on for life.

I glimpsed his face. He was consumed, crazed. His drive for the Gifts had turned him psychotic. And now, I had glimpsed his reasons. He'd been dogged by it his whole life. And that thing he'd said in the Clock Tower—had his father died in the search? Was it Sandor's fault?

"Sandor—you can't reach it. It's too far." My mind raced; maybe I could talk him down.

"No. It's mine," he snarled. "I have to get it. I cannot live unless I—"

Sandor reached and stretched, and I watched with horror as his fingertips brushed the Egg. He was trying to swing us closer, but it wasn't enough. He planted his feet on the clock's arm and used it to push, holding on to the rope with a single hand. He reached out impossibly far, and—

He lost his grip on the rope. In slow motion I saw his face turn back, too late. There was air between his hand and the rope, and nothing but air beneath him.

All the oxygen left my lungs as I watched him fall, screaming. I lost sight of him before he hit the ground, swallowed up by the night air and the heavy fog. I turned away, cringing.

When I opened my eyes, I saw the Egg, glistening, balancing, teetering just a little. The Egg was about to fall down from the full height of the Clock Tower to smash on the ground beneath.

I couldn't let that happen.

I focused on the Egg and reached for it. I strained as far as I could, holding the rope with one hand. I could feel the pull on my harness. It wouldn't hold much longer, the straps were loosening. But I almost had it. If I could just reach a little further. I could touch the surface of the Egg now, but I needed to grab it, to cradle it in.

"Catherine, let it go," came a steady voice on my far side. I turned and saw Brooke. She must have roused from her trance, perhaps when Sandor fell, and climbed back up beside me.

But I couldn't let the Fabergé go. I reached with my hand and caught sight of Penny's ring. This Egg was everything right now. I'd sacrificed so much for this chance to put things right.

But if you don't let it go, it's going to be your death, said a voice in my head. Just like it was for Sandor.

Frustration made me want to rip my skin off in shreds. I'd come so far. I was so close. But it was down to this: I had to choose, here, between saving the Fabergé, and life.

I couldn't fix the past but I could live, right now. Suddenly I saw that the Egg was just a thing. It couldn't truly change the past. It was not salvation, not redemption or penitence. It was time for me to stop looking for symbols of forgiveness. I needed to forgive myself. And live.

I pulled my hand away. The Egg wobbled a little. Then it teetered, and rolled off the clock hand, falling into the mist.

Bleak failure punched my stomach. The Fabergé was gone. The Gifts of the Magi were destroyed, smashed upon the streets of London. All that remorse, all those generations of people trying to correct the original mistake made by two thieves so long ago—it was all gone and shattered on the ground.

I had failed.

And yet . . . in the back corner of my mind, just out of sight, there was a lightness of being. Because alongside the Fabergé something else lay destroyed on the ground. It was my own personal burden: the guilt I'd been carrying for years about Penny.

Brooke's hand was on my arm. "Cat. We need to move."

I looked into her eyes. I snapped back to the present predicament. We needed to get out of there.

"There's no way we can go down now," she said. "A crowd will be gathering—a man just fell to his death."

We needed a new plan. Trouble was, every palace exit would be blocked now, whether by Sandor's people or by the police. We were trapped. And we couldn't waste time climbing back up to the belfry.

Brooke lowered down, just below the clock face, and kicked through a window. At the sound of breaking glass, Ethan roused a little, shifting slightly and mumbling incoherently. Brooke pushed the glass shards away, clearing a hole, then helped me and Ethan through, grasping firmly to my arms and sides. We stood up inside and got our bearings. We were in the clock repair room, just behind the face. How were we going to get out of there? I recalled the schematics of the building in my mental image-finder. A plan began to formulate.

"Brooke, can you help me carry Ethan? We're going to have to run." She sized him up and nodded. She was able to put a little weight on her leg, enough to get us out of here. "Okay. Follow me," I said.

Brooke grunted as we lifted Ethan into a two-person carry. We hobbled down a spiral staircase and then stumbled through corridors as fast as we could, heading south. We bolted through darkened libraries and dressing rooms, pushing on. Intruder alarms rang and clanged and wailed as we raced through but we ignored it all. The city lights filtered in through endless rows of windows, flashing like strobe lights as we raced past. I was operating on pure adrenaline now, in that space between exhaustion and nervous breakdown.

Along the way, Ethan slowly regained consciousness. We carried him a little further as he struggled to come to. At this point, however, Brooke was limping badly. Her leg wound had started bleeding again. We put Ethan down and the three of us toiled onward.

At last we reached a vast room at the very end of the south wing: an office of some sort, with a single desk, two club chairs, and massive oil paintings on the walls. Tall windows overlooked the foggy Thames. On this far corner of Westminster there was no terrace below. It was just a straight drop, seven stories down, into the river.

"We're going out that way," I said, clawing for breath.

"*What* way?" Brooke said.

I pointed to the river. "There."

Ethan nodded, and immediately began looking around for places to attach the rappel anchors.

I shook my head vigorously. "No time for rapelling," I said. They stared at me with bewilderment. "We just have to go."

"Do you mean . . . jump?" Brooke said.

"Yes."

She stared down at the Thames far below. The fog was thinner now. We could make out what was below: dark, choppy, charcoal water.

Ethan raked his hand through his hair and exhaled. He knew as well as I did this was our only viable option. He glanced down at Brooke's leg; she was unable to put any weight on it at this point. Ethan, on the other hand, was beginning to rally. He was unable to use his left arm but was otherwise functional. "Okay. I'll take Brooke," he said. "We'll meet at Blackfriars Bridge. But not right away. We'll separate, then rendezvous in two hours. I know where to go, to get these injuries seen to."

We worked quickly to wrench the window open. Then, without belaboring the task, Ethan went over the window ledge foot first, carrying Brooke down with him. They dropped down, Ethan silently slicing through the night sky like Batman. It was a long drop down. I watched the icy water splash as they submerged. I held my breath. After several seconds two heads bobbed to the surface. I closed my eyes and exhaled. *They made it.*

But now it was my turn. My head swam and my stomach flip-flopped.

And then, there was a great clattering of boot steps and the door smashed open and a swarm of armed men burst into the room. Whether they were security guards or Sandor's people I didn't know, but it didn't matter at this point. I spun and saw firearms pointed directly at me. "Stop right there!"

My trepidation about jumping vanished and I lunged for the window, leaping into the open night air. I was sailing, flying, then falling. . . .

Chapter 40

The pavement over Blackfriars Bridge glistened beneath street lanterns, slick with moisture. The mist was clearing now. I stood at the old carved railing and stared at lantern reflections in the slow-moving water of the Thames. Everything felt black and white and silver, like some kind of 1930s noir film.

"Are you going to be okay?" Ethan asked me.

I nodded soberly. "Actually, yeah. For the first time, I really think I am."

I had hidden for a long time—huddled along the bank of the Thames—after jumping from Westminster. When it was safe I'd clambered out and gone to Charing Cross train station, where I had stashed a change of clothes.

My muscles were starting the slow burn that came from a long night of strenuous activity. Brooke was quiet, standing beside me on the bridge.

I looked at her. "You okay?"

"Never better." She winced a little as she readjusted herself on her crutches. After climbing out of the river, Ethan had taken Brooke to the back door of a very exclusive, very private clinic. It had been a place he'd used on a job in London years ago. An exceptionally capable—and discreet—physician treated both of their gunshot wounds, and confirmed that Ethan's head injury was not as serious as it seemed.

"You know, Ethan, someday you're going to have to tell me how you got those combat skills of yours," I said teasingly.

"Someday, Montgomery," he said, shrugging. He grinned. "So anyway, what are you going to do now?"

I thought about this for a moment, gazing at the trees lining the south bank. Hundreds of tiny blue lights illuminated their branches. "Probably stay low for a little while. Then head back to Seattle."

"To continue working for the Agency?"

I nodded. "With a little luck, everything will be fine with AB&T." It seemed to be the only thing that hadn't become totally screwed up, against the odds. I would slip back into my life in Seattle.

I saw a flicker of approval in his eyes. "That's my girl," he said. Had he wondered if I would give it all up? That was the last thing I would consider now.

A warm glow of calm suffused my being. Because I knew who I was now. And, more importantly, I knew *why* I was this way. I had always thought my drive to be a thief came from trying to correct the wrong I'd done Penny, long ago. But that was not what it was.

In that moment when I thought I'd atoned for Penny, in the Westminster vault, I realized I didn't want to give up my life as a thief. *This* was who I was. And that's because—right or wrong—being a thief was my own way of being special, of living a life less ordinary. And it was the one thing I could do in the world at which I could be . . . the best. So how could I walk away from that?

No. This was what I was meant to do.

A small shadowy doubt tiptoed into the edge of my brain. But— did that mean I'd *always* be driven to be a thief? Until it killed me?

I pushed that shadow down. That was something I'd have to deal with at another time.

I glanced at Ethan again, taking in his injuries, his battered self. His wounds were my fault. But they were sustained because he came here to help me. No personal gain involved. "You know," I said to him, "you're not as much of a villain as you make yourself out to be." He looked surprised, then grunted noncommittally. "There's a hero inside you, Ethan Jones. You just have to let him out."

He looked at me earnestly for a moment. Then his face took on a wicked expression and he moved closer. "Maybe if I had a good influence in my life—someone who was always rushing around trying to do the right thing—that person might rub off on me. Hmm?"

My stomach fluttered and my pulse sped up. "Well, I don't know . . . but it might be worth a try. . . ."

I bit my lip as Ethan moved even closer.

Brooke cleared her throat. "Um. Do you two mind continuing this conversation elsewhere? The police have combed the water once already, but they're probably going to return. Also, being a third wheel is not familiar territory for me and I am quite disinterested in trying it out—"

Ethan and I stepped apart and laughed, awkwardly, at that. But she was right. We did need to make ourselves disappear again. I pulled my coat tightly around myself and turned.

And then, everything changed.

Three figures appeared in silhouette walking along the bridge, toward us. Three men in trench coats, striding purposefully. Panic seized my brain and I looked for a clear path of escape. In that moment, though, I recognized Templeton's face among the men.

He was flanked by two other men: the Chairman of AB&T and a thin, wiry man I didn't recognize.

The floor dropped out beneath me. And just like that, my one constant was gone. I stood, staring, saying nothing. What could I say? They were obviously there because they knew what I had attempted to do.

Templeton looked at us grimly. "Catherine," he said, nodding at me. "Jones. Brooke," he said, addressing them in turn. He carried a black umbrella. His eyebrows were low and his mouth was a hard line.

"Templeton . . . I can explain—"

"Cat," he said, interrupting my stammering. "Stop. It's over."

I closed my eyes. *How did they find out?* My gaze was drawn slowly, inexorably, to Brooke.

She stared back. "Don't look at me, Cat," she said flatly. "It wasn't me."

Templeton nodded. "This time, it wasn't."

"But then—"

"Catherine Montgomery," the Chairman interrupted, addressing me directly in the manner of a sentence hearing. He was a short, round man with a fleshy face. "You directly disobeyed an order from AB&T. You disregarded our rules. You have compromised our entire corporation."

I nodded, slowly. My chest constricted. This couldn't be happening. I was about to hear my dishonorable dismissal. No more glorious climb to success, no Elite status, no international assignments. This was the end of my career with AB&T. Quite possibly the end of my career as a jewel thief.

No. Just at the moment I finally understood that being a thief was my one true thing. I tasted bitter irony on my tongue.

I stared into the river, at the bridge lights reflecting in the water. A double-decker bus lumbered over the bridge, swishing along the wet pavement. I waited for the guillotine.

And then I heard the Chairman say, "*However . . .*" I raised my eyes. "There's something you need to know."

I glanced at Templeton. Under the surface of his grim expression I saw a flicker of something else. His eyes darted to the Chairman and then back at me. Like he was eager to see my reaction to what was going to come next. *What was it?* My pulse rocketed.

"It's something not many of us, within the Agency, are aware of. Only a small faction. Even Templeton didn't know about it until tonight."

I couldn't speak. What was he going to say? The Chairman looked at the wiry man I didn't recognize. "Wesley, why don't you take it from here?"

The man called Wesley spoke. "Cat, you're aware that AB&T has a very long history. Yes?" He smiled, and I noticed he had an awful lot of teeth. But there was something trustworthy about his demeanor. "Yes."

"In fact it stretches many centuries back. And when we formed, our charter included a very specific quest." He paused, rubbing the back of his neck. "You know the legends mention two groups descended from the original thieves, right? One wanted to regain the Gifts for malevolent purposes—"

"The Caliga Rapio."

"Right," he said, nodding. "Well, Cat, the other group—that's us."
I blinked. And then it clicked. *Of course.*

"So all along," I said, thinking it through, "when I thought I was working behind your backs, I was actually working for you? The Agency is the other side?"

"Well, truthfully, we're just a part of it. A hundred generations later, it's a very big network. We do know that the tradition has given rise to some of the great thieves of history."

I had a mental image of all the legendary thieves throughout time. Robin Hood, Bonnie and Clyde . . . was I, too, part of that pedigree?

I looked at Wesley. "So that's the whole reason AB&T exists— to find the Gifts?"

He nodded. "We perfected the art of thievery, waiting for our chance. Over the years we expanded beyond that original goal, but we never fully lost sight of it. We've always had a team assigned to it."

"Okay," I said slowly, thinking. "So where's that team now?"

The Chairman smiled. "Well, that's why Wesley is here. Wesley Smith has been handling that side of things."

"Our team, it seems, was one step behind you," Wesley said. "We were duped, fed bad information, and led away to the other side of the city. Nicole Johnson's handiwork, as a matter of fact. We didn't know the true location was Westminster, until a core member of our team in Seattle figured it out and notified us right away, through Templeton. I believe you know him: *Jack Barlow.*"

My mouth dropped open. "You can't be serious."

And suddenly, it all made sense. Jack, so secretive. At the masquerade ball. His warnings. And in the restaurant, he had known the Aurora Egg had been stolen. He'd wanted to know if I'd had anything to do with it.

"Are you telling me Jack has been working for AB&T all this time?" I asked. How could this be?

"No, not exactly," Wesley said. "He's more of a . . . consultant. We've approached him many times to come and work for us, but he's always refused. But his father was a part of the team seeking the Gifts. Jack Barlow always respected that. Otherwise, he's been trying as hard as he can to stay clear of our way of life."

"Goodness knows *why*," Templeton quipped, grinning.

"So . . ." I could hardly even ask. "Is Jack here?" My stomach was cartwheeling.

"No. He couldn't make it in time."

I nodded, but I couldn't help feeling a pinch of disappointment. "And what about Nicole?" I asked, trying to stay focused on the other issues at hand. "You mentioned her. Did she get away?"

Wesley's face stiffened and his lip curled with distaste. "Unfortunately, she did get away. Nicole was Caliga, had been all along. She'd been under deep cover within the FBI for a few years. You can be sure the FBI will be hunting her down now, though."

It wasn't a lot of comfort. I didn't like the idea of her out there, at large.

The dome of St. Paul's Cathedral loomed, floodlit, beyond the bridge. The Chairman smiled at me. "The good news, here, Cat, is that we're not going to be firing you. How could we fire the one person who helped us achieve our two-thousand-year-old goal?"

And here, I cringed. "But, I didn't, actually." With a wave of nausea I envisioned the Fabergé plummeting, disappearing into the fog. I could barely bring myself to tell them. "It's gone. It's destroyed." I described how I let it fall from the height of Big Ben.

The three men exchanged a peculiar look. "In fact," said Templeton, "it's not quite so simple. Because nothing has yet been found. Despite having a team do an exhaustive search of the area."

I frowned. "What do you mean?"

Brooke laughed. "What, it just disappeared into the mist?"

"Well," Wesley said, "we're not sure. But, it's something like that. We'll find it. Eventually. This has . . . happened before."

This was too much to think about just now. They seemed fully prepared, however, to handle whatever came next. I was fully prepared to let them.

I turned and looked over the water, half listening as the others discussed an exit strategy and a plan to return home. At that moment a riverboat glided out from under the bridge, on the far side of the river. A figure in a hooded slicker stood on the back of the boat, gazing in our direction. I narrowed my eyes. There was something familiar about the man's face. . . .

Wait a second. Was that *Professor Atworthy*? My French lit professor at UW?

I squinted to get a better look in the gloomy darkness. Another boat passed by, obscuring my view for a moment. By the time I could see him again, the man had turned away and his hood was up. I couldn't make out his face anymore. I frowned and shook my head—was I seeing things now? Why on earth would Atworthy be here? No. I must have been imagining it.

I glanced back at the group, wondering if anyone else had noticed the riverboat, when a big black London cab pulled up beside us. The passenger door opened and out stepped Jack Barlow.

The instant his foot touched the wet pavement his gaze went immediately to me, face full of concern. My heart gave a lurch of excitement. *He's come for me.* . . .

Which was ridiculous. Of course, he was just here to help AB&T. "You're too late, Jack," I said, all business. "Your team has already told me everything."

My eyes slid to Ethan. He had stepped back and was watching Jack carefully. His jaw was clenched and his mouth was set in a grim line.

Jack nodded. "I know." He walked directly to me, barely casting a glance at anyone else. His eyes raked me over, presumably looking for injuries. He looked relieved when he found none. "I came here because I needed to find someone."

And then, as if it were on the the Cyclone at Coney Island, my heart surged again. Just briefly. But I quickly scolded myself. He'd come to London for Nicole, of course. *Stupid,* Cat. He must have been worried sick once he learned her life was in danger. Nicole, I now know, was only with Jack to monitor Caliga enemies. But Jack had no such calculating motives.

And just like that, my heart was breaking all over again. I wanted to scream. But what I said was: "I don't know how to tell you this, Jack, but Nicole is not who you think she is—"

"I know," he interrupted. "I didn't come here for Nicole." I stared at him, like an idiotic deer in headlights.

"Cat . . . I'm here for *you*," he said.

"You—you're what?"

"It's always been you, Cat."

The bridge tilted. Jack didn't appear to care that we had an audience. He cradled my face in his hands and pulled me into a deep kiss. My heart burst like hot popcorn. I forgot about everything else that was happening.

"I promised myself I wouldn't hesitate if I got this chance again," he murmured. "I need you to know that I was wrong. So wrong . . ."

I pulled away, gazing into his eyes. "Wrong about what?"

"That I could live without you. It was stupid. And I'm sorry. I just can't stand being away from you. Maybe you're toxic, but I can't help myself." He smiled a crooked smile. "I'm hoping I haven't screwed things up too badly," he said, looking down sheepishly. Suddenly he looked nervous. He shifted anxiously, like an awkward teenager asking a girl to dance.

My head was spinning. This was all happening so fast.

I remembered, then, everyone else standing with us on the bridge. My eyes swiveled involuntarily to Ethan. He had turned away; his hand scrubbed his face as he gazed over the shifting water. I frowned and felt a twist in my chest.

But I turned back to Jack. Here he was, laying his heart out at my feet, saying the exact words I'd fantasized about him saying.

"Jack, let's just take it slow," I said. "This is all so much to deal with. . . ."

"You're right," he said, nodding and brushing a strand of hair from my face. "There's no need to rush. How about this—let's just start with dinner." He smiled. And those familiar, melting-chocolate eyes gazing into my face made my knees wobble. "How does that sound?"

The night sky was just barely beginning to lighten, washed with the chalkiness that heralds sunrise. Morning civil twilight is a sacred time of day for thieves: many ancient laws specified that, with the first light before sunrise, the nighttime crime of burglary was less wicked. Daybreak offered a sliver of forgiveness for crooks.

I heard the swish of tires as glossy black cabs slid over the bridge; the city was just beginning to wake. In the distant sky a jet plane was climbing out of Heathrow.

And my heart aimed for the moon.

I took a full, deep breath. "Dinner sounds perfect."

Look for the next AB&T novel by Kim Foster,
coming in June 2014 from eKensington!
And visit Kim at www.kimfosterwrites.com
for more news about upcoming projects.

Acknowledgments

First, I would like to thank my agent, Sandy Lu, for playing the role of fairy godmother and plucking my manuscript out of her inbox. "I'm not scared of books that cross genres," she said. "I like them, in fact." Bless her brave soul.

I want to thank Peter Senftleben, my editor at Kensington, for championing Cat's cause, criminal though it was. His ideas are fabulous, his humor is wicked, his editing eye is sharp. He has been the best Sherpa a debut novelist could ask for.

I owe a debt of gratitude to the following mentors, teachers, and early readers of Cat's story: Don Maass, Cameron McClure, Elizabeth Lyon, Carolyn Rose, and Lisa Rector Maass. My education as a writer would have been sadly lacking without their guidance.

A big hug goes to Eileen Cook for all manner of writerly support, and for holding my hand as I jumped into the abyss.

Thank you, Starbucks, for letting me share office space with you. And providing fuel.

I happen to have the most amazing support network a mom-writer-blogger has ever had. To Erica Ehm and all the awesome bloggers at the Yummy Mummy Club, and to all my fellow writers and bloggers and social media goddesses (you know who you are): I raise a glass of wine (or two) to you all.

Cheers and hugs go to my sisters, Deb and Vivi, for being my best friends, my first readers, and my unconditional fan club.

I give kudos to my father for exercising extreme restraint when faced with a fully trained, licensed, and practicing physician-daughter unaccountably chasing a deep desire to actually be a writer instead.

I will forever thank my mother for sharing her love of words with me, and for teaching me that dangling participles are at least as dangerous as dangling from tall buildings.

My heart is full of gratitude for my husband Ken. I want to thank him for embracing his solitary side and entertaining himself while I spent countless hours writing. Even more so for entertaining the kids. But mostly, for taking on the laundry. Around the third draft of this manuscript, he had mastered the division of colors and whites. Around the twelfth draft, he had achieved fifth level fitted-sheet fold. Ken, you ground me, you make me laugh, you keep me sane.

Finally, I want to thank my boys. Quite simply, you are my jewels.

25280940R00192

Made in the USA
Charleston, SC
20 December 2013